PICTURE PERFECT

A wedding. The scene coming to life in front of me, created by my own hand, was that of a wedding. More details were added, and then, finally, the pencil moved to the couple about to walk back down the aisle, hand in hand. My breath caught in my chest. Was this it? Had I finally found the key to my soul mate's identity?

The bride's dress was traditional, with plenty of lace and pearls. This surprised me, because I am not a lace kind of girl; but the picture had to be of me. Who else? I continued to draw, continued to shade. Shivers coated my skin. My eyes watered and I needed to blink, but I refused to, too afraid that the magic would stop and the groom's identity wouldn't be completed. I had to finish this.

My heart raced and I swallowed, trying to calm myself. My baby danced inside of me, and I laughed. Through all of this, the magic swirled, the colors increasing in vividness around me, the lights growing brighter. And then I began drawing the faces of the couple. Would it be Ethan as the groom? Kyle? One of the many half-naked men my grandmother had trooped through my apartment…?

Other *Love Spell* books by Tracy Madison:

A TASTE OF MAGIC

Tracy Madison

a Stroke of Magic

LOVE SPELL NEW YORK CITY

*To my grandfather, Elmer Palenske, with all my love and thanks.
I think about you every day, and wish with all of my heart you
were still here with us.*

LOVE SPELL®

July 2009

Published by

Dorchester Publishing Co., Inc.
200 Madison Avenue
New York, NY 10016

ISBN 10: 0-505-52811-8
ISBN 13: 978-0-505-52811-7
E-ISBN: 978-1-4285-0702-9

Acknowledgments

Thank you to the greatest critique partners of all time: Natalie Damschroder, Connie Phillips, and Liane Gentry Skye, for your input, words of wisdom, and continuous support. I don't know what I'd do without you gals. Let's not find out!

A huge thanks to my fabulous editor, Chris Keeslar, and my fantastic agent, Michelle Grajkowski, for helping me make my words, my stories, so much stronger.

And a final thanks to my family, who always supports me, even when I go a "little bit crazy." I know it can't be easy, but I so appreciate it!

a Stroke
of Magic

Chapter One

Pregnant women had taken over Chicago.

At least, it seemed that way to me, because every single place I went, there they were. Women with glowing skin, shiny hair, smiling faces, stomachs in various shapes and sizes, and—the far majority of the time—with men at their sides. It boggled my mind, really. I'd lived in or near Chicago my entire life, and I'd swear on a stack of one-hundred-dollar bills there had never been so many expectant mamas.

Now, once again, I was surrounded by them. Literally. Of course, seeing as I was sitting in an obstetrician's waiting room, this didn't exactly shock me. But the phenomenon occurred at the grocery store, the library, when I went out to buy art supplies over the weekend, and even at the car wash. Rationally, I knew there weren't *more* of them, just that I *noticed* them more now. But that didn't make me feel any better. It also didn't help that all of the women in this room had someone with them. Except me. I was alone.

"Alice? Alice Raymond, is that you?" The way-too-perky voice came from my right.

I thought about ignoring whomever it was, because come on—unless I lifted my head and acknowledged them, they would assume they'd made a mistake and leave me alone. Because I really wanted to be left alone, I continued pretending to read *Your Pregnancy and You*. In actuality, I'd already read the dang pamphlet cover to cover. Three times.

"Alice?" the woman said again. "From Mayfield High?"

Oh, hell. *Now* I recognized the voice. How I'd ended up in the same doctor's office as Shelby Whitaker, otherwise known as crazy-cheerleader-chick from my high school days, was beyond me. This girl? I'd disliked her with a passion for four years running. Don't get me wrong; cheerleaders in general didn't annoy me, just this specific one. And yep, I continued to ignore her. I was in no mood for a reunion.

A man spoke next. "Honey, she's obviously not who you think she is."

"Oh, she is too. I'd recognize her profile anywhere. I sat next to her in almost every class we had together." A hand, presumably Shelby's, touched my arm. "It's me, Shelby Whitaker. Well, Harris now. It's so great to run into you here! When are you due?"

"My name isn't Alice." I kept my eyes on the pamphlet. Lying didn't bother me. I hadn't seen the man-stealing, self-involved twit in more than a decade, so I'd likely never see her again after this.

"That's so odd! You look just like her. Sound like her too."

"Sorry. Not her." Leaning against the arm of the chair, I used my right hand to block her view. "But they say everyone has a twin."

She didn't respond, and the chatter in the room that had momentarily died down picked back up. Relieved, I focused on what I would say to the doc when I finally saw him. Some weird symptoms had cropped up since my last visit, and I wasn't all that sure about the best way to broach them. Probably, he'd think I was a nutcase. Honestly, that might not be so far off.

I heard the soft slide of the door opening across the carpet. "Alice Raymond? The doctor's ready for you now."

"I knew it!" Shelby all but screamed.

I really should know by now not to lie. It always bites

me in my ass when I do. A flush of heat swarmed my cheeks. Oh-so-slowly, I replaced the pamphlet on the table in front of me.

After I stood, I confronted the cheerleader. Shelby Harris née Whitaker didn't look all too different from the girl I remembered. Same Kewpie-doll mouth, same wide blue eyes, and the same perfectly styled ash blonde hair—albeit a different, shorter style. The big difference, and I do mean *big*, was her stomach. Either her due date had long since passed, or she carried a baby elephant.

"Hi, Shelby."

Humor lifted her lips at the corners. Her left hand, adorned with a megasized diamond ring and wide gold band, rested on her belly. "Why'd you say you weren't you?"

"Sorry about that. I was focused on reading and didn't want to be interrupted."

A flash of surprise, and maybe hurt, whisked over her expression. "I see. I'm sorry for interrupting you then."

Her eyes shifted away, and a tiny bit of remorse crept into my consciousness. Dealing with the realities of being single and pregnant, with an out-of-his-mind and delusional ex, hadn't exactly made me a happy-go-lucky person. But I hadn't meant to make Shelby feel bad. "I'm kind of uncomfortable around doctors."

A lame excuse, but she seemed to accept it. Swinging her gaze back to me, she smiled again. "It's been a long time." She turned to the man next to her. "This is my husband, Grant. Grant, this is Alice. We went to school together."

Grant Harris had almost the same shade of hair as his wife, cornflower blue eyes that shone brightly behind his glasses, and an open, engaging smile. So totally not the type of guy Shelby used to go for. I wondered which of her friends she'd stolen him from. He nodded in greeting. "Any friend of Shel's is a friend of mine."

"Um. Sure. Well, it's nice to meet you." I didn't bother stating his wife and I had never been friends. Hell, we hadn't even been *friendly*. What we'd had in common was one friend whom she'd stabbed in the back repeatedly.

"Miss Raymond?" the nurse said. "Can you come with me?"

Yay. Saved by the bell. "Gotta go. Good luck with everything."

I'd almost made it to the nurse when Shelby whispered, "She never liked me much. I don't know why."

For a millisecond, I considered turning around and reminding her of *why* I hadn't liked her much. But really, it had been a lifetime ago, so why bother? What is it they say: let bygones be bygones? Something like that, anyway. So I did the mature thing and kept walking, without even a flinch as a response. My sister would have been quite proud, as I wasn't known for keeping my mouth shut.

On the other side of the door, the nurse motioned me down the hallway. We stopped in front of a scale and I cringed. Before this whole pregnancy thing had occurred, I'd never thought twice about my weight. Now, with my body changing shape so rapidly, I'd begun to worry about the pounds. Though it couldn't be too bad yet. At barely four months along, and with nearly constant nausea screwing up my appetite, how much weight could I have possibly gained?

I stepped on, and the nurse fiddled with the bar until it balanced out. "Ten pounds," she said as she wrote the number in my file.

"Ten pounds in a month? Are you sure?"

"That's what it says."

"That's too much, isn't it?" Following her into an examination room, I mentally did the math, and it didn't look good.

"You were on the thin side to begin with. You'll likely even out. There's nothing to worry about yet."

Everything I'd read said most women gained an average of between twenty-five and thirty-five pounds over nine months. Seeing as I'd already gained fifteen altogether, I'd probably beat those averages. "What if I don't? Even out, that is."

She set the file down. "We'll cross that bridge when we come to it. If you're concerned, talk about it with the doctor."

Swallowing my worries, I pushed up my sleeve when she grabbed the blood pressure cuff from the wall. After she finished with me, I only waited a few minutes before Dr. Layton came in. With his warm eyes, curly brown hair, and slightly round body, he was like a cuddly teddy bear come to life. Plus, Dr. Layton radiated kindness, compassion, and expertise. Exactly what a girl like me needed at a time like this.

"The nausea hasn't abated at all?" he asked, reading from the notes the nurse had written in my chart.

"Not really. It's pretty constant."

"Have you tried any natural remedies? Peppermint, ginger, soda crackers, or dry toast might help." At the shake of my head, he said, "Give it a try. You might also try some candies called Preggie Pops. A lot of my patients have had good results from them."

Preggie Pops? Why were things created for pregnant women given such cutesy names? I worked at an advertising firm, and I still didn't get it. But hey, at this point, I'd give anything a go. "Okay, thanks."

Rolling the stool over, he sat down with my file in hand. "I'd like to set up an ultrasound before your next appointment. Just so we can take a peek at how the baby's growing and ascertain that everything is good."

The room spun slightly as I took in what he had said.

"Do we need to do that now? I'd rather wait another month or two."

"It's up to you. If you'd rather wait, that's fine. But is there a reason?"

I didn't know what to say, how to explain what I didn't understand. Intellectually, I knew I carried a baby. I did everything I was supposed to do so the baby would be healthy. But emotionally I wasn't prepared, and the first time I saw an image of my child I wanted to be prepared. "I'd prefer to hold off a little longer."

"Okay. We'll talk about it at your next appointment. Let me know if the nausea gets any worse."

"I will." Deciding to take the plunge, I said, "And I have a question about some odd symptoms I've been having."

"That's what I'm here for. What's going on?"

My mind played over the events of the past several weeks, and I tried to find a way to articulate what I wanted to say without sounding like a complete idiot. Because nothing came to mind, I put it the best way I could: "Are weird dreams and hallucinations normal?"

"Dreams, yes. Hallucinations? That's a new one to me. Why don't you tell me exactly what has you concerned?"

Clasping my hands, I took another breath. "It started a few weeks ago. I have the same dream, over and over. Nothing really happens in it, but it fascinates me. There's a woman with a lot of colors around her, and she opens her mouth as if she's talking, but I can't hear her."

"Do you recognize the woman?"

"She looks a little like my sister. Long brown hair, brown eyes, but she's tall . . . and whatever she's trying to say, I think it's important."

"You're tall. And you have long brown hair and brown eyes," he pointed out. "Could this woman be you?"

Startled, I thought about it for a second, brought the image of the woman to the front of my memory. "My sister and I are similar in appearance, so I guess if I think she looks like Elizabeth, she probably looks like me too. But, no, it's not me."

He opened my file and wrote something down— probably that I was insane, and to check my family history. "It's not uncommon for pregnancy to cause unexplained dreams. My guess is that this woman *is* you, but you can't hear her because your life is changing drastically. This dream is simply a manifestation of your fears."

"Really?" I said.

"I can't guarantee it, but I've had patients who've had some out-there dreams." Dr. Layton laughed. "Trust me. As you become more accustomed to what's happening, your emotions will even out, and the dreams will likely end."

Relief poured through me. What he said made sense. "Awesome. Thank you. I feel better already."

"Now, tell me about these hallucinations."

I'd almost forgotten that part. Suddenly, I worried all over again. "The hallucination is exactly the same as the dream, except the last time I had it, I wasn't sleeping. Well, I *had* been asleep. But I woke up because it was muggy in the room. I remember sitting up and wishing the bedroom windows were open. That's when it happened. She sort of halfway appeared, but I still couldn't hear her."

"Were you afraid?"

"Not at all. But then she vanished, and I fell back asleep pretty much right away. So, that's a hallucination, right?"

"I don't think so. Have you ever had a dream where you thought you were awake but then you really woke up?" At my nod, he continued. "You probably either never woke up to begin with, or you fell back asleep and didn't realize it."

"I don't know. I'm pretty sure I was awake."

"Let me ask you this, then. Have you had this happen in the middle of the day? Like at work, or cooking dinner, or any other time that wasn't immediately preceded or followed by sleeping?"

"No. It's only happened once."

Another smile. "Okay, then. There's your answer. Trust me, Alice, this is all normal."

Rather than argue with him, I took the easy way out. The more I pushed, the crazier I'd sound; and really, it's not like the hallucination scared me or anything. It was just weird. Really, really, weird.

After reminding me to set an appointment for the following month, he left the room. I gathered my belongings and thought about what he'd said. Yeah, probably I'd be able to believe him, except for one very specific thing I'd neglected to mention. That night? When I'd seen the mystery woman in my bedroom? My windows had most definitely been shut, and I had most definitely not gotten out of bed to open them. Nor had I ever before had an incident of sleepwalking. When I woke in the morning, a cool breeze blew through the room. Somehow, at some point, those windows had been opened, and I was almost 100 percent sure I hadn't done it myself.

After leaving the doc's office, I did the responsible thing and returned to work. My new position as a graphic designer with Enchanted Expressions Advertising didn't leave me with a lot of squeeze room, and risking my recently acquired steady paycheck was out of the question. Not in this economy, with a baby on the way.

Even so, I'd be lying if I said I didn't miss my prior job at a local art gallery. Before baby, I'd carved out a life that was nearly a perfect fit. Twenty hours per week at a job I loved, helping to show other artists' paintings, and plenty of nonwork time to focus on my art. It had just started paying off too. With a couple of solid placements in national art competitions, and as a featured artist at a local art fair, my paintings had finally begun to sell. But not quickly enough, and not for nearly enough money, to support the added responsibility coming my way.

I'd thought I could handle working full-time and continuing to paint, at least until the baby was born. Unfortunately, that hadn't panned out so well. Mostly because I was so freaking tired every minute of the day. Including now.

Glancing at my coworkers, I saw glazed-over eyes, twitchy arms, and barely restrained bodies. With the AC on the blink, the surprising May heat in the cramped conference room had notched up to just this side of the Inferno, and the couple of fans circulating air didn't alter the temperature any. Sweat dribbled down my neck and I wiped it away. My blouse and skirt stuck to my skin, and I wanted nothing more than to take a cool shower.

Because I needed to make a good impression, I attempted to pay attention to the staff meeting currently in progress. Not such an easy task. My eyelids refused to stay open. I envisioned propping them up with a couple of toothpicks, like in the cartoons I used to watch as a child. It had worked okay for Tom the cat in *Tom and Jerry*. But, seeing as I'm not a cartoon cat, or crazy enough to actually put little pointy sticks in my eyes, I hoped the image alone would be enough to keep them from slipping shut. So not the case. A heavy weight, almost like a drugged feeling, pushed down on me.

The owner of Enchanted Expressions, the dark-haired, ridiculously long-lashed, smoky-eyed Ethan Gallagher, was running through our current list of clients, asking for a progress report from each of the leads. His deep voice carried through the room, and with it, a faint Irish brogue that had most of my female coworkers entranced. For me, the result was more sleepiness. Every time he spoke, it was as if he were telling the most mesmerizing bedtime story ever written, delivered with the perfect cadence and rhythm.

My eyelids drifted shut again, and I pinched my thigh as hard as I could, hoping to send a burst of adrenaline through my system. I yelped. Every gaze in the room swung toward me. Geez, I'd wanted to be forced awake, but not like this!

"Sorry," I mumbled.

Ethan cocked his head to the side, eyes sweeping over me. "Everything okay, Alice?"

Prickly heat crawled along my skin, inch by inch. "Um. Yeah. Couldn't be better."

"People don't normally yell out in pain without reason. Are you sure there isn't a problem?" He stared at me, his eyebrows raised.

"Not pain," I replied. "Excitement. I just get so darn excited at these meetings, I can't keep it to myself."

"I see. Do you often say 'ow' when you're excited?"

"No. Of course not. That wouldn't make much sense, would it? I said 'Wow!' as in . . . well, you know . . ." *Great.* Any hope I'd had of making a good impression had just flown out the proverbial window.

A few quiet giggles from my coworkers sent another wave of heat to my face. I just knew I'd be the topic of conversation at the water cooler for the next several days, if not weeks.

Ethan's long lashes grazed the top of his cheeks as he blinked at my statement. "Okay, then. While I'm pleased you're excited, let's try to stay focused, shall we?"

"Yes. Of course. That's me. Focused. One hundred percent."

Amusement flickered in his eyes as he nodded, which bugged me a little. My embarrassment was fair game for a chuckle? Evidently so. It didn't matter that if the same situation occurred to someone else I'd find it funny; Ethan

Gallagher got to me. Not for the first time, I wondered why. It was as if, when he looked, Ethan saw the real me. He saw the Alice I didn't show anybody. Which was kind of freaky, but also kind of cool. But since I hadn't figured out what he thought of what he saw, I didn't like the idea of him laughing.

He flipped a page in his binder and moved on to the next account, asking for an update. With the pressure off, I stared at him for a minute, enthralled by his easy confidence, by the way he took charge of a room just by being present. Whenever he was close by, I knew it instantly. This awareness perplexed me, as I'd never before experienced anything like it.

Even stranger, I was fairly sure he felt it too. There was this ongoing vibration between us, almost a connection, and in different circumstances, I wouldn't have hesitated to make the first move. But with things as they were, most days I just tried to keep Ethan out of my head.

Opening my notepad while Ethan talked, I doodled a cartoon character with toothpicks holding its eyes open. If I started to get sleepy again, maybe the image would snap me out of it. But instead of heavy eyes, my stomach swirled and then somersaulted.

Not again. Not now.

Based on my doctor's claims of ginger being a good cure for nausea, I'd grabbed a can of ginger ale from a vending machine right before the meeting. Taking a cautious sip of the now tepid beverage, I prayed it would do what it was supposed to. My stomach gurgled in response.

After a hard swallow, I tried to even my breathing. Getting sick now would be bad. Horrifically, horribly, humiliatingly bad. Between the encounter with Shelby and my outburst in front of my coworkers, I'd been humiliated enough today, thank you very much. I clamped my lips together and willed my traitorous stomach into obedience.

"Missy had to leave early today," Ethan was saying, picking up a tiny, nearly paper-thin remote off the table and pointing it at the monitor in the front of the room. "But she has the preliminary commercial ready for the Kendall account. I watched it earlier, but let's take a look together."

He pressed a button and the monitor came alive. I squirmed as it did. This was one of the accounts I'd been working on, and honestly I thought the commercial was way off base. Not that Missy, the lead for the account, was interested in my opinion, but I'd still given it to her. Politely, of course.

Our advertising agency logo flashed, followed by the client's name. I scrunched lower in my chair. A mommy and a daddy penguin stood in the center of the screen with a group of children penguins all around. With dripping ice-cream cones in hand, they began to dance to an upbeat jingle.

As silly as this was, it was about to get even sillier. Cartwheeling polar bears holding melting Popsicles came next, their furry white bodies jiggling in rhythm. As if anybody could cartwheel while holding a Popsicle, especially large lumbering polar bears. For whatever reason, Missy thought this commercial would bring the residents of Chicago to Frosty's Ice Cream Shoppe.

When the monitor finally flashed off, a sigh of relief escaped my chest. I'd drawn the images the animator had referenced for the commercial, but I still wasn't on board with the overall design.

Ethan turned toward me just as my stomach burbled again. I slapped my hand over my mouth and eyed the door. How long would it take for me to run to the ladies' room?

"What are your thoughts on this, Alice?" he asked.

I sipped my soda, hoping like hell it would stop the

sloshing in my gut. "I think we accomplished Missy's goals." Why did the door seem farther and farther away as each second passed?

"What about the client's goals?"

Sweat moistened my forehead. Not only did I have to fight getting sick in front of everyone, I needed to be tactful. Many of Missy's friends were seated at the table, and anything I said would get back to her. I really didn't want to piss the woman off.

But an answer was expected, and I couldn't ignore a direct question from my boss, so I forged ahead. "One of Mr. Kendall's requests was to suggest his place is fun for children, and I think this commercial certainly does. It is fun. For children." I mentally patted myself on the back, for I'd oh-so-neatly sidestepped his question.

I started to stand, so I could excuse myself, when I realized it wasn't going to be that easy. All of Ethan's attention was centered on me. Other than the slight up and down movement of his chest, he stood completely still. The combination of absolute confidence and patience unnerved me, made me feel like I had to say more. It was the perfect boardroom tactic, and this man did it better than anyone I'd ever met. Not that I'd been in that many boardrooms, or met that many men who spent their time in boardrooms, for that matter; but I could still tell.

"Missy mentioned you had other ideas for this campaign," he remarked. "I'd like to hear them."

"Um . . . but . . . I'm just an artist," I said.

He shook his head, the gray of his eyes darkening. "Nobody is *just* anything here. We're a team, and everyone's opinion is important. That includes yours."

Ha. He should tell Missy that, as she certainly hadn't thought much of my ideas.

Once again, his stare went right through me—not the most pleasant of feelings. To buy a few extra minutes, I grabbed my soda . . . then instantly changed my mind. One sip and I'd be done for. I wished it was just out of the fridge, icy cold peppermint tea instead of flat ginger ale.

All at once, a shiver rippled through my body and tiny bumps coated my arms. The strength of the feeling surprised me, and I inhaled a long slow breath until the sensations gradually bled away.

"Alice? We're waiting."

"Well . . ." I cleared my throat and reminded myself to be tactful. Before I could speak, the soda can grew cold beneath my fingers. I swear! But that was impossible, right?

I dropped my hand and tried to focus on Ethan. "Mr. Kendall wants a campaign that promises fun for everyone who loves ice cream. While the commercial is cute, I think the cartoon limits the appeal to children and to those who have children." Swallowing to moisten my suddenly dry mouth, I forced myself to finish my thought process. "His place looks like a soda shop from the fifties. I think if we tie this shop to old-fashioned fun but also make it clear it's perfect for whatever people celebrate today, it would have a broader appeal, beyond families with kids."

"You visited the ice cream store?" Ethan asked.

"Well, yeah. That's how I came up with the idea. Walking in is like stepping back in time to when people did more together than they do now. Let's show them that celebrating at Frosty's is fun . . . no matter what the occasion." I shrugged. "I'm new at this, but it seems to me we should use that angle. Celebration, fun, and old-style togetherness."

"I like that. Put together some specific ideas by next week's meeting. We'll go over them then." And with that, he moved on to the next account.

Flattered, but also more than a little nervous, I sat back down and waited for my legs to stop shaking. Being in group situations, unless it was with my rather large family, was something to which I was unaccustomed. It knocked me off balance.

My stomach jumped again. It seemed Ethan was wrapping up the meeting, so I chanced another sip of ginger ale. But as I tipped the can, I had to force myself not to spit the drink back out. Oh my God, what the heck was happening?

You know when you're expecting one taste and you get another, how completely freaky that is? Even if the secondary taste is appealing, it doesn't seem that way because your brain's expecting something else. Slanting the can forward at an angle, I waited for the contents to seep over the edge to pool in a little puddle on the top. It was light amber in color—which really didn't tell me anything.

Raising the can, I sniffed. The unmistakable scent of peppermint met my nose. My skin chilled and my pulse sped up. I slammed the can back down on the table and watched it closely, as if it would break into dance like the cartoon penguins, which was ridiculous, because unless I'd crossed over into la-la land that was pretty much impossible.

Yet, how could room-temperature, flat ginger ale, in a freaking aluminum can, instantly turn into cold peppermint tea? No reasonable explanation presented itself. Was I hallucinating? Maybe pregnancy hormones had created a chemical shift in my brain and I truly was going insane. Did this happen to other expecting women?

On the heels of that thought, I recalled the mystery woman in my dreams and bedroom, and the windows opening on their own accord. I might have been able to convince myself, over time, that I'd gotten out of bed in a freak sleepwalking encounter and opened my bedroom windows that night. *Maybe*. But now I had two impossibilities staring me in the face. As much as I wanted to, I couldn't ignore that.

I looked at the can of soda again. Another shiver struck, this one a shiver of apprehension mixed with a little bit of fear. My world, as crazy as it had been, had just gotten a hell of a lot wackier and I had absolutely no clue what to do about it.

Chapter Two

"Why are you so freaked out? I think it's cool," said my best friend, Chloe Nichols, as we sat at my retroish dining room table Thursday evening. She'd recently cut her luxurious Lucille Ball red hair into a short style that framed her now even more pixieish face. The haircut definitely suited her, but I wasn't quite used to it yet.

"Cool? It's weird. And scary. Not to mention impossible." Chloe was the only person I told everything to. She already knew about the dreams and the window, but this was the first she'd heard of my changing-ginger-ale-into-tea story.

She shrugged, her light green eyes dancing with humor. "Nothing is impossible. Besides, I've always thought you were extra sensitive about things. Maybe being pregnant has heightened that awareness."

Chloe is a true believer in anything mystical. I was fairly sure she had a string of psychics on speed dial, ready to assist her at a moment's notice with any question she might have. She even owned a little store specializing in all things crazy.

"Did you hear me?" I asked. "I'm not talking about awareness here. I wished my ginger ale was tea and it *became* tea."

"I heard you. Have you tried again? To see if you can make it happen on purpose?"

"No." Why hadn't I thought of that? "Should I?"

"Yes!" She jumped up and then dashed into the kitchen. A minute later, she reappeared with a glass half filled with orange juice. After placing it in front of me, she returned to her seat. "Try to turn that into something else."

"Okay. Let me think." Did I really want to do this? I figured I might as well try, so I closed my eyes and concentrated. "I wish I had grape juice instead of orange juice." Then, to be sure, I thought the wish a couple more times. Opening my eyes, the same half-filled glass of orange juice met my gaze. I didn't know if I was disappointed or relieved. "Crap. I swear it happened."

"Try again. Maybe you're not concentrating hard enough. *Imagine* it turning into grape juice. See it with your mind's eye, and when the image is crystal clear, wish again."

I laughed. I didn't mean to, but she had that voice people use when they're telling ghost stories. But she knew more about this kind of thing than I did, so, funny or not, I took her advice. Unfortunately, other than pain at my temples, thirty minutes of effort brought me nothing except warm OJ. "Forget it. Nothing's happening. Maybe I did imagine it."

"I guess that's possible," Chloe admitted. "Maybe you wanted iced tea so badly, your brain made you think you had it? But I wouldn't give up entirely. Try again later."

I shrugged. "Maybe. I think I'm better off if I can forget it, though." The last few days had been a giant pool of nonproductivity, what with my thoughts of the strange and unexplained. So, yeah. Definitely it would be better if I shoved those aside and focused on more important things. Like keeping my job.

Ethan expected my ideas for the Kendall account by Tuesday's meeting, a mere five days away, and at this point I'd basically done nothing. Maybe I'd jot down some thoughts later that evening and put it all together over the weekend. It might mean skipping Sunday brunch with my sister, but I figured she'd understand.

"You never mentioned how your doctor's appointment went." Chloe was also one of the very few people who even knew I was pregnant.

"It went fine." I filled her in on everything Dr. Layton had said about my dreams. "But you'll never guess who I ran into."

"Who?"

I took a breath before answering. Chloe could be unpredictable, and I wasn't sure how she'd react. But I had to tell her. We had a no-secrets-allowed type of relationship. "Shelby Whitaker."

She gasped, and her already pale face paled more. "Seriously? If there's any justice in this world, you'll tell me she's grown a third eye and has a hairy mole on her chin."

Laughing, I shook my head. "No mole, and only two eyes, but she's huge. Well, her stomach is, anyway. She sounded the same, and looked mostly the same, but she was actually kind of nice. That was the biggest difference."

"Impressions can be deceiving. Once a spoiled brat, always a spoiled brat."

While Chloe had an open mind about almost everything, there were a few things in her life I didn't think she'd ever get over or forgive. Seeing as how Shelby had swooped in and stolen not one, not two, but *three* boyfriends away from her in high school, I was pretty sure Shelby would remain on Chloe's evil-eye list forever.

It was the third boyfriend that had really done it. The first two Chloe had gotten over relatively easily, as her emotions hadn't been completely involved. But the third boyfriend, Kyle Ackers, she'd fallen head over heels for. He'd broken things off with Chloe right before graduation, and all the plans they'd begun to make were forgotten. It had been a long time ago, yes, but that didn't mean it hurt Chloe any less today than it had back then. Especially because she and Shelby had been friends before the first boyfriend-snatching incident.

"It doesn't matter. I'll probably never see her again. You've been over Kyle for years now, anyway. Right?" I remarked.

Chloe blinked before answering. "Sort of. I guess I've always wondered if fate played out correctly, or if Shelby screwed up my one chance at happily ever after. Sometimes you only get one shot. I'd hate to have had it stolen."

"One chance? I don't believe that," I replied. "Just because you haven't found your knight in shining armor yet doesn't mean you won't. Look at me. I'm still alone."

"But you want to be alone," she pointed out. "I don't."

All at once, the man I tried very hard not to think about entered my thoughts. Troy Bellamy, the father of my unborn child, was a thief, a jerk—and, oh yeah, married. No. I didn't know he was married when we were dating. His wife demolishing my then-apartment in a fit of rage clued me in to that little detail.

Just thinking his name brought about images better left forgotten. I shuddered. "After a man lies to me, steals money from me, and acts like an escapee from an insane asylum, alone is pretty much all that's left."

A glimmer appeared in Chloe's eyes. I knew that look, so I braced myself. Always, right before she had some crazy idea, she'd get all lit up from the inside and almost glow. "What?" I asked, not sure I really wanted to know.

"You just reminded me! When Troy came to your old place to pay back your money, you said he stated some far-out things. Do you remember?"

Like I'd ever forget. "Of course. He was ill and thought I'd cast a spell on him. Said his mother was a witch and had done the same exact thing to him, and begged me to take it off. And then he pointed to my sister as being the cause!" I grinned at the thought of Elizabeth casting a spell on anyone, for any reason whatsoever. My sister?

She was almost as practical as our mother. Definitely not witch material, if there even was such a thing.

Chloe stood and paced the dining room. "Don't you see what this means?"

"No. Why don't you explain it?"

"You're pregnant with Troy's child. Troy's mother is a witch. So, maybe the baby is too, and that's how your soda turned into peppermint tea."

Chloe's words slammed down on me like a block of cement. I gave myself a minute to take it all in, because let's face it: this was the first semireasonable, if totally crazy, explanation I had. But after that minute passed, I remembered one key fact. "Troy's a liar. We can't believe anything he said. His mother is probably a sweet old lady who bakes cookies for his kids."

Chloe pulled a chair out next to me and sat down. "Well, there is that, but my skin is tingling." She shoved her arm in front of me. "See? Goose bumps. I always get them when I'm on to something like this. Just the other day, one of my customers told me about how she thought she saw a ghost, and the same thing happened. Goose bumps everywhere."

"Sweetie, that's just your body giving you a physical reaction to something you're excited about," I told her. Someone had to keep Chloe's feet on the ground. Witches weren't real. Not the magic-producing, twitchy-nosed kind like in *Bewitched*.

"What's Troy's mother's name?" Chloe asked.

I'd never met her, but he'd talked about her here and there when were together. "It's Beatrice. Beatrice Bellamy."

"Is she local?" Chloe pushed.

"I think so, but I don't know for sure."

"Where's your phone book?"

"You are not going to call her and ask her if she's a witch, Chloe!"

"Don't be silly. It's not like she'd tell some stranger on the phone. I just want to see if she's listed. So, where is it?"

Sighing, I stood. "I'll get it." After grabbing the phone book from the living room, I returned to the dining room and plopped it down in front of my friend, troublemaker that she was.

"What's his dad's name?"

"I don't know. He never talked about his father."

She flipped through pages until she found the Bs, and then ran her white-tipped fingernail down the list of names. "Wow, there's lots of Bellamys but no Beatrice."

"Maybe she's unlisted. Or maybe I'm wrong and she doesn't live around here."

Sliding the phone book my way, she said, "You still haven't been able to get a hold of Troy?"

I shook my head. Against my sister's advice, I'd attempted to reach Troy several times over the past month. Because, jerk or not, I felt he had the right to know about the baby. Only none of his numbers were still in service. I'd even checked the health club he'd worked at when we dated, only to find he was no longer an employee. They had no idea where he was, or if they did, they weren't telling me. So, as of now anyway, he didn't have a clue I was pregnant. Maybe good, maybe bad. But at least I'd tried. "I don't know where else to look for him."

"I'll do some checking around. About him and his mother. If she's really a witch, someone I know will know of her."

"You don't seriously think this is a possibility, do you?" I asked.

"Like I said before, anything is possible. Even this. And come on, how cool would it be to have a witch in the family?"

"Your idea of cool doesn't quite mesh with mine. And even if this is more than a far-fetched thought, it still doesn't explain my weird dreams."

"That might be one thing your doctor is right about. Maybe the woman *is* you, Alice. You've gone through a lot of stuff lately. Most of the time, dreams are all about our subconscious worries, fears, and fantasies. You know that."

Weird, but for some reason, it was far easier for me to write off the other, more tangible things to imagination and hormones. But the dreams were just too real, in every way. It was hard to let go of that. This woman? She wanted to tell me something. I'd never been surer of anything in my life. "My gut says it's more than that, but you could be right," I ceded.

"Time will tell." Chloe squeezed my hand. "I'm going to take off. I want to find out more about Beatrice Bellamy, and I think I know where to start." Rising from her chair, she almost bounced to my front door. "I'll call if I learn anything."

I'd known Chloe long enough to realize that once the twilight zone portion of her brain is engaged, there's no pulling her away from something. "Okay. We're still on for Wednesday next week, right?"

"Absolutely. My treat, since it's your birthday. And maybe I'll have some answers for you by then."

After she left, I rubbed my belly and thought again about Troy and that day he'd been at my place. He'd been so insistent that either I or my sister had cast a spell on him to make him sick. That was the reason he'd paid me back. Somehow, he'd had it in his head that once he did, the pain in his stomach would dissipate.

Troy was most definitely a liar. There were no ifs, ands, or buts about it. But that didn't mean he'd lied about everything. So maybe this thing about his mother was the truth—at least as far as he believed.

Hell. Did witches, *real* witches, exist? I glanced at the door Chloe had exited through and hoped, really, truly hoped, she'd discover something to disprove the notion.

Because, in all seriousness, the thought of raising a baby with magic in his or her bloodline freaked me out more than anything else possibly could. My new motto in life was all about control. And come on: there was absolutely nothing I could control about this. If it proved to be true.

Pushing the situation out of my mind, I made my way to my desk. A few hours of work on the Kendall account would certainly bring things into better perspective. After all, that was one thing I *could* control.

As to the rest? I'd just have to wait and see.

The telltale shuffle of my coworkers walking toward the elevator clued me in that it was time for lunch. I felt like the odd girl out. It wasn't that the people at Enchanted Expressions weren't nice. They were; they just didn't think to include me in any of their out-of-the-office activities.

Usually this sort of thing didn't bother me. But today, for whatever reason, a hint of disappointment settled in when I was once again alone in the office I shared with two others. I shrugged it off. So it would be a working lunch. No big deal. Opening my sketchbook, I decided to flesh out some of my ideas for the Frosty's Ice Cream Shoppe account.

The ice cream counter went in first, with a line of stools in front. Behind the counter, I added a couple of employees and the large menu that hung on the wall. My hand moved quickly, the pencil making that *swoosh* sound I'd always loved, and I didn't stop to think about the image emerging: I just wanted a rough sketch to begin with. The tables went in next. One by one, I filled the chairs with people spending time together, enjoying ice cream.

Everything around me disappeared as I worked. Creative energy flowed from me to the pencil to the page, my hand in perfect harmony with my mental vision. While this feeling wasn't completely unusual, it hadn't occurred in far too long—since before the drastic change in my life, and never at Enchanted Expressions. On many occasions in the past, I'd begun a painting or a sketch and hours had disappeared without me being truly aware of it. When I looked at my work later, I'd remember every stroke I made with brush or the pencil, but the process itself was pure magic. Coming out of this trance was like waking up slowly from an afternoon siesta, without any outside intrusions.

In other words, pure heaven.

Not this time. A series of shivers erupted over my body, as if someone had dumped a bucket of freezing water down my back. Startled, I dropped my pencil and waited for the effects to subside, lifted my chin and glanced at the vent high on the wall. They must have fixed the AC, which was good, because summer was not that far off. Still, I made a mental note to grab my sweater from my car.

Cracking my neck first to the left and then to the right, I appraised my nearly complete drawing. Definitely rough, it also had the air I'd been aiming for: celebration, fun, family, and friends. The center table showed a family of four sharing a huge sundae. Around them were other families, a group of kids in baseball uniforms celebrating their win, and a young couple sharing a malt while staring romantically into each other's eyes. Very Norman Rockwell. I liked it.

Thinking I'd grab some lunch before sketching in the finer details, I pushed my chair out from my desk. Ethan appeared, though. My office was large, but with three easels, three desks, three computers—each with two monitors, along with various other paraphernalia, plus the dividers separating the work spaces—there wasn't that much elbow space left over. And Ethan was a tall guy, so as soon as he entered, even that minuscule space seemed to diminish.

As did my ability to breathe. Forcing a smile in greeting, I reminded myself to stay calm. To act professionally, to not show how much his presence affected me.

"Have plans for lunch, Alice?" he asked in his sultry Irish brogue.

Friday was casual day, and he'd chosen to wear black jeans and a white short-sleeved shirt. His tan, muscular arms caught my attention, and I had to admit once again that, boss or not, Ethan Gallagher was one hunk of a man. "Um. No. Why?"

"I'm heading out now. I thought you might want to join me."

"For what?" I asked, then realized quite suddenly that I was staring at his chin. How had I never noticed the cleft before?

"Lunch. It's a meal between breakfast and dinner. Surely you've heard of it," he teased.

"Lunch. Uh-huh." And the jaw itself? Strong. Angular. My hands itched to touch it, to draw it.

He must have noticed my gaze was not directed at his eyes, because he rubbed his chin. "Do I have something there?" he asked.

"Hmm? Oh. No. Sorry."

He didn't say anything, just stood there watching me with an inquisitive, teasing expression. As if he had a secret he couldn't wait to share. Finally, I said, "Um, did you need something?"

"I asked you to lunch, if you'd like to go," he reminded me.

"Oh. Sure." My stomach flip-flopped. "When?"

He laughed. "Now. Is this a good moment for you to step away?"

I hesitated. Ethan got under my skin, and I didn't completely understand why. Sure, he was sexy in a *Remington Steele* sort of way, but I was pregnant. No man anywhere should be getting to me at this juncture of my life. So, spending an hour with him alone made me more than a little nervous. But I couldn't exactly say no to my boss, now could I?

"It's fine," I mumbled. "I just need a minute and I'll be ready to go."

"I'll meet you in the lobby then. Sound good?"

I nodded in agreement just as his gaze caught the sketch I'd been working on. "Hey, that looks pretty good." He bent over to get a closer view, and as he did, the clean, fresh scent of his cologne wrapped around me. "Is that us?"

"What?" I so wanted a bottle of whatever he was wearing.

He pointed with his index finger to the couple sipping the malt. "I know it's rough, but that looks a lot like you and me."

"Don't be silly. Why would I draw us as a couple?"

Straightening, he winked at me. "I don't know, but the likeness is uncanny. Take another look."

I leaned over, all ready to point out the myriad differences between my hurriedly sketched figures and us, but as my eyes took in the drawing, I gasped. The profiles of the man and woman were, indeed, eerily familiar. Why had I done that? I certainly hadn't done it on purpose. Heat tickled my cheeks, and I said, "There's not enough detail to tell."

"Actually, I was thinking they had more detail than any of the other people in the shop."

The tickle of embarrassment turned into a blast. I imagined flames shooting out from my cheeks; they were that hot. And since a person should change the subject when there's no hope of the floor opening up to suck her away, I did. "Lunch?"

"Of course. I'll meet you downstairs." He turned to leave, saying over his shoulder, "I think it's cute. That you put us in the picture."

Cute? More like freaky. Did the fact that I'd coupled myself with him in pencil mean I harbored fantasies I hadn't fully admitted to myself? Or was it yet another sign of hormones gone wild? Hell if I knew, and I didn't have time to figure it out. Tucking the picture away in a drawer, so no one else would see it, I went to meet Ethan.

First, though, I stopped in the restroom to check my appearance. I was pleased to see I looked mostly okay. Except for my shirt. I'd been in a hurry that morning and grabbed the first clean one I'd come across that fit. Soon I'd have to give in and go buy maternity clothes. Not something I looked forward to.

I tugged at the drab olive green blouse. The cut and style suited me well enough, but the color did nothing for my skin tone. Primary hues were best. Blue, especially. If I had to go to lunch with someone as dashingly sexy as Ethan, it'd be nice to feel confident.

"I wish you were blue, you ugly green shirt," I said as I turned on the faucet.

A long, rolling tremble began at my toes and inched its way up my body. I grasped the edge of the counter to steady myself and inhaled. The walls closed in and, for a minute, the entire room swirled around me. I thought I might faint. I bent over and splashed my face with cold water, which helped. After another minute passed, everything settled and I took another shaky breath.

I didn't get, at first, what had happened. Seeing as I hadn't eaten since breakfast, I assumed my body wanted some calories, and that was that. But after I dried my face off, when I turned to leave the restroom I caught sight of my reflection out of the corner of my eye and stopped. I forced the air out of my lungs and then back in. I wanted to freak, truly I did, but I think I was in shock.

Holy shit.

Turning orange juice into grape had apparently been too difficult, but somehow, changing the color of my blouse wasn't? Again I tugged at my shirt, now a bright peacock blue. Seriously, the fabric itself had changed color. How was that even remotely possible?

Most women would probably think this was cool, but not me. I preferred ginger ale to stay ginger ale and green garments to stay green. Besides, I was about to meet Ethan, and he'd just seen me, so unless he was color-blind, he'd notice. How the hell would I explain a chameleonic shirt?

My mind jumped around all the possible things I could say, and nothing I came up with seemed realistic. If I wished it blue, maybe I could wish it back? "I wish this shirt was its original color," I whispered. Nothing happened, so I tried again. "Please, please, please be green."

Zip. Zilch. Nada.

With shaking hands, I whisked out my cell phone and dialed Chloe. Only she didn't answer. Maybe I'd just stay in the bathroom and hide? No. He'd eventually come to find me, and that would be so much worse. Which meant I needed to figure this out. And fast.

I was about to try wishing the color back again when the restroom door opened and Missy entered. The woman wore a constant frown, though maybe that was only when she dealt with me. She glared as she crossed to the row of sinks. "I just saw Ethan in the lobby. He wanted me to check on you."

"Oh. I should go then," I said.

She didn't respond, so I left. Whatever her beef with me was, it would come out sooner or later. Right now, I had more important things to think about.

Ethan's gaze skimmed over me when I met up with him in the lobby. "I was beginning to worry." Cupping my elbow with his hand, he led me toward the door. "Everything okay?"

"Yes. Sorry it took me so long." Hey, if he didn't mention my shirt, I wasn't going to.

"Not a problem. I thought we'd go to Roméo's, since it's within walking distance and it's a beautiful day. Do you like Italian?"

"Love it."

Fifteen minutes later, we were seated in the restaurant. We'd already placed our orders, and now I didn't know what to say. After the sketch incident and the magically changing shirt, I pretty much had nothing. Besides, he'd likely invited me to lunch for a reason, so I assumed he'd take control of the conversation at some point. Until then, I was content to nibble on a roll and drink my water.

"How are you finding Enchanted Expressions?" His tone held nothing more than interest and mild curiosity, but a knotted ball of tension curled between my shoulders.

"What do you mean?"

"You're not very happy, are you?"

Oh, no. Was this one of those *take the lousy employee out to a public place to fire her so she wouldn't make a scene* type of things? "Why would you say that? I'm thrilled. I can't wait to get to work every day!" So I exaggerated a little. It didn't hurt anything.

His smoky eyes met mine, and again, my instincts told me he saw straight through me. "A little overkill on the excitement, don't you think?"

I fiddled with my water glass. "I don't want you to fire me," I admitted softly. "It's a good job, and I'm grateful to have it. There are a lot of things I like about it. I'm still adjusting, that's all." I shrugged. "I never saw myself in an office for forty hours a week."

"Then why are you?"

Because being a single mother required a decent income, that's why. Of course, I couldn't tell him that. It wouldn't be right when most of my family remained clueless. "Time to grow up, I guess," I said instead.

"Remind me. What did you do before taking this job?"

"Lots of things. After college, I decided to try my hand at being a working artist. After a year of that, I decided I was tired of eating only ramen and mac and cheese, so I accepted a part-time gig at a gallery. The gallery's owner, Maura, is a huge supporter of independent artists, and helped me gain a little notice." My fingers curled together on my lap. "It was a good fit then, but things change," I explained, not wanting to give more details.

"Why did you wait so long to enter the field you went to school for?"

While his tone still only held general interest, my nerves ramped up another notch. Not sure what to say, I settled on, "It was the right time."

The waitress brought our food, but my appetite had vanished. Not because of nausea, for once, but out of stark, cold fear. I didn't know what I'd do if I lost my job. Ethan's appetite seemed to be fine, so rather than eat my food I watched him eat his. And for a few minutes, I was pleasantly distracted watching his jaw move as he chewed.

"I'm not firing you. I should have said that straight off. I apologize."

In a blink, all my anxiety evaporated. "Oh. Well, good. You made me a little nervous."

"I asked you here because I sincerely wanted to know if you're happy." He took another bite of his food. "I also plan on visiting Frosty's on Sunday, and hoped you'd come with me."

And just like that, a spark of energy passed between us. At a different time, with a different man, I'd think I was being asked out on a date. Of course, that couldn't be the case here. But wow, I liked that idea. Way more than I should. Silly, really, because becoming involved with a man was not in my newly formed plan for the future. Even so, I'd be lying if I said I didn't miss the side effects of being in a relationship: having someone to talk to, share dreams with, cuddle and laugh with. Because I did. In a huge way.

And let's not forget the sex thing. I really, really missed that. Especially lately.

"Alice?"

"Hmm?"

"What are you thinking?"

"That I miss sex," I admitted.

A raging inferno lit my cheeks on fire. *Again.* "Um. I didn't mean that. Well, I did, but I shouldn't have said it. I tend to speak without thinking. I'm trying to stop that."

Little lines crinkled around his eyes as he laughed. He had a good laugh, strong and warm, like a bubbling brook, and the sound of it relaxed me immediately. "You have to be the most curious woman I've ever met."

"Just outspoken. I'm actually kind of boring." Or I used to be. I didn't know what I was any longer. Paranoid? Delusional? Maybe the mother-to-be of a witch? None of those choices thrilled me. At all.

"Sex is a good thing to miss. It makes it all that much better when you have a chance to revisit it."

Ha. He had quite a way with words, didn't he? *Revisiting sex.* I liked that.

"About Sunday? Are you available?"

"To go to the ice cream shop? I'd love to." But even as I answered, something hovered on the edge of my consciousness. Almost a déjà vu feeling but not quite.

"Great. It's a date. I'll pick you up around two, if that's good."

A date? My mind fixated, though it was probably just an expression. Still, a tingle of anticipation made me smile. "Two is perfect."

Whether it made sense or not, in a flash everything seemed a little brighter than it had. My appetite resurrected itself, so I dug into my pasta. It was nice to have something to look forward to. Nice to have a plan for the weekend. And yeah, it was nice that that plan involved Ethan Gallagher.

"Now, I have a strange question for you," he admitted.

"Shoot."

"Weren't you wearing a green shirt earlier?"

Swallowing my bite of food, I decided to be honest. It wasn't like he'd believe me, so why not? Besides, I couldn't give him an explanation when I didn't even have one for myself. "Actually, I was. But I wished it blue and it turned blue." I snapped my fingers. "Just like that."

Confusion clouded his eyes for a second, but then he grinned. "Yes. Definitely the most curious woman ever."

I couldn't argue with that statement, so I didn't.

Chapter Three

I crave Saturday mornings the way my sister craves coffee—earnestly, with a passion, and pretty much non-stop. Saturdays are about sleeping in, and then a full day doing whatever I want, with the knowledge I still have one more day off. Sundays are different. Sure, I can still sleep in, but the reality that Monday's just around the corner makes it not quite as special. On Saturday, all things are possible. So when my coffee-addicted sister phoned me way too early on Saturday morning, begging me to babysit her boyfriend's nephew, to say I wasn't jumping for joy is a mega understatement.

Elizabeth had to work, and her boyfriend had been called in to work unexpectedly, so they needed some help until the boy's mom could pick him up. Because my sister didn't ask for favors often, and because she really sounded stuck, I'd dragged myself out of bed and driven to her place. Lucky for her, watching Sam had been kind of fun. But now I was glad to be home.

Yawning, I climbed the steps to my condo and then stopped. Why was my front door open a crack? Had I left in such a hurry that morning, I'd forgotten to close and lock it? I couldn't discount that possibility, not right away. But as I mentally retraced my steps, I distinctly remembered turning the lock on the knob and shutting the door behind me. My skin grew clammy and a rush of lightheadedness had me gripping the porch railing so tightly that my knuckles turned white.

Scooting to the edge of my narrow front porch, I tried

to peek inside, hoping to discover who, if anyone, was there. The door wasn't open wide enough for me to see anything but the russet-painted wall of my entryway. No way was I walking in there. For one, I'd always hated those movies where people ran pell-mell into danger when they could have avoided it by being somewhat intelligent. For two, well—I'm not stupid.

Retreating to my car, I figured I'd go find a friendly police officer to help me out, when a thread of laughter hit my ears. I knew that laugh. It came from my younger brother Joe, who never, and I mean never, visited me alone. So if he was at my place, that meant the rest of my family was also. Swiveling on my heel, I checked out the cars that dotted the parking lot. Yep. My parents' ten-year-old boat of a car, my sister's falling-apart Volkswagen bug, my older brother's sparkling new SUV, Joe's refurbished Trans Am, and my Grandma Verda's Mini Cooper were all lined up in a nice, pretty row.

A new type of uneasiness slid in. Had my sister spilled the beans? If so, then my entire family being at my place was not a good sign. They'd have questions. Lots and lots of them, and they'd expect answers. A shudder rippled through me. No way, no how was I going into that mess until I knew. So I did what any her-family-doesn't-yet-know-she's-pregnant woman would do. I ran and hid.

Kneeling behind my car, I called my sister on my cell phone.

"Alice? Where are you?" my sister asked when she answered.

"I'm outside. Why are you all at my place?"

"Waiting for you, you goof. Come inside."

"Did you tell anyone about . . . you know?"

Elizabeth's voice lowered. "Of course not! I told you I wouldn't."

Patience was not one of my virtues, but I tried. Really, I did. "Spell it out for me then. Why are you all here?"

She huffed into the phone, as if *she* were exasperated with *me*. "What day is today?"

"It's Saturday. Yesterday was Friday, and tomorrow is Sunday. That doesn't tell me anything." As soon as I spoke, though, I realized. "Oh, crap. Is this some early surprise birthday thing?"

"Well, it's not now, is it?"

All at once, the early morning phone call made sense. "You set me up! You didn't need a babysitter."

"Oh, stop. We had to find some way to get you out of the house for a few hours. Just get in here." She giggled, clearly pleased with herself.

"Maybe I don't want to. Maybe I'll just get back in my car and take off. How'd you guys get in, anyway?" Damn. I was not in the mood for a birthday gathering. After a week of weirdness, I just wanted to be left alone. At least until Chloe had more information.

"You're a dork. Grandma still has a key." Her voice lowered again. "Get in here before Mom figures out I'm talking to you. She's glaring at me from across the room."

Before I could respond, my phone beeped and the call ended. So . . . great, just great. If I didn't make an entrance quickly, my sister would bring everyone outside.

For half a second, I contemplated leaving anyway. But that would just add fuel to the already roaring fire. Annoyed, I stared at my cell phone for a second. Then, tucking it back into my purse, I stood and straightened my oversized white shirt. Was it voluminous enough to cover my ever-growing baby bump? I wasn't huge by any stretch of the imagination, but I'd definitely begun to show. It had been several weeks since the last time I'd seen any of my family. Would they notice?

Probably. And that thought made me grab my sweater out of my car. Thank goodness I'd left it there. I'd have to tell everyone soon, but not today, and not all at once.

That would be a level of hell into which I wasn't ready to descend.

I pulled on the sweater. I hated surprises. Well, let me rephrase: It was the *being surprised* portion of surprises I didn't like. Planning out surprises for other people was a totally different story. For some reason, though, my family had failed to catch on to this. Or maybe they just ignored it.

"No time like the present," I muttered, taking the steps, once again, to my condo. Pushing the door open, I stepped inside. From the entryway, the dining room opened to the right, and I saw a huge birthday cake sitting on my table. The living room was on the left, and my family had decorated it with balloons and streamers. A *Happy Birthday!* banner hung over the entrance to my hall. And everywhere I looked, too many freaking people met my gaze.

Weirdly, no one noticed me right away. Again I thought of sneaking out, but before I could, all eyes turned toward me.

"Surprise!" my family yelled, in almost perfect unison.

I put a fake smile on. "Wow. I had no idea," I said. "Especially since my birthday isn't until Wednesday."

Grandma Verda, decked out in a turquoise running suit with orange piping matched with almost fluorescent purple sneakers, approached me. "If we'd waited until Wednesday, then it wouldn't have been a surprise, now would it?"

"I guess not." I gave her a quick hug.

"Besides, you probably have plans with your girlfriends on your birthday. This is for family only."

She was right. I did have plans with Chloe on Wednesday, but that wasn't really the point. "You guys should have let me know you were coming over."

"That wouldn't have been nearly as much fun." Her faded blue eyes zeroed in on me. "How are you feeling?"

"Surprised, I guess. Why?" I tugged at my sweater, worried it wasn't enough coverage to hide my condition. Besides, my grandmother? She wasn't just smart; she had this creepy and often right-on-target intuition about things.

"Just wondering. You're wearing a heavy sweater in the middle of May. I thought you might be ill." Her hand reached toward my stomach. I pivoted slightly away, so it landed on my hip instead.

"It was chilly when I left this morning. That's all," I lied. "Maybe I'm coming down with a cold."

"Uh-huh. How are you eating? Nutrition is important. I hope you're getting plenty of fresh fruits and vegetables." She clutched my arm. "Oh! And protein. You need protein."

"Um. Grandma? What are you talking about?"

"You've always been so skinny. I worry. That's all."

Hmm. Probably she wasn't being honest, but I'd take the out she gave me. Happily. "You don't need to worry. I'm eating plenty." Another fib, but what the heck, I was on a roll.

Luckily, she didn't question me further, just retreated to the couch where her seminew boyfriend sat. Vinny was a nice guy, and because they'd decided to live together, Grandma Verda had given me her condo. At the time I hadn't considered her reasoning behind the gift. Now I wondered how much she knew, and how long she'd known.

I made my way to my mother. Isobel Raymond stood near the kitchen, watching everyone with an eagle eye. She was dressed in one of her many housedresses, this one a pale green, and she held her body ramrod straight. Perfect posture and all that.

Her lips turned upward in a smile. "Happy birthday, sweetie."

"Thanks. Who planned this?"

She reached over, tucked a strand of my long hair behind my ear. "Your grandmother. She insisted. It came together wonderfully, didn't it?"

"Sure. Wonderful."

"Your grandmother seems to think you need cheering up." Her brown eyes, so similar to mine, bored into me. "Is there something going on you'd like to share?"

"Just busy at work." I didn't mention the other stuff. She'd drag me to a psychiatrist before I could say *Boo!* Though maybe that wasn't such a bad idea.

"Oh! I forgot to tell you. An old girlfriend of yours from high school called the house the other day. Since your number is unlisted, she couldn't find it. I gave it to her, so you'll probably hear from her soon."

For the life of me, I couldn't think of who would be phoning me from that many years ago. "Do you remember her name?" I asked.

"Shelby something. She was very nice."

"Shelby Whitaker? Harris?" My first reaction was fear. What if she'd told my mother she'd seen me at the OB's office? Almost as quickly, I calmed down. If my mother knew I was pregnant, she wouldn't hesitate to tell me.

"That's her. She gave me her number. I left it on the counter for you."

Before I could reply, my other brother, Scot, came up behind and wrapped his arms around me in a tight squeeze. "How's it feel to be thirty-three?" he asked in my ear.

Pulling out of his embrace, I faced him. "I'm still thirty-two, so ask me again on Wednesday." Scot was the typical big brother who'd taken great pains to pick on me every chance he got while we were growing up. Every now and then, our relationship echoed the past, but for the most part we got along well.

Other than—to my mind, anyway—he'd gotten all the looks in the family. Dark brown hair, almost black eyes, and eyelashes any girl would kill for were just window dressing on his tall frame and fit body. For some unknown reason, he'd remained single all these years.

His eyes skimmed over me and I sucked in my belly as much as I could. Then I curled my arms around myself. Scot tended to notice things. Other than my grandmother, he was the one most likely to catch on.

A quizzical expression flitted across his features. "Are you hot? Your face is red."

My mother interjected, "You do look flushed. Why don't you take that sweater off and get something cool to drink?"

I grappled with something to say that would make sense, but sadly, I had nothing. Thankfully, Elizabeth saved the day.

"Let's do cake and ice cream," my sister announced, stopping next to me. "It's your favorite, Alice. Dark chocolate and whipped icing."

My sister owns a bakery called A Taste of Magic, and normally the chance to eat anything she bakes is a walk this side of Heaven. Due to my pregnancy predicament, and the almost constant nausea, this was no longer the case. Of course, I couldn't say that. "Sure. Cake sounds great."

Elizabeth called the rest of my family to the dining room, and they gathered around the table. Verda and Vinny stood on the fringes, my grandmother's eyes suspiciously on my stomach. I sucked it in tighter. Next to them was Joe, who, with his fair complexion, blue eyes, and shaggy blond hair, resembled a surfer boy hankering to catch the next wave. Funny, really, when my brother was a total tech geek.

He smiled at me. I smiled back. I loved all my siblings, but Joe had a special place in my heart. Mostly, probably, because all the annoying older sibling lessons I'd learned from Scot and Elizabeth, I'd been able to inflict on Joe. At least with him I'd always had the upper hand.

My father, Marty, an older version of Joe (except for his receding hairline) leaned against the wall of my dining room. I was calmest around my dad. He never poked his nose into anything, just accepted everyone for who they were and what they wanted to say. Gotta love that in a dad, you know?

After everyone sang, I leaned over to blow out my candles—all thirty-three of them.

"Don't forget to make a wish!" my grandmother interrupted. "Wishes are important!"

I ignored her and blew the dang things out. I'd had enough issues with wishes lately, and until I figured those out, I didn't plan on making any more. Besides, I wanted to push the party along and send everyone home. I needed to talk to Chloe. Badly.

"What did you wish for, Alice?" my grandmother asked, accepting a piece of cake.

"Health, happiness, and prosperity," I quipped. I finished handing out cake, and then took mine to the living room. Sitting down on my battered red papasan chair, a throwback from my college days, I tried to tune out the chattering all around.

The first bite of cake went down smoothly enough. So did the second, thank goodness. Not wanting to push my luck, I set the plate on an end table and leaned back. My family had clumped into groups. My brothers were chatting in the dining room. Vinny and Verda were back on the couch. My sister was on the phone, probably with her boyfriend, Nate.

My father approached, my mother right behind him. He offered me a card. "We didn't know what to get you, so I hope cash is okay," he said.

"Marty! Let her open it before telling her what's inside," my mother scolded.

"Oh! Are we doing presents now?" This question came from my grandmother.

"Cash is always good." Opening the card, I read the birthday sentiment and a rush of emotion hit me. No matter how completely insane my family could be, they were all about love and sticking together. Maybe it was time to tell them about the baby.

Glancing up, I saw my sister watching me. She nodded, as if reading my thoughts. Before I could gather my courage, though, my grandmother slid a brightly wrapped present toward me, by way of my mother.

When the present reached me, I gasped. *Oh, no.* The paper had women, in varying stages of pregnancy, all over it, with the word CONGRATULATIONS in huge pink and blue letters. Quickly I ripped the paper off and crumpled it up into a ball, hoping no one else would notice. No one said anything, so I must have been successful.

Under the paper was an unmarked white box. I sent a silent prayer upward that it didn't contain anything pregnancy or baby-related, like a breast pump. I picked off the tape holding the lid shut and slowly opened it. A jade green blouse lay inside, along with a gift card to a maternity clothes shop.

Heaven help me.

Tucking the gift card beneath the blouse, I tipped the box around to show everyone. "Thank you, Grandma. It's a beautiful color."

"That *is* pretty! Let me see," my mother said.

Because it was all too likely it was a maternity shirt, and no way in hell was I going to hand it to my mother, I set the box down beside me. "I'll try it on later and model it."

We finished with gifts. My brothers and my sister had banded their resources together to buy me some new art supplies—always a welcome choice. Using my foot, I pushed the box from my grandmother farther back, so that it sat beneath the frame of my chair, then grabbed a folded blanket and shoved it over the top.

That moment earlier, when I'd almost confessed all? I'd had second thoughts. Better to wait and do it slowly. Like, maybe tell them from the hospital when I was in labor. My stomach twisted and a wave of nausea had me clamping my mouth shut.

"I'll be right back," I said, jumping up and running to the bathroom. I sat on the edge of the tub, willing my stomach to settle. I hated this, the loss of control. My body did what it wanted to do, when it wanted to do it, and that freaked me out.

Hushed voices drifted in—my grandmother's and my sister's voices, to be precise, and they must have been right outside the bathroom door. Maybe it was rude to listen, but it's not my fault they chose that particular spot to chat. So yeah, I eavesdropped.

"Have you told her yet?" asked Grandma Verda.

"No. Miranda said to wait. That I'd know when the time was right." This came from my sister.

"Elizabeth! She needs to know. It's been almost a month since you gave it to her. You know how unpredictable it can be. How much longer are you going to wait?"

"Shh. She'll hear you. I'll tell her, but not yet. Miranda said she'd come to me."

My mind worked through what I'd heard, but it was like trying to decipher Russian. Gave me what? And who was Miranda? I started to stand, but a soft knock on the door stopped me. "Yes?"

"Alice? It's me, Elizabeth. Are you okay?"

"I'm fine. You can come in."

She entered and closed the door behind her. Kneeling in front of me, she grasped my hand. Like me, she had our mother's brown hair and eyes. But she had been blessed with the curvier body, and was about two inches shorter than my five feet eight inches.

"Shouldn't the morning sickness be over with by now?

I thought once you hit your second trimester you'd be feeling better," she said.

"That's what all the books say. My doctor says it's different for everyone. If anything, it's gotten worse."

"I'm sorry." She hesitated a beat. "You're going to need to tell everyone soon. You can't keep it quiet that much longer. Grandma already knows."

"I sort of figured that one out. Did you tell her?"

"Nope, not me. But she's known almost since the beginning, I think. She was making baby booties a few weeks ago."

Baby booties? *Great.* Grandma Verda was not normally the stay-at-home-and-knit sort of gal. If everything earlier hadn't been enough to seal the deal, that was. Really, I was lucky she hadn't told my mother yet. "I heard you guys talking. Who's Miranda?"

Elizabeth's cheeks paled. "You must have misunderstood. We were just wondering if you were okay or not."

"I distinctly heard the name Miranda. 'Fess up, sis."

"That's just someone Grandma wants to introduce you to."

I stared at her. That wasn't what I'd heard, was it? No. But prying secrets out of my sister before she was ready to tell was an impossible feat. "I don't believe you, but it doesn't matter. I should get back out there."

She left and I splashed cold water on my cheeks. I kind of wished I'd made my birthday wish earlier, when I had blown out the candles on my cake. Nothing crazy. Just a simple one. I whispered it now: "I wish everyone would go home."

A warm shiver slipped across my skin, followed by the sensation of butterfly wings flapping around in my belly. Then came tingling, as if someone were running her fingers ever so lightly up my spine, that made me shiver again.

Whoa. Okay, that was more than a little strange. I sat

back down and waited to feel it again. Nothing. No more butterfly wings. Goose bumps appeared on my arms, though, even under the heavy weight of my sweater, and I tried to rub them away. I'd read enough books to realize I'd just felt my baby move, and instead of the happiness most women probably experienced at that moment, I was flat-out terrified.

For the first time since the little line had turned pink, I truly understood that another person lived inside of me. I didn't have a husband, or even a boyfriend, to lean on. I didn't have a plan. I didn't know how to be a parent, or how to do all the things I was going to need to do. Right then, in a millisecond, my world shifted again. I ignored the tears weighting my eyes. I ignored the shivers that refused to stop.

Somehow, I needed to find control. And with that control, maybe I wouldn't be so freaking afraid of what was going to happen. I forced myself to breathe slowly, and, bit by bit, the fear receded and my shivers abated.

I stared at the door. I didn't want to walk through it. Yet again, I wished everyone would leave and go home. My family meant well, and I loved them, but I needed some space. I wanted to curl up on my couch with a blanket and close my eyes. I wanted to pretend that my life wasn't on the wickedest, tallest, topsy-turviest roller coaster ever invented.

Because I had zero choice, I pulled myself upright and returned to the oh-so-fun birthday celebration. Elizabeth and our mother were cleaning up the food and dishes, my brothers were taking down the streamers and balloons, and my father was straightening the living room. My grandmother and Vinny were standing by the front door. When Grandma Verda saw me, she beckoned me over.

"We're going to take off. Vinny's tired," Grandma said, patting her beau's arm as she did. The older man smiled but didn't say anything.

I gave her a kiss on her soft cheek. "It was nice to see you."

"We'll get together soon. You, me, and Elizabeth." Another sharp-eyed stare. "We need to talk. When you're feeling better."

She didn't say anything about her present, or the pregnancy, and I was grateful for it. It didn't matter that she knew. I wasn't ready to confront her.

Once they drove off, I went to help my mother and sister with cleanup duty, but they were already done. As were my brothers and father, with their tasks. In fact, less than fifteen minutes later, after more kisses and hugs, I was completely alone.

Wow. My family had never before fled so quickly from anyplace, especially not all at once. This was one wish I appreciated coming true.

With my soft, fuzzy blue blanket and a big fluffy pillow, I curled up on the sofa. Closing my eyes, I pushed everything else away. Sleep was my savior. When I slept, no worries, no sickening fear of how I was going to manage, no remembrances of the man I'd thought I loved revealing himself to be a complete jerk, intruded. It was just me, warmth, peace, and bliss.

I'd barely closed my eyes when I caught a whiff of something. Flowers? Being prone to allergies, I didn't tend to keep flowers around, so I was probably imagining things. But then the scent grew stronger and tickled my nose. A tingling, almost prickly sensation crept from my head to my toes, as if my body were telling me to pay attention. But to what?

I opened my eyes. A pale light shimmered in the middle of the room. Tightening my hold on my blanket, I sat upright. The light grew brighter and colors bled into it; a soft rainbow shimmied and danced all around. And just as in my dream, excitement ran through me. This wasn't scary, not one little bit.

Entranced, I watched and waited. In my dreams, she stepped right out from the center of the light and walked toward me. Anticipation had me scooting to the edge of the couch, my eyes never leaving the light. A warm breeze, filled with the scent of flowers, touched my cheek. And then, suddenly, there she was. She had long, billowy chestnut hair, dark brown eyes, and she wore a dress that seemed to capture the colors that swirled around her.

She smiled, and the light grew even brighter, but I could still see her clearly. Rationally, I knew I should be afraid. What was happening in front of me should have had me running from the room screaming. Instead, I felt weirdly at ease—comfortable, even.

"Hello, Alice. I've waited such a long time for this." Her voice skimmed over me, through me, and the sound of it was as joyful as ringing bells.

"Are you an angel?" I asked.

Another laugh. "Not hardly. I am your great-great-great-grandmother. We need to talk about something vitally important."

My mouth moved, but nothing came out.

"I won't be able to stay long. Listen carefully, and take my words to heart. Your daughter is special. She'll need to be raised in a home of pure love, and she'll need the guidance of one particular man. Your soul mate. It is of the utmost necessity that you find him before she is born, so you can secure her future. *Your* future."

I tried to process everything she said, tried to make sense of her message, but at that moment, I couldn't. "Who are you? How do you know these things?"

"I already told you. I am Miranda, your great-great-great-grandmother. Your sister and Verda have the answers. Talk to them, but don't forget what I said, Alice. You need to find your soul mate—there's no time to waste!"

Then, as if someone had pulled the plug, she, the scent

of flowers, the breeze and the colors disappeared, gone as quickly as they'd appeared. I closed my eyes for a second and then opened them again. Yep, everything seemed to be pretty much back to normal, as if I'd imagined the entire episode. Except for one tiny thing. My heart thumped, my breathing came fast and uneven, and goose bumps coated my skin. A rose petal floated in the air directly in front of me, as if held up by an invisible hand, and slowly weaved its way to the floor. When it landed, I leaned over, picked it up, and then stroked my finger along it, feeling its velvety smoothness, proving to myself it was real.

My baby moved again, another flutter of butterfly wings. As if she were equally entranced by what had just happened. Something so odd. So mystical. Awe-inspiring, even. And she'd called herself Miranda.

I trembled as I mentally replayed the whole scene. Soul mate? My daughter?

I had questions. Tons of them. And I knew who to get the answers from. My sister and my grandmother had a heck of a lot of explaining to do. It appeared Grandma Verda was right—we *would* be talking soon.

Tonight, if I had any say in it.

Chapter Four

"Elizabeth, it's Alice again. You need to call me back ASAP. No matter what time it is," I said into the phone. This was the third message I'd left for my sister in the past several hours, and honestly, annoyed didn't begin to express my feelings. "It's about Miranda, who appears to be a ghost, and who said you and Grandma were the people to talk to. Call me back."

Not knowing what else to add, I hung up the phone and returned to my prior position of staring at it. As if by sheer force of will I could make it ring. It so wasn't happening. I'd even tried wishing she'd call me back, but no dice. If wishes were real, why were mine so fickle?

Tiredness seeped in and I yawned, but I didn't allow myself to give in to exhaustion. As much as I wanted to sleep, I needed to be awake and alert when my sister finally phoned. But I needed to do *something*. Sitting around doing nothing made the entire situation worse.

Grabbing the remote, I flipped on the TV and channel surfed for a minute. When nothing caught my interest, I shut it back off. I hadn't called my grandmother yet. I thought about doing so now, even though I'd wanted to talk to Elizabeth first, but one glance at the clock changed my mind. While my grandmother often stayed up late, Vinny was always in bed early. He'd had a heart attack not that long ago, and I didn't want to disturb him. But, dear God, I wanted answers.

Now that several hours had passed, I'd begun to doubt what I'd seen. What I'd experienced. Maybe I had fallen asleep and dreamed the entire episode. But then, just like before, I saw the rose petal now sitting on my coffee table. I picked it up again, holding it between my thumb and index finger. How could it feel so normal? You'd think something appearing out of thin air—on the heels of a ghostly woman—would somehow feel different. But it just didn't.

It bothered me, and not just because of how it had appeared, but because in the several hours since it had showed up, it hadn't changed. Fresh and soft, supple even, as if it had been plucked from a rose mere seconds earlier and wasn't several hours old. All things being normal, it should have been drying out by now, the edges curling up, the texture becoming brittle. But it wasn't. Not that any of this was normal, but this one little detail bugged the hell out of me.

I sat on the couch, tucking my legs underneath me, resting my head on the cushion, not really lying down but not fully sitting up, either. My finger and thumb still pinched the petal, so I dropped it into the palm of my other hand. Deep red against the pale white of my skin, it stood out, and as I watched, it seemed to lose shape until it was no longer the petal from a rose. It pooled in my palm, warm and liquid, then spread, easing into the creases between my fingers, slipping through to drip onto my denim-covered legs in a plop. Then another. Like the soft sound of a slow rain against a window.

Plop. Plop. Plop.

The color changed from red to dark purple as it oozed into my jeans, merging with the blue fabric. This, whatever *this* was, felt familiar. Anger came first, then sadness, and together, they became an empty, clawing pit of emotion that I'd never before experienced yet somehow recognized. I closed my hand into a fist, the warm stickiness of the melted petal against my skin.

Pain came, sudden and swift, down the center of my

palm. Opening my hand, I saw a cut from the bottom of my thumb that stretched diagonally across, meeting my little finger. Not deep. Not jagged. But enough of an injury to explain blood. My arms trembled and my stomach sloshed.

I tried to swallow the sickness away, to no avail. Again, I noticed the stickiness on my palm, and a tremor of fear skittered in. What was happening? *Why* was it happening? My brain shifted through all of the various possibilities, trying to piece it together, trying to make sense of it all. The room dipped and twirled around me; the walls elongated and stretched, morphing themselves into another shape, another place. Oh, God. *Another time.* Don't ask me how I knew this, because I can't say. I just knew.

With a sudden yank, it was as if I separated from myself, as if two parts of a whole were split down the middle and pulled apart. One and the same, but not. I floated upward, and weirdly it seemed I was in two places at once: hovering in an unknown space, and also sitting below me, directly within my view.

The pain in my hand disappeared, and when I looked, the injury was gone. I wanted to believe *this* was the dream. This wasn't happening. But it was too real, and it was happening, to me *and* to the woman below me, who sat on the ground, in a tentlike shelter, with just enough light to see her clearly.

In the space of two heartbeats, I knew she wasn't me. "Miranda," I whispered. Her hands, which had been slowly rubbing her rounded belly, stilled, as if she'd heard my voice. "Miranda?" I said again. "Can you hear me?"

Long dark hair hung loose, flowing around her face like water. She tipped her head up, gaze searching, shoulders shaking. Lightning flashed bright and hot in her eyes as they explored the small space. "Mama? Is that you? You can't stop me. He deserves to be cursed, for all he did, for all his lies. For my pain. For my baby."

She shook her head as if refocusing, slanting her gaze downward. In front of her were several objects lying in an uneven row on the bare ground. She picked up the object on the end—a knife—opened her hand, and lightly cut the skin from thumb to pinky, like I'd just seen on my own hand. Really it wasn't more than a deep scratch, but the blood bubbled out and the pain returned once again and I curled my hand into a fist.

"No," I said. "Stop."

This time she didn't hesitate, didn't turn her head to search the shadows. She held her bleeding hand over a bowl. *Plop. Plop. Plop.* It dripped slowly, not in a gush, into the bowl, and as it did, her lips moved silently. I couldn't hear her, but I knew to the depths of my soul what she was doing. And *why* she was doing it. Power hung in the air, as heavy and forceful as an oncoming storm, and I wanted to tell her to stop. I wanted to tell her not to curse the man who'd hurt her, the father of her unborn child who hadn't lived up to his promises, like Troy hadn't. It wasn't worth it, even if I understood the agony she felt. But when I opened my mouth, nothing issued forth. I'd been silenced; I no longer had a voice.

With a shaking hand, the one she hadn't cut, she picked up a hairbrush and pulled strands of hair from it. Holding them over the bowl, her body swayed and her lips moved. Light and color swirled around her, and I knew—just knew—that the second she dropped the hair into the bowl, the die would be cast. And that it would be a mistake of such magnitude, it could never be corrected.

I screamed soundlessly for her to stop. The power grew stronger, rushing through the little tent like fabled giants crushing people beneath their feet. I closed my eyes. I didn't know why I was being shown this, but I didn't like it and I didn't want to see any more.

My baby moved, as if to say *Hey, Mom, what do you think you're doing?* Not the flutter of nearly weightless butterfly wings, but a solid kick with way more pressure behind it than was even possible at this stage. I laughed at the surprise of it, at the strength of it, and as I did, the power in the room evaporated.

Oh-so-slowly, I peeked through half-opened eyes. Miranda still sat there, her body tight, frozen. Her mouth hung open, her complexion drained of color, and a whip-cord of tension emanated off of her. One hand remained clenched over the bowl; the other rested on her stomach. I waited . . . watched . . . compelled by the unknown to somehow comprehend. And with a slow, deliberate movement, she pulled her arm back and dropped the hair—not into the bowl, but to the ground.

A breath of relief slipped out and I began to relax. Miranda tipped her head to the side, waiting for something. A sign, perhaps. I continued to watch, sure there was more I was meant to see. More I was meant to experience. She dumped a jug, spilling water onto her hands, washing them briskly, as if she couldn't clean them fast enough. At that moment, my baby—her baby?—kicked again, even more forcefully than before. She gasped, cradled her arms around her stomach. Tears rolled down her cheeks, fast and furious, in a flood of emotion.

Wetness on my face surprised me. I brushed the tears away with my fingertips, and as I did, a heady swirl of sensations swept into me, through me. Once again, I was *her*, but I was still *me* too. This time, a light of hope took center stage, instead of anger, instead of retribution. This hope mixed with happiness, and while the sadness still existed, it wasn't the all-consuming, gnawing pain of earlier.

Miranda stood and paced the small space, her arms never leaving her stomach. Even if I couldn't feel what she felt, the expression on her face, the brightness in her eyes, would have told me all I needed to know. Whatever hex she'd almost placed on the man who'd hurt her, who'd

abandoned her, was forgotten. Now, all that was in her
mind, in her heart, was her unborn baby. A daughter.
Her daughter.

Through Miranda's mind, I saw her daughter as a baby
just born. And then, I saw *her* daughter, and then the next.
This last daughter was my great-grandmother, whom I
only knew from pictures; and then came my grandmother,
my mother and my sister, along with other women I
didn't recognize but somehow knew to be family, connected to me in some form or fashion. They all appeared
before me at lightning speed, in a vision that didn't make
any sense. At the tail end, another baby appeared, and I
saw her grow into a little girl. She had big brown eyes
and chubby cheeks, and a smile that melted my heart. In
barely a breath, I knew who she was.

My daughter.

I hadn't thought I was ready to see an image of my
child, but now? I wanted to stare at her, memorize every
detail, and pull her into my arms; but the vision abruptly
ended, leaving me with an ache—an empty place deep
inside—and it hurt like nothing I'd yet known. Miranda's lips moved again. The power returned, and while it
was just as strong as before, it didn't scare me. It didn't
fill me with foreboding or urge me to scream out warnings. Instead, it washed over me in a hazy glow, like a
rainbow appearing after a storm on a sunny day. *This*
display of power had an enchanted feel—without darkness, without evil.

As her lips continued to move, the colors grew brighter,
the power stronger. I watched, once again completely
enthralled. While I couldn't hear her voice, I heard her
thoughts as if she spoke them directly to me.

*A gift, from daughter to daughter, to be passed on through
the generations. The gift of magic. My gift. My magic. My
daughters. My legacy.*

Somehow, I understood that *this* was the message I was

meant to hear. But even with that knowledge, I couldn't quite grasp it fully. It hovered there like a pesky mosquito I couldn't squash, evading me at every turn. Before I could give it any further thought, the scene below me changed yet again. The colors and the energy still swirled together, like a rainbow whipping around at top speed, but the colors strengthened in hue to a brilliance I couldn't see through. Shielding my eyes with one hand, I tried to see past the glare, past the brightness, to no avail. My eyes watered, the wetness seeping out, dripping down my cheeks.

Ringing filled my ears. Loud, obtrusive, it went on and on. I cringed at the sharpness of the noise and moved my hands to cover my ears. At first I didn't recognize the sound, because it didn't belong in this place, in this time. The second I realized *what* the sound was, everything in front of me, everything around me, stopped, as if I'd hit the pause button on my DVD player.

The energy pulled at me, tugged at me, and with one hard yank I was only myself again, on my couch, clutching the rose petal in my fist. The phone still rang, blaring through the room incessantly. My sister? It had to be. And for that, I was grateful.

With a trembling hand, I reached for it. "What took you so long? You won't believe what happened." My voice came out in a rush, the words merging so that they were almost incomprehensible. I inhaled deeply and gave it another go. "I need you to come over here now. No ifs, ands, or buts. Just do it." After a thought I added, "Please."

When she didn't answer immediately, my exasperation climbed to a whole new level. "Are you there? Why didn't you tell me about Miranda? And the gift?"

Still no reply. And really, the fact she *hadn't* answered should have been enough to clue me in that I'd been mistaken about the caller's identity. Sadly, it didn't. I was too preoccupied for coherent thought. "Elizabeth?"

"Have I phoned at a bad time?" The sexy Irish drawl held a bit of humor, along with a touch of concern.

Heat rushed my face, embarrassment that somehow had become the norm around this man. "Oh. You're not Elizabeth. Sorry, Ethan," I managed to mumble. "What can I do for you?"

"You sound a little a distracted. Are you all right?" The timbre of his voice helped soothe my agitation. Not something I expected, but I appreciated it.

"I'm fine. Just—um—a little busy at the moment. What's up?" My phone beeped, signaling another call. This time, it *was* my sister. Finally. "Oops, I have another call. Can you hold for a sec?"

"Of course. Take your time," he said.

I pushed the button. "I've been waiting forever for you to call."

"Sorry, sis. My cell ran out of juice and we were at Nate's parents' this evening. You said something about Miranda?"

People who didn't know my sister as well as I do wouldn't have heard more than a faint twinge of curiosity in her voice. But after years of sharing—and keeping—secrets, I heard the *Oh my God, I've been wanting to talk to you about this forever.* And that little nuance calmed me even more. *She* would have my answers. *She* would understand the weirdness. I was sure of it.

"She showed up here tonight. A lot of crazy stuff happened that I'd rather talk to you about in person, so when can you come over?"

"What kind of crazy stuff?"

"Elizabeth! You've been holding out on me. You *and* Grandma. Don't you think I should have known our great-great-great-grandmother's ghost pays house calls to her relatives? And drags them out of *their* time to visit her in *her* time?"

Elizabeth sighed, long and plaintively, as if she'd been the one secrets were kept from. "I know we should have told you, but I didn't expect her to just show up. What did she say? And what do you mean she dragged you to her time?"

"Like a time warp. Seriously. I visited Miranda in *her* time." My phone beeped again, reminding me that Ethan still waited. "Hold on. I was on the other line when you called."

"Okay. But are you sure this time-warp thing really happened? You are pregnant, you know, and hormones can do crazy things. Maybe the visit from Miranda spooked you enough that you dreamed the rest?"

"Just hold on!"

I switched back over. "Hey, Ethan. I think this call might take a few minutes. Can I call you back?"

"Actually, all I wanted to know was if we could go to Frosty's tomorrow after dinner, instead of at two. Does that work for you?"

I was about to say yes, but then I figured I'd better check with Elizabeth first. A nice, lengthy, face-to-face chat with her and my grandmother was most definitely in order—not to mention way overdue—so I didn't want any scheduling conflicts. "Um. Probably. Let me make sure, though."

I clicked the button. "This was not a pregnant hallucination dream thing! How can you believe in ghosts and not a time warp?"

Nothing but silence met my ears, followed by a long, slow intake of breath. *That*'s when I realized I might have made a mistake. "Elizabeth?" *Please, please be Elizabeth*, I prayed.

"Nope. Still Ethan."

I waited for him to say something else, anything else, but he didn't. He was probably trying to decide how crazy I actually was. "I'm really sorry. You shouldn't have heard that. Can we just forget all about it? Would that be possible in any way whatsoever?"

He cleared his throat. "Let's agree to set it aside for now, but we'll come back to it at a later date. Will that work well enough?"

No. "Um. Sure. I guess."

"Good. We're in agreement. About tomorrow?"

I still hadn't checked with Elizabeth, but no way, no how, was I chancing mis-clicking a second time. "I think after dinner will be fine. Around six or seven?"

"Let's say seven. And Alice?"

"Yes, Ethan?" I braced myself, waiting for the pregnancy question. Because it was bound to come. And now, because of my big mouth, it was going to happen sooner than I'd planned. Chicken? You bet.

"Do you want to ride with me or do you want to meet me there?"

"Meet you." Then, worried that I might have sounded rude, I said, "I'll be out around then anyway. Easier on me."

He hung up and I swallowed in relief. I knew it wouldn't last long, but I was happy for the delay while I had it. I clicked back to my sister. "I'm sorry it took me so long. No, it wasn't a dream. Yes, it really happened. I'd prefer to talk about it with you and Grandma at once, though."

"Oh, come on. You can't do that to me! I want to hear everything. Just tell me!"

I was tempted. Really, really tempted. But I was also exhausted. As much as I wanted answers—all of them— my body wanted to sleep. And I didn't think my brain would process much of anything until I did. "How about tomorrow morning? Instead of going out for brunch, come here for breakfast. And bring Grandma Verda with you."

Another wounded sigh floated through the phone line. "Fine. We'll be there at nine. You better have coffee made when we get there! And not that instant crap, either."

I promised I would and then disconnected the call. With a sigh reminiscent of my sister's, I curled up on the couch again. I thought about what Miranda had shown me, and I was pretty sure I understood her message. The magic—the wishes—were a gift she'd created for her daughters, and it seemed now I had it. I didn't get how it worked, but at least part of the picture was clear. The rest would come into focus soon enough.

Weirdly, though, I wasn't nearly as surprised about the entire revelation as you'd expect. Rather, it was as if a cloud I'd always known existed had finally been lifted. The magic itself didn't scare me as much as it had before, either. But even so, I wasn't so sure I wanted it. What I did want, though, was to know *everything* about it. Every last detail.

On the top of my need-to-know list was finding out who else in my family had experience with it, and why I hadn't been told about it before. I mean, really, shouldn't I have known my entire life? *Yes.* If for no other reason than to be prepared when it arrived.

Maybe my family hadn't learned that lesson, but *I* certainly had. And that was one thing that was going to change here and now. No more secrets.

Beginning with *my* daughter.

"So that's the story." I sipped my tea, now lukewarm. I'd decided to tell my grandmother and sister about everything that had occurred, so they could fill in the blanks.

"Wow," Elizabeth said. "Something similar happened to me, but instead of seeing Miranda's past, I saw my own. With Marc."

"*Ew.* Let's not bring him up." My sister had made her peace with her ex-husband, but I never would. He'd broken her heart, walked out on her, and *then* had the gall to hire her bakery to make his wedding cake—for his wedding to the woman with whom he'd cheated on her.

"Water under the bridge. Besides, my magic started with Marc."

Now I was interested. "That's when you got your witch powers?"

"Not witchcraft. Gypsy magic." Grandma Verda's eyes shone. "Miranda was a gypsy, and the gift she passed on to us has nothing to do with witchcraft."

"Oh. Wow." The cloud lifted a bit more. "But why was she trying to curse the father of her baby? I didn't understand that part of it, other than he'd hurt her."

"When she told him she was pregnant, he revealed that he was married, and wanted to take the baby from her to be raised in his home," said Grandma.

Pain sliced through me fast and hard. While different in some ways from my experience with Troy, it was also eerily similar. The lies. The betrayal. An invisible thread of unity existed between me and my great-great-great-grandmother, tying us together in a way I'd never known with anyone else. "That sucks. But how does it work?"

Grandma Verda gave a small smile. "The magic is different for each of us, and each of us can manifest it in different ways, but it's about wishes."

"Wishes? Like three wishes from a genie, only there's no limit?" I asked.

"Well, close. While there isn't a limit, not all wishes come true." Grandma's forehead wrinkled in thought. "Miranda had far more power than any of us, so maybe she had more luck with that than we have. Her magic also extended beyond wishes. But for us, for everyone that's followed . . . our magic has been solely about wishes. Mine was in my writing. Elizabeth's was in her baking. I'm assuming yours will be through your artwork, like my grandmother's was."

I thought about it, then shook my head. "I don't think so. The wishes that have worked? All I did was think them. No art involved. And they were completely accidental." I filled them in on my wish experience thus far.

Elizabeth frowned. "That's strange. It's never worked like that before."

"It worked that way for Miranda," I pointed out.

"Well, yeah, but she's the source. The beginning. My magic is only there if I put it into something I bake and then someone eats it. That's how I gave you the magic, Alice. I wished to pass it on to you when I baked that lemon meringue pie for you last month."

"Wait. You're telling me you gave me magic via a *pie?*"

"And like any gift you give someone else, ownership changes hands, so to speak, and it becomes uniquely connected to the receiver," Grandma Verda interjected. "So neither I nor Elizabeth has it any longer. Only you."

Elizabeth cleared her throat. "Er. Well. That's changing."

Grandma's razor-sharp gaze turned to her. "What do you mean? You still have it?"

"I do. I was going to tell you, but I didn't want to hurt your feelings. Miranda said I was the first in the family who was strong enough to keep it and pass it on, and that it would continue that way from now on."

"Well, I think that's delightful news. How wonderful, the magic is growing and changing!" Excitement tinged Grandma's cheeks pink.

"I'm more confused now than I was before. What the heck is happening with the gift now that I have it? Can you answer that?" I said.

Grandma gripped my hand. "I don't know, sweetie. I wouldn't worry about that just yet, as time will tell. But there is something you should be aware of with wishes."

I braced myself. "What now?"

"Just that magic is unpredictable. Crazy things can happen, so use caution."

"Trust her on this. I almost ended a few friendships and ruined a life or two because I screwed up some of my wishes," Elizabeth said.

"*Trust me.* I plan on striking the word 'wish' from my vocabulary. At least until I understand this more."

Elizabeth chuckled. "Well, I made a wish before I even knew about the magic—and it came true. In fact, you were the one who told me it came true, Alice."

"Really? What was it?"

She blushed. I rarely see my sister change colors, so it amused me immensely, and that amusement helped ease my tension. "Remember the day you overheard that girl in the gym talking about Marc's honeymoon?"

"Oh." It took a second, but when it hit, I laughed. I couldn't help it. "When Marc couldn't get it up?" I loved that my practical-to-the-core sister had wished *that* for her ex on his wedding night. *Priceless.* "That's awesome. I didn't know you had it in you."

"But that's why you need to be careful. The thing with Marc worked out okay, but really, I was lucky. Magic can be fun and empowering, but dangerous too."

Something else came to mind. "Did you cast a spell on Troy, like he thought? When he got so ill?"

Her lips twitched. "That was me. He'd hurt you. It made me mad, so I tried to fix it."

"God, Elizabeth. He was in a lot of pain. I mean, thank you for wanting to protect me, but that's a little scary."

"Not as scary as he is. He came to the bakery one day, trying to get back the money he paid you. I scared him off." She twisted her fingers together. "Don't be angry with me. I did what I felt was necessary."

I shouldn't have been surprised that Troy would stoop to such a level, but I was. Even after everything that had happened, I had a difficult time reconciling the man he actually was with the man I'd thought him to be. Though I knew one thing for certain: I hadn't loved him. Not really.

"I'm not angry." I pushed Troy out of my head. "Let's get back on track. My wishes don't seem to be connected to anything in particular, and certainly not to my artwork." I gasped when another thought hit. "Maybe something did happen, but not like you've explained."

"But something has? What?" That came from my sister.

"I was working on a sketch for an ad campaign, and I drew me and my boss sitting at a table as a couple at Frosty's Ice Cream Shoppe. Later, over lunch, he asked me to go there with him. But that's not the same."

"Did you wish you'd go there with him when you were drawing it?" asked my sister.

"Not exactly. I was lonely and wishing someone would ask me to lunch or something, but I'm not sure. I was in the zone." But then I realized. Ethan *had* asked me to lunch that day. Did that mean it was only a wish-induced invitation? Ick. I hated that thought.

A tiny grin popped up on my grandmother's face. "Do you have a crush on him?"

I ignored the whisper of desire that teased at me. "He's cute. And really nice. I haven't thought about him in that way, if that's what you mean." Just a little lie.

"I think—maybe—there are two different things going on here," Elizabeth mused.

My grandmother lit up even more, if that's possible. "This is so exciting! Aren't you excited, Alice?"

"No! It's scary and strange and if I can't figure it out, then things are going to get even weirder." How many times in a day did I wish something would happen? You know, those random thoughts like *I wish it was five so I could go home,* or *I wish it was Saturday,* or . . . or anything, really. "I could screw things up without even meaning to!"

Grandma huffed. "Screw what up? You should be thrilled. This is our legacy; this is who we are. Grab on with both hands, Alice! Your life will never be the same."

But that was the problem. I wanted my *old* life back. I wanted order to prevail. Change was the polar opposite of what I wanted—what I needed. "Can I give it back? Or pass it to someone else?"

"I don't know," Elizabeth said. "You can try, but I'm pretty sure you're stuck with it now."

A spasm of fear rolled into me. "That's just terrific. You should have kept this little gift to yourself, Elizabeth."

"Oh honey, I'm sorry. I was trying to help you, not make things worse. We can figure this out, though. Why don't you tell us what Miranda said to you? Maybe that will shed some light on why your magic is so different from anything we've experienced."

"She said my daughter was special—"

"You're having a baby girl! I knew it!" my grandmother exclaimed. "I dreamed about it, you know."

One question answered. "Ah. That's how you figured it out. I was going to ask."

"Go on, Alice," my sister prodded. "What else did Miranda tell you?"

I repeated her words to them, and then I shuddered. "It's crazy. I don't need or want a soul mate. I can raise my child with all the love and guidance she'll ever need. On my own."

Elizabeth tipped her head to the side and appraised me. My sister had that look: the one that told me she wasn't saying something she definitely should say.

"Spit it out."

Her dark brown eyes bored into mine, searching. "Miranda told me you were having a daughter too. But she also said . . ." She inhaled a deep breath.

"This is about me and my child, so you better tell me,

Liz." Still, even as I made my demand, a whoosh of light-headedness had me gripping the arms of my chair.

"She said your child would be the strongest of us all. Stronger than Miranda, even. And that she'd be around to help. So, maybe you don't want to blow off the soul mate thing. I've found Miranda usually knows what she's talking about."

Energy, similar to what I'd felt the night before, whipped through the air. It almost buzzed in my ears. "So the ghost is sticking around because of me? And my baby?" Connection or no connection, I wasn't sure how I felt about sharing the next many years with a long-dead relative. "My daughter's going to be magical some day, I get that. But unlike me, she'll know about it long before it affects her."

"Actually, I'm thinking it might mean she's magical *now*. Think about it. Your wishes are different from ours. Maybe it has something to do with how powerful your daughter is . . ."

Ugh. "Chloe and I had a similar conversation." Still, I'd pushed that away. With the possibility facing me again, I liked it even less than before.

"There's one other thing. I didn't want to mention it . . . but maybe I should."

"Yes?" I rubbed my stomach, hoping to ease my queasiness.

"Didn't Troy say his mother was a witch?"

Oh, hell. Something else I'd already set aside. "Yes . . . Chloe is looking into it for me."

Grandma Verda leaned over the coffee table. "Goodness. If that's true, it means your child has magic from *both* sides of her family. Oh my."

"Oh my, indeed. I think that's why she's going to be so powerful, Alice." My sister's voice was calm enough, but worry was evident in the tight way she held herself. "I've thought about it a lot over the last month or so."

"Maybe if you'd talked to me, rather than only thinking about it, we'd have some answers by now." The walls closed in around me. Everything spun in circles. "Dizzy," I whispered, reaching my hand out for support.

My sister's grasp centered me and helped reel in the craziness, but the room still spun.

"Put your head between your knees." My sister's voice sounded far away and foggy, but I did as she asked. Almost at once the spinning slowed.

"Breathe slowly," my sister instructed.

"This isn't going so well," my grandmother said. "Should we call nine-one-one?"

"No! I'll be fine. It's getting better." And yeah, the dizziness was fading—thank goodness! But the rest of it? I had to wonder if anything in my life would ever be fine again.

Magic. Soul mate. Pure love.

God help me.

Chapter Five

I sat at a little round café table at the ice cream shop, waiting for Ethan to show up. Granted, I was way early—like thirty minutes or so—but I couldn't concentrate on anything at home so figured there wasn't much sense in staying there. Besides, I'd needed a change of scenery and a quiet place to think. In a big way.

There weren't many people in the shop. I didn't know if that was the norm or just a by-product of a rainy Sunday evening, but at the moment it suited me perfectly. I made a mental note to stop in at various times throughout the next week, just to get a better sense of the store's customer flow. This wasn't part of my job, at least not officially, but having that information couldn't hurt. It might even help.

My eyes drifted to the front door again. I fidgeted in my seat. I'd chosen a table on the other side of the room from the one I'd drawn myself sitting at with Ethan, just to be sure no mystical love mojo was at play. Silly? Maybe, but it made me feel better. All I needed was to get through the next hour or so, and then I was meeting my sister and grandmother back at my place.

To discuss the *soul mate* issue. Apparently, Grandma Verda had some ideas on how to find my soul mate, and she wasn't taking no for an answer. Unless I wanted her moving in with me, it was smart to at least listen. But no way was I going to go ahead with anything soul mate related.

My stomach roiled with unease. Not just about the magic stuff, or the soul mate stuff, but about seeing and talking to Ethan. I'd decided to take the bull by the horns and bring up my pregnancy on my own. Like a responsible adult. Something I should have done in the interview process but hadn't because I'd still been reeling from the news.

But after last night, I no longer had a choice. Plus, out of all the things I'd blurted to Ethan, the pregnancy topic was, believe it or not, the one with which I was most comfortable. Maybe if I brought *that* up, he'd forget the rest. Because how I'd explain a ghost and a time warp to him was beyond me. I didn't even want to go there. Not just because of my job, but because I really, really didn't want Ethan to view me as a loon.

Fiddling with the straw in my soda, I tried to come up with the best way to raise the subject. I didn't allow myself to wonder *why* Ethan's opinion of me mattered so much. It just did, plain and simple.

"You look lost in thought," said the man in question, pulling out the chair across from me. Startled, I twitched slightly in my seat. Lifting my chin, I smiled, trying to look at ease. Of course, that didn't work so well, because Ethan Gallagher defied the laws of nature. Today, he was even sexier than normal.

He looked as if he'd come straight from a hike or some other outdoor activity. Mussed hair, khaki shorts, and a sort-of-tight, sort-of-rumpled blue T-shirt made my smile widen. He appeared more natural dressed like this, more approachable. Not to mention more real, rather than a perfect specimen of an Irishman. But what really got to me was, instead of the smooth, clean-shaven look I'd become accustomed to, dark stubble—probably about two days' worth—graced his jawline. So he had that just-tumbled-out-of-bed, sexy-as-sin thing going on. Heaven help me.

"I didn't hear you come in," I managed to say. Maybe he looked as if he'd just tumbled out of bed because he had? Was there a woman waiting for him now? I ignored the pang of jealousy that hit, because let's face it—whom he slept with was none of my business. "I was just wondering if the shop is usually this slow on a weekend evening." Even with my prior thoughts, the urge to reach across the table and run my finger along his stubble almost overcame me.

I resisted. Barely.

"Good question." His gray-eyed gaze pinned me, searching. "But before we talk about that, I have another question for you. I'd like you to answer it honestly."

Great. No beating around the bush for this guy. Time to suck it up and deal, right? Right. Pushing my inappropriate musings aside, I said what needed to be said. "I know what you're going to ask, so I'll just answer. Yes, I'm pregnant. I know I should have said something earlier, but, um, well, the father isn't involved and I've been trying to handle everything on my own." *Okay.* Not nearly as hard as I'd thought it was going to be. "I'm sorry about that."

He rubbed a hand over that sexy jaw of his, never taking his eyes from mine. Which, oddly, wasn't uncomfortable at all. I saw compassion, understanding, and not one iota of pity. That helped me relax a little more.

"That actually wasn't my question, but now that you brought it up . . ." Breaking off, he shook his head, as if clearing cobwebs. He opened his mouth again, and then clamped it shut just as fast.

What was it with people not wanting to tell me things lately? It wasn't like I had FRAGILE, PROCEED WITH CAUTION stamped on my forehead. "Go ahead. You can say it. Whatever it is."

Uncertainty whisked over his features, which surprised me. In the short time I'd known Ethan, I'd never seen him appear anything but completely in control and comfortable.

"It's like this." He exhaled a short breath. "I've known about your pregnancy since shortly after you were hired. I've been curious about why you didn't bring it up, but it's a personal topic, so I wasn't shocked or put off at all last night."

He knew? His statement more than perplexed me; it dumbfounded me. "How did you find out?"

"Let's just say someone told me out of concern for you."

"Someone told you? Who?"

"I promised I wouldn't say. But it's nothing to worry about. Her intentions were the best."

I mentally went through the list of people who knew, which took like one second, because I'd only told two people. Out of those two, my money was on Chloe—but even that seemed hard to believe. "Chloe?" When he shook his head, I said, "Elizabeth wouldn't have said anything. I'm positive."

"That's your sister, right? The one who owns the bakery?"

"Yes. But how did you know . . . ?" And then, without a shadow of a doubt, I had my answer. "You spoke with my grandmother, didn't you?"

Now, rather than centering on me, his gaze floated somewhere behind me. But his lips lifted at the corners for just a second. Ha! He'd wanted me to guess. My grandmother hadn't counted on that. "It *was* Grandma Verda, wasn't it?"

"Your grandmother called me a week or so after you started working at Enchanted Expressions. She asked if she could take me to lunch." His words were slow, and he watched me as if I'd dump my soda on him. You know the look: sort of a worried, what's-she-gonna-do, and should-I-get-the-heck-out-of-Dodge? kind of expression.

My jaw dropped. My eyes widened. I'm absolutely positive I looked like a gaping fish. "She took you to lunch?" I reminded myself that I loved my grandmother.

And then I reminded myself again. Because at that instant, I kind of wanted to throttle her.

Ethan reached over and pushed my soda to the side. It wasn't necessary. I'm not the type of woman to dump a glass of anything on anyone. But that one little action told me that somewhere in Ethan's past existed a woman, or women, who'd done that to him. Even in my distress over my grandmother, curiosity flared.

"Yes, she did. Quite a feisty lady, your grandmother." The grin he'd tried to shield earlier emerged. "She impressed me. Intrigued me too."

"How long was this lunch? And what did she say?" Out of all the possible topics my grandmother could come up with regarding me, there were maybe only two—tops— I'd be okay with. Even those were a little iffy.

"Several hours, at least. But it wasn't all about you, so you can stop panicking."

Stop panicking? Not hardly. "What did you talk about?"

"Irish fairy tales and myths for the most part. Oh, and she asked me if I was a pomegranate. Do you have any idea what she meant by that? I found it the most curious statement."

Biting my lip, I shook my head. "She's a little quirky. I hope she didn't say anything, um, really out there."

Questions filled the air. "As I said, she had a particular interest in Irish folklore. She also said a few things about magic and ghosts that I found—"

"What things?" She wouldn't have told him about Miranda. Would she?

"You mentioned ghosts on the phone last night, as well. And a . . . what was it? Time warp? I take it you're a believer in the supernatural?"

"Oh. Hmm." How to answer without lying? Taking a page from Chloe's book, I went with, "I believe almost anything is possible. There are a lot of things in our world that can't necessarily be explained by hard cold facts." And yes, I purposely avoided mentioning anything to do with my short trip to what I assumed was the 1800s.

"I agree with you."

He didn't say it, but there was an exception there. I heard it loud and clear. "But?" I prodded.

Those perfect lips of his straightened into a line. "It's all well and good to believe in fortunes, magic, ghosts, and the like, but when these things lead people to make choices that defy the facts in front of them . . ." Coldness edged his voice for a millisecond, but then a grin came forth. In a warmer tone, he continued. "It disturbs me. Decisions should never be made based on anything but fact and intuition."

"But isn't intuition the same as the unexplained?" Even as I asked, I couldn't help wondering if he spoke from personal experience.

"Unexplained, maybe. But trusting one's intuition is quite different from changing your life because of a tarot card or a cheaply bought fortune at a fair."

Wow. Such passion. Definitely personal experience. What would he think of Miranda's warning? Would that count as fact, because the warning itself was real? Or would he place it under the "cheaply bought fortune" heading?

Because I couldn't ask, no matter how much I wanted to, I put the conversation back on track: my loud-mouthed grandmother. "Why did Grandma Verda tell you I was pregnant?"

"She loves you. She just wanted me to be aware that you're in a fragile condition. She worries about you working such long hours when you're not used to it, that's all. Quite innocent, really. And very sweet."

"Fragile condition? I'm not fragile," I muttered. "Besides, I've always worked long hours, just not like this." I so couldn't wait to talk to her later. Of course, I'd have to be careful, because I didn't want to upset her. But she was going to know this wasn't something I appreciated. At all.

"I understand that. But don't be too hard on her."

"And you . . . why did you promise you wouldn't tell me?"

A ruddy flush stole from the top of his angled cheekbones down to the edge of his jaw. For once, *he* was blushing around *me*. Kind of cool, even if I wasn't all that happy about the reason.

"You see, Alice . . . she sort of sneaked that in. I never saw it coming." He drummed his fingers on the table. "What can I say? She reminded me of my own grandmother, and I fell for her charms."

My anxiety disappeared in a flash. A man who could be charmed by a slightly wacky, weirdly dressed elderly lady softened everything inside of me. "She is pretty charming. But that doesn't make it right. It should have come from me."

"It would have been nice but not necessary. The law protects you on this. Surely you know that."

"Yes, but it's about more than that. I was getting around to telling you, really. I just haven't shared this with most of my family yet." Which was clearly going to have to happen soon, before Grandma Verda decided to do it for me.

My announcement seemed to startle him. "I assumed your family was close. Is there a reason you haven't said anything?" As soon as he asked the question, he held a hand up. "Don't answer that. I'm sorry. I don't mean to pry into your personal life. It's none of my business."

"I don't mind." And weirdly, I didn't. "I didn't plan this. The timing hasn't been right yet. That's all. But it's not like I'll be able to keep it a secret forever."

The compassion from earlier returned. He reached over, grasped one of my hands, squeezed, and then let go. In the less than ten seconds our hands touched, a glimmer of something passed between us. Desire? Yes, but something more. And since I barely knew this man, it more than confused me. It scared the hell out of me.

Suddenly, the moment became too much. In an effort to bring the conversation around to the less personal, I said, "So, what was the question you were going to ask me before I jumped the gun?"

He hadn't anticipated the change of topic; that was evident by the flicker of light that hit his stormy gray eyes. But he went with it, no questions asked. Well, except for one.

"Oh. Right." He cleared his throat. "Is something going on with Missy that I should know about? I've noticed there seems to be some type of friction between the two of you."

Yep. The man noticed the details. "I have no idea. I don't have a problem with her, but she sure doesn't like me. Or at least that's my impression. Has she said anything to you?"

"She hasn't. But her behavior is unusual. The entire time I've known Missy, she's proven herself a valuable employee, happy to work with others, and has thrived in our team environment." He scrunched his eyebrows together in thought. "I hope everything's okay. I'll have a chat with her later this week."

"Please don't. Please." At his puzzled glance, I explained, "That will only make things worse. Especially if there is an issue I'm unaware of. I'm sure it will come out. And if I need your help then, I'll let you know. Deal?"

He hesitated for a few seconds but then nodded in agreement. "Be sure to let me know if things get out of hand. We're a fairly relaxed company, as I'm sure you've noticed. To continue being that way, signs of trouble need to be stomped out quickly."

At that point, our discussion finally moved on to Frosty's, my ideas for the campaign, and his thoughts.

The next hour passed quickly. By the time we left, I had a firm handle on what I wanted to officially present at the next staff meeting, and in a strange way, I felt as if I'd made a friend.

Naturally, I ignored the voice in my head that told me I wanted much more than friendship from Ethan. And I pushed away the surreal feeling that we were supposed to be . . . well, something we weren't. I also ignored the signals my body repeatedly gave me in his presence. Sweaty palms, heart palpitations, and the like were nothing more than symptoms of an excess of hormones. They had to be. Because I barely knew the guy, and I had more than my share of complications in my life as it was.

So, yeah. Friendship was good.

It'd be enough—one way or another.

When I returned home, I walked into a mess. Literally. The majority of my art supplies were scattered from the dining room to the living room, sitting on every available surface except for the couch, which held my sister, my grandmother, and Chloe.

"What's going on?" Not that I really wanted to know, but it had to be asked.

Chloe jumped up, her cheeks flushed, her eyes bright. "I came over earlier to check in on you, and your sister and grandmother filled me in on everything. I am so jealous! You have *magic*. And a ghost for a grandmother. And you went to another time. How can you stand it? It's so unbelievably cool!"

"Chloe! Calm down before you keel over," I told her.

"But it's wicked exciting. Anyway, I told them about Beatrice and how I haven't found any dirt on her at all, but then we talked about the soul mate problem." Her eyes gleamed even brighter. "We figured out how you're gonna find him. *Tonight.*"

My stomach tightened in knots. For the moment, I

turned away from Chloe and focused on my sister. She tended to be the calm one. "What's she talking about?"

"Your magic should be in your artwork," Elizabeth said slowly. "So we thought you might be able to draw a picture of your soul mate. Once we have a picture, maybe we'll be able to find him."

Grandma Verda stood. "I'm hoping it's that cute Irish boss of yours, Alice."

"You mean that cute Irish boss of mine who you took to lunch? And told I was pregnant?"

"He told you?" Her mouth stretched into an uneven line. "He's definitely not a pomegranate if he broke a promise. I had such high hopes for that young man."

"Grandma! Stop with this fruit thing. None of us even knows what it means. Besides, he didn't tell me; I guessed. And why'd you do it? You know I love you, but you stepped out of bounds with that one."

She looked contrite for about half a second, and then she grinned. "I'm so glad I wasn't wrong about him. Maybe he's the one for you."

I sighed. I'd hoped for an apology, but that *so* wasn't happening. "The one what?"

"She means your soul mate. For some reason, she has it in her head that this boss of yours is the man you're destined to be with," Elizabeth said. "I have no idea why."

"Call it instinct." Grandma Verda winked at my sister. "I was right about Nate, wasn't I?"

My sister just about glowed at the mention of Nate's name. She nodded. "Point taken. So maybe it's not such a farfetched idea. What do you think of him, Alice?"

Even though searching out a man was the last thing I wanted, I had to admit that the thought of Ethan being that man wasn't so bad. Of course, I couldn't let this continue. "I barely know Ethan! And about this drawing my soul mate thing—how am I supposed to draw a picture of some man I've never met?"

For no reason that I could discern, Chloe ran into the kitchen. She returned almost immediately with a chocolate-frosted cupcake balanced in the palm of her hand. "Eat this first. Then draw."

"What are you talking about? I feel like everyone is speaking in a different language."

"It's easy! Since Elizabeth still has her magic, she baked the cupcakes with the wish that you'd be able to draw a picture of your soul mate. If you eat it, the magic should do its thing, and we'll know who he is without even leaving your condo. Isn't that terrific?" Chloe pushed the cupcake toward me.

"It *is* a good idea." Grandma nodded toward the cupcake. "Let's give it a go. What can it hurt?"

With another sigh, I accepted the treat. "Didn't you two just get done explaining how unpredictable magic is? That we should be careful and all that jazz? What if you said the wish wrong, Elizabeth? What if instead of drawing my soul mate, I draw the exact opposite of my soul mate?"

"I've learned my lesson with wishes. I'm very careful with how I word everything." She crossed her arms. "It *should* work. But if you don't want to do it, it's totally okay. This is your thing. We're just here to help."

Help. Yeah, right. Elizabeth would agree with whatever my decision was, I knew that. But Grandma Verda and Chloe? They'd nag at me in their own special ways until I gave in. And I'd eventually give in, so why bother putting up a pretense?

I sat at the dining room table. "Fine. All I need is a sketchpad and a pencil. I don't know why you brought every art supply I own out here."

Chloe rushed to get the pad and pencil, while Grandma Verda and Elizabeth perched in the chairs across from me. Elizabeth smiled faintly in my direction, probably to reassure me. Call me bratty, but I didn't return the gesture. Grandma Verda clasped her hands together and jiggled in her seat, bits of glitter from her sparkly lavender shirt landing on my table.

"We weren't sure if you'd want pencils or charcoals or if you'd want to paint or whatever." Chloe placed my requested items in front of me. "So I brought everything out. Sorry about that."

"Not a big deal." I glanced at Elizabeth, who still watched me intently. "So, all I do is eat this and then instantly it should begin? Just like that?"

"Ideally," she replied.

"Ideally?"

"You know, that whole magic-is-unpredictable thing," Chloe interjected. "We hope it's right away, though. Don't we?"

She'd certainly taken to all of this nice and easily. Too bad she wasn't truly a member of the family, or I'd pass the magic on to her in a second. If I even could. "Okay. Here goes nothing."

I picked the paper off the cupcake and then tore a small chunk from the bottom. Popping the bite in my mouth, I somehow expected that *this* time I'd notice a difference in the taste, with magic as an extra ingredient. But no, it tasted like any other chocolate cupcake my sister ever baked: moist, flavorful, but completely normal.

The first bite went down easily, so I took another. And another. The entire time I ate, Chloe hovered next to me, while Grandma Verda and Elizabeth stayed seated, eyes never leaving my face. After I swallowed the last bite, I brushed crumbs off my hands and stood. "I need some milk."

"Do you feel any different?" Chloe asked. "Can you tell if the magic is working?"

"Are you ready to draw your soul mate?" asked Grandma Verda.

"Give her a few minutes, girls. Geesh." That voice of

reason, which I oh-so-appreciated, came from my sister. Bless her heart.

In the kitchen, milk in hand, I leaned against the wall. Did I feel any different? No. I didn't. Did that mean the magic hadn't taken hold? Most of me hoped that was the case, but I'd be lying if I said there wasn't a small part that had wanted this scheme to work. After all, even with the weird crap going on, I was still a woman who'd once been a little girl, who'd once had dreams about finding her real, true love. But there was no prince in shining armor waiting around the bend for me; Troy had taught me that.

I put my glass in the sink and went to give them the bad news. Returning to my chair, I clasped my hands together and said, "Okay, guys. I don't feel any different at all, so I'm pretty sure nothing's happened. Can we forget this? Please?"

"You have to *try*," Chloe said. "Like with the juice the other day. Give it a chance, at least."

"She's right, Alice. All you've done is eat the cupcake. I don't think you'll feel anything until the magic begins to work, which probably won't happen until you begin to draw," said Elizabeth. "If nothing happens then, we'll know."

For once, my grandmother didn't say a word. And I wanted her opinion. "What do you think, Grandma?"

"I think you're the only one who can decide." Her steady gaze met mine. "But if you don't try, won't you always wonder?"

I couldn't argue with that, so I nodded. "Okay, then. I guess I'll give it a go."

My palms were damp—probably from nerves—so I rubbed them on my pants before opening my sketch-book to a clean page. Curiously, as soon as my fingers took their normal position around the pencil, everything relaxed inside of me. What was there to be nervous about, though? It wasn't like this was going to work. Inhaling a short, quick breath, I put pencil to paper, not even sure what I was going to draw.

I didn't have any image in mind. Not a face, or a place, or anything at all. Closing my eyes, I tried to picture the person, the *man*, I was supposed to draw. Still nothing.

"It's not happening."

"Give it a little longer," my grandmother said. "Don't think too hard about it."

Trying to follow her advice, I cleared my thoughts. Instead of attempting to see an image, I focused on not seeing anything, on not hearing anything. But nope, that didn't work either. A few years back, I'd taken a meditation class with Chloe. Let's just say I hadn't excelled. It seemed this wasn't going to go any better than that twelve-week course, because I couldn't stop thinking about what I was *supposed* to be doing, which was drawing the face of a man I was meant to be with. And because I couldn't stop thinking about that, I couldn't think of anything else.

Because I wanted this over with, I decided to give them the show they were after. Only I'd have to fake it, because this magic thing? It so wasn't happening. But I needed a man to draw, and after a minute, I had the perfect one.

Elizabeth's boyfriend, Nate.

Besides, my sister had given me this gift I didn't want, so I owed her one. I'd do this just to tease her. She'd probably freak out, but once I told her it was a joke, maybe everyone would forget this ridiculous idea and leave me alone.

I thought of Nate, remembering his features. Normally I didn't like drawing people without at least a picture of them in front of me, but I figured I'd be able to get a close enough representation based on memory alone.

"Oh! I'm feeling something," I fibbed. "I think it's working!" My lips quirked and I fought to stop myself from breaking into laughter.

Chloe squealed. My grandmother hushed her. Putting pencil to paper, I began to draw.

In a millisecond, everything changed. Tingles sped down my arms into my hands, and just like that I was drawing a picture that wasn't Nate. I didn't have any other image in mind, so I saw what the others saw, as it came to be on the paper in front of me.

My hand moved quickly, drawing lines, shading them in, moving on to another area of the page to do the same. The tingles increased, sort of like when your arm falls asleep and you get that numb but not quite numb feeling. That was exactly what it felt like, except it affected my entire body.

As weird as this was, I also knew I had the power to stop. That if I wanted to drop the pencil, I could. But something I couldn't explain pulled at me, pushed at me, and I felt as if I had to finish this drawing. That nothing else mattered at that moment but completing the picture in front of me.

So, I drew. And drew. And finally, after I don't know how much time, the image began to make sense. Sand met a water's edge; a pile of seashells and a toy bucket with a shovel came into view. After that, a dog with big, floppy ears and a sideways grin. I have to admit, that made me chuckle. Here I was, supposedly drawing my soul mate, and a dog stared up at me from the page. Cute as he was, I doubted he was my forever after.

But then my hand drew the image of a little girl. And I recognized her from the vision I'd had with Miranda. This was *my* child. My daughter. Garbed in a sundress, she sat on one side of the dog, her hands digging into the sand, building the beginnings of a sand castle.

My heart raced and my breath caught in my throat. My daughter. I had a picture of my daughter before she was even born. How many people could say that?

My hand continued to move, but every part of me

remained focused on the child. Her smile was wide, open, and carefree. She looked healthy and well taken care of. Which meant I hadn't screwed up too badly yet. Yay for that.

When I heard Chloe gasp, I realized I was finally drawing the form of a man. My attention switched to him, and I waited with bated breath as my hand continued to move, continued to shade, continued to draw. All my prior arguments flew out the window. Because, guess what? I wanted to see his face.

If this man was truly my soul mate, then hell yes, I wanted to see his face. My hand moved faster, so fast that my arm began to cramp. My fingers gripped the pencil tighter, sending another spasm through my arm. Ignoring the ache, I waited for the image to be finished.

And then, finally, it was. I dropped the pencil on the table. It landed with a soft *clack* before rolling off, soundlessly hitting the floor below.

"Oh, no," Chloe whispered.

"What?" Grandma Verda stood and then walked over to us. "Well, that's not good."

"It can't be that bad." Elizabeth followed in Grandma Verda's footsteps, stopping on the other side of me. She bent forward, the movement causing her hair to cover her eyes. Pushing it away, she sighed. "All right, that sucks."

Disappointment I hadn't expected brushed against me, drowning out my anticipation. I ran my fingers over the drawing I'd just completed, and let out a sigh of my own. Maybe this man in front of me, put on paper by my own hands, really was my soul mate, but I'd never know who he was. At least, not based on *this* image. He knelt on the other side of the sand castle, across from my daughter, but all I could see was his backside. From the soles of his bare feet past the edges of his swim trunks, up to his bare back, to the—yep—back of his head. Not one part of his face showed.

"He must be nice, this man. I mean, he's building a sand castle with someone else's child, so he must be a good man, right?" I muttered.

"How do you know she isn't his child?" Chloe asked.

"Because she's my daughter. I saw her last night, when I was with Miranda."

"Oh!" My grandmother squeezed my shoulder. "She's beautiful."

Tears filled my eyes. I pushed them away. "Yes, she is. And she looks happy."

Elizabeth spoke softly over my right shoulder. "Of course she does. You'll be a terrific mother."

Maybe. But what if this man, whose face I couldn't see, was part of the reason why my daughter looked so happy? I heard Miranda's warning again, and the part about my daughter needing the guidance of one particular man reverberated inside of me. As quick as I'd been to laugh at the idea of finding my soul mate, this changed things.

"Miranda said she needed to be raised in pure love. She said it was of the utmost importance I find my soul mate before my baby is born. It could be she's this happy because this picture represents the best-case scenario, assuming I can find him."

But what would the results be if I couldn't? Prickles of unease popped up, coating my skin from head to toe. I didn't know the answer to that question. I stared at my daughter again, taking in her smile, the happiness in her gaze, and at that second I knew something I hadn't known before: I would do anything—*anything*—to ascertain this image became reality.

"I think I need to find him," I whispered. Once again, I ran my fingers over the sketch, wishing I could turn the picture of him around by force of will so I could see his eyes. Were they gentle? Kind? I wanted to know. I wanted to know so badly that it startled me.

"How are you going to find a faceless man?" my grand-mother asked.

This was another question for which I didn't have an answer. At least, not right away; but as I stared at the drawing, searching for something, anything I could use to identify him, I found it. My answer *and* the identify-ing mark.

"He has a scar." I pointed to the jagged mark on his right shoulder. "See it? It's not that large, but it's there."

"Let me see that." Grandma Verda reached for the sketchpad.

I gave it to her. Then I stood and paced, working out the kinks in my legs from sitting so long.

"You're right! It's definitely a scar. Or a birthmark. It's hard to tell for sure."

She passed the sketchbook on to my sister, who said, "Hmm, I think it's a birthmark. But Grandma's right; it could be either."

Elizabeth then gave it to Chloe, who barely looked before returning it. "Would more magic work? Can't you bake a new batch of cupcakes, Elizabeth? But wish for Alice to draw the *face* of her soul mate."

"We can definitely try. I'm just not sure how success-ful we'll be. I was pretty clear in this wish, and that's what we got. Of course, Alice should be able to use her magic for this too."

Grandma Verda crossed her arms. "There's no need. The back of that man could be Ethan Gallagher. The body looks about the right size, and he has dark hair, just like Ethan." She pointed at me. "All you have to do is get a look at him without his shirt on."

"That's it, huh? How am I supposed to do that?" And yes, I realized that the chance of Ethan being the man I'd drawn was slim to none, but I also knew that until I ruled him out Grandma Verda would be of no help. In fact, she'd be a hindrance.

Her faded blue eyes sparkled. "Well, dear, I'm sure we can come up with something."

While I'm sure she meant to reassure me, coming from Grandma Verda, that statement did anything but. Her ideas tended to fall on the wild and wacky side of things. "I'll figure it out. Just don't do anything. Okay?"

She huffed. "What do you think I'd do?"

Knowing her? Take him to lunch again and ask him to remove his shirt.

My eyes fell on the sketch again. I noticed something I hadn't before. While I couldn't see his face, I *could* see his left hand. It was outstretched, as if he were about to grab another fistful of sand to add to the sand castle. Adorning his ring finger was a wide band, most definitely a wedding band.

Did that mean, if I found him, there was a wedding in my future?

The butterfly wings came back then, and it felt as if my daughter were dancing a jig, they were that strong. A shiver rippled from the bottom of my neck all the way down the length of my back. Call me crazy, but I'm fairly sure my daughter was giving me her approval.

Tilting my head, I looked at Chloe, then Grandma Verda, and then, finally, my sister. "Let's figure this out. We have close to five months."

Chloe clapped her hands. "This is going to be *so* much fun!"

Finding my soul mate through magic and a scar on his shoulder. Yeah. Sure. *Fun*.

Chapter Six

My alarm blared way too early on Monday morning, and I groaned. Slamming the obnoxious noise off, I yawned, curled up in bed, knees to chest, and tried to wake up. The night before hadn't passed in blissful slumber. Rather, it had been a night spent thinking about my daughter, magic, and soul mates, and wondering exactly how my life had turned into an episode of *Ripley's Believe It or Not*. Or maybe *Mission: Impossible* was more like it.

I sat up in bed. Definitely *Mission: Impossible*. Because after a night of thinking, tossing, turning, and thinking some more, finding the man I'd drawn certainly didn't feel like a cakewalk. Bleary-eyed, I headed for the bathroom to begin my morning routine. My stomach forced a nasty morning-sickness routine instead.

It did it again after I finished my shower. And again after I tried to eat some dry toast. Thinking my nausea would pass—or at least lighten—I took to the couch, one eye on the clock. I didn't have to leave for another thirty minutes, so maybe, just maybe, I'd be lucky and this feeling would go away.

Unfortunately, that didn't happen, and thirty minutes later the nausea was even worse than before. I debated about what to do: go to work, since I was still such a new employee; or stay home because I didn't really think I'd be able to get much work done in my current condition. Another rush of nausea answered my question, so I called in and left a message on Ethan's voice mail.

Back in my bedroom, I pulled off my too-tight-at-the-waistband work pants and searched through my drawers for something more comfortable to wear. Finally, I settled on a pair of extra-large pajama bottoms and a long, loose T-shirt. Well, it used to be loose. Now it sort of hitched up slightly at my waist, clinging around my midsection.

After brewing a cup of tea, I grabbed my sketchpad and pencil from the dining room table and plopped down on the couch. Placing the pad on the cushion, I sipped my tea, my eyes taking in the drawing again. It really was a heartwarming picture, and so totally not the type of art I tended to create. While I'd done my fair share of portraits and scenic paintings over the years—mostly because they sold pretty well—I liked bolder, more abstract artwork.

But this? The finer details blew me away. My hands itched to add color to the picture, to put some blue in the water, a touch of pink in my daughter's cheeks and on her lips, a dash of red on the dog's lolling tongue—not so much coloring between the lines as adding depth to certain areas. But not now. I didn't feel well enough to do the work justice; and besides, there was something else I wanted to try.

I sipped a little more tea, hoping the warmth would ease the ongoing churning in my stomach. Setting the mug down, I picked up the pencil and the pad. Turning to a clean sheet of paper, I closed my eyes and brought back everything I'd learned about the magic. About the wishes. Elizabeth had said I should be able to use my magic to do this, so why not give it a try?

What did I want to accomplish? That was easy to answer. I wanted to see the face of the man I'd drawn. But somehow, I didn't think wishing it in that way would do the trick, so instead I said, "I wish I could draw the beach-scene picture from another angle, so I can see the man's face more clearly."

I put pencil to paper. I waited for the magical zing I'd felt during each of the other instances I'd cast a wish that came true. But this time nothing happened. No shivers, trembles, swirling rooms, or anything else. Frustration zipped through me, and without thought, I said, "Oh, come on. This isn't fair, Miranda! You give me a warning, and I'm trying to do what you want, but this is silly. I need to know who the guy is, don't I? Help me out a little."

Suddenly, the magic was there. It zapped into my body like a bolt of lightning, only it didn't hurt. It was more like a sharp buzz of electricity. My hand gripped the pencil tighter. I began to draw. This time, the strokes were broad, the scene rapidly appearing before my eyes. Barely a few minutes had passed before I realized I *wasn't* drawing the same scene as before.

No sand met a water's edge. There wasn't a dog, a sand castle, or a toy bucket. Instead, the scene before me was of a woman in a wooden rocking chair holding a baby. Not a newborn, either, though probably no older than a few months. At first, I thought I was drawing myself, rocking my daughter to sleep, but as the woman's features became clearer, I realized it wasn't my face that stared back but another, older face. And I didn't recognize her.

The child—and I assumed she was my child—had her cheek pressed against the woman's chest. The woman's arms were wrapped around the tot, holding her snugly. Her expression was one of peace, and the child's was one of sleepiness—from what I could see, anyway. When my hand finally stopped moving, the ripple of magic seeped away, and it was just me again, sitting on my couch, holding a pencil.

I looked at this new image, trying to make sense of what I saw. There were no indicators of time or place, just the rocking chair, the woman, and the baby. And while I *thought* the child had to be my daughter, I couldn't see enough of her face to be absolutely sure. Who was this woman holding her? Where was I?

Fear took hold of me, and I dropped the pencil in surprise. If the other picture, the one from the previous night, was the best-case scenario like I'd guessed, did that mean this one was the worst-case scenario? Meaning someone else was raising my child? If so, why? What happened to me? I stared closer at the baby, trying to determine for sure if she was my daughter or not. I flipped the page to the other drawing, so I could compare the two, but the original sketch depicted a child years older than the one in the second drawing.

But really, it had to be her. Who else?

Before I could give it any further thought, my phone rang. I reached over to the coffee table and grabbed it. "Hello?"

"Is this Alice Raymond?" a voice chirped in my ear.

The perkiness of the caller should have tipped me off to her identity. It didn't. "Yes, this is she."

"Alice! This is Shelby. Shelby Harris. We saw each other a few days ago at the doctor's office, remember?"

I held back a sigh. "Of course I remember."

"Doesn't life do funny things? Imagine running into each other after all these years. Your mom was nice enough to give me your number. I hope that's okay!" Before I could reply, Shelby continued. "Anyway, I was wondering if we could get together soon and catch up? None of my girlfriends are pregnant, and I'd love to have someone to talk about everything with."

I didn't say anything, because the last thing I wanted was to hang with Shelby or chat about our mutual belly bulges. Yes, she seemed nice enough now. I got that. But for one thing, I didn't want to upset Chloe. And for another, other than pregnancy, I didn't see how I'd have much in common with Shelby. Especially now.

"Things aren't that great at the moment. Can we catch up another time?"

"Oh. Sure. If that's what you want . . ." She broke off, a twinge of disappointment evident.

Again, just like in the doctor's office, I felt like a heel. "I'm home sick today. This nausea isn't going away and I can barely function, let alone have a conversation and make any sort of sense."

"Isn't it terrible? I've had the same problem, but I'm carrying twins."

"Oh. Wow. Well, I'm not. I'm just sick all the freaking time."

"Have you tried Preggie Pops? Or one of the other brands? They've helped me a lot."

"Not yet. They really work?"

"They're not the be-all, end-all, but they do make a difference." She stopped talking, and I heard her take a deep breath. "Since you're home today, and I have nothing going on, I could bring you a bag of them. Maybe they'll help. And we could catch up a little."

I hesitated. "I'm in my pajamas and don't feel like changing. Maybe another time?"

She giggled. "Don't be silly. I don't care if you're in your pj's. And I don't have to stay long."

Checking the time, I saw that I had hours before there was any chance of Chloe showing up, and it was nice of Shelby to offer. And I did feel miserable. "If you really don't mind, that would be great."

I told her where I lived and she rang off, presumably to pick up some Preggie Pops and come right over. I wasn't sure how I felt about that, but I didn't see how spending an hour or so with Shelby was going to hurt anything. Chloe would understand.

At least, I thought she would.

Ha. Actually, that was a lie. Chloe would definitely not understand, but she loved me, so she'd get over it.

My place still resembled a disaster zone, with all my art supplies strewn around, so I took a few minutes to straighten up. Then, after one more curious peek at the new drawing, I closed the sketchpad. I put that and the pencil on my coffee table, and went to put on some real clothes, because no matter what Shelby said, I was not greeting her in my pajamas.

Nearly an hour later, my doorbell rang. Then I did something I never thought I would do in a million years; I opened my door and invited Shelby Harris née Whitaker, aka crazy-cheerleader-man-stealing-self-involved-twit, into my home. Weird, how things change.

Weirder still, she gave me a hug as if we were long-lost friends, finally reunited. Because I didn't know what else to do, I hugged her back. Dressed in crisp white pants and a collared, short-sleeved yellow shirt that stretched tightly over her abdomen, she looked like one of those perfect models on the covers of pregnancy and baby magazines. But even so, her expertly applied makeup didn't hide her fatigue, and when she advanced farther into the entryway, her movements were slow and awkward.

"It was really nice of you to offer to come over," I said, leading the way into the living room. I pointed to the couch. "Why don't you relax and I'll get you something to drink. If you'd like something?"

She immediately crossed to the sofa and sat down. I tried not to stare at her stomach, but it was kind of difficult to miss, it being huge and all. "I'd love some ice water, if you don't mind. I'm always so warm."

"No problem." In the kitchen, I pulled out two glasses, filled them with ice and water, then returned to my guest. "Here you go."

She accepted the glass. I took the chair across from her, and tried to think of something to say. Nothing came to me, so I relied on the most obvious topic. "So. Um. When are you due?"

Grimacing, she placed her free hand on her stomach. "Not soon enough. My official due date is mid-July, but twins tend to come about a month early. So probably next month sometime. What about you?"

"September. It seems so far away. Are you ready? I mean, twins! Were you surprised?"

"We were relieved, actually. I didn't conceive easily." She hesitated and then leaned forward. "We spent a lot of money to have these babies, and I don't think we'd ever be able to do that again. It will take us years to get out of debt. So we're happy we're having two. But no, we're not ready."

"I haven't even started." My admission startled me, but somehow, hanging with Shelby wasn't nearly as horrible as I'd expected. "Right now, my extra bedroom is my art studio, but I'm going to have to turn it into the baby's room. I'm thinking about painting a nursery scene on the wall."

"I wish I were that creative. Or my husband." She laughed. "Grant has been meaning to paint the nursery forever, but he still hasn't gotten around to it."

I almost offered to paint a scene for her but held my tongue. Right or wrong, it seemed traitorous to Chloe. "It sounds like you're really happy."

"I am! What about you? How's the father-to-be?"

"He's not involved," I said quickly. "I, ah, prefer not to discuss that. Or him."

"I'm so sorry," Shelby said. "I can't imagine going through this without Grant. Most of my friends . . ." She broke off, sipped her water, and then set the glass down on the end table. "They're not at the same place in their lives, and they're not sure how to handle this." She gestured to her stomach. "So . . . well, they've kind of vanished. And Grant has to work so many hours, I'm alone a lot. That's why I wanted to see you."

"But we were never really friends," I remarked. "Don't

get me wrong. It's nice to chat, but it's a little confusing." Though, based on what she'd just said, her behavior made a lot more sense.

"You were really nice to me once, a long time ago. I've never forgotten it. When I saw you at Dr. Layton's . . . well, I thought maybe . . ." She stopped speaking and twisted her fingers together.

"Maybe what?" Even as I asked, I tried to remember when I had been really nice to Shelby.

"I don't know. I'd hoped we might be able to be friends now."

"Oh. The thing is—" My stomach gurgled and nausea climbed the back of my throat. In one quick move, I set my glass down and slapped my hand over my mouth. Jumping up, I ran from the room, hoping like hell I'd make it to the restroom in time.

When I finally returned, some ten minutes later, I said, "I'm so sorry. It comes in waves, and normally I can deal with it. Today has been bad."

Understanding gleamed in her gaze. "Don't even think about it. I get it, believe me." She opened her purse and pulled out a bag. "I should have given this to you right away, but I was so happy to see you, I forgot. They didn't have Preggie Pops, but this brand works really well too."

I accepted the bag and opened it. Inside was a package of lollipops. The words on the outside of the package promised they would "Stop queasiness in its tracks." Choosing one, I unwrapped it and stuck it in my mouth. "Thanks," I said, talking around it.

"No problem. Hey, do you mind if I put my feet up? My ankles are hideously swollen." Pink blossomed on Shelby's cheeks, as if the admission embarrassed her. "I promised my husband I'd keep them up as much as possible. He worries."

Even as I said, "Go ahead," and "Isn't that sweet?"

jealousy whipped into me. Mere minutes earlier, I'd felt a little sorry for her, because of her vanishing friends. But now? The pang of envy grew stronger. What would it be like to have a husband hover around, making sure you were okay, worrying about you, taking care of you? If he were the right guy? It would be wonderful.

Shelby smiled gratefully. Kicking her shoes off, she started to swing her feet onto the coffee table but then stopped. "Let me move this first." Reaching over, she picked up my sketchpad. "Oh! I remember you were always the artsy type. Mind if I look?"

I was still thinking about how lucky she was to have a husband who so obviously loved her. "Go ahead. They're just sketches, though."

Shelby scooted around, settling into a half sitting, half prone position. Once her feet were up, she sighed. "So much better." Opening the sketchbook, she flipped from one page to another, oohing and ahhing as she went. Me? I kept sucking on the lollipop, and guess what? It was working. For the first time all morning, my nausea, while not gone, was nowhere near as bad as it had been. I had a strong hunch I'd be buying out my local pharmacy's supply.

"Oh! This looks like someone I know," Shelby said, her eyes glued to the sketchpad.

"Really?" There were a lot of pictures in that book, but most of them weren't of people, so immediately the hairs on the back of my neck stood up. "Which?"

She flipped the book around, so I could see the page she looked at. "This one. I can't tell for sure, because I can't see his face, but from the back, he looks like an old boyfriend." Another flush gathered on her cheeks. "He introduced me to Grant, actually."

I opened my mouth. The lollipop fell to the ground. "You know him? Who is he?" I tried to sound natural and calm, but yeah—that didn't happen. "And how can you tell from his back?"

She gave me an odd look. "I can't for sure. Like I said. And it probably isn't him, anyway. Lots of men would look the same from the back. Don't you think?" Her eyes returned to the page, and she puckered her lips.

"There's a scar on his shoulder. Or maybe a birthmark, I'm not sure," I offered.

She nodded. "I saw that. That's one of the reasons why I thought it looked like Kyle. But that's silly. Isn't it?" Her gaze flickered over to me. "Who is it? I'm sure I don't know him, but now I'm curious."

Kyle? No. Not that Kyle. Impossible.

"Oh, nobody. I mean, I drew the picture with no one in particular in mind. Kyle who?"

"Ackers. You probably don't know him. We dated for about a year, and then he introduced me to Grant." She shrugged. "Love at first sight. We've been together ever since."

Her forgetfulness annoyed me. Big time. "We went to school together, Shelby. Remember? Of course I know who Kyle is. I'm surprised you don't remember *why* I know who Kyle is." Now I was more than annoyed; I was a little peeved. Sure, the incident between her and Chloe had happened forever ago, but—to me—if you're going to be classless enough to steal a girl's guy, you should at least remember it!

The terseness of my voice must have tipped her off that she'd trodden into a danger zone. Her blue eyes clouded for a second, as if she were searching back in her memory, trying to find whatever piece of information to which I'd alluded. Then they widened, and she looked a little like a deer caught in oncoming headlights. "Oh. That's right. I'd forgotten. It was a long time ago."

Leaning over, I picked up the sucker I'd dropped. "When someone's feelings are hurt, they don't forget. Especially when your heart is involved." My anger increased. How could she not remember? Of course, she wasn't the one who'd held Chloe while Chloe cried her eyes out, day after day, for nearly a year. Shelby wasn't the one who'd helped Chloe dispose of all the little mementos she'd collected throughout her relationship with Kyle. That had been me. Because that was what friends did for each other.

Afraid I was about to say something I'd later regret, I stood. "I'll be right back." I strode to the kitchen, tossed the lollipop in the garbage and leaned against the wall, waiting for my temper to lessen. Part of me wanted to order Shelby out of my home, to never contact me again. But that reaction was based on the past, and how fair was that? Everything I knew about her now suggested a nice woman in a good marriage, happy about beginning her family. People change. And while I'd never forget the misery Chloe had gone through, it wasn't all Shelby's fault. A large portion of the blame went to Kyle. Which, oddly, Chloe had never admitted. Not verbally, anyway.

Suddenly, what Shelby had said hit me again and I almost doubled over. No way was that picture of Kyle. That would be far too cruel a joke. But I couldn't blow it off. I couldn't ignore it. Especially because the information had seemingly come out of nowhere, not long after I'd begged Miranda to help me. So, like it or not—and I didn't, by the way—I had to look into it. But I truly didn't believe my soul mate was the same man who'd devastated my best friend.

I left the kitchen, only to find Shelby yakking on her cell phone. When she saw me, she said her good-byes and disconnected quickly, tucking her phone into her purse. Apprehension skittered over her expression, and again I reminded myself that she wasn't the same person she had been in high school.

"You're right, Shelby. It was a long time ago. Let's just leave it alone."

She smiled in relief. "Thank you. Things change, and

now that I remember what I did, I feel horrible. But I can fix it!"

Oh, no. "Fix it?"

"That was Kyle on the phone. Once I realized how much you must still be hung up on him—I mean, you drew his picture—I decided to fix you two up again. Just like the old days."

"Um. Shelby? I never dated Kyle. It was my friend Chloe. Chloe Nichols. You remember her, right? You guys were really good friends for a long time."

"Kyle dated Chloe? Are you sure? I thought you dated him."

An exasperated sigh slipped out. "Yes. I'm positive."

She tilted her head to the side, and her gaze took in the drawing again. "Why'd you draw him then? Does Chloe know how you feel?"

"Shelby! I didn't draw Kyle. I just drew a man. I don't know who he is."

"Wow. That's bizarre, huh?"

"I guess." I laughed at the ludicrousness of me being hung up on Kyle Ackers. "He's not exactly my type, you know," I said.

"What do you mean?" She looked truly perplexed.

"He's just a little"—I searched for the right word—"callous."

Shelby's blue eyes filled with sadness. "He actually has a great deal of compassion; he just doesn't let many people see it."

I shrugged, ready to bring the subject back to the drawing. "It's been years since I've seen him, so I can believe he's changed."

A quick grin wiped away the sadness. "Oh, I wouldn't go that far. He still doesn't have the greatest social skills, but trust me . . . he really isn't as bad as he comes off."

Her eyes drifted to the drawing again, so I switched gears. "How sure are you that it looks like Kyle?"

Amusement flitted over her. "Oh, pretty sure. I've seen his back a zillion times." I must have looked puzzled, because she laughed. "Not like that! Not for a long time, anyway. We have a pool, and Kyle likes to swim, so he's over a lot. Did I mention he's really good friends with my husband?"

"Yes, you mentioned that." My head hurt from taking in so much information at once. How could anyone be so dang chipper all the time?

"So, anyway, Kyle remembered you. And we're having a cookout on Saturday. If it's warm enough, we'll be opening the pool. Want to come? You can bring Chloe, if you'd like."

No, I didn't want to go. No, I didn't want to see Kyle. And no, I didn't want Kyle to be the man I'd drawn. But for some reason, what I said was, "Sure. Sounds like fun. I'll check with Chloe."

Shelby hung around for another hour or so, and while I tried to be sociable, I probably wasn't that successful. After she left, I picked up the sketchpad again. Turning to the beach scene, I stared at the man. "Who are you?" I whispered. "And why is it so important I find you?"

"You're going to Shelby's house. For a barbeque. And Kyle will be there." Chloe's voice had that monotone thing going on. That, combined with the stiff way she held herself, worried me. Because when Chloe isn't animated, something is very wrong. "How exactly did all of this take place?"

We were sitting in the living room of her minuscule one-bedroom apartment. Rather than give her the chance to come to my place, I'd been waiting for her when she got home from work. I'd already explained how Shelby had stopped by, but I'd sort of zoomed ahead to the cookout invitation, thinking Chloe would be so excited at the chance to see Kyle again that the rest wouldn't matter. Wrong.

"Well. It's kind of funny, actually."

Her light green eyes darkened a shade. "I could use a laugh. Go on."

"Shelby . . . ah . . . you see . . ." Maybe this wasn't such a good idea, after all. Chloe is tiny, just hitting five feet tall in her stocking feet, but she's tough. Even with my eight extra inches of height and God only knew how many pounds, if she wanted to flatten me, she probably could. But more than that, I worried about her feelings. Possibly, it would have been a better idea to have gone to the stupid cookout, ascertained Kyle was not the man in my drawing, and never breathed a word of it. But yeah, like I said before, we didn't keep secrets from each other.

"Just tell me."

"She saw my sketchbook and wanted to look through it. I told her sure, because it didn't occur to me to say no. Besides, that would have been weird, don't you think? And kind of rude." I looked to Chloe for affirmation, somehow wanting her approval of my actions before I explained any further.

"I'm still trying to comprehend how Shelby 'Man-stealing' Whitaker ended up in your home, and how that turned into a get-together at her place with Kyle."

"Um. So. She flipped through the pages. When she came across the picture I drew last night, she stopped. She thought she recognized the man, Chloe! My soul mate! So, I kind of have to go to this thing. Just to be sure."

A spark of interest darted over my friend. "Really? Well, I guess if anyone in this world could recognize a man by nothing but his bare back, it'd be her."

"Stop that. She's not the same girl we knew back then. She's pregnant, she's happily married, and she's been with the same guy for a long time. Seriously, Chloe. You might even like her now."

Chloe scowled. "What did she do to you? Suddenly you're all chummy with the enemy." When I didn't say anything, she heaved a breath. "Fine. Who does Shelby think this guy is?"

"Well." I cleared my throat. "The thing is, it's nearly impossible to identify someone by just his back. Even with that scar and all. The most we can really do is *rule out* men. If they don't have a scar . . . or a birthmark . . . or whatever that mark is, or if it looks different . . ."

Comprehension dawned and, as it did, Chloe's entire body slumped forward. As if the weight of the understanding was greater than she could bear. "It's Kyle, isn't it? Shelby thinks the man you're destined to be with is Kyle."

I reminded myself to proceed with caution. "She thinks there's enough of a resemblance; it intrigued her. But she doesn't know why I drew that picture. She doesn't know about the magic or anything else. She just thinks it's kind of funny I happened to draw a man who reminds her of someone she knows. It's probably nothing, Chloe. Really. It's a ludicrous idea, but think of the good side. You get to see Kyle again."

"And have my heart broken for the second time when you discover he's your soul mate? How much would that suck? No thanks."

"Gee, there's the pessimist Chloe I haven't seen in years. Can't say I've missed her much," I teased.

A small smile appeared. "So I'm overreacting. I know I'm being stupid, but I'll never forget what it felt like when he dumped me. I had so much invested in him. And I don't know if I even want to see him again. So this time, my friend, you're on your own."

"I need your help. I need you to come."

She stood and marched toward her kitchen. Well, it was more of a kitchenette. She didn't even have a full-sized refrigerator, just one of those mini ones like college students get.

"Where are you going?"

"I'm getting a glass of wine. I need a drink." No full-sized fridge. She did, however, have a nifty little wine cooler she'd had installed under her counter. Priorities, you know?

I followed her and waited while she poured herself a glass of Chardonnay. "Look, I know this seems horrible, but maybe it won't be. It might even be fun. If nothing else, you can show him how amazing you are today, and rub his face in the fact that he lost out on someone as gorgeous, funny, smart, and spectacular as you are."

Swallowing half of her glass of wine in one gulp, she shook her head. "I can't do it. Besides, I don't think I can be polite to Shelby."

"Stop."

Her eyebrow raised in question. "Stop what?"

"This. Kyle was a jerk back then. Shelby was too," I admitted. "But I know she's not the same, so maybe he isn't either."

"The way Kyle broke things off wasn't cool. But he wasn't always a jerk." She sighed, as if trying to pull herself together.

"Put the past to rest, Chloe. Come on. Please come with me. Besides, aren't you curious about what he looks like now?" I smirked. "Maybe *he's* the one with the third eye and hairy mole."

She laughed. A little bit of color returned to her complexion, and I was glad for it. "Fine. You win. So, what's the plan?"

"I don't know. That's why I need you. I'm terrible at making plans."

"Well, obviously we're going to need to see his back—so we can compare it to the drawing." Her face lit up. "You need to invite Ethan to come too."

"Why?"

"Because then, whatever plan we come up with we can use on him at the same time. In case your grandmother is right."

"And then what? Let's assume neither of them is the right man. Then what?"

She finished off her wine. "I don't know. Let's focus on this first."

Suddenly, everything was okay between us again. I wasn't truly worried about Kyle being a match to the drawing, because you'd think if he were my soul mate, I'd have clicked with him back in the day. That just the very thought of being with him now would fill me with anticipation. Want. Desire.

Yep, you got it. Pretty much the way I felt about Ethan.

Chapter Seven

I strolled into work on Tuesday morning feeling much more like myself. I'd barely made it on time, but hey, I was there, and I wasn't late. Points for that.

On my way in, I'd stopped to pick up three more bags of the lollipops that made my nausea bearable. That—if nothing else—was one thing I could thank Shelby for. At my desk, I dumped one of the bags into my top drawer, for easy access, and another in my purse. The third I'd left in my car to take home with me.

The office buzzed with the morning sounds of chatter and people getting coffee. Kind of weird, maybe, but I'd noticed that as the workday went on, people became quieter, more fixated on their tasks. But mornings? That was gossip and chitchat time. I'm not a chatterer in the morning, so I kept to myself.

I turned on my computer and desk light, and then checked to see if I had any messages in my voice mail. Nope, not a one. To anyone else, this was a normal workday. For me? Not so much. For some reason, Grandma Verda's insistence about Ethan being the man in my drawing refused to leave my mind. I mean, come on, she was right about so many things on such a regular basis, I couldn't ignore it. And I'd be lying if I said I hated the idea. Because I didn't. That was why I was so nervous. Today, I needed to ask Ethan out on a *date*. Because let's face it, no matter how I worded it, it was a date. And seeing how smart Ethan was, there was no way he wouldn't catch on. I'd thought about every word spoken between us, every little nuance, and I was pretty sure the sparks I felt weren't one-sided. But who knew how he'd react to something a little less professional than what we'd previously shared?

Plopping down in my chair, I grabbed a hand wipe and cleaned the surface of my desk. Not because it needed it, but because I was in heavy procrastination mode. Next, I clicked on my e-mail box and read all of my e-mails—even those I'd read before. Nothing needed my attention, but as I stared at my little file with its thirteen e-mails, I wondered if it would be appropriate, in any way whatsoever, to just invite Ethan to the cookout electronically.

Yeah. I know. Not. But still, I gave it some more thought. This way, if he said no, it would be easier to take. Plus, it had one huge advantage: distance. It saved me from the face-to-face; I wouldn't be able to smell his melt-my-knees cologne, and I wouldn't be distracted by the cleft in his chin or his dimples.

Deciding to type out an invite and see how it looked, I opened up an e-mail he'd sent me the prior week, clicked *Reply*, deleted the old subject line, and typed:

Morning, Ethan!
A friend of mine is having a cookout this weekend. Want to come?
There will be food, fun, and games.
Oh! And if you get hot enough—swimming!
Anyway, let me know,
Alice
P.S. Thanks for Sunday. I enjoyed it!

I stared at the e-mail, read it again and then again. My cursor hovered over *Send*, but I couldn't make up my mind. But when I considered walking into his office instead and verbally asking him, the decision seemed simple. I sent a quick prayer upward and did what I had to. The screen flashed and it was gone. Almost instantaneously, a new e-mail appeared in my in-box. It was an *Out of the Office* reply to the e-mail I'd just sent, but not from Ethan.

What? I blinked. I blinked again. I really hoped I'd read it wrong, but no. I broke out in a cold sweat. My stomach dipped. I checked my Sent file. Opening the e-mail I'd just typed, I scanned the recipient list. Leaning forward, elbows on desk and chin in hands, I tried very hard not to freak out. Because yeah, apparently I'd clicked *Reply all*, which meant every person who had something to do with the Frosty's account was getting my carefully thought-out note to Ethan. And that meant I was about to become water cooler topic number one. Again.

The whole freaking point of the freaking e-mail was so I wouldn't have to invite Ethan in person! Now, I had no choice. Because in case he hadn't yet seen the e-mail, I needed to warn him. So if anyone cracked a joke or made a comment, he'd at least know what the deal was.

Grabbing a lollipop from my drawer, I shoved it into my pocket, just in case. Walking to Ethan's office felt like it took forever, instead of the less than a minute it actually did. Luckily, most everyone still stood around gabbing over coffee, so I doubted anyone on the reply-all list had actually seen my e-mail yet. But it wouldn't be long.

I stopped outside of Ethan's door. It was closed, and his assistant wasn't at her desk. Knock or come back later? I debated for a couple of minutes. Even though walking away sounded like a great plan, that would only put off the inevitable. So I shored up my courage, forced a smile, and knocked.

His voice came through the door. "Come in."

Twisting the knob, I pushed open the door and stuck

my head in. "Do you have a few—?" I broke off at the totally unexpected vision that met my eyes. Normally, just being in Ethan's office calmed me. The room, from the chocolate brown painted walls to the big, comfy leather chairs and sofa, to the splashes of green throughout, resonated warmth and comfort.

Not this time. Ethan sat behind his desk, looking a little rumpled. His hair was mussed, as if he'd just run his hands through it, and his suit jacket was draped around the back of his chair. Another chair was pulled up next to his, and in it sat my grandmother in a bright purple and green paisley dress. Seriously. Grandma Verda. At my place of employment. Behind closed doors with Ethan, the man she thought was my soul mate. I reminded myself to stay calm.

"What's going on?" I managed to ask.

Grandma Verda's lips twitched. "Ethan's showing me how to go through the mail." A stack of mail in front of them, plus the fact my grandmother wielded a letter opener, verified her statement.

"Why would he be doing that?" My voice squeaked on the last word.

"So I know how to do it. Why else?" She sliced open an envelope, stacked it neatly to the side, and moved on to the next.

I looked to Ethan for an answer, but he seemed a little dazed. So I asked again. "Why are you showing my grandmother how to go through the office mail?"

"Angela quit yesterday without notice." He cleared his throat. "Verda happened to show up right afterward."

"Angela? Your secretary? But what does that have to do with—?" *Oh, no.* I got it, and I didn't like it. "You hired my grandmother? Seriously?"

"Just for the interim, until I can find a replacement. It seemed like a good solution yesterday when Verda offered." His gaze floated off to my left somewhere.

"Grandma? Why?" Ouch. I instantly regretted asking that. Because I knew why.

"Why not? It'll be fun being around you, and I can earn a little extra money. I worked as a secretary for years, you know that." A simple enough statement, which would make a great deal of sense to anyone else. I nearly bought her oh-so-innocent explanation too, but then I noticed her hand—the one wielding the letter opener—moving in the direction of Ethan's shirt.

She wouldn't actually slice his shirt off. Would she? I tried to keep an eye on her while I spoke. "But you're so busy all the time. With Vinny. Maybe you should reconsider."

"I won't be coming in every day, dear. Just two or three mornings a week. To help out." She winked at me, and her hand inched closer.

Okay, I needed to stop this before she did something crazy. "Grandma? What are you doing?"

"There's some lint on Ethan's shirt. I'm just going to pull it off."

"What? That's not—" Ethan's hand went to his shirt at the same time Grandma's did, but she was quicker. Not to mention sneakier.

"Already got it!" She pretended to drop the invisible piece of lint on the floor, and scooted back to her former position, grinning like the cat that swallowed the canary. Her free hand tightened into a fist.

I dashed to her side and grabbed the letter opener. "What's in your hand?"

"Oh, dear. All the chatter distracted me." Grandma Verda batted her eyelashes innocently at Ethan, her voice as sweet as southern iced tea. "I'm so sorry, but it seems I somehow removed one of your buttons." Then she opened her fist, and lying there was the button in question.

"Yes. *Somehow*. I wonder how that happened?" I glared at my grandmother. Or I tried to, but she didn't look at me.

Ethan held up a hand. "It's not a big deal. I have plenty of other shirts at home. Not a problem." He grinned at Grandma Verda. "Remind me not to chatter around you when you're opening mail, though," he teased.

"I'm so terribly sorry. You know what? I'm positive I have a travel sewing kit in my handbag. Why don't you slip that shirt off for me and I'll fix it right up. I'll be done before you know it!"

My God, she was good. I had to admit, even I was a little impressed, and I'd grown up witnessing her antics. I thought I'd seen it all. Curiosity got the better of me, and I walked back around to the other side of the desk and took a seat. So I could watch her in action.

"That's a very nice offer, Verda," Ethan said, "but it isn't necessary. It's just a button."

"Young man, you are in a position of authority here. You need to look the part. It will only take a minute," Grandma Verda said.

"Really. It's okay. Let's finish the mail so I can have one of the girls show you how to use the phones."

Grandma Verda pouted. I tried not to chuckle, because as sorry as I felt for Ethan, I knew she'd win. He didn't have a chance. And nope, I wasn't going anywhere.

"I'll feel badly all day unless you let me mend your shirt." She sighed pitifully. "But if you're sure." She rubbed her eyes, and I thought—maybe—she was taking it too far. But then she sort of did a heavy shrug, as if the weight of the world rested on her shoulders. "Okay. Show me the rest of the mail," she said with a sigh.

Ethan glanced at me and then back at my grandmother. "I don't want you to feel bad about this, Verda. It's no big deal."

"Don't worry about me. I'll be fine," she said, her voice cracking slightly. "I hate the thought of you walking around all day with a missing button . . ."

Humor glinted in Ethan's eyes as he gave in. "If it's

that important to you, I'd be quite pleased if you'd mend my shirt."

That was all Grandma Verda needed to hear. Without hesitation, she began unbuttoning his shirt for him. I put my hand over my mouth to cover my grin.

"It's the right thing to do," she was saying.

With a slight tilt of her head, she winked at me. I winked back. Poor Ethan. I reminded myself to scold my grandmother later, because her actions were wrong. But for now? I waited on the edge of my seat. Literally.

"I can take care of this, Verda." He gently removed her hand from his shirt, turned slightly away, and finished unbuttoning it himself. His position couldn't have been better. As soon as the shirt came off, I'd have a perfect view of his right shoulder. Anticipation had me scooting closer. I leaned in a bit more. Was this it? Was Grandma Verda right? Was I actually about to find out if Ethan was my soul mate? I leaned in even farther. And waited.

Grandma Verda watched in rapt attention. He lifted his shoulders, pulled the shirt back and off his arms, and . . . I almost chewed my lip off in frustration. Because instead of the bare back I'd expected to see, what greeted me was a white T-shirt. Sure, it fit him like a second skin, and the urge to touch him blasted through me, but it seemed—for now, at least—my question was to remain unanswered.

Settling back in my chair, I pulled my lollipop out of my pocket, removed the wrapper, and stuck it in my mouth. Because while I wasn't exactly queasy, my stomach swirled as if I'd just stepped off of a roller coaster. My grandmother appeared just as frustrated. She slumped forward for a second, but then she got to business. In less than five minutes, she had the button sewn back on and was handing the shirt to Ethan. "There. All fixed."

"Thanks." He shook his head, a bewildered haze once again settling around him. "I . . . ah . . . appreciate it."

"You're such a delightful man. I'm so going to enjoy getting to know you better." She patted him on his arm. "Oh! And the rest of the family will adore you. Especially Isobel, Alice's mother. She'll think you're perfect!"

His confusion deepened. "That's . . . nice. Thank you, Verda."

Before she could say anything else, I jumped in. "Hey, Grandma? I kind of need to talk to Ethan for a minute."

"Well, go ahead. Cat got your tongue?"

"Grandma!" I threw my gaze from her to the door. Luckily, she got the message.

She wrinkled her nose. "Since my granddaughter wants your undivided attention, I'll take the mail to the desk out front and finish opening it. That way you two can talk." She grabbed the pile of mail. When she reached me, she held out a hand and I dropped the letter opener in it.

When the door closed again, Ethan put his shirt back on. It didn't bother me, because it wasn't like I could see anything anyway. "Did I miss something there?" His Irish lilt was a little more pronounced than normal.

I pulled the lollipop out of my mouth. "I warned you. My grandmother is a little quirky. Things seem to happen when she's around."

"I'm still not sure how she talked me into hiring her. I was all set to say no, because I worried it might be awkward for you, but somehow I ended up saying yes. And this morning, I was going to have someone else show her the mail, but . . ." He blinked. "Well, let's just say your grandmother should give lessons in charm. She'd be a millionaire within a month."

The realization that he liked her, even with all her manipulations, made me like him even more. "Grandma Verda's kind of an original."

He chuckled, and the warm rolling sound eased into me. Rather than sitting in his chair, he took the one next to me. "Something about that generation, maybe. As I said before, she reminds me a great deal of my own grand-mother."

Dear God, he smelled good. The scent punched into my brain, interrupting my thought processes. "Um, Ethan? What cologne do you wear? I'd like to pick some up."

"As a gift?" he asked.

I opened my mouth to say what I was thinking, that it was more along the lines of dousing one of my night-shirts with it, but luckily, rational thought won out. "Um. Yes. As a gift . . . for . . . one of my brothers."

He reached across the desk and grabbed a pad of Post-its. After scribbling on the top sheet, he handed it over. "I don't think you can buy it locally. I wrote down the Web site I purchase it from."

"Oh. Okay. Thanks." I folded up the little yellow paper and shoved it in my pocket.

He waited expectantly, his eyes never leaving mine. I tried to remember what I needed to tell him, but sadly, my mind remained a total blank.

"There's something I wanted to ask you, but you go first. What did you need to talk about?" he said.

All at once, it came back to me: The e-mail. The invitation. Awesome. Better to just get it over with, you know? "Well . . . I sort of sent you an e-mail this morning. See, I meant to send it only to you, but somehow I clicked wrong, and it went out to several other people."

"Is this a problem?"

"Not really, but I thought you should know. Because . . . well, I sort of . . . Not sort of. I did. And . . ." Crap. This was hard. Really, really hard.

Then he did something completely unexpected. He wrapped his hand around mine. His touch set off little tiny explosions in my brain, making it even more diffi-cult to think. And to breathe. "You did what?"

I still couldn't think. Probably I needed oxygen, so I

sucked in a large mouthful of air. Only, instead of helping, it made me a little dizzy. My mouth went dry. "Um."

"What is it, Alice? It can't be that bad."

"I asked you out on a date. In the e-mail. And by now, probably everyone knows about it, so, well . . . I needed to tell you." I hoped he understood me, because no way would I be able to say it all again.

He didn't reply, but he didn't let go of my hand, either. A light of interest—and humor?—gleamed in his eyes. "Let me make sure I have this right. You asked me out on a date via an e-mail, which you accidentally sent to several other people here at Enchanted Expressions. Is that correct?"

"Um. Yes." He didn't appear taken aback by the idea. At all. That propelled me forward. "On Saturday. To a cookout," I blurted.

The gleam in his eye grew brighter. "Ah, yes. The American tradition of broiling meat over a grill in the great outdoors. And you'd like me to escort you?"

"Should be fun," I offered. "And you'll be able to meet my friends."

He didn't respond right away, which worried me. Maybe I'd gone too far? Maybe I'd misinterpreted everything? Or, even worse, maybe I was delusional. I should have known better than to listen to Grandma Verda. But then he squeezed my hand, sending another thousand volts through my brain. "I'd love to go. I'm just sorry I didn't ask you out first. I was planning on it."

"Really? You were?"

"Yes, I really was. But you beat me to it."

Wow. Warmth centered into me, flowing through my body like water. "So . . . you're not upset about the e-mail?"

"Not at all. Are you?"

Hmm. How much to say? "Not upset, but worried,

maybe. You are the boss. I don't want people thinking bad things about you. Or me."

"We're allowed to have a personal life, Alice. And as long as we don't let it affect what happens at the office, then I don't see any issues." He grinned. "Besides, I think you'll find most people here won't even care."

Well, okay. He had a point. There were already several couples, a few of them even married, employed at Enchanted Expressions. And, as he'd said before, it was a laid-back office. But it still worried me.

Even so, that worry didn't stop the tingle of excitement from knowing he was interested. In *me*. "Maybe you're right."

"I am. I'm not saying there might not be some teasing here and there, but I've worked hard to create an environment that respects personal space. Give the people here a little credit. They're not going to care what we do in our off time."

All at once, his shoulders stiffened. "Unless you're not comfortable with this. That's an entirely different matter. I'd like to date you, Alice. And seeing as you sent me that e-mail, I'm assuming you feel the same. But what's most important is your comfort level. You can take the invitation back if you're having second thoughts."

"No! I'm not. I definitely am not doing that," I murmured.

"Then don't worry about the e-mail. I'll take care of it," he promised.

This thing happened then; I'm not sure exactly how to explain it. But the air became charged, and all I wanted to do was lean forward, stroke his cheek with my hand, and kiss him like he'd never been kissed before. As if he could hear my thoughts, he blinked. His eyes darkened from their normal light gray to a smoky black.

The yearning grew stronger. I stuck my lollipop back

in my mouth and willed my body to chill out. My skin flushed, and I knew, without even looking in a mirror, I was likely red all over. I tried to find control, I really did. But as he leaned forward, I knew if his lips touched mine, I'd lose any and all control—and dear God, what a pleasant thought that was.

His eyes found mine again, still dark, searching. I needed to cool down. Fast. Before I did something I shouldn't be doing—at least not here, and not now. I wished for an icy cold shower, because honestly, being doused with frigid water was about the only thing that would stop this moment that was about to happen. Tickles of anticipation dotted my skin. And then a long, slow series of shivers began.

Oh-so-gently, he removed the lollipop from my hand and pulled it from my mouth. Dear God, he was really going to kiss me.

"Alice," he sighed, "I find you in my thoughts constantly. Even when I'm supposed to be focusing on other things, you're there, making it quite difficult to concentrate on anything." His head bent down. I gave up the fight, closed my eyes, and waited for our lips to touch.

My stomach swirled, the shivers grew stronger and, right or wrong, too fast or not, I couldn't wait for his kiss. His hand grasped my chin, tipped my face upward, and another tremble whisked over and through me.

Just as our lips should have met, a blast of icy cold water poured down on my head, slicing through my clothes to my skin. I gasped. Pulling back, I opened my eyes. "It's raining!" I choked, wrapping my arms around me.

"Not rain!" he called over the downpour. "The sprinklers have gone off. Come on, we need to get out of here. There must be a fire in the building."

He pulled me from the chair. Before we even made it to the door, however, we realized the rain had stopped. Just like that. And that's when it hit: I'd wished for an icy cold shower, and that was what I'd gotten. Maybe this was good, maybe bad, but at least I had time to think about the kiss that had almost happened.

"Hmm, that's a little strange," Ethan remarked. We turned back to appraise the room, and what we saw was even stranger. Because the only wet spots were the chairs we'd just sat in; everything on Ethan's desk remained dry, and the rest of the office was untouched. "I'm going to make sure everything's okay," he said, heading for his phone.

Another thought occurred: Not all of my wishes came true. But this particular wish had. Was that because Ethan *wasn't* my soul mate, or was it just because it was too much, too soon? Or perhaps it was the wrong place? I didn't know. But, somehow, whether with magic or without, it needed to be figured out.

I tugged at my wet clothes and then pushed a strand of sopping hair behind my ear, waiting for Ethan to finish his call. When he hung up, he said, "Everything's fine. But the sprinkler company is sending a technician over to see if they can figure out what happened."

"At least your computer and everything is okay," I pointed out. I felt kind of bad, because I knew the technician wasn't going to find anything wrong.

"Thank goodness." He took in my wet appearance, and then glanced down at his own soaked clothes. "Go home and change. I'm going to do the same. If it weren't for that staff meeting today, I'd suggest we play hooky. Go take in a movie or something."

Honestly? I was kind of glad for the staff meeting. Because I kind of thought a little distance before spending any more alone time with Ethan would be a good plan. You know, just to get things straightened out in my head.

I remembered that feeling right before the kiss that didn't happen—how much I'd wanted to kiss him, to touch him, to taste him. I shook my head to push the sensation away.

"That would have been nice," I mumbled.

"Another time," he promised.

"I'm . . . um . . . going to go do that now—go home and change," I said. And with that, I swiveled on my heel and attempted to walk naturally out of his office. I was pretty pleased I didn't fall on my face.

Later that afternoon, dressed in dry clothing and after the staff meeting, I gathered my belongings and headed for my desk. Other than a few snickers from my coworkers regarding the mass-delivered e-mail, not to mention my soaking wet departure from Ethan's office that morning, the meeting had gone well.

True to his word, Ethan had put a halt to the giggling. He'd made a quick announcement about how we were a team, and that every person within the team also had a private life that sometimes bled into the workplace. He reminded us to respect each other, and to keep the focus on work. His message did the trick, because the sidelong glances ended.

Beyond that, we were going to move ahead with my design ideas for the Frosty's account as well as Missy's, and present both to the client in a few weeks. So, points for me.

Missy had glared at me throughout the entire meeting, however. I didn't know if it was over the account or the date e-mail, or maybe both, but Ethan was right. I needed to confront the issue and deal with it. Her attitude bugged me. A lot. Don't get me wrong, I'm not one of those women who needs everyone to like her, but if someone's going to dislike me, it'd be nice to know why. I was pretty sure it wasn't just because we had divergent views on the ad campaign.

After I dropped my stuff at my desk, I made my way to

Missy's office. She'd moved up the ranks enough to have her own space, which was convenient. I really didn't want to have this conversation with other people in hearing distance.

When I reached her office, I knocked on the door, even though it hung open. She looked up from the file on her desk. Her lips turned down in a frown. "Do you need something, Alice?"

"I'd like a few minutes of your time. Can I come in?"

Even though she nodded, it was clear she wasn't happy with the idea. But hey, too bad. I stepped in and closed the door. "We should talk."

"You heard Ethan. We're working on both of our ideas for Mr. Kendall, so I can't see what you need to talk to me about," she snapped.

"This isn't about the account. Or maybe it is. I don't know." I crossed my arms. "Look, it's been fairly obvious since day one that you have an issue with me. Seeing as I'd never met you before I began working here, I'd like to know why."

She laced her fingers together and rested her chin on them, her hazel eyes centered on me. "I'm not sure we should be having this conversation." But she wanted to. I could tell by the anger that sizzled off of her in waves.

"Well, I'm not leaving until you tell me what the deal is, so just say it." I plopped down in a chair to punctuate my statement. "Besides, Ethan's noticed and he's concerned. So unless you want to talk to him about it, you'll talk to me."

That pissed her off more. "Yeah, well, you're already the teacher's pet, aren't you? Are you trying to get me fired?"

The venom in her voice shocked me. "No, Missy. He came to me and asked me what the issue was. I told him the truth—that I don't know. He then suggested he should talk to you, and I asked him not to."

Somehow, and I'm not sure how, my words calmed her a little. Not enough to remove all of the fire blazing in her eyes, but at least she didn't appear ready to strangle me. Clobber me, maybe. "Trust me. You don't want to get into this," she said.

"I've worked here for a little over a month. Somehow, in that minuscule time frame, I've done something, said something, acted in a way that irritated you. My preference would be to get along, but I don't see how I can do that unless you tell me what needs to be fixed."

She brushed a flyaway strand of brunette hair off her cheek. "What you did has nothing to do with Enchanted Expressions. I dislike you as a person. You can't fix it."

What the hell? I kept my voice calm. "How can you dislike someone you don't even know?"

She leaned back in her chair and studied me. "Maybe that came out incorrectly. You're absolutely right: I don't know you. But I know what you represent, and I know you're missing something that all decent people have."

Whoa! I felt a little like I had when Miranda had sucked me away into her time, but at least that had made some sense. "And what would that be?"

"A conscience, Miss Raymond."

Whoa, again. I reeled in my temper and tried to remind myself that this woman didn't know me. That her opinion of me didn't matter in the slightest. "That's not something you say to a person without a very good reason to back it up."

"Oh, I can back it up." In one quick motion, she grabbed a photo frame that sat on her desk facing her, and turned it toward me. "This picture should answer your questions."

I glanced at the photo and the blood drained from my face. I looked from the picture to Missy and then back. "Oh, God," I muttered.

"I figured that would bring it all in line."

I shook my head in an attempt to think clearly. Picking up the photo, I looked at it closer, hoping, somehow, it wasn't what I thought. But of course it was. The picture was of two couples sitting at a picnic table in a park somewhere. One of the couples was Missy and a man I assumed to be her husband. Even in my distress, I noticed they appeared happy. Good for them. But as my eyes took in the other couple, my heart sank.

"You're friends with Troy and his wife," I said.

"Used to be. Now I'm just friends with his wife. She has a name. Do you know what it is?"

I shook my head again.

"Of course not. Why bother learning her name, right? You were far more interested in Troy. His wife and children were of no consequence to you."

"I get why you dislike me now, but it's not what you think. I didn't know Troy was married. He never told me, and he didn't wear a ring. The day I found out was the same day I ended things."

"You were with him for a year," she pointed out, her words dripping disdain. "I cannot fathom how in those twelve long months you never deduced he was lying to you."

"I tend to believe people when they tell me things," I snapped. She had a point, though. I'd asked myself that same question repeatedly, and kept coming up blank. "I thought I loved him. I truly didn't know until the day I came home and found him and his wife screaming at each other in my apartment."

Missy's mouth tightened. "She told me about that. She'd hired a private investigator. He came back with your name. Pictures." Her eyes narrowed. "That's how I recognized you. Anyway, she followed Troy that day because she wanted to see for herself. But she didn't expect that . . . confrontation."

All my energy evaporated. My body went limp. "I

didn't expect it, either." I didn't bother filling Missy in on the other details: my trashed apartment; the stolen money; or even how Troy had showed up at my sister's bakery. It wouldn't have mattered to her. Just as, if our situations were reversed and Chloe was the woman wronged, it wouldn't have mattered to me.

Missy rubbed her hand over her eyes. A little more of her anger slipped away. "Terri and I have been friends forever. I didn't like Troy from the beginning, but she loved him so much, I accepted him as family. She still loves him. She's forgiven him."

"So, they're back together?" I don't know why I asked. Probably because I'd watched my sister deal with the fact that her husband had cheated. I hoped Terri had found happiness, with or without Troy.

Missy's face closed down. "I shouldn't be talking about her. Not with you. Because even if what you say is the truth, she wouldn't like that we're having this conversation."

"God. This entire situation bites." Too many things happening in such a short time frame had left me a little off balance. Okay, a lot off balance. "I'm sorry for my part in all of this. But I need you to believe I didn't know, if for no other reason than that we can work together without friction."

She laughed, but it wasn't a happy, merry sound. "I've tried to set my personal feelings aside. I'll try harder."

Probably, for now anyway, that was the best I'd get. "Okay. Fair enough." Another thought drifted in, and while I should have known better than to ask, I couldn't stop myself. "Missy? Do you know how to contact Troy?"

She paled to a deathly white. "You're a piece of work. I was almost ready to believe you, and then you ask for Troy's phone number. What? You want to start things up again?"

"No! Not at all!" I sighed. "There's something I need to talk to him about."

"If, as you say, he lied to you and you didn't know, what subject is important enough to talk to him about now?" Her hands closed into tight fists. "I'd think you'd never want to see him again."

"It is. Important. I wouldn't ask otherwise." Without thinking about it, my hands went to my stomach.

My movement caught her attention. Her eyes drifted down, saw my hands cradled over my abdomen, and her eyes widened. Blotchy pink spots appeared on her cheeks. "You're pregnant."

I didn't deny it, but I didn't speak either. I lifted my chin, squared my shoulders, and returned her gaze without flinching.

"Oh my God, this is going to kill Terri." Shaking her head, she pointed to the door. "Please leave. I . . . I'll have to talk to you about this later. I just can't right now."

"I really do need to speak with him," I said softly.

"Whatever I tell you or don't tell you will be up to Terri." Her voice softened. "We don't keep secrets from one another, so I need to figure out how I'm going to handle this."

I got that—the no-secrets thing—so I nodded and slipped out of her office, closing the door behind me. As if things hadn't been complicated, confusing, and freaky enough as it was. Now Troy was back in the picture, and I didn't really know how I felt about it.

I mean, it wasn't that I wanted to tell Troy about the baby, because honestly I'd have preferred never to see the man again. But someday my daughter would be old enough to ask questions, and I wanted to be able to look into her eyes when she did and tell her I'd acted responsibly.

Tears burned my eyes. I'd barely made it to the restroom and ensconced myself in a stall before they erupted. Leaning my forehead against the door, I let everything out. I'd cried plenty over the past few months, but this? This eruption of tears chewed right through me, leaving me empty and drained when it finally stopped.

I washed my face and pulled myself together the best I could. Returning to my desk, I buried myself in work until, thankfully, the end of the day arrived. As I left the office building, the only thing I had on my mind was curling up in bed and going to sleep. That way, for a little while, I could flat-out forget about everything.

Chapter Eight

The following evening after work, after my birthday dinner with Chloe, I sweet-talked her into going shopping with me. It was a huge testament to our friendship that she agreed, because Chloe hates the mall. She loves to shop, but only at thrift stores and little, independently owned boutiques—the more off-the-beaten-path, the better. Seeing that she owned her own off-the-beaten-path boutique, it made perfect sense to me.

Twisting sideways in front of a mirror, I scowled at my reflection. The bright orange summer dress wasn't nearly as appealing on my body as it had been on the hanger. In fact, it was the exact opposite of appealing. I resembled a Halloween pumpkin. "Ugh. Every single thing I try on makes me look pregnant. This is hopeless."

"It's not *that* bad." Chloe collapsed on the small bench in the dressing room and frowned.

"It's not good," I shot back.

"I've never seen you like this. Normally you grab a bunch of stuff and we're done in less than thirty minutes." She checked her watch. "Honey," she added in that calm voice mothers use on cranky children, "we've been here for two hours. You've tried on nearly every article of clothing this store carries. Please pick a few things so we can get out of here. Please."

"But I don't like anything. And Saturday is the cookout, and I want to look nice—and not pregnant—for Ethan." A tight ball of frustration curled between my shoulder blades.

"You have a slight problem then," she teased. "But he knows, so why are you worried about it? If Shelby's as huge as you say, he won't even notice *your* tiny bump. Especially if you wear something loose."

"Yeah, I guess." She had a point. But somehow, that didn't matter. The yearning to feel like my old self swarmed over me and my frustration increased. All I really wanted was one measly day to be the former Alice, but not only was that impossible, I didn't want to try to explain it to Chloe. "Hush. It's my birthday, so just pretend you're happy to be here with me."

Exasperation floated off of her. "I'm not that good an actress, but I'll give it a go." With a huge, albeit fake smile, she said, "Go for it. Try it all on again."

I sorted through the few things I'd yet to try, hoping to find something that appealed. It didn't happen. Because my feet hurt and my friend was miserable, I took the pumpkin dress off, pulled my way-too-tight slacks back on, then slipped my shirt on over my head.

"What are you doing?" Chloe asked.

"You win. I won't put you through any more torture. Let's get out of here. I can come back tomorrow or Friday."

I figured she'd hop up and run for the door, but she didn't. Instead, she stared at me, curious glints in her eyes. "That's not like you. Since when do you give up without a fight? What's going on?"

"Nothing," I said. This was not a discussion I wanted to have. While I'd already shared with her my conversation with Missy, as well as Grandma Verda's sudden employment at Enchanted Expressions and the sprinkler mess, I hadn't told her how all of it had made me feel. Mostly because I didn't know how to explain it. "Let's get out of here," I repeated.

"Avoidance isn't going to work."

I pretended to look through another stack of clothing.

"Hey. It's me you're talking to, the girl who knows you better than almost anyone else. What's wrong?"

"It's nothing. I'm just a little scattered tonight. Maybe this one isn't so bad." I blindly grabbed a pale pink blouse from the pile. "What do you think?"

"Um . . . that you hate pink?" When I said nothing, she sighed. "Okay. That's it. You're going to tell me what's bothering you. Now."

I dropped the blouse. The charade was up, but I still didn't turn. "It's the birthday. This time in a year from now, everything will be different. I guess it just sort of hit; that's all."

"This time in a year from now, everything will be wonderful. You'll have your beautiful daughter, you'll be in a great relationship, and you'll be so happy that I'll probably be green with envy," Chloe promised.

I finally looked at her. "I'm scared. About all of it. Hell, Chloe, I can't even make a decision about clothes; how am I supposed to figure out the rest of this stuff? Everything is slipping through my fingers, and I don't know what to do."

"We're a team. We'll figure it out together. Starting now."

Standing, she gave me a look I'd seen many times in the years we'd known each other. It was her I'm-taking-charge-and-you're-gonna-deal-with-it look. That look had led us down some interesting paths in the past—and not always good ones.

"Do you trust me?" she asked.

"Why?"

"Just answer. Do you trust me?"

"Usually. Depends on what you're talking about."

She sniffed. "Just wait for me out there." She pointed in the general direction of the shop. "And don't look for anything else to try on. Just stand there and wait. Please."

I did as she asked, because honestly I was tired—oh-so-tired—of shopping. Plus, if I stood there any longer, I'd start to cry. I didn't feel like crying.

When she emerged from the dressing room a few minutes later, she held about six items. She crossed to the rack on which we'd been putting my discards and flipped through them, grabbing another handful of clothes. She was a flurry of movement, and I just stayed out of her way.

Finally, with her arms completely full, she turned to me. "Give me the gift card from your grandmother."

Her voice held no room for argument. I didn't argue. I dug in my purse until I found the gift card and then passed it to her. "It's generous, but I don't think there's enough on it for everything you're holding," I remarked.

She barely glanced at it. "Close enough, and the rest is my birthday present. And don't worry. I have excellent taste. You'll be thanking me tomorrow."

I nodded and then walked out of the store, into the mall, watching other shoppers as they strolled past. Once again, it seemed every woman had a pregnant belly and a man walking beside her. Of course, that wasn't really the case but it sure felt like it. Before the magic thing and the soul mate possibility, I'd pretty much accepted the fact that I'd be doing this whole parent thing on my own. Now, I wasn't so sure. I hovered between anger at feeling forced to find my soul mate and a blind hope that I actually would.

When Chloe exited the shop some fifteen minutes later, she carried three very large bags with the maternity boutique's name and logo emblazoned all over them. She handed me two. "See? All done. Let's go get an ice-cream cone and chat."

"Sure. If you'd like," I allowed.

We headed toward the food court in silence. Because it was a weekday evening, the mall wasn't crowded. Neither was the food court. Most of the restaurants had no lines, and the vast majority of the tables were empty. We bought our cones and then found a table near the fountain in the center of the food court. I dumped the two bags I held in the chair next to me, and Chloe put hers in the chair next to her. Sitting down, I sighed in relief.

We enjoyed our cones in silence for a few minutes. It was obvious Chloe had more she wanted to say, as her green-eyed gaze followed me. I figured she'd spit it out—whatever it was—soon enough. Until then, I was keeping my mouth shut.

"So . . . um . . . how was work today?" she asked. "Anything else happen with Missy? Or with Ethan?"

I shook my head no.

"Did Ethan wish you a happy birthday? Or give you a present?"

"Nope. But he didn't know it was my birthday. And a present would have been kind of odd, don't you think?" I was pretty sure I knew where this was leading, and it had nothing to do with Ethan. Not really, anyway.

"You almost kissed him. I think a present would be nice. Didn't Grandma Verda tell him?" At my confused expression, she added, "That today is your birthday."

"She must not have. And she wasn't in today. Otherwise, yeah, she probably would've," I admitted.

"Oh." She took another lick of ice cream from her cone. "Do you think Grandma Verda is right? Could he be your soul mate?"

Uneasiness settled in my stomach. I *definitely* knew where this conversation was headed. And I didn't like it. "I have no idea."

"Do you want him to be?" Her light tone sounded forced.

I finished the last bite of my cone to give myself a minute before answering. Then: "I don't know. Physical attraction is one thing. We're talking about a guy I don't know that well yet."

"Oh," she repeated. She played with an invisible speck on her shirtsleeve. "It might also be Kyle. Are you ready for that?"

Bingo. This was what I had been afraid of. I said simply, "Until we see his shoulder, we only have Shelby to believe. Maybe she's wrong. Or maybe it's on his left shoulder. It's not worth stressing over yet."

"Weren't you the one stressing a few minutes ago?" she pointed out.

"Yes, but not about Kyle. He's barely entered my thoughts." I chewed a bit on my lip after saying this. While it wasn't a complete fabrication, it wasn't exactly the truth. But for now, until Chloe had a better handle on whatever she was going through, I was sticking to my guns.

"I'm not sure I really want to go," Chloe admitted softly. "To the cookout. Since Ethan is going, do you mind if I skip out?"

I reined in my impatience. We'd already had this conversation about a dozen times, and I was a bit tired of it. "I can't make you go, but I'd like it if you did. Besides, if it's miserable we'll leave. I promise."

She nodded. Just like she had the other times. "Okay, but I've been thinking a lot about this." She bit her lip. "There's another promise I want from you."

This portion of the conversation was new. I said, "Anything. Well, anything within reason."

She wiggled in her chair. "If it turns out that Kyle is the man in your drawing, then don't worry about me. Or my feelings. What's most important here is that you do what Miranda says." Her eyes met mine again. "Promise me that."

I snorted. "No way am I promising that. Of course I'm worried about your feelings. Besides, when I think about Kyle all I feel is irritation. There's no excitement or attraction. We've gone over this," I reminded her as calmly as possible.

"But that's my fault, because of what happened with me. You might feel very differently if I'd never dated him. If I'd never been hurt by him. You can't rule that out. You really need to keep an open mind."

"About Kyle? I don't think that's possible."

"Don't you get it?" she pushed.

"Get what?"

She exhaled loudly. "Everything happens for a reason. You know that! It's like fate is playing her hand right now. She has been for a while, actually. And you have to pay attention to it."

"Pay attention to what? I have no idea what you're talking about. Lots of men likely have marks on their shoulders. This doesn't have to mean anything. You know that."

"That's not what I mean," she argued.

"Then tell me what you mean."

"It's the order of events. The timing of everything." I must have still looked perplexed, because she sighed again. "Don't you think it's just a little unreal? From running into Shelby, to her seeing the picture and thinking it's my ex? That sort of stuff doesn't just happen."

"Coincidences happen all the time."

Chloe sucked in a breath. "But if it's fate, then it's all supposed to happen this way. That's why I think it is Kyle. And that's why I don't think I should go on Saturday."

My stomach hurt. I ignored it. "Maybe it is fate. Maybe you're right about that. But it could be a different outcome. We don't know anything yet." I hesitated but decided it was better to forge ahead. "Besides, isn't how I feel important?"

"I'm not saying it isn't. But you can't ignore—"

"What I'm trying to say is that I feel things for Ethan. Not Kyle." Another thought occurred to me. "And I could make the exact same fate argument about Ethan."

"No. You can't." Chloe lifted her chin.

"Oh, yes I can. One: I haven't worked with him for that long. Two: he called the very night I first heard about the warning. Three: I drew him with me in a sketch, without meaning to. Four: I think about kissing him all the time."

Stress rolled off her in one long wave, though a small smile appeared on her face. "Fine. I admit you have a point. But that doesn't mean I'm wrong, so you still have to be ready to move forward if it turns out Kyle really is the one. Deal?"

So tired of talking about this, I put my hands up in defeat. "Okay, Chloe. If you need to hear that, then okay. Deal."

As soon as I agreed, she blinked in surprise. Her jaw dropped but she snapped it shut. Her expression tore my heart in two. "Why did you push for this so much if that's not what you wanted to hear?" I asked.

"That's not it. I'm . . ." A tremble passed through her body and she admitted her mistake. "I want what's right for you. I just hate that it might be with him. And I hate myself for feeling that way. I'm trying to do everything right. I'm trying to say the right things. But just now, when you agreed . . . it hurt. I know that's dumb. You're my best friend. And . . . well . . . I love you. But I loved him too. This is just really hard."

The tears came then, dripping down her cheeks in quick succession. I reached across the table and clasped one of her hands. "Right now, at this minute, there's nothing to worry about. Let's save this discussion until there is something. Because I don't think there will be." At least, I hoped there wouldn't. "Besides, how do you know this isn't about you and Kyle? Maybe fate is pushing you two together again."

"I doubt that. But you're right about the other stuff." She laughed, wiped the tears away. "I still have this strange feeling that everything is going to change on Saturday. That's dumb too, huh?"

I had the same feeling, but I'd been trying to overlook it. "Not dumb. You're just thinking too much. Let's focus on what we know, and not the stuff we don't."

"Good plan. I'm going to go wash up."

She let go of my hand and then headed for the restroom. Me? I cradled my arms on the table and laid my head down. Right or wrong, I was frustrated with Chloe. I understood why she was so upset, but I'd trade places with her in an instant. Her big anxiety was seeing Kyle again. And with everything I was handling, I wasn't managing her emotions all that well.

She returned and sat back down. I didn't lift my head.

"I'm sorry," she said. "I know you're dealing with heavier things than I am."

And with those words, everything settled inside.

Sitting up straight, I smiled. "It's cool. We're fine. But we still haven't come up with a plan for Saturday. I can't think of one thing that will get both men to remove their shirts other then Shelby's pool, so let's hope for a hot, sunny day."

Chloe chuckled, her own good mood obviously restored. "Well, one positive thing happened as a result of all my freaking out—I had a possible idea that just might do the trick. It's not very creative, but if it's successful, who cares?"

"I don't care if it's creative. What's the plan?" I asked.

A voice came from somewhere to my left, interrupting. "Hey! Fancy running into you two here!" Cocking my head to the side, I saw Scot, dressed in blue jeans and a brown T-shirt, loping toward our table. "Happy birthday, sis. It's Wednesday. How's it feel to be thirty-three?"

I stuck my tongue out at him. "Exactly like it felt to be thirty-two. What are you doing at the mall?" Because, you know, as a guy, he enjoyed shopping about as much as a dental appointment. But I have to admit, it was nice seeing him.

He held up the bag he carried. "Just expanding my CD and DVD collections."

"For all your lonely nights at home?" I joked. But instantly I felt bad, because while I was only teasing, he sort of froze. His gaze swung from me to Chloe.

I was about to apologize, but he grinned. "Nah. For those nights I need a break from all the women." He winked at Chloe and then pulled out a chair.

Yeah, right. My older brother rarely dated, but I wasn't going to swing the axe at his macho attitude a second time, so I stayed silent. My packages were in his seat. He grabbed them and went to put them on the floor, but then he stopped. His jaw clenched and the muscle in his arm pulsed. Pivoting his head, he shot me a look filled with questions.

I didn't get—at first—what had my brother so nonplussed. My eyes followed his arm to his hand to the bags he still held. Then I froze. Because that's when I got it. My pay-attention-to-the-details brother had noticed the maternity shop's name on my packages. And for once, he was startled enough that he didn't know what to say.

This was so not the way I'd wanted him to find out. I'd envisioned a calm discussion where I slowly spilled the beans after making sure he knew I was okay with everything. But this way? It looked like exactly what it was: a secret I'd kept for far too long.

I opened my mouth, all ready to confess, when he dropped the bags to the floor and shifted his gaze to my friend. In a quiet voice he said, "Chloe? You're pregnant?" The softness of his tone didn't fool me. I heard the mix of disbelief, worry, and another emotion I couldn't quite identify. Me? I think I was as shocked as she.

Her eyes widened. Her face blanched. She looked at me, and I saw in her gaze the truth—that if I wanted her to, she'd play along with his assumption. She'd take the heat for me until I was ready to confess all. Chloe is, hands down, the best friend a girl could have. But not only was that unfair, it was time—beyond time—for me to be honest with my family.

It seemed I'd be beginning with Scot. Grabbing his wrist, I tugged until he turned to me. "Scot," I said, speaking as calmly as possible. "It's not Chloe who's pregnant."

Relief washed over his expression, which kind of surprised me. He ran his hands through his hair. "Whoa. For a minute there . . ." His eyes swept over me, down to the bags on the floor, and then back. Comprehension dawned and his jaw clenched. "You, Alice? You're having a baby?"

I swallowed before answering. "Well, not yet," I said, hoping to make light of the situation, hoping I'd be able to get a grin from him. I failed. "But in September, yes."

He did the math. "You're four months along? And you haven't told any of us?"

"Chloe and Elizabeth know. And Grandma. But no, not anyone else in the family." I clenched my hands together, trying to make them stop shaking. Why hadn't I taken care of this earlier? Rhetorical question. I knew why. Avoidance with a capital A.

His gaze stayed centered on me. "Are you okay?"

"I'm better than I was, and I'll be okay. It's getting easier every day." His arm came around me in a tight clutch. My forehead touched his shoulder, and he squeezed me again. Being hugged by my big brother felt good. So good, I had to work to steady my emotions. Crying would freak him out.

"Who's the father?" he whispered, his mouth right by my ear.

I pulled back. "I don't want to talk about that. At least not here. Not now."

"Then when?"

I cleared my throat. "After I tell everyone else."

"And that will be when?" he pushed.

"Soon. I promise."

"Don't you trust us?" A twinge of hurt darted over him, and that made me feel worse. "Don't you trust me?"

"That's not it. Not at all." I took another steadying breath. "Of course I trust you, Scot. My not telling you had nothing to do with trust. It had to do with being afraid and wanting to have a plan so that I wouldn't look like such an idiot to everyone."

The tightness in his shoulders eased—just a little— and the hurt in his eyes evaporated. Thank God for that. "You're not an idiot. I wish you'd come to me, that's all."

I touched his cheek with my hand. "This is a personal thing. I needed some time to deal, but I've been planning on talking to you—to everyone—for a while now."

He gave me another hug. Then he did the coolest thing any big brother could possibly do in that situation. He sort of shook himself, as if to clear the air, and then he let me off the hook. "So what's going on for you this weekend? Maybe we could go catch a movie or something."

"We have plans on Saturday," Chloe interjected.

"What sort of plans?"

"Just a cookout at a friend's house," I said.

Chloe snorted. "Uh-huh. *Friend*."

I gave her the evil eye. "I'm telling you, you're going to like her now. If you give her a chance, anyway."

This piqued Scot's interest. "What's going on? Where are you going?"

Chloe wrinkled her nose. "Shelby Whitaker's house for a barbeque with her, her husband, and Kyle Ackers."

The color drained from Scot's complexion as he glanced at her. "Kyle Ackers? That guy from high school? The one you thought you were going to marry? Are you dating him again?"

"How'd you know I dated him? It was forever ago. But

no, I'm not. It's just a thing we're doing." Chloe shot me a curious glance. I shrugged. I was as surprised by Scot's behavior as she was.

"Like anyone in our house didn't know you dated Kyle. Or what he did." He leaned forward, toward Chloe. "Don't go out with him. I know men, and we don't change. What you see is what you get."

Wow. A little intense for my brother. "Scot, chill. I ran into Shelby again not that long ago, and she has changed. So you can't say people never change."

"I didn't. I said *men* never change. At least men like him."

Okay, this conversation was getting weirder by the second. I wasn't sure how to respond, but luckily, an announcement that the mall was closing reverberated throughout the food court. Yay. Saved by the bell. "We need to go. Walk us out to Chloe's car?"

"Of course."

The three of us shuffled out together. At the car, Scot gave us a both a stiff hug. "Let me know when you're ready to tell everyone. I'll be there," he said in a low voice.

"Thanks. I appreciate it."

And I did. But this was one birthday I was glad to see come to an end. A girl could only handle so much weirdness at a time. The slippery slope I stood on seemed to be getting slipperier by the minute. I needed something to grab on to, something to give me a bit of traction as I figured out the rest. My stomach fluttered with nerves, and I wondered what Saturday would hold: good news; bad news; or nothing new at all.

People were laughing. Loudly.

The noise pushed through the wall of sleep and I dragged my eyes open to darkness. Sitting up in bed, I yawned and focused my attention on the sound. It came from the direction of my living room, but that made zero sense. Unless I'd left the television on.

I scooted from bed, thinking that was what I'd done. It wasn't until I reached my bedroom door that I remembered I hadn't turned the television on that evening. Dinner, shopping, and the unexpected confrontation with Scot had left me exhausted. After returning home, I'd brushed my teeth and gone directly to bed.

Another wave of laughter streamed into my room. Yep, definitely the television. Seeing as the only other person who had a key to my place was Grandma Verda, and it was doubtful she'd come all the way over just to watch TV in the dead of night, a flicker of fear stopped me in my tracks. I almost turned back to grab my phone, but the same curiosity that killed the cat pushed me forward. I crept into the hallway, my bare feet soundless on the carpeting.

Shivers of unease slipped over me, coating my skin with bristly bumps. I paused again and listened. Other than the television and the sound of my own breathing, nothing else met my ears. Maybe I'd forgotten I'd had the television on? Anything was possible.

A couple more silent steps and I stopped. The heady fragrance of roses weaved itself around me, tickling my nose. The scent was so strong, so real, that if I didn't know better, it would have been easy to believe I stood in the center of a rose garden instead of in my hallway. Which meant it was quite likely that Miranda was in the house.

Adrenaline kicked in, replacing the fear. I ignored the urge to run into the living room and pummel her with questions. I mean, what if I were wrong and it was a liberally perfumed thief who was inside my house watching TV? Yeah, I know. Not likely. But just in case, I continued to move softly and silently.

At the end of the hallway, I peered around the corner. There was Miranda, sitting on my couch, ghostly eyes glued to an episode of *Three's Company*. And even though I'd expected it to be her, the sight still startled me.

My shivers came back, but for a different reason. In a weird way, I felt as if I were witnessing a moment I shouldn't see. She looked so *real*. I took a step backward, but not far enough that she left my view. Her ghostly form shook with quiet laughter as she continued to watch the show. Who knew ghosts enjoyed old sitcoms? Not me, that's for sure.

During every other instance I'd seen my great-great-great-grandmother, a rainbow had swirled around her, colors seemingly bouncing off of each other in a sparkling, breathtaking display. Not this time, and their absence surprised me. Other than the slight glow, she really could have been a normal, flesh-and-blood person hanging out in my living room.

My instincts were still to run forward and toss all the questions I had at her, and to demand answers, but something continued to hold me back. After all, Miranda certainly had the capability of waking me up or invading my dreams if she wanted to talk to me. Since she'd done neither, I had to assume that wasn't the case. Besides, barging in on a ghost didn't seem to be that smart a plan, no matter who the ghost was.

Should I go back to bed? Stand there and wait? Or creep in and quietly take a seat? I lingered, trying to make up my mind. She ended the debate for me.

"I know you're there, Alice. Come join me. This boy is absolutely adorable."

I took one step forward. "What boy?"

"This one. Here on the box. Jack Tripper."

One more step, and I hovered just inside the living room. "Yeah. He is." I sidled over to my papasan chair and sat there. For some reason, weird or not, sitting next to Miranda on my couch didn't feel right.

We sat there for the rest of the sitcom, neither of us speaking. When the credits finally rolled, Miranda waved her hand and the TV blinked off. "I decided not to wake you," she said. "You haven't been sleeping well since you've learned everything. You need your sleep."

My brain numbed at her words. Imagine a ghost being worried about waking someone. The entire situation seemed surreal, and for the first time I wondered if I were dreaming. If, at that moment, I was actually in bed sound asleep.

"The TV was kind of loud," I pointed out. When she didn't respond, I said the next thing that came to me. "Where are all the colors and lights that are normally around you?"

Her eyes twinkled. "That's for effect. People pay more attention with all of that. They are more likely to believe I am who I say." She laughed. "Besides, I have to have some fun, don't I?"

"Oh. I see." I didn't, really, but who was I to question a ghost? "Have you done this before? Been here while I sleep, I mean."

"It's easier for me to stay longer when no one realizes I'm here. But you're getting stronger now. Your daughter is getting stronger every day. I think I'll be able to stay longer than normal." Her image shimmered slightly. "You have questions. I'm afraid there's not much I can tell you. You need to find the answers for yourself, Alice. Otherwise, I might lead you in the wrong direction."

"But that's not fair!" I complained. "Do you know who my soul mate is? If you wanted to, could you tell me his name?"

"I could tell you, but I won't. I can't."

"Why not? It's important enough to come to me, important enough to warn me, but you can't tell me a name so I can make sure everything works out right?"

Her voice skimmed over me. "That's just it. It won't be

right if I tell you. And I've been around you for a very long time. There are things in your life that are there because of me. You just didn't know. There are a lot of things you don't know yet."

I let all of that slide. For now. "Why can't you tell me who he is?"

She sighed. "You need to find him on your own, so you'll never doubt that he's the right man for you. Think of what might happen if I told you, if I did give you his name. Years might pass where you'd be content, but someday, at some point, you'd begin to question the validity; you'd begin to wonder if all you feel is only because of what I told you. Everything could fall apart."

"Maybe not. You don't know that for sure."

She shook her head, her hair billowing around her like a cloud. "Trust me. You'll never believe in your heart, in your soul, that this man truly is your soul mate unless you fall in love with him entirely on your own."

"Okay . . . but why now? Why this particular time to warn me?"

Her ghostly body rippled with a shiver. "Your heart was broken, Alice. You wouldn't have gone looking for the right man for a very long time. The timeline here is essential, so the warning was needed to push you along. But I can't tell you anything else. In this area, I've interfered as much as I'm allowed." She snorted in a very human manner. "We have rules we must follow."

"Seriously? Rules?"

"If I want to stay here—and I do—then yes. I must follow certain rules. But that's neither here nor there. What's important is that you believe in what I have told you, that it's vital you find your soul mate before your daughter is born. If you believe nothing else, believe this."

"That's it? That's all you can say? I'm truly on my own in this?"

Turning her head so that her brown eyes met mine,

my great-great-great-grandmother stared at me. She didn't speak right away, but the silence wasn't unnerving. Instead, calmness seeped in and annoyance drifted away. "You're not on your own," she said. "Your magic, your power, will give you answers as you need them. Trust in that, and use it to help you find your way."

She was talking in riddles, and that annoyed me. "None of that makes sense! None of that helps. What happens if I don't find him? And how will I know if I do?"

She laughed her tinkling laugh. "Such an impatient one you are. There's so much more you need to know, more I will be able to share—but not quite yet. Remember what I said. Find him, Alice. It really is within your power."

My eyes watered, so I blinked. In the space of that blink, Miranda disappeared. "Great," I muttered. "You could have at least said good-bye."

Knowing sleep was definitely not going to happen now, I turned the television back on, more for the noise than for entertainment. My mind once again went over everything I knew, every detail. She'd said to trust in the magic, so maybe whatever I needed to do I hadn't done yet. More wishes? More drawings? I unfolded the blanket draped over the back of the couch and lay down. Maybe if I stared at the TV long enough, I'd fall asleep. If I were really lucky, maybe I'd wake up in the morning with the answer.

One could always hope.

Chapter Nine

Grant and Shelby Harris lived in a neighborhood teeming with kids, pets, beautiful houses, manicured lawns, and blooming spring flowers. Their house was a pale yellow Cape Cod–style home with brilliant blue shutters, a matching door, and a vibrant splash of tulips and daffodils lining their front walk. It was as if we'd left the real world and somehow driven into an alternative universe that wasn't exactly *The Stepford Wives* but was pretty darn close.

Ethan pulled into Shelby's driveway. Chloe had decided to drive herself—probably so she'd have an easy escape route if she deemed it necessary. I couldn't blame her. Besides, it had given me the opportunity to explain a few things to Ethan on the ride over.

"Chloe dated Kyle; then Shelby dated Kyle. Now they're only friends and Chloe hasn't seen either of them in years, but will today at the cookout. Anything else I need to know?" Ethan tucked his car keys in the pocket of his jeans. "I feel like I should take notes," he teased.

Wow. What had taken me fifteen minutes to say, he'd distilled down to one sentence. "No, those are the basics. I wanted you to know the background, in case there are some weird undercurrents." I'd left out far more than I'd shared, because it was private, but the little I'd told him had made me want to confide all of my secrets to him. The magic. Miranda. All of it. Of course, I hadn't. Based on our conversation at Frosty's, he didn't hold the supernatural in high regard. So, for now, I had secrets I'd keep to myself.

Unbuckling his seat belt, he angled his body toward me. My heart beat a little faster. Mark Twain once said, "Clothes make the man," but in Ethan's case, the opposite was true. Even in casual clothes—faded blue jeans and a navy sweatshirt—he looked just as dashing, just as sexy, just as male as he normally did. No dark stubble covered his jaw today, which was a pity. I liked that rough and tumble look. But he was still hot, clean-shaven jaw and all.

His eyes met mine and I thought—maybe—that he was going to kiss me. My stomach did a somersault. He leaned closer, and I slanted myself forward too.

"Ready to go in?" he asked, unbuckling my seat belt before reaching across me to open my door.

"Oh. Um. Sure." No kiss, but at least I'd gotten to sniff him without him realizing. Not such a bad trade-off. But when I stepped from the car, my knees almost buckled. Somehow, I managed to stay upright.

Chloe parked in the street in front of Shelby's house, instead of in the driveway. I recognized the maneuver for what it was. She didn't want to get stuck behind someone else's car. Again, I didn't blame her. That morning, we'd both laughed over the fuss I'd made at the mall, because when push came to shove, I went with my standard jeans (albeit a new pair) and a long-sleeved red tunic.

She wasn't laughing now. When she reached us, my heart went out. Her pale complexion told me she was even more nervous than I.

Ethan must have noticed too, because he tucked one of his arms through mine, and his other through hers. "I'm a lucky guy, escorting two such beautiful women," he remarked.

Chloe shot him a smile. A real one, because it reached her eyes. "You're very sweet to say that."

"Just stating the truth," he responded. And then, arm in arm, we walked to the front door.

Even though I'd already known Ethan was a good guy, this gesture, as small as it was, made it even more apparent. Soul mate or not, I was lucky to have met him.

Disengaging my arm from his, I rang the bell and then wiped my palms on my pants. Shelby opened the door almost immediately—so fast, she must have been watching for us through the window. Dressed in khaki capris and a long white billowy blouse, she had the same cover-model perfection from the other day going for her. She still looked tired though, and while I wouldn't have thought it possible, her belly seemed even larger. "Hi, Alice! This must be Ethan? It's nice to meet you. I'm Shelby." After he nodded, she said, "And Chloe, I'm glad you decided to come. It's great to see you again."

"Thank you for the invitation," Chloe replied, her voice polite but with zero warmth. "You have a beautiful home."

"I second that sentiment," Ethan said.

"It's nice to see you," I offered. "And Chloe's right. I love the flowers."

Shelby blushed as she motioned us inside. "Well, thank you. And welcome. Grant's playing with the grill. He can't seem to get it fired up." Her eyes twinkled. "I'm sure he'll figure it out. Eventually."

We trailed behind her. Hardwood floors graced the entryway and hall, gleaming as if they'd just been polished. The hallway opened up into a large and airy kitchen. The floor, counters, and appliances were all white, but baskets of dried flowers, pictures, and candles placed throughout made the room warm and inviting.

Shelby nodded toward the sliding door on the other side of the kitchen. "Grant's out back. Come say hi, so he doesn't think we're ignoring him."

As soon as we stepped outside, Grant quit fussing with

the knob on the grill and stood straight. His smile was wide, sincere. After the introductions were complete, we all stood in a slightly awkward half circle. I tried to think of something to say or do that would break the ice. Sadly, I came up blank.

Grant stepped up. Turning to Chloe, he said, "It's great meeting Shelby's friends from high school. You've known each other for a while, right?"

Chloe blinked. I nudged her. Inconspicuously, of course. "Um. We met in grade school, actually."

"Over a game of hopscotch. Remember?" Shelby asked, trying to follow her husband's lead.

That pulled a grin from Chloe. "That's right. We kicked butt."

But then the silence returned, and I shifted from one foot to another. Man, the rest of the day was going to be painful if something didn't change. I tried drawing attention to the covered pool in the very back of the yard. "Hey, that's a great pool."

"Thanks!" Grant said. "Too bad it's not warm enough today to enjoy it. You'll have to come later in the summer when it's hot enough to use. Isn't that right, Shel?"

"Oh, yes! That would be fun!" But then came more silence. Shelby fidgeted, as if trying to find something else to say. It didn't seem like she came up with anything. "Okay, you guys chat. I need to finish up the potato salad. Let me know if you need anything."

"I'll get them whatever they need, hon," Grant promised. "Maybe Chloe can help you in the kitchen? That way you two can catch up. Since it's been such a long time." He winked at my friend. "You don't mind, do you?"

Humor at the ludicrousness of the whole situation bubbled up inside me. I fought it. However, as Chloe hadn't yet responded, I tilted my head toward the kitchen. "That's a great idea! Go catch up. We'll be fine out here."

She sent me a look that told me exactly how unhappy

she was, but she nodded and played along. "Sure. I'm happy to help."

When Shelby and Chloe were gone, Grant gave me a look. I grinned, realizing what he'd done. "Remind me never to get on your bad side. You're a little sneaky."

"Not so much sneaky as proactive. Shel's been worried about talking to her, and I'm guessing by Chloe's reaction that she's had the same worries. Might as well let them hash it out so we can have a good day." He grimaced at the grill. "Of course, we might not be eating if I can't fix this."

"Shelby said it's not firing up. No idea what's wrong with it?" Ethan shoved his hands in his pockets even as a gleam of interest whisked over him. I knew what that meant: the male bonding ritual was about to take place. I took a step backward.

"We haven't used it yet this year, and it's not cooperating." Grant scratched his head. "Do you know anything about propane grills?"

"Nope, but we can probably figure it out. How hard can it be?"

In seconds, they were engrossed in the nonfunctioning grill, not much different from two little boys playing with a really cool toy. While it was kind of cute, I wasn't sure what to do, myself. Going inside and interrupting whatever conversation Chloe and Shelby were embroiled in was a bad idea, but standing too close to two men screwing around with flammable objects held no appeal, either. After all, both had the possibility of exploding in my face.

I settled for sitting at the long table on the far end of the deck. It was enough of a distance away to offer me some safety, and for the moment I let myself relax and enjoy my surroundings. The backyard was as well taken care of as the front. What would it be like to live in a home like this, with a husband and two babies on the way? The thought of it was so far out of my realm of reality that I couldn't decide if it was something I'd want or not.

The husband part was easy, because if the guy was right, I could definitely do the marriage thing—I didn't have any doubts about that. Rather, it was the house part, the yard part, the living the so-called American dream part. For most of my life, I hadn't wanted those things. I loved living in the city, so even moving to Grandma Verda's condo had taken some getting used to.

But this? I tried to imagine myself in Shelby's place. Tried to see myself coming home every day to her neighborhood, to this house and everything that came with it. I couldn't. And what did that say about me? I was having a kid; shouldn't I want this stuff?

"Hello, beautiful." An unknown voice interrupted my musings, followed by a long, slow whistle.

I blinked, pushed everything away and brought myself back to the real world. A man stood in front of me. My eyes whisked over him, taking in his appearance in one full sweep. His black jeans were a smidge too tight, as was his black T-shirt. And I don't mean in a hot, sexy way, either. More like he wore clothing two sizes too small. Not much taller than me—I'd put him at about five feet ten inches. He had light brown hair, light eyes, sunglasses pushed up on top of his head, and a million-watt smile. Sadly, no third eye or hairy mole. Kyle Ackers had arrived.

Apparently, I'd taken too long to respond, because he whistled again. "I'm talking to you, gorgeous."

Pursing my lips so I wouldn't laugh, I nodded. "Hi, Kyle. Did you just get here?"

He pulled out a chair and sat down. White teeth gleamed in another light-bulb smile. "Yep. Came in through the garage. You're . . . Alice, right?"

"Right."

Kyle stared at me, as if trying to find my face in his memory. "We dated? I'm sorry, but I don't recall going out with you. Though you do look a little familiar." His grin faded to something more realistic, if a little sheepish.

"Oh, no. We never dated." Damn it. Shelby had obviously forgotten to correct that bit of information.

"I thought Shelby said we did. That's why she was so up on us getting together again." He winked. "Not that I mind. You're a doll."

Yeah. Doll. Whatever. "She was mistaken. You dated my friend Chloe. For almost two years. In high school."

"Chloe Nichols?" He slapped his forehead. His sunglasses nearly fell off, but he caught them and set them on the table. "Now I remember you! You're Alice Raymond!" Another whistle. "Wow. You look really good."

I fidgeted again. "Um . . . thank you." There was no way he didn't remember me. Unless he'd had a brain injury in the last decade. Which, taking his current behavior into account, was entirely possible. "Chloe's actually here. Right now. In the kitchen." I motioned in the general direction, hoping he'd get a clue and go find her. Because Kyle did nothing for me. Nothing at all. Which should have relieved me, but it didn't. For that to happen, I'd need to see his shoulder.

He either ignored the hint about Chloe or didn't realize it was a hint, because he leaned back in the chair and put his hands behind his head. As if he planned on staying a while. Lucky me.

"Cool. Shelby said you're pregnant and the dad isn't involved. That must be wild."

"Yes. Wild," I concurred. Quirking my head to the side, I tried to catch Ethan's gaze but didn't manage. He appeared heavily focused on the little tube thing that ran from the propane tank to the grill. Grant was messing with the knob again. I scooted my chair a little farther back. For safety reasons.

"What do you do for a living? You could be a model. Or an actress." Kyle leaned over the side of his chair and peered under the table. "Definitely a model. You have the legs for it."

"I'm wearing jeans. You can't see my legs."

"But they're long. Long enough to be a model."

"Well, I'm not. But thanks. I think. I'm an artist at an advertising company." I nodded toward Ethan. "See that guy over there with Grant? I work with him. He came here with me today." Another hint. Another hint that Kyle let slip right by.

"Cool," he said again. "Have you thought about modeling? Stand up and spin around."

Was this guy for real? "No, thanks."

"Aw, come on." He stood and then, before I realized what he was doing, pulled me to my feet. "There, just spin around. Let me see what you got."

"If I spin, I'll get dizzy." I returned to my seat. "Did you hear me say that Chloe's inside? I bet she'd like to say hi." I curled my fingers into a fist, so I wouldn't wave him off like you do a pesky insect.

"I definitely want to see her, but let's talk more. Shelby hooked us up, and I don't want to annoy her. Ever since she's been pregnant, ticking her off isn't a good idea." Rubbing his arm with his other hand, he shrugged. "She has a solid punch."

Now here was an image I enjoyed. My lips twitched. "You probably deserved it. What did you do?"

"I didn't say I didn't deserve it." He picked his chair up and set it down at an angle. Resuming his seat, he stretched his legs out, crossing them at his ankles. "I stopped by last week with tickets to a ball game. Thought me and Grant could go, have a few beers, hang out for a few hours. He was stuck at work."

"That's it?"

"Nah. I hadn't seen her in a while, and—" He fiddled with his sunglasses. "There should be a manual that tells guys what not to say to pregnant women."

I gave in and grinned. "What did you say?"

His eyes shifted away from mine. "Are you gonna punch me too?"

I laughed. Okay, so the guy wasn't my type, but he wasn't all bad. "Maybe," I admitted. "Because if it had to do with her size, you're in trouble. You can't talk about a woman's size ever. Especially when she's pregnant."

"Like I said. There should be a manual."

A flicker of movement caught my attention. Chloe and Shelby approached from behind Kyle, but he didn't see them. "Come on—'fess up. Why'd she punch you?" I asked again.

"He wanted to know if I had to have the dress I was wearing specially made," Shelby said, stopping next to Kyle. "To cover my—what was it you said? Girth?" She squeezed his shoulders, leaned over and kissed the top of his head. "This guy is good at heart, but has some lessons to learn."

Kyle smiled the first real smile I'd seen yet. He reached one of his hands up and tugged at Shelby's hair. "Hey. I'm learning. You feeling okay?"

"I am." Shelby took the chair next to Kyle and motioned to Chloe. She rounded the table and pulled out the chair on the other side of me, directly across from him.

I noticed the two women seemed more relaxed around each other. Good. Chloe's eyes skirted over Kyle, and she gave sort of a half smile. He didn't notice; his attention was still on Shelby.

With a grin, Shelby asked, "Hey, Kyle, have you told them about your work with Habitat for Humanity?"

Kyle shifted uneasily in his chair, and then shrugged. "Nope."

"You work for Habitat for Humanity?" I asked.

Shelby shook her head. "No, he's a volunteer. He gives up a ton of his weekends and a chunk of his vacation each year to help build houses for people who need them." She reached over and squeezed his hand. "Aren't you taking off again soon?"

Wow, talk about seeing someone in a different light. Especially because it was something I never, in a million years, would have guessed about Kyle. "Really? Where to?"

Obviously uncomfortable, Kyle slid his sunglasses back on, hiding his eyes. "Two more months. I'm going to New Orleans again." Before I could ask anything else, he nodded toward Grant, and asked Shelby, "He hasn't figured it out yet?"

"Nope, and I'm not positive, but I don't think we filled the tank at the end of last summer."

"I brought another tank like you asked. I left it in the garage. How long are you going to let him play with it?"

She shrugged. "Not much longer. But it'll be better if he figures it out for himself."

"Wait a minute." I laughed. "You're saying the grill isn't broken?"

"I don't think so, but shh. Grant's an engineer, so he tends not to think of the easiest, most obvious solution right away." Shelby grinned conspiratorially. "Besides, he's getting to know Ethan, so it's all good."

Chloe still hadn't said anything, but she also hadn't taken her gaze off of Kyle. I cocked my head toward him and gave her the eye, but she ignored me. Deciding to step away for a minute and let Chloe handle this one all on her own, I said, "Shelby, may I use your restroom?"

"Of course. It's the second door on the left, coming from the kitchen."

I excused myself and escaped. I didn't really need to use the restroom, so instead I leaned against the counter in the kitchen. Maybe by the time I got back out there, Chloe and Kyle would have acknowledged each other and actually struck up a conversation.

The sliding door creaked open and Grant stepped in. "Hiding out?"

"Is it that obvious?"

"A little. Why do you think I'm here?" He crossed the room and opened the fridge. "We figured out what was wrong, by the way. I swear we filled that tank last year, but apparently we didn't. Hey, you want a soda or something? I'm getting a beer for the guys and Chloe."

"Kyle brought a propane tank, I guess. He said it was in the garage. And no, thank you. But maybe it will help loosen them up."

He grabbed the beverages. "That's my hope. And yeah, Kyle's hooking up the tank now, so I'll start cooking soon." I trailed after him, thinking I'd reclaim my seat now that I had Ethan to talk to, but Grant stopped me. "Wait here, okay? I'd like to chat with you for a second. I'll be right back."

"Um. Sure." I tried to think of what he might want to say to me, but nothing came to mind.

I didn't have long to wonder. In less than two minutes, he'd returned. Pushing his glasses up on his nose, he said, "Thank you for being so nice to Shelby. It's been tough lately."

"Oh." Was he being sarcastic? I certainly hadn't been all that nice when I'd originally seen Shelby at the doctor's office. "Um. I don't know if I was that nice, or if I deserve a thank-you. I sort of ignored her. It was a gut reaction."

"But you were willing to give her a chance when she called you. She was so excited that night when I came home." He grabbed a large white platter from a cupboard, placing it on the counter. "It'd be great if Chloe gives her the same chance."

"I can't speak for her. I have no idea how she's feeling at the moment."

"I know. But Shel's a different woman now, and she had reasons for behaving the way she did." He swung his gaze to the door, as if making sure no one was about to walk in. "You comforted her once, a long time ago. I think you guys were in junior high. Do you remember?"

This piqued my curiosity. I thought back, tried to bring forth whatever moment Grant was referring to, but nothing came to me. "I don't. I'm sorry."

"She was crying. You found her in the restroom, and you asked her what was wrong," he offered. "Does that ring any bells?"

Suddenly, the memory returned. How had I forgotten? Had I even realized that was Shelby? "Oh my God. Now I remember. Her dad had just moved out. She was upset her parents were getting a divorce." I shook my head. "Wow. I'd pretty much forgotten that."

"Her dad walked away one day and never returned. She hasn't seen or heard from him since," he said, anger evident in each abruptly spoken word. "She was young. Confused."

"I had no idea."

"She missed her dad. She was pretty much alone all the time then, because her mom had to work a couple of jobs to keep the bills paid."

In a flash, I understood what he was getting at. "I'm so sorry."

Grant ran his hand over his face. "Look. I know this doesn't change how she hurt your friend, but I hope it gives you a little insight into her and what she was going through at the time. Shelby is a good person. She just made a lot of mistakes."

A sigh escaped. I felt bad for Shelby. "I hope we can remain friends. But . . ." Ugh. How to say what I had to?

I didn't have to; Grant understood. "I get it. You're

tight with Chloe and she might have issues with this. I hope it works out. Shelby could use a friend. A real one, and not someone who will disappear." He hesitated. "Can you do me a favor?"

"Maybe. Probably. What's the favor?"

"If you decide, for whatever reason, you can't associate with Shelby . . . tell her. Don't just ignore her phone calls. That will just hurt her more. Okay?"

"Of course!" I agreed. "She's a lucky girl. I'm glad she has you." And I was glad. But at that moment, the green-eyed monster roared to life inside of me too. Not over Grant, but because of the love and concern he had for his wife. I didn't think—no, I knew I'd never experienced that with a man outside of my family.

"We're both lucky. But we work really hard at it." He angled his eyes toward the door. "Ready to go back out there?"

"I am. Thanks for sharing this with me."

"You're welcome! And I hope we see lots of each other." Opening a drawer, he pulled out an apron. Also white. Tying it around his waist, he said, "Go on. Ethan's waiting for you. By now, things might have loosened up a bit."

I nodded and let myself outside. Ethan was in the chair I'd vacated, but there was another empty one next to him. As I approached, his eyes caught mine and he smiled. Anticipation shivered down my spine. More good news met my gaze. Apparently, they'd all played musical chairs or something, because now Chloe sat next to Kyle. And they seemed to be in the middle of a discussion.

Except, she didn't appear comfortable. At all.

When I reached the table, Shelby stood. "I'm going to help Grant. You guys keep chatting and we'll get the food all set."

"Wait, Shelby," Chloe spoke up. "Let me help Grant. You should rest."

"I'm fine! Besides, you're our guests." Shelby disappeared into the house.

"Shouldn't she be on bed rest or something?" Chloe asked. "She looks so uncomfortable."

"Shelby on bed rest? Not likely. The woman doesn't know how to sit still," Kyle replied. He took a long swig from his beer bottle. "Grant says she's doing good, though. He goes to all her appointments, so he'd know."

I sat in my chair, happy to be next to Ethan. "He definitely seems like an attentive husband. I think that's great."

Kyle nodded. "Those two are meant for each other. If you believe in that stuff."

"What stuff?" Chloe asked.

"Happily-ever-after love stuff."

"You don't?" Chloe frowned. "So, you don't believe in love? You don't think there's a soul mate for you out there somewhere?"

Oh, God. I couldn't believe she was going there.

"Soul mate? What is this, the romance hour or something? Nope. I'm not saying love doesn't exist, but it's not what most people think." Kyle picked at the label on his bottle.

Chloe arched an eyebrow. "Is that so? And what do most people think love is?"

"Hell, I don't know. Rainbows and puppy dogs. All I know is I've dated a lot of girls and I've never felt the need to propose to any."

Her eyebrow arched higher. "Really? Do you remember dating me?"

"Of course I do. We had some great times together."

"We did." She nodded, a slight smile appearing on her face. "We talked a lot about the future. You don't remember that?"

Oh, God. He was in trouble. And the poor guy didn't

have a clue. "We never talked about rings, Chloe," he replied. "It was all about college and having fun. Maybe living together. But that didn't work out, and it was a long time ago."

She snorted. "Not *that* long, you dolt. I remember our conversations and our relationship very clearly. I certainly believed that after college we were planning on a wedding."

Things were getting out of control fast. Fortunately, Kyle seemed to finally recognize he'd made a misstep. He drained the rest of the beer from his bottle and then sent a pleading look at Ethan. "What about you? Have you ever thought about proposing?"

Ooh. Good question. I turned to Ethan, awaiting his response.

He looked startled, and at first I thought he wasn't going to answer, but then he cleared his throat. "I proposed once. We never made it to the altar, though."

Before I could even think about this oh-so-surprising bit of information, Chloe stood and stomped away from the table. She could have waited a second, because I'd really have liked to hear more about Ethan's proposal. But, "I should go talk to her," I said, pushing my chair back.

Kyle shook his head. "Nah. It's my fault. I'll go apologize."

"You might—" I was about to say he should stay out of her way for now, but when I glanced in her direction, Chloe was shaking her head at me. It took me a few seconds, but when she held up a beer bottle, I realized what she was doing. "Oh. Okay. That's a good idea," I said, settling back in my seat.

"I need to buy body armor," Kyle muttered. "Wish me luck."

And then, for the first time since arriving at Shelby's, I was alone with Ethan. "I'm so sorry. I knew today might be a little awkward, but I didn't know it would be this bad," I explained.

"I'm enjoying myself, madness and all. Besides, I'm here to be with you." He turned toward me. "I've thought about you all week."

The words were simple enough, but something about the way he looked at me set off a spark of longing. "I've looked forward to this too. There's so much I want to know about you."

"Really? Ask away," he said.

I wanted to ask him to expand on his answer to Kyle's question, but I didn't. Instead, I stuck to a general—and safe—topic. "You grew up in Ireland?"

"I did, but I was born in Chicago. My father died when I was young, so my mother and I moved to Dublin and lived with her parents."

"Oh. Wow. I'm really sorry."

"Don't be," Ethan replied. "He drank himself into the grave, and while my mother still mourns him, I only have the faintest recollection. I was quite young."

"Still, that had to be tough. Growing up without your dad."

"It was. But realistically, I had three parents: my mother, grandmother, and grandfather. It was a good childhood. Probably better than it would have been."

I thought of my dad and how important his support had always been to me. No way could I imagine growing up without his presence. And even though Ethan seemed okay with it, I felt sad for him. For missing out on that. Then I thought of my daughter, and how strong the possibility was that she'd grow up without a father. "Did you miss him?" I asked softly.

"I'm not sure if I missed him, per se, or if I missed having a dad in general. But family helps." His hand found mine under the table, and he grasped it. "Are you worried about that? Your child missing out on a father?"

"Maybe a little. But there's nothing I can do about it."

He paused, then said, "May I ask a personal question?"

"Go for it."

"The father—he doesn't want to be involved?"

I chewed on my lip. After the Missy incident, I worried Ethan would think the same things she did: That I'd known Troy was married. That I hadn't cared. "This is going to sound bad, but give me a chance to explain."

"I'm happy to listen," he promised. "And I don't make judgments without knowing all the facts."

"His name is Troy. We dated sporadically for about six months, and then more seriously for another six." My voice caught. What a stupid mistake it had been. "But he was married the entire time we were together. I didn't know."

He took my words at face value, which I appreciated. "I'm sorry that happened to you."

"Me too. It was a bad time and I've blocked a lot of it out—other than feeling completely stupid for not recognizing he was lying. He said all the right things and I foolishly believed they were true." My throat felt dry and tight.

"It happens. Don't beat yourself up over it. He knows about the baby?"

I shook my head. "He's moved or something. I can't find him." I almost told him about Missy, but decided not to. This wasn't the time or the place. Besides, I still had hope she'd give me the information I needed.

He let go of my hand. "You have something in your hair." Then his fingers touched my hair and gently pulled. "Just a piece of lint. See?"

This action, as small as it was, brought my attraction to the surface. Warmth climbed through me, saturating my entire body in barely the time necessary to take a breath. "Thank you."

"What are you thinking right now?"

"I'm not thinking. I can't think."

"I feel much the same."

Ethan scooted his chair closer, leaned in, and before I could blink, his lips touched mine and I forgot about everything else. Every*one* else. A swirl of sensations began in the pit of my stomach, crawling up and out, until my entire body shivered with them. His hand came to my chin, and then to my cheek. The kiss deepened. We could have been sitting anywhere in the world, and I wouldn't have known it. Because all I knew was his scent, his taste, his touch. Every part of me yearned for Ethan, and that startled me. Maybe it even scared me a little.

I pulled back. As we separated, I sighed. "Wow."

"Wow, indeed." He brushed my hair away from my face, kissing me softly on my forehead. His gaze moved past me, and he blinked. Then he half smiled. "How odd. Chloe has dumped her beer on Kyle's head."

"What?" I tried to make sense of his words, but his kiss had muddled everything. When I realized what he'd said, I leapt up and said, "I should make sure she's okay."

I strode toward Kyle and Chloe, trying to forget how Ethan's kiss had made me feel. This wasn't easy, because my lips still tasted like him, but I refocused and attempted to appraise the scene ahead of me. I should have been there the whole time. After all, Chloe had emptied her beer on Kyle for me. Well, *mostly* for me.

Chloe's arms were crossed. Kyle was tugging at his now-wet shirt. By the time I got to them, he was pulling it up. I stopped and held my breath. Chloe stared at me, obviously waiting for my reaction because she stood in front of Kyle. It was as if everything stopped and then started again, but in slow motion.

He lifted the shirt more. I stepped closer. The slow motion sped up, and in one fast yank, his shirt was off. I tilted my head to the side. I took another step closer. My heart stopped and then dropped like a dead weight into my gut, because . . . Shelby had hit the bull's-eye. The scar was in the exact right place on Kyle's right shoulder. And from what I could tell, it was a close match. I couldn't be sure if it was perfect without my sketchbook, but I knew it was really, really close.

Kyle Ackers. My soul mate? "No way," I whispered. "I don't believe it."

Chloe spun on her heel and headed for the house. I knew without asking that she was leaving. And, for the third time that day, I didn't blame her.

Kyle grinned. "I'd forgotten how spunky she is. I love a woman with red hair." He winked at me and set off after Chloe.

Me? I sort of crumpled to the ground, wishing it would open up and swallow me whole. Of course, that was another wish that didn't come true.

My fingers touched my lips. Here I was, just beginning to get to know Ethan, feeling things for him I'd never felt with anyone else, and now what? I was supposed to turn away and focus on Kyle? That was not only something I didn't want to do, but I didn't think it was something I *could* do. Because somehow, in the space of that very short kiss, my heart had become involved.

It was another thing I hadn't expected.

Chapter Ten

Clutching my pencil tighter, I stared at the page in front of me. My breathing came in fast, shallow huffs. My anxiety grew. Why wasn't this working? Maybe I wasn't focusing hard enough. Closing my eyes, I imagined every muscle in my body relaxing.

Maybe if I'd paid more attention when I'd taken that meditation class, this wouldn't be so difficult. I concentrated on what I wanted to happen. On what I *needed* to happen. My breathing slowed, and suddenly the slightest of tingles swept through my fingers. It was there. I could feel it.

Opening my eyes, I put pencil to paper. The tingles increased, and shivers cascaded down my spine. My fingers twitched. The pencil began to move. I told myself to remain calm, to not do anything that would interrupt what I'd worked so hard for all morning. Hell, all week. But then, for no reason that I could discern, the shivers, tingles, and magic disappeared. Bam. Gone.

Snapping the pencil in half, I threw the pieces across the room. They hit the wall with a soft *clack* and then fell to the floor. The urge to toss my sketchbook in the same direction came over me. I resisted. Because no matter how upset I was, there was no reason to behave like a spoiled child. My eyes rested on the blank page, and I swear it mocked me, inanimate object or not.

"Oh, hell with it," I muttered. Giving in to the urge, I flung the sketchpad as hard as I could. It sailed through the air, hitting the wall with an oh-so-satisfying smack.

Yep. It made me feel better. For about three seconds.

But of course my aggravation returned. A week had passed since the cookout, and I still didn't understand anything. Like: what would happen if I didn't find my soul mate before my daughter was born? Even if I did, how would I know for sure I'd found the right guy? And of course, how could a man I had zero attraction for possibly be the key to my daughter's future?

It would also be helpful to understand my magic a bit more, such as why it worked sometimes and why other times I got nothing. Sighing, I willed myself to calm down. I so wanted to talk to Chloe about it. Unfortunately, I couldn't. She'd asked for a temporary time-out, just until things chilled out a little. I understood, but I didn't like it.

At least I still had Grandma Verda and Elizabeth. They were coming over later to see if the three of us could figure out what I alone hadn't been able to.

Thank God for that.

The phone rang, interrupting my thoughts. Hoping it was Chloe, I answered immediately. "Hello?"

"Alice? It's Ethan." My heart slammed against my chest at the sound of his voice.

"Oh! Hi. What's up?" I tried to be cool and collected, but I probably failed. You see, I'd avoided having any personal discussions with Ethan this past week. Even so far as turning down a lunch invitation, claiming I had other plans. "Are you calling about the Kendall account? I stopped by Frosty's again the other night, just to check out their weeknight traffic."

"Really? And how was it?"

"Um. Busy." I bit my lip, wishing I hadn't brought up work.

"That's great, but it's not why I phoned. We've barely talked since the cookout. I've missed you."

He missed me? Wow. Spidery tingles danced along my skin. I liked that more than I should. "Really?"

A low rumble of laughter slid through the line. "You sound surprised."

"Not surprised, exactly. Well, okay. Yeah. Maybe a little." God. Everything about this man made me believe I could fall for him. In a heartbeat. Part of me wanted to run full speed ahead and see what happened. The other part? It wanted to run in the other direction at warp velocity. "I'm glad you called."

"I'm glad you answered," he teased. I smiled wider. "I know this is last minute, and I should have asked you days ago . . . but are you busy this afternoon? I thought we could see a movie, maybe get some dinner afterward."

Excitement hit fast, and I almost said yes. But then I remembered my grandmother and sister were coming over soon. *Very* soon. Disappointment fluttered in. "I'd have liked that, but I have plans today."

"Ah. Well, I understand. Maybe another time?"

"Definitely another time. I could probably cancel . . ." I trailed off, thinking it over. I so wanted to go with Ethan, but I'd waited all week for this family powwow. "No, I guess I shouldn't. Responsibilities, you know?"

"As I said, this was last minute. Let's plan something for next weekend?"

Yay! I couldn't stop my heart from pounding, even though I knew this complicated everything. "Yes. Next weekend is . . . um . . . perfect."

We talked for a few more minutes about nothing in particular, but it was still nice. I loved that he'd taken the time to call, to check in, and yeah, to ask me out. When we hung up, some of my bad mood had evaporated. Funny, how a ten-minute chat with Ethan could make that happen.

When the phone rang again, I thought maybe—just maybe—it was him calling back to see if I was busy the next day. Sadly, it wasn't. Rather, it was my brother Scot, who claimed he wanted to know how I was feeling. But he hemmed and hawed so much that I realized there was something he wasn't saying.

"Okay, what's going on, Scot?" I picked up the broken pencil pieces and my sketchpad as I talked.

"What do you mean?"

"Is there something else you need?"

"Not really. I . . . I was wondering how last weekend went. With Chloe and Kyle." The stress in his voice should have tipped me off. It didn't.

"Interesting. A little weird. Why?"

"Weird how? Did . . . uh . . . something happen with Chloe?" When I didn't answer, he exhaled. Loudly. "Is Chloe dating him again?"

And that was when I got it. "You like her, don't you?"

He cleared his throat, as if something thorny was stuck in it. "Like Chloe? Of course I like her."

"Come on, bro—you know what I mean." Why hadn't I seen this before?

"It's not like I'm in love with her or anything. I just want to make sure she doesn't get hurt again."

"Oh, Scot. She thinks of you like a brother."

"It's not like it's a huge deal. Look, I need to go. Do me a favor and make sure she's okay. Please?"

After promising I would, we hung up. Was Chloe the reason Scot had never gotten serious with anyone? Maybe, but I hoped not. She'd put him in the family category a long time ago, and I didn't think that status was likely to change.

I was still mulling it over when my sister and grandmother arrived. We took our positions in the living room and I caught them up to speed on the cookout happenings. When I finished speaking, I could almost see the wheels turning in Grandma Verda's head.

"There has to be a reason you haven't been able to use your magic while drawing," she said. "We're missing something."

"I know. But I don't know what."

"Never mind that for now." My sister grabbed my sketchpad and flipped to the page of the beach drawing. "How closely does Kyle's scar match this one?"

I brought the image of Kyle's shoulder back to mind. "I don't know. It's really close, but it's not like I took a picture."

"Maybe you should have," Grandma Verda pointed out. "Because then you might not be so worried. And why didn't you dump something on Ethan's head? It would've been easy!"

"It didn't seem the appropriate thing to do. That's why." This wasn't the complete truth. To be honest, I wasn't ready to see his shoulder. Because if he didn't have a scar, I'd have to turn away. And that was something I wasn't ready to contemplate.

"It might not be Kyle *or* Ethan. You've thought of that, haven't you?" my sister asked. "It could be someone else entirely. I thought the plan was determining if Ethan or Kyle *could* be your soul mate, and then going from there."

"Which is why you should have gotten Ethan's shirt off," said Grandma.

"Okay, Grandma. I think you've made your point."

"I'm just saying . . ."

I held my hands up. "So what am I going to do?"

"Well. Since the magic doesn't seem to be working, it's time to be more practical. You need to be out there meeting other men. Just in case. I have the perfect idea too." Coming from my grandmother, that didn't exactly fill me with confidence.

"I thought you were sure Ethan was the man."

She leaned forward, her pale blue eyes serious. "I still think he's a likely candidate, but you need to expand your horizons. There're a lot of men in this world to choose from."

"She's right. As much as I hate to admit it." Elizabeth chewed on her bottom lip. "Maybe you should do one of those online dating things! In your profile, just write down that scars turn you on. I bet you'd get tons of responses!"

Before I could voice how very much I disliked that idea, Chloe showed up. When I let her in, the first thing she did was hug me. Stupidly, I assumed this meant everything was okay between us. So I hugged her back. "I've missed you."

"I've missed you too. But that's not why I came over." She pulled away. When she saw my grandmother and sister hanging out in the living room, she frowned. "Let's go to your bedroom to talk. There are some things I need to say, and I'd rather do it privately."

Rather than argue, I followed her to my room. "So, why are you here?"

She pulled herself up straight and focused on me. "I don't understand why you haven't called Kyle—or even Shelby, so she can set up a date. Or something. This is driving me crazy, Alice. I need to know," she blurted.

Oh, no. "Have you fallen for him again? This is the guy who completely broke your heart!" I reminded her.

Unshed tears glistened in her eyes. "I don't know. Maybe. And I know you don't understand it."

"Then explain it."

"He was just there, Alice. No matter what crappy thing happened, he was there." She blinked. "Remember the summer before our senior year? Your family went on that month-long vacation to Europe?"

"Of course I remember; you were supposed to go with us."

"Right, and I got sick. Pneumonia. I couldn't go. Kyle knew how bummed I was." She paused, as if bringing the memory back. "He planned pretend vacations for me. Every day was a new one. He'd bring these crazy decorations over and he'd tell me we were in Milan, or London, or wherever." Lifting her chin, she focused on me. "It probably sounds silly, but it wasn't to me."

"I don't think it's silly at all." I understood so much more now. "Why didn't you tell me about this before?"

She shrugged. "I didn't want you to know how bummed I was."

"He still broke your heart," I pointed out. "He continued to make plans with you, even after he started dating Shelby."

"You're right. But I can't forget that summer, or how sweet he was. So yes, I might be falling for him again, but I can't do anything even if I have. Because if I start dating him again, only to find out he's supposed to be with you . . ." She fisted her hands. "That would just be too hard. So you need to move ahead like you promised."

Why the hell had I made that promise? "I don't feel anything for Kyle, so how can he be the right man? And if you think he's right for you, don't wait for me, Chloe. Go for it."

"I can't. It would hurt too much later. He's calling me every day. How can I keep saying no to him when I want to say yes? I can't avoid him forever." She paused while she gathered her thoughts. "This is your thing. You need to figure it out."

"I'm trying. That's why Grandma Verda and Elizabeth are here. To help me."

Temper darkened her eyes. "Why can't you use your magic to find out? It doesn't make any sense."

"It's not that easy," I reminded her. "A bunch of stuff I've tried hasn't worked."

"But why not? You're probably doing it wrong. It seems pretty simple to me. You make a wish, and then it comes true. It can't be *that* difficult!"

My anxiety turned into frustration. "I wish you had

the magic, Chloe, so you could see how difficult it is for yourself."

"Yeah, I wish I had it too. Because I bet I'd be able to get to the bottom of this."

"Right. It should be a friggin' cakewalk." I rubbed my arms to chase away the goose bumps that had appeared. "I'm sorry. I don't want to fight with you."

"I don't want to argue, either. But—" She sort of lurched forward then, and grabbed the edge of my dresser for support. Her snow white complexion sent a jolt of concern through me.

"Are you okay?"

She nodded. "Just a little dizzy. I haven't slept well this week."

And that made me feel worse. "Aw, Chloe. I'm sorry. Sit down. I'll get you some juice or something."

"I'll be okay. *We'll* be okay. Just work this out. I really like Kyle, but I can't do anything until I know my heart isn't going to get broken again."

"Oh, honey, regardless of what happens, there's no guarantee of that."

"True, but this is one thing I *can* rule out. So for both of our sakes, will you try?"

Slowly, I nodded my head. "I've been trying, but I'll try harder."

"Thank you. Let me know what happens." She started to leave my room, but suddenly turned back. "You know how lucky you are, don't you?"

The change of subject confused me. "Are you talking about the magic? Because it's not as cool to me as it is to you."

"No. Well, that too. But I'm talking about your family. Grandma Verda, your sister, your brothers—all of them. Don't forget you have family who really care about you. Even if I wasn't around, they'd all stand by you and help you out."

Oh my God, this felt like a breakup talk. "Are you planning on going somewhere?"

Chloe's eyes widened. "No! I guess . . . well, this past week showed me how alone I really am. I barely talk to my family." A small laugh. "If I became pregnant, I could go until the child's first year before any of them would even know."

Her words broke my heart. Chloe's parents had passed away when she was young. Her aunt had taken her and her younger sister in, but they weren't close.

"You're a part of my family," I said.

She shrugged, but a sliver of sadness existed. "It's not the same, though."

"Well, maybe not exactly, but I love you as much as I love Elizabeth."

"I know. But it's still not the same." Rubbing her hand over her eyes, she said, "I'm sorry. I'm just a little melancholy. I think I should go home and go to bed."

She left then, and I sat on the edge of my bed, my thoughts centered on everything we'd discussed. Was my inability to find any answers this past week my fault? Maybe. Because somehow, suddenly, I wanted to ignore the whole freaking mess. But I couldn't. Even without knowing exactly why, my instincts screamed that Miranda spoke the truth. Which meant I needed to make a decision. If my magic wasn't going to be of help, then I'd have to figure it out without it. And that meant—yep—I needed to see Kyle.

The room spun slightly. I took a couple of breaths to stop the wooziness. Of course, there was that *thing* about Ethan that resonated with me. No way was I giving up on him yet. I couldn't. Even if I should.

Besides, I hadn't seen his shoulder yet. So that meant, as far as I was concerned, Ethan Gallagher was most definitely still in the running.

* * *

Saturday's craziness stayed with me through the rest of the weekend. So much so that when Monday rolled around, my obnoxious alarm barely fazed me. Getting up and going to Enchanted Expressions gave me a much-needed reprieve. Just the simple act of performing my job allowed me to put all the other stuff on the back burner, at least for a little while.

But now it was lunchtime. I'd taken a later break than most of the other staff, so I had the break room to myself. People strolled in every now and then to refill their coffee cups, or to get a soda from the fridge, but for the most part I was left alone. That was okay by me. I'd had plenty of social interaction lately.

I spooned the last bite of lemon yogurt into my mouth and then set the container down. Other than some faint queasiness in the morning, my nausea had, thankfully, all but disappeared. And that had bolstered my spirits in a big way.

Missy entered the room. She paused for a split second before aiming for my table. Dressed in black slacks and a long black tunic belted at her waist, she made me think of the wicked witch from *The Wizard of Oz*. Not a fair comparison, because Missy certainly hadn't done anything wrong, but the image refused to leave.

Maybe it was intuition, or a sense of foreboding, because when she stopped in front of me, an icy chill skittered from my neck all the way down my spine. She crossed her arms. "We need to talk."

I fiddled with my empty yogurt container. "About the Kendall account? I'm still on break."

"No, Alice." She glanced around the room to make sure we were still alone. We were. "I need to talk to you about Troy."

In an instant, what remained of my good mood vanished. "Is this about his contact information? If so, you can just e-mail me."

"No. That's not it." She paused, as if trying to decide what to say. "We should go somewhere else for this conversation. Somewhere private."

I almost argued with her. Not because I disagreed, but because my innate muleheadedness had kicked in. Luckily, I was able to set it aside. "That leaves your office or the conference room." Standing, I cleaned up my lunch debris.

"Wherever you're most comfortable."

"I don't think I'll be comfortable anywhere," I snapped. I hadn't meant to. Sighing, I mimicked Missy and crossed my arms. "Sorry. Your office is fine."

She nodded once and then pivoted on her heel.

Trailing behind her, I tried to prepare myself for whatever she was going to say. Of course, I couldn't. Before we reached her office, another thought processed, and panic edged in. What if Troy waited for me now, in this woman's office? As quickly as the panic had come, anger slammed in on top of it. If he'd decided that an unannounced visit was a way to push my buttons, then not only had he underestimated me, but he was even more of a jerk than I'd given him credit for. Maybe I'd wish him into a toad or something.

When I arrived, however, the room was empty save for Missy. I stepped in and closed the door behind me. Already seated behind her desk, she motioned to another chair. "You might want to sit down for this."

Nope. Not happening. I just wanted this, whatever *this* was, over with. So I kept my stance near the door. "I'm fine. Tell me what this is about."

Twisting her long silver necklace with her fingers, she didn't speak. The air weighed heavily, almost stagnant with apprehension. Both mine and hers.

Not able to take another moment of silence, I decided to start the conversation. "You've told him about the baby?"

Missy's hazel eyes skated to the side of me. She released a breath. "No, I didn't. But I did tell Terri, and she told Troy. She's going through hell right now."

"I can imagine. I'm sorry about that." And I was, but that didn't change my circumstances or my feelings in any way. "So what's going on?"

Her fingers still played with her necklace. "He called me this morning." She grimaced. "It wasn't a pleasant conversation."

I thought I knew where this was headed. My stomach turned upside down, and my nausea roared to life with a vengeance. "He's coming here, isn't he?"

A quick shake of her head. "No, that's not it. He gave me a message to pass on to you."

"What is it?"

"I really think you should sit down." Letting go of her necklace, her hands went to her desk, palms flat on its surface.

"I'm not going to keel over. What's the message?" I asked again.

"Look. This is awkward for me. If I weren't Terri's friend, I wouldn't be doing this." She shuddered. "I hate that I'm doing this. I hate that I'm even involved. But here we are, so I'm just going to say it, even though it's not very nice."

I backed up against the wall for support. "That's fine. Go for it." I could handle it if it came at me fast. At least, I thought I could. Sort of like ripping off a Band-Aid. The faster you did it, the quicker the pain left.

"I'd feel better if you'd sit down." When I didn't move or respond, she sighed. "Okay, then. Here goes." She whisked a strand of toffee-hued hair off of her forehead. I braced myself. "Troy has no desire to be involved with you or the baby. In any way."

Something strange happened then. I'm not sure how to explain it, but it was as if everything around me, everything inside of me, stopped, and then drained away. I felt nothing. Absolutely nothing. "That's it?"

"No. Troy, the asshole that he is, would like you to sign a legal document that removes his rights as a parent. He doesn't want to pay child support; he doesn't want his name even connected to the baby." Her eyes didn't meet mine as she spoke. "And if you refuse to sign the document, then he's going to insist on DNA testing."

The entire situation seemed unreal. As if I were watching a play or a really bad movie, none of it affected me. I knew I should be feeling *something*, but weirdly, everything was numb. "DNA testing doesn't bother me, because Troy's the father. That being said, I prefer for him to stay away, so you can tell him I agree to his . . . demands."

"I know this is a crappy thing. I'm sorry to be the one to deliver the news."

"It's fine." For some reason, I found myself staring at the back of the picture on Missy's desk. The one with her, her husband, Troy, and Terri. Maybe I felt something, after all? Because I definitely wished I could walk over, pick that photo up, and slam it down on the desk. Productive? Not at all. So I tucked the urge away.

"There's more," she said softly.

"More? What more could there be?"

"While Troy isn't interested in knowing the child, his mother is. She would like to set up a meeting."

Finally, I really felt something: stunned disbelief. "Doesn't the very fact that Troy is excising himself from his child's life pretty much wipe out any familial connections?" Besides, I knew nothing about Beatrice Bellamy other than that she'd raised a jerk. Oh, and that she might be a witch. Neither of those things endeared her to me.

"It's completely up to you. I know Beatrice fairly well. She won't push. Or, I don't think she will. But she wanted me to ask." Missy spoke calmly, but it sounded forced.

I'm sure she wanted this discussion over with. Which made two of us.

"Why did Troy even tell his mother?"

"I don't think he did. Terri has always been close to Beatrice. It probably came from her."

"Oh." Not that it mattered. Making a decision about Beatrice wasn't going to happen. Not right now.

Missy walked over to me. "I was so angry at you. Now I'm just angry at him."

A choked laugh spilled out, but I didn't speak.

"You're white as a ghost. Do you need to lie down or something?" The concern, so evident in her voice, pushed me forward.

Lifting my chin, I plastered a smile on my face. "I'm okay, Missy. Tell Troy to send his papers here and I'll have an attorney go through them. Assuming there are no issues, I'll be happy to sign. As for Beatrice . . ." Suddenly, I lost steam. "I'll need to think more about her request."

She reached out, as if to touch me, but then stopped. "Okay. I'll let him know."

A tight, uncomfortable haze surrounded me. All at once, the only thing I wanted was to get out of that room. I walked to the door. "My break is about over. I should go."

"I need to say one more thing."

"Yes?"

"I'm sorry. For everything. I don't really know what happened between you and Troy, but I do know what kind of man he is. I should have been nicer to you."

"I appreciate that." Still numb, I twisted the doorknob, but before I could make my escape, something crashed behind me. Turning around, my gaze landed on Missy's desk. The framed photo was facedown.

Setting it upright and looking surprised, Missy held her other hand up as if testing the air. "There must be a breeze in the room."

"Yeah. Must be."

This particular wish coming true probably should have put me in a better mood, but it didn't. Other than shock, I still felt nothing. Because there was nothing else to say, I marched from Missy's office, keeping my head up and my back straight. Then, rounding the corner out of the hallway, I concentrated on getting to the rest-room, where I could lock myself in a stall and let myself feel whatever I was going to feel. Because surely, when the shock wore off, I'd feel something.

You'd think I'd be happy. Wasn't this what I'd wanted?

So focused on moving forward, I didn't see Ethan un-til a millisecond before colliding with him. The impact sent me staggering backward a few steps, and the file he held flew through the air before dropping to the ground, all of its contents spilling out in a messy fan shape.

"I'm sorry," I mumbled. Kneeling down, I grabbed one loose paper after another, stacking them up in front of me.

"Where are you going in such a hurry?" he teased in his Irish accent. Balancing himself on the soles of his feet, he helped me gather the pages. He was so close. Too close. The scent of his cologne, which normally had me in a near-drooling state, almost unhinged me. I wanted to turn to him, lean on him, gain comfort from him, and that was utterly stupid. Because as nice of a guy as Ethan was, he didn't need to deal with this mess. Hell, I had no choice, and I still didn't want to deal with it.

I tipped my face away from him. "Nowhere. I wasn't paying any attention. That's all." My voice shook, and I hated that it did. I finished picking up the last few pages strewn around. Grabbing the entire stack, I slid it into the file and then handed it to him. "Here. They're all out of order now. I'm sorry," I repeated.

"It's okay." He stood and then helped me to my feet. I averted my gaze.

A shudder rippled through me. The numbness had begun to wear off, and I wanted it to come back. "I'll talk to you later," I mumbled, and went to walk around him.

"Alice?"

Funneling every bit of strength I had, I smiled as brightly as I could and faced him. "Yes, Ethan?"

He looked down at me, his smoky eyes searing. Once again, it was as if he could see everything about me, everything inside of me. I blinked to break the moment, but as soon as I did, a tear dripped down my cheek. And then another. Hell. I hadn't even realized I was that close to crying. I swiped them away. "Not here," I managed to say.

That was all he needed to hear. With one hand on my elbow, he guided me forward. I let him, because as much as I'd wanted privacy before, now I craved his presence.

We maneuvered toward his office in quick, short steps. Luckily, Grandma Verda wasn't at her desk. I didn't know if she'd already gone home, or if she was off somewhere else, but it didn't really matter. What mattered was that she wouldn't see me in this condition. Not only would it break her heart, but she'd likely go find Troy and break his legs. Seriously, she could do it too. Of that I had no doubt.

Ethan closed his office door and then led me to his couch. "Sit down," he ordered. Good timing, because at that minute my legs trembled, and I didn't think I would have been able to stand much longer, anyway. I sort of collapsed on the couch. He joined me and angled his body toward me but kept silent.

A weight sat on my chest, heavy and unrelenting. All of a sudden, anger whipped in, followed by a blast of pain so strong that I gasped. Not physical pain. Emotional pain. And it pissed me off even more. Because how could Troy hurt me? When had I given him that power?

"Do you want to talk?" Ethan's deep baritone sifted through the haze, offering me support, comfort.

I shook my head. I didn't cry, and that surprised me. Not only because I'd just about burst into tears a mere few minutes earlier, but because now that the shock had worn off, the hurt inside of me was so huge, you'd have thought the tears would come pouring out. But they didn't. So I sat there while all these emotions tore into me.

My chest tightened even more. I forced myself to breathe. In. Out. In. Out. Slowly, too slowly, the sharpest edge of the pain—of the anger—began to subside. And the entire time I went through this, Ethan watched, remaining calm, waiting to be or do whatever I needed.

That knowledge also surprised me. But it was there. I saw it in his eyes, in the way he looked at me, by the way he held himself. It reminded me of Grant and the way he was with Shelby, and the power of *that* nearly took my breath away. I mean, I knew it wasn't the same. Not exactly, anyway, but it was the closest I'd ever gotten. And even in the fallout of Troy's latest betrayal, I recognized it as important.

With that realization, I was finally able to talk. "Missy delivered a message from Troy." My voice shook. "It hit me in a way I didn't expect."

Ethan reached over, stroked the line of my jaw with one finger. "I'm sorry. I wasn't aware Missy and Troy knew each other."

Oh, yeah. I never had gotten around to sharing that connection with him. "She's a friend of Troy's wife. That's where all the pent-up friction came from." In halting speech, I told him the rest. When I finally finished, I sighed and waited for his response.

White-hot anger blazed over his expression. "He's a spineless coward. People who don't take responsibility for their children deserve . . ." His eyes snapped shut. When he opened them again, the fury was either gone or well hidden; I wasn't sure which. "Troy should have had the decency to talk to you himself, rather than sending a message through his wife's girlfriend."

"I'm actually okay he didn't. I don't want him involved, anyway. That's why my feelings confused me so much. The anger makes sense. I'm not sure why it hurts."

Lifting my chin, he stared into my eyes. "It's not about you. It's about your child."

That was when it hit. I'd already hardened myself to Troy's betrayals. Old stuff, in the past, done and over with. But this betrayal wasn't really about me. It was about my daughter, and she'd done nothing wrong. So it made sense. The pain I experienced was the pain of a mother. "My first lesson in motherhood. I wonder if the rest will hurt this much," I whispered, mostly to myself.

Ethan pulled me into his arms. My cheek rested on his chest. His arms tightened around me, and the rest of my tension evaporated. Being held by Ethan? It felt right. It felt real. And that made absolutely no sense. "Some will. Some won't. I wish I could give you more advice, but what do I know? I haven't faced the joys of parenthood yet."

He kissed the top of my head, and we disengaged from each other. "Thank you for listening. It seems you're always seeing me at my worst."

"You do seem to have the most curious group of people you surround yourself with. But it adds to your charm." Then, as if getting back to business, the take-charge Ethan appeared. "I'd like to help you when you get the papers from Troy. I'll have my attorney go through them for you, if you'd like."

"That would be great." I watched him curiously. I could almost see him checking off a list in his head.

"He should, at the very least, be financially responsible. Are you sure you want to give up your right to monetary support?"

"I am. I really don't want any connection to Troy." Beatrice flickered into my mind, and I groaned. "His mother wants to meet me, though. She'd like to be a part of the child's life. I don't know what to do about that."

"Is she going to go for legal visitation?"

"Oh. I don't know. Can she?"

"If she wants to try, she can. It doesn't mean a judge will give it to her." I must have looked panicked, because he squeezed my hand. "Don't stress over it. You might want to consider meeting her, even if just to rule out that possibility."

Ugh. "Yeah. I guess. But the thought of meeting the woman who raised Troy doesn't exactly fill me with happy feelings."

"She might be a perfectly nice person who happened to end up with a not-so-nice son. It happens, Alice."

Another point I couldn't argue. "I'll have Missy set up a meeting."

"If you want company, I'd be pleased to go with you."

"Yeah. I might. I'll let you know."

"Good." He must have decided business was taken care of, for now, because the other Ethan returned. His voice softened. "You scared me, when I first saw you out there. You were so white, and your eyes were filled with so much pain." He paused. "You look more like your normal, beautiful self now."

And then, out of nowhere, that *thing* passed between us. "I really like you," I blurted.

"I really like you too. I wasn't lying when I said I find you in my thoughts constantly."

"No. I mean I really, *really* like you. And it startles me." Why had I said that? I so needed to learn to keep most of my thoughts to myself.

Desire, strong and deep, darkened his eyes. But he didn't reach for me. "There's nothing wrong with being startled. It reminds us we're alive. It makes us think. We have plenty of time to get to know each other. Plenty of time to see where this goes. There's no rush."

"Right." But did we? Maybe. Maybe not. D-Day was approaching faster than I'd anticipated, and I definitely heard the clock ticking away.

"Hey. What's with those worry lines?" He rubbed at the skin around my eyes with his thumb. His touch sent a zillion little trembles zipping over me.

How to say what I couldn't explain? "Lots of things are changing for me soon. I'll understand if it's too crazy for you."

"If you take it one day at a time, then changes come really slowly. Let's just see where this takes us. I'm not going anywhere."

I thought about what he'd said, and I nodded. "Fair enough."

"I had a thought. Are you busy on Saturday?"

He'd changed the subject so fast, I didn't get—at first—what he was leading to. "Nope. No chaos is planned for this weekend. For once."

When he grinned, my heart tumbled. It was just that simple. "Are you still up for that date? I'd like to spend the day with you. I'm fairly certain I can guarantee a chaos-free day. I might even get a laugh or two out of you."

And I did, more than anything, want to spend Saturday with him, so I said, "Yes." Suddenly, everything brightened, and my good mood fully returned.

Just like magic.

Chapter Eleven

The next three days passed excruciatingly slowly. Not only because I couldn't wait for my date with Ethan, but also because I missed Chloe. And that situation didn't appear to be changing anytime soon. Here it was Thursday afternoon, and I still hadn't connected with Kyle. But it wasn't like I hadn't tried, because I had. After getting his number from Shelby, I'd called three times and left three different messages. He just hadn't returned them.

I'd try again tonight. But geez, you'd think if he were my ever after, he'd have shown a little bit of interest by now. And that raised my hopes for Ethan. Because *there* was a man who'd definitely shown some interest.

On arriving home after work, my entire plan for the evening was to eat dinner, try to contact Kyle, and then maybe talk Chloe into coming over. I wanted to see how she was doing. I also wanted to tell her about Troy and the upcoming meeting with Beatrice. Of course, this plan went down the drain the second I unlocked my front door, because what greeted my eyes wasn't merely the unexpected; it was the craziest of the crazy. Five men—complete strangers, by the way—sat at my dining room table. Each of them seemed to be filling out some type of paperwork. Not only that, but they were all shirtless. Seriously.

I might not have known what was going on, but I certainly knew who was behind it. My eyes narrowed. Speaking to the entire room, I asked, "Where is she?"

One of the guys—the very blond, artificially tanned one—looked up from his form. "Are you the artist?"

"Where is she?" I asked again. Weirdly, I wasn't even angry. Just a little perturbed. When no one answered, I raised my voice. "Grandma Verda? Where are you?"

The response came from my bedroom. "In here! Come see, Alice!"

Lordy. Why wasn't I surprised to come home and find half-naked men in my home, with my elderly grandmother shouting at me to get to my bedroom? Well, actually, that was sort of a question that answered itself. After all, we were talking about my grandmother.

Before I went to see what she was doing in my bedroom, I stopped next to the man who'd just spoken. "What is this about?"

"A modeling job," the blond beefcake said, nodding to the form in front of him. "There were a bunch of us here earlier, but the old lady sent away everyone who didn't have scars or birthmarks on their backs."

"Oh. I see." And I did. Way too clearly. "So, what are you filling out?"

"It's a part résumé, part medical history, part IQ test thing." Then, lowering his voice, he pointed to one of the questions. "Who was the sixteenth president of the United States? The choices are Abraham Lincoln or John Adams."

"It must be a trick question, because the sixteenth president of the United States was George Washington," I whispered. I expected him to laugh. Truly, I did. So when he drew a very straight line underneath the other two choices and wrote in George Washington's name and then circled it, I didn't know if I should feel badly or laugh.

One of the other guys looked up. With rich auburn hair, bespectacled green eyes, and a splash of freckles on his cheeks, he appeared intelligent, friendly, and more than a little of the apple-pie variety of cute.

He frowned at me. "That's mean."

"I didn't think he'd believe me. It was meant to be a joke," I shot back.

"What? It's not George Washington?" the blond guy asked. "Why'd you tell me that?"

I sighed. "I was teasing. It's Abraham Lincoln."

He glared at me doubtfully. "Are you teasing again?"

"Alice! Come here!" Grandma Verda screeched.

"No. I'm not. I swear. Just mark it. You'll get that question right." Though maybe not many others. Not that it made a lick of difference, because I was having no part in whatever scheme Grandma Verda had set up.

Deciding it was time to find out exactly what that scheme was, I strode to my bedroom to find her perched on the edge of my bed with my sketchpad open next to her. Yep—to *that* drawing. She'd brought my sixth dining room chair into the room, and it sat at the far end of the bed. And in that chair sat another man, also without his shirt on. And, of course, he was seated so that his bare back faced my grandmother. I watched in partial disbelief, partial respect, and partial annoyance as, with a fancy digital camera I'd never seen, she snapped a few more pictures. For one, she got so close to the poor man's back that she could have counted his hairs. Of which, I'm sad to say, he had plenty.

"Okay. Thank you, Will. We're finished."

Standing, he pulled on his T-shirt. "When will you be making a decision?"

"Oh, I'm not really sure. But we'll contact you either way. Just be sure to leave your application, completely filled out, on the dresser there." She pointed. I followed her finger and gasped. The stack of forms sitting on the dresser was huge. Really huge.

Will did as she asked, and then left the room. Me? I reminded myself that my grandmother had the best intentions, and only half shrieked, "What are you doing?"

"Come here, Alice. Take a look at the pictures I have so far."

"No! How many men have you paraded through my bedroom today?"

"If you'd come here and look at the photos, you'd be able to see for yourself. There're a couple who I think match your drawing, dear. Most don't. But I figured it didn't hurt to get the photos so you'd have a bigger pool to choose from."

"Um. Grandma? If the scar doesn't match, why does it matter how large the pool is?"

Wait a minute. Oh my God; she'd done it. She'd dragged me into this conversation.

Blithely ignoring me, my grandmother continued, "I also made them fill out paperwork, so you'll know something about them before you set up any dates. I think it will be quite useful."

Yes. *Useful.* Sure. "Please explain to me how you accomplished this," I said, fighting to remain calm.

She clapped her hands. "Oh, it was simple. I put an ad in the paper, asking for artist's models, and ran it all last week. I got so many responses! I had to stagger their appointments. I've been doing this since Monday afternoon, after leaving Enchanted Expressions."

"You've been bringing strangers into my home since Monday?"

She sniffed. "Yes! All for you. Unfortunately, most of them I had to send home, because the newspaper neglected to print my ad correctly. It was supposed to say 'scar or birthmark on right shoulder' in the description, but they left out the 'right shoulder' part."

"And how did you get so many of them to apply?"

"I think the bonus did the trick," she said, still browsing through photos.

"And what is the bonus?" I knew I shouldn't ask.

"Just money." She sighed and shook her head—I wasn't

sure if it was at me, the bonus, or the picture she perused. "A *lot* of money for a job like this. But only one bonus for one person. Oh, and only if he's your soul mate. Of course, I didn't say that part."

I had more questions. So. Many. More. But I gave myself a minute to be sure I really wanted to know the answers.

Deciding full disclosure was for the best, I said, "Okay. Let's start at the beginning. Why did you decide to place this ad? Did you find out something about Ethan that you haven't shared with me?"

Her light blue eyes skittered to me and then back to the camera. "I don't know anything for sure."

"But you know something? What is it?"

"I still think it could be him. I just wanted to give you more possible soul mates to choose from. You do have a time limit, you know. Your baby won't wait to be born."

"Quit evading the question. What new information do you have that shows it might not be Ethan?" And yes, this question was one I didn't really want answered. But I needed to know, like it or not.

"Oh, for heaven's sake. It's not a big deal. I was telling him about all the scrapes you used to get into as a child. Climbing trees, falling off your bike, that sort of stuff."

"Go on."

"And I asked him if he'd ever injured himself as a child. Anything that would leave a scar, for instance."

A small amount of relief slid in. It didn't sound as if she'd actually seen his bare shoulder. "And?"

Wrinkling her nose, she laid her camera down in front of her. "The only scar he has is on his leg. At least, that's what he said. He was playing one day when he was young, and he knocked a glass vase over. He fell on the broken pieces and ended up with ten stitches. Can you imagine?"

"So you know for sure he doesn't have a scar on his

shoulder?" It was as if someone had punched me in the gut; the agony was that strong, that sudden. "Why didn't you tell me this immediately?"

"Because he might have a birthmark there. Or something else." She shrugged. "He might even have a scar there he doesn't know about. It's not like we look at the backs of our own shoulders every day." And then, in an obvious move to prove her statement, she crooked her neck at an awkward angle, trying to see her own shoulder. "See? It's nearly impossible."

"Nice try, Grandma." But she was right about the birthmark part—it was still a possibility. Picking up my drawing, I peered closely. Yeah. It could definitely be a birthmark.

I pretended I didn't hear the little voice in my head. The one insisting it resembled a scar far more than a birthmark. "If he's still in the running, why all these men? Why the ad?"

"When I'm done here, I'm going to have all these pictures printed, and then I'll label them. Each man will have his own file with his application and photos! Then, you, Elizabeth, and I can go through each and figure out the men who match the best."

"You really don't think it's Ethan, do you?" I whispered.

Finally, she looked at me. "Oh, honey, I don't know. But we need to have a backup plan."

Before I could respond, the auburn-haired model stuck his head in. "I've finished filling everything out. What's next?"

My grandmother's face lit up. "Well, come right in here then." She held out her hand for his paperwork. He gave it to her, and she glanced at it. "Hello, Aaron. Take a seat in that chair, with your back to me, and we'll get this finished nice and quick."

I let her do her thing and left the room. Cloistering

myself in my art studio, soon to be my daughter's bedroom, I pushed my disappointment away. Well, I tried
to. But it wasn't that easy. I tried to convince myself that
all hope wasn't lost. That Grandma Verda could be
wrong. Or, if she wasn't, that just because Ethan didn't
have a scar on his shoulder didn't mean anything. He
could still be "the one."

With a heavy spirit, I hung up the phone. I'd spent the
last hour in a heart-to-heart chat with my sister, and for
the first time since she and her boyfriend Nate had gotten together, an air of trouble stirred in their relationship. Well, I didn't think so, but she did. Or rather, she
worried there might be trouble. Apparently Nate had a
new partner at work—a very young, beautiful, and
blonde female cop.

Elizabeth said she was fine, but I'd heard the undercurrents in her voice that told me she was concerned.
You couldn't find a much better guy than Nate. He was
about as good as they got. So, I was fairly sure the blame
for her discomfort didn't rest with him, but came from
her experiences with her ex-husband and his blonde and
willing receptionist. Also, my sister's feelings were natural. After all, she and Nate had only been together for a
few months, so she was bound to cross this bridge eventually. But that didn't make the crossing any less of a
struggle.

Sighing, I tried to push her fears out of my mind so I
could focus on the picture I'd been attempting to draw.
"'Your magic, your powers, will give you the answers as
you need them,'" I murmured, repeating the last bit of
advice I'd received from Miranda.

Okay, then. So why—no matter what I tried—did I
continue to come up blank? "Damn it! I just want to know
what's going to happen."

A spark zapped into me. It began at my toes, rushing

up my body at lightning speed, pulsating through my arms, and then, with an electrifying tingle, it zapped straight into my fingertips. Tiny sparkles of light danced from my fingers to the pencil, like a miniature display of fireworks. They grew and grew until the sparkles bobbed in the air, the light of them blinking like a thousand fireflies on a summer night.

In that moment, I felt the magic like I never had before. It was inside of me. It was all around me. It *was* me. The energy continued to flow, the strength of it so great, I nearly dropped the pencil in surprise. But I held on, captivated by what was happening, enthralled by the very power. My hand trembled, and the pencil began to move.

Just like before, no image met my mind's eye, but without me having the slightest inkling of what I was creating, the magic took control. No hesitation existed in my strokes; they were solid and sure, and they swept across the page, creating the barest of outlines. Two people, a man and a woman, took shape. They stood at the front of a wide room. Candles and flowers filled the space around them. I drew more quickly, the pencil going from broad strokes to small, fine ones, filling in details throughout. From the stained-glass windows, to the wooden pews filled with people, to the flickering flames on the candles. A flower here, a pair of hands clasped there, and a crying baby all came into view. Oh! My parents were there too, in the front pew.

A wedding. The scene coming to life in front of me, created by my own hand, was that of a wedding. More details were added, and then, finally, the pencil moved to the couple about to walk back down the aisle, hand in hand. My breath caught in my chest. Was this it? Had I finally found the key to my soul mate's identity?

The bride's dress was traditional, with plenty of lace and pearls. This surprised me, because I am not a lace kind of girl, but the picture had to be of me. Who else? I continued to draw, continued to shade. Shivers coated my skin. My eyes watered and I needed to blink, but I refused to, too afraid that the magic would stop and the bride and the groom's identities wouldn't be completed. I had to finish this.

My heart raced and I swallowed, trying to calm myself. My baby danced inside of me, and I laughed. Through all of this, the magic swirled, the colors increasing in vividness around me, the lights growing brighter. And then, when I began drawing the faces of the couple, my movements slowed. I pulled air deep into my chest and then huffed it out, my eyes never leaving the page, the couple before me.

When the last line was drawn, the final detail sketched in, and there was no shading left to be completed, the magic whooshed out of me as quickly as it had come. The colors disappeared, the lights dimmed, and everything returned to normal. My hand shuddered to a stop and I dropped the pencil. My wrist ached; the muscles in my arm were tight, taut. I rubbed, first at my wrist and then at my arm, trying to ease the soreness that had come from drawing so fast.

All the while, I stared at the picture, taking it in, trying to understand why I'd drawn this specific image. I pushed a breath out. I sucked another back in. I tried to feel nothing but happiness, but a shroud of disappointment existed, heavy and unrelenting, and I couldn't quite erase it. Envy churned inside of me. Maybe that made me a bad sister, but I couldn't help it and I couldn't stop it.

For the picture wasn't of me. Though, on closer appraisal of the wedding, I was there too—at the far end of the first pew, holding a baby who was likely my daughter. A man sat next to me, but only his arm, swung over my shoulders, could be seen. The bride and groom were smiling. Love shone brilliant and clear in their eyes.

No, it wasn't me. It was my sister and Nate, on *their* wedding day. Which, apparently, was going to happen sometime in the next year, based on the age of my daughter. I peered closer at the drawing, trying to gather as much information as possible, but honestly—as far as my dilemma went—there wasn't much to see. An arm, a hand, the ridge of his shoulder, the edge of his watch peeking out from beneath his sleeve. Not enough of anything. Nothing distinctive. But then my eyes landed on his hand again, his left hand. And, assuming it was the same man from the first drawing, in this representation the wedding ring was absent.

Interesting, but completely unhelpful.

My doorbell rang, and I hesitantly set the sketchpad down and went to answer. It was Chloe, and while I was happy—no, thrilled—to see her, my heart still ached.

"I don't like things like this," she confessed, standing barely inside my door.

"I don't either. I've called Kyle four times, though. He's not calling me back. So, if you're here to get mad at me again, please don't. I can't take it tonight."

She tucked a strand of red hair behind one ear. "I've been an emotional, whiny witch. I'm sorry." A slight pause. "None of this is your fault."

"Well, I haven't exactly been calm and serene. And it's not your fault, either."

Her lips tipped up into a faint smile. "Okay. So. Where does that leave us?"

"We're friends, Chloe. Nothing has changed." And in the snap of a finger, the tension between us lessened. "Come on in."

She did, and her eyes swept the room and then me. "There's something wrong, isn't there?"

"Nate and Elizabeth are getting married." I led the way into the dining room, plopping myself into the chair I'd just vacated.

"Wow! That's great news! Why do you look so down about it?" She settled next to me.

"I'm happy for them, but I thought I was drawing my wedding." I shoved the sketchbook toward her and then let her in on what had just occurred, not leaving anything out. "It doesn't make any sense!"

Chloe's eyes clouded. "You're right. It doesn't. Almost as if something is blocking you. Or someone. Is that possible?"

I thought about it for a minute. "No. I don't think that's it. It's more like I don't know the rules, or am missing some critical component." Another thought wove into my brain. "You know that first drawing? I don't think that was me at all."

"What do you mean?"

"That one was Elizabeth's magic, not mine. I'd bet money on it." Glancing down at the wedding picture, I continued, "And this one was my magic. The difference in the two, as far as what I experienced, is huge."

"So what does that mean?"

"I don't know." Suddenly I remembered the other drawing: the one with the older woman rocking my daughter. Grabbing the sketchbook, I flipped to that page. "This one was different too. No colors or lights, just the static electricity stuff."

"Let me see that." Chloe pulled the drawing to her and dipped her head forward. "Who's the woman? And what were you doing, or wishing, when you drew this?"

Shrugging, I said, "No clue about the woman. It was the day after you all were here, right after I found out everything. I wished to draw the beach scene from a different perspective, thinking I might be able to see the man's face. Nothing happened. So I sort of yelled at Miranda, and that's when I drew it."

Chloe's green eyes rounded. "She was here?"

"No. Or, if she was, I didn't see her. But I was frustrated . . ."

"What did you yell? Do you remember?"

"Um. Let me think." Hesitating, I brought back the moment. "I stayed home from work because I didn't feel well. I don't remember all of it, but I know I asked her to help me."

A sizzle of excitement whipped through Chloe's body. "And you drew this then? Right away?"

"Yep." I shuddered. "This picture scares me. I've been trying to forget about it."

"Scares you how?"

"That's my daughter." I pointed to the picture of the child. "And I have no idea who that woman rocking her is. So it makes me believe that this picture is what will happen if I don't find my soul mate. That someone else will raise her. And that makes me afraid of what will happen to me."

Chloe paled. "Yeah, that is scary. I didn't even think of that. I was thinking that maybe this woman, whoever she is, knows who your soul mate is."

I tried that idea on for size, then shook my head. "I don't think so." Out of nowhere, I thought of Beatrice, my child's other grandmother. "Oh my God. Maybe I do know who she is."

"Who?"

Forcing myself to chill, I caught Chloe up to speed on Missy, Troy, and the fact that his mother had requested a meeting—which I'd agreed to. Whereas before I'd been fairly ambivalent about the meeting, now I felt real anxiety. "So, if it turns out this woman is Beatrice Bellamy, then what?"

"Well, maybe your hunch is correct and Beatrice would raise your daughter if you don't find your soul mate, but maybe it isn't. The picture still might mean she knows the identity of your man."

"It's not Troy. I'm positive of that." The very notion sent a wave of nausea through me. "No. It's not him."

"That's not what I meant. You know, this could just mean that Beatrice becomes a part of your life after the baby is born. Don't get all worked up. It could mean anything. Or nothing."

"You know what? Let's put this discussion on hold until I meet her. Because right now, there's way too much that's up in the air." My gaze hit the drawing again and I shivered, because no matter what Chloe said, I knew it meant something.

My friend didn't push the issue. We talked a little more about Kyle, and how I'd keep trying to get a hold of him. Things got a little weird then, and I worried we might be headed into another danger area, so I switched subjects and related Grandma Verda's latest exploit.

"She's awesome. And it's a good idea. I'll help you go through the photos when she has them ready." Chloe stifled a yawn. "I'm tired. I hadn't expected to stay this long. Mostly I wanted to make sure we were still okay."

I nodded. "I'm glad you did. We've talked nearly every day for the last fifteen years . . . it was odd not checking in with you. Not knowing how you were doing. But I wanted to give you space, like you asked for, so I didn't bug you."

After our make-up moment was over, Chloe let herself out and I readied myself for bed. The next day was my date with Ethan—something I'd looked forward to all week but now approached with more than a little nervousness. Somehow I needed to question him about the scar thing without being too obvious. I also wanted to know more about the woman he'd proposed to. Of course, that was nothing but pure nosiness.

Ambling into my bedroom, I saw the rose petal from Miranda's initial visit. I hadn't thought about it in weeks, and I was positive I'd put it away for safekeeping. But there it was, sitting on top of my jewelry box. And yep, it still looked just as fresh, just as newly plucked, as it had the first moment I saw it. Weird.

Picking it up, I stroked the petal with my finger. It didn't alter, morph, or bleed through my fingers like it had earlier. But as I held it, dizziness whirled into me. Backing up, I sat on the edge of my bed, willing the light-headedness to stop, but it didn't, so I closed my eyes and struggled to find my balance. My stomach whooshed, my hands grew clammy, and quivers itched along my skin.

When I opened my eyes again, I was no longer sitting in my bedroom. It didn't surprise me, nor did it scare me, as somehow strangeness had become the norm. The realization of that bothered me more than the actuality of what was happening around me. This time, at least, my feet were solidly on the ground, and I stood outside a large white Victorian-style house.

The scent of spring drifted through the air. Where was I? This didn't look anything like the short vision from before. I turned around in a circle, looking for something—anything—that would clue me in on what I was supposed to be seeing, on what I was supposed to be learning. Nothing jumped out at me.

Trusting my instincts, I walked toward the house. Before I reached the porch, the front door opened. A woman and a little girl stepped out, sitting down on the front step. The child appeared to be five or six, her long hair curled around her face in ringlets. I didn't recognize the woman. Of course, they didn't see me. I was only a spectator. Nothing but a ghost, really. And they didn't have any idea I stood so close to them. There didn't seem to be anything odd happening, nothing that made me understand why I was there.

I blinked, and in the space of that blink the scene changed again. Now I stood somewhere else. Still outside. Still spring. My eyes swept the area, and instead of the grand Victorian home, the house in front of me was quite small but well kept. I waited for someone to walk outside, but the door stayed firmly shut.

A lighthearted giggle floated through the air. Following the sound, I walked to the back of the house. When I reached the corner, I saw Miranda—a slightly older version of the pregnant Miranda from my earlier time warp—hanging laundry on a line. Next to her, a little girl sat in the grass, playing with a doll. The same child I'd just seen. Except her clothes weren't quite as fancy, and her hair was styled differently; instead of ringlets, it hung straight around her face. Confused, I tried to make sense of what I'd been shown, but nothing clicked.

I blinked again, and this time, at the end of that blink, I was back in my bedroom. Stunned, I dropped the rose petal and watched it float to the floor. What in heaven's name was Miranda trying to show me?

Suddenly, from somewhere deep inside, I knew the answer: Miranda hadn't had one child; she'd had two.

"Twins?" I whispered.

"You're such a smart girl." Miranda's voice shimmered into me, but when I searched the room, she was nowhere to be found.

"Are you there?" I asked. The scent of roses tickled my nose.

"I am here, in a way. What's important is that you are correct. I indeed gave birth to identical twins, but was only allowed to know one of them."

"Allowed? Who made that decision for you?" I so wished I could see her. Talking to the air felt a little like I'd lost my mind.

"Her father. He bribed the people closest to me. If I'd only had one daughter, he would have taken her."

Pain, fast and furious, dug into my heart. How could anyone do that? How had my ancestor lived with it? "Why didn't you go get her?"

Her voice lost its tinkling bell quality. Sadness reverberated in every word she spoke. "By the time I found her, it was too late. She was happy, deeply ensconced in her family, and even though it was the hardest thing I'd ever done, I decided to let her stay. But now everything has changed. It's time for the truth to come out."

"What do you mean? She's long gone." Okay, that came out badly. "Sorry . . . but it's not like she's still alive."

Miranda's voice was firm. "My family, my daughters, need to recognize each other, to help each other. I can't rest until the circle is complete. I need your help for that to happen. I need you to close the circle."

"But how? Do you know where her descendants are today?"

Breath touched my ear. "All in good time, Alice. But the answer exists inside of you, around you. If you search, you'll find it."

I knew without asking that she'd left. What I didn't know was why this vision, this knowledge, was so important. Did it have anything to do with my soul mate search? Or was it just another piece of a puzzle that was too huge to see all at once?

It seemed the only one with all the answers was Miranda. But she'd already said her piece, so once again, I had a whole bunch of questions with no clear answers. Awesome.

Chapter Twelve

The sudden jangle of my telephone interrupted my early-Saturday-afternoon preparations for the date with Ethan. Worried it was him calling to cancel, I flipped the phone over to catch a look at the caller ID. It read: Chloe Nichols. To say I was relieved is a massive understatement. Besides which, I'd finally talked to Kyle that morning, and we'd set up a date. Or, to my way of thinking, a meeting, because no way could I consider it anything else. But I hadn't yet told Chloe.

"Hey, Chloe. What's up?" I asked, cradling the phone between my ear and shoulder, all set to give her the news she'd been waiting for.

"Oh my God, Alice! We've been doing this wrong."

I removed the lid from my eyeliner and leaned close to the mirror. "What are you talking about?"

"Last night. Your magic. You were still thinking about Elizabeth, and her worries about Nate, and that led you to draw a picture of their future."

"Uh-huh." Finished with one eye, only half listening because I was still thinking about Kyle, I moved the kohl brown pencil to my other eye.

"I have goose bumps. This is so cool."

"What is? You're confusing me."

"It's precognition! Maybe your magic isn't so much about wishes coming true as it is about telling the future."

Her words hit me hard. My hand stumbled, and instead of the larger-than-life eyes I'd been going for, I had a thick brown line edging down my cheek. "Sec," I mumbled, wiping the mess off of my face. Well, I tried to, anyway.

Could she be right? I mean, the magic had certainly been much more forceful with the wedding drawing than with anything else that had happened, including the accidental wishes. "If that's the case, then why haven't I been able to draw a clear picture of my soul mate?"

"I think it's because you can't see your own future, only the futures of those around you. It lines up with what you said, that this time you thought it was your magic and not Elizabeth's."

Ignoring the bruiselike smudge on my cheek, I collapsed onto my bed and considered my friend's words. Was my gift somehow different from my grandmother's? From my sister's? Theirs had to do with wishes, and from what my grandmother had said, it had always been that way. But . . .

"So now I'm a fortune-teller or something? And what about the wishes that have come true?"

"Who knows? You're pregnant with a magical baby. Maybe your wishes coming true are only because of her. Like, an excess of power in your system."

I choked out a laugh. "Very funny. You make it sound like hormones."

"Maybe it is like that. The wish stuff didn't happen right away; you were what—four months or so along before it started?" She sighed, clearly unsure. "Okay, I don't know. But it's a possibility, and right now, until you talk to Miranda again, it's a good guess. If it's true, I think I know how to use it to our advantage."

"Go on," I said.

"Instead of trying to draw your soul mate or your future, instead of trying to wish for anything to happen, try to draw *Ethan's* future. Or Kyle's." She hesitated. "Or mine."

I exhaled. "I'm pretty sure it needs to be more exact than that. Like, a specific thing in their futures." And then another thought occurred: "And maybe there has to be a reason for me to even be able to use the magic in that way."

"What do you mean?" Chloe asked.

I didn't know, exactly. But a thread of knowledge teased at me, pulled hard. It was right there, only I couldn't quite grab it. "Elizabeth was upset . . . so somehow that set the magic off? Like an inciting incident, maybe?" I sighed in exasperation. "It's not coming out right. But I don't think it's as easy as sitting down with a pencil and saying, wishing, *whatever*, 'Show me so-and-so's future.'"

"Maybe not. But it doesn't hurt to try," Chloe pushed.

"Try what, exactly?"

"To rule out either Kyle or Ethan. Pick one and try to draw his wedding day."

I hesitated. I hadn't told Chloe about the very high possibility that Ethan didn't have a scar, and I didn't think I was going to. At least, not now. Not until I knew for sure. Because that would only make her focus even harder on Kyle, would make our relationship even more strained. Especially now that I'd done what she wanted and set up a meeting with him. "I can't now. Ethan will be here soon. But . . . I need to tell you something."

Chloe wouldn't be dissuaded from her earlier point. "But later? You'll try later? This could be it, Alice. The key we've been missing."

"Yeah. Of course I'll try later," I promised.

"And. Um. Can you also try to draw my wedding day? Or even just a picture of the guy I end up with?" Her voice was soft and tentative, but a giant vat of want lurked beneath.

"Sure, Chloe. If that's what you really want. But it hasn't worked so well for me," I reminded her.

"Right, but I'm not you. So yes, please, see what you come up with." Her tone went up a notch in excitement. "Your turn now. What was it you wanted to say?"

"Oh." Swallowing, I made myself continue. "I got hold of Kyle this morning. We're meeting for lunch on Monday."

The responding quiet seemed louder than any scream I'd ever heard. Finally Chloe said, "Okay. That's good. It needs to happen. You'll let me know how it goes?"

"Of course I will. But are you really feeling things for him again? Seriously?"

Another pause. "I don't know. There's something there, but it might just be leftover stuff from our past."

"Be careful, okay? There are other guys out there, you know. Guys who are interested in you."

She snorted, her good humor returned. "Yeah? Like whom?"

"Scot, for one." Oh, God. How had that slipped out? My brother was going to kill me.

"Scot? As in your brother Scot?"

"Uh-huh."

"Are you trying to set us up? Because if so, just stop. He's a nice guy, and I'm sure he'll make some woman incredibly happy someday. But not me. He's family to me, Alice."

Deciding to leave it at that, because come on, I already knew she felt that way, I faked a laugh. "Can't blame me for trying to make you an official member of the Raymond family."

She laughed too, and then we hung up.

I continued to get ready, but my conversation with Chloe refused to leave my brain. Maybe if I had time before Ethan showed, I'd see if her thoughts about the magic were correct. The thing was, what I hadn't admitted to her, what I'd barely admitted to myself, was that it felt right. So why, then, did I want to do anything but draw Ethan's future?

Ha. I knew why. I was too afraid it wouldn't be me in it.

When Ethan arrived at my door, a ball of nervous energy had me pausing before opening up. He wore jeans that were just snug enough to show every luscious detail of his muscular thighs, a dark green long-sleeved jersey-type shirt, and a smile that made my belly quiver. A blast of rain-soaked wind followed him inside.

"Whew. It feels more like October out there than June," I said, slamming the door shut behind him and then wrapping my arms around myself to warm up.

Sliding his umbrella closed, he tipped it against the wall. "It's actually quite chilly." His lips lifted into a semi-sheepish grin. "I planned the most perfect day today, taking every last detail into consideration—except, it appears, slashing cold rain."

Laughter bubbled up in me, but I swallowed it back down. "And what was on your perfect sunny day plan?"

He chuckled. "I'm not telling. I'll save it for another day."

Wow. He was already planning another day. With me. The tease of a shiver touched my skin. "Oh, come on. Just one hint?"

"Absolutely not. But I've come up with another plan, also a secret until we get there. While not nearly as romantic as the original, it should do well enough to pass the time." Uncertainty sparked into his eyes. "I hope you won't be too disappointed."

I laughed. "I'm sure it will be wonderful. Just let me grab my jacket and I'll be ready."

Ten minutes later, I sat next to Ethan as he drove toward our mystery destination. I'd thought so much about this date, I should have been prepared. Unfortunately, my mind refused to focus. Instead, it meandered between my conversation with Chloe and her new magic hypothesis to my latest time warp. The whole Miranda-birthed-twins twist still boggled my mind. I mean, somewhere out there were relatives I hadn't known I had. Sure, it wasn't the same as finding out you had a long-lost sibling, because we were talking about cousins many, many times removed, but it still fascinated me.

"What are you so quiet about over there?" Ethan asked. Strangely, the sound of his voice soothed my jumbled nerves.

"My crazy family."

"Aren't all families crazy?" he asked.

I pivoted so I could see him better. Once again, my eyes found that cute cleft in his chin. "Not like mine." A crack of thunder reverberated overhead, and lightning flashed through the windows. "We could've stayed at my place, where it's dry. Watched a DVD, ordered in Chinese or pizza or something. I should have thought of it."

"But then I'd have had to rely on my wicked sense of humor, magnetic personality, and charming repartee to impress you. I'm not sure I could've pulled it off."

A laugh I'd held back emerged. "Somehow, I don't think it would have been a problem. You've already impressed me."

"Well, then, maybe we can do the DVD and Chinese later. After I woo you with my brilliant date-planning techniques," he teased. "Today, I'm all yours."

All mine? For not the first time, I wondered what it would be like to have Ethan in my bed, his hands on me, mine on him, our limbs entwined. An image of the two of us doing just that struck, and a hot rush of desire mixed with longing swarmed over me. I pressed my legs tightly together and forced myself to breathe evenly.

My reaction was startling. This was not the time for fantasies—not when Ethan sat so close.

It was hard to let the image go. Pushing it away the best I could, I asked, "So, no hints on where we're going?" Not that I really cared, but I hoped it was something laid-back, somewhere we could actually talk to each other.

"Nope. But you're free to guess. I'll tell you if you're correct."

"Hmm." My mind browsed through the various possibilities. "A movie theater?" He shook his head. "One of Chicago's fine museums?" Another shake. "Okay, then. I give up."

"We're almost there. I just hope you're not a poor loser. Because what we're going to do is something at which I'm exceptional."

"Wow, just a little modesty there." My smile widened to the point that my cheeks hurt.

"I can always give you some pointers." His right hand skimmed my knee for just a second. A delicious curl of want licked at me. "In fact, I'd love to give you some pointers."

When we pulled into the parking lot of our destination, I laughed again. "Bowling? You are so in trouble. I'm going to kick your butt. I'll be giving *you* pointers."

"Is that so?"

"I grew up in a large family. Whenever there was an argument between us kids, my dad would take us bowling." I grinned. "We had lots of fights, so we spent a lot of time at alleys. You're so going to lose," I teased.

Unfastening his seat belt, his eyes met mine. "So . . . you're not disappointed?"

"Not at all!" I told him. "I think this is the perfect way to spend a rainy few hours." Well, I could think of one other indoor recreation that I'd also enjoy, but bowling worked well enough. It was casual, fun, and maybe I could squeeze in a few questions between frames.

"Then let's get to it. Wait here. I'll come around with the umbrella." He did, and we ran inside together, his arm draped lightly around my waist. And guess what? Wind, rain, and gloomy skies did nothing to alter my pleasure or excitement.

That feeling didn't change over the next several hours. I won the first the game. He won the second. We were halfway through the third—the tiebreaker—and I still hadn't managed to ask him anything of merit. But at that moment, I didn't care. I was having way too much fun.

"You're better than I thought you'd be. They have bowling in Ireland?" I asked.

"No, Alice. Ireland is sadly lacking in bowling alleys, miniature golf courses, and any other types of recreation," he deadpanned. "A few soda bottles, a rubber ball, and my backyard was the closest thing I had." He sighed. "It was a difficult youth. You should take pity on me."

I couldn't help it; I laughed. "Nice try, but I'm still going to win."

And I did.

Two hours later, after eating dinner out, we pulled up in front of my condo. "I had a great time with you today. You're quite the worthwhile opponent," Ethan said, shutting the car off.

"I loved today," I admitted, then hesitated before forging ahead. "It's still early. Want to come in for a while?" I desperately wanted him to say yes.

"I was hoping you'd ask. And remember, the romantic date I had planned is still on the table. Maybe we'll have the weather for it next weekend."

"I can't wait," I replied.

But what if everything changed by then? Everything in me only wanted to get to know Ethan better. I wanted to follow my instincts full speed ahead and see where we might end up. Why couldn't I do that? Why did I have to make some choice based on nothing but a vaguely worded warning? Maybe, regardless of how I'd felt earlier, I didn't have to? I mean, wasn't it up to me? This was my love life, after all.

Ethan followed me inside, but my thoughts were still preoccupied. "Want some tea or something? I think I might have some wine left in the fridge, if you'd like that," I offered.

"Nah. I just want to talk to you." He clasped my hand in his, and pulled me toward the living room. We sat on the couch, and as his arm came around my shoulders, awareness rippled through me. "How are you feeling?"

"I'm good. Really good." Physically, anyway. But as I looked at him, I saw something simmering below the surface. I found myself wishing he'd tell me exactly what he was thinking, and as the thought whipped through me, a strong shiver followed. I gasped.

"Are you okay?" he asked, tightening his hold on my shoulders.

"Um. Yeah." Even as I spoke, I recognized something had changed. The air between us was charged with unseen bolts of electricity. My heart hammered in my chest, so loudly that I was surprised he didn't hear.

He blinked, his long lashes sweeping downward. "I wasn't going to bring this up yet, because I don't want to send you running." A slight twinge of indecision colored his tone, his features. "But maybe I should, just to clear the air."

"Um, Ethan? It's okay. You don't have to say anything."

The indecision fled. "Actually, it's better if I do, even if I hadn't planned on it. Just promise me you won't run until I say it all."

"I won't run, Ethan. What is it?" I tried to sound confident. I was sure I failed.

"My feelings for you are stronger than I anticipated." Shaking his head, as if trying to clear a daze, he continued, "I've only felt this way once before, and that didn't end as I'd hoped. I just want to make sure we're on the same path here."

"And that path is going where?" I probably shouldn't have asked, because it was my stupidly thought wish that had started this conversation, but I couldn't help myself. I wanted to know. I needed to know.

Smoky eyes steadily held mine. "I can't answer that yet, because neither of us knows what the future holds. But Alice? I'm not interested in other women. I'm only interested in you, and moving forward, and seeing what the future is." His hand played with my hair. "But you're about to become a mother, and your life is going to change quickly."

"And you're worried about what, exactly?" Maybe the baby was a deal breaker. I couldn't blame him if so, but if that was the case, I needed to find out before my heart became further entangled. Before I made any decisions.

"I'm not asking you to make any promises. I just want to know that, right now, I'm the man you want to spend time with." I must have looked perplexed, because he sighed. "Let me try this again. Are you dating anyone else right now?"

At first, a blast of happiness made me more than a little dizzy. Ethan wanted to be with me as much as I wanted to be with him! I opened my mouth to tell him just that, but out of nowhere, Kyle came to mind. Did he count as someone I was dating? Ugh. Not really. Not yet, anyway. But what if that changed?

Deciding to answer the question he'd asked, I said, "At the moment, you're the only man I'm dating. The only man I even want to date." Even though that was the truth, I felt as if I'd lied.

Still, the worry in his gaze disappeared. "I want you to be happy. I hope I make you happy."

"You do." My own worries eased away. In any other circumstance, where a warning from a long-dead relative wasn't in play, I'd be head over heels by now. Maybe the best thing I could do was grab hold and trust my instincts.

"Come here," he growled. His hands tugged at my waist, and he pulled me toward him. I took things a step further, pivoting my body so I was sitting on his lap, my legs on either side of his, facing him. Exactly where I wanted to be.

One of his hands came up behind me, his fingers threading through my hair, pushing my head forward. His other hand rested on my back. Our lips met, and just like before, everything else melted away. All my worries, thoughts about soul mates, magical mishaps, and the rest of it evaporated. Ethan's scent wrapped around me, intoxicating. How could this be wrong? And even if it were, I wasn't so sure I cared.

His tongue teased at my mouth, plunging in, pulling me deeper into his kiss. The taste of him, the feel of his erection against me sent a wave of desire rolling through my body, so strong and so fast, my head spun. Everything about this man resonated with me, and I didn't think, I just reacted. My hand tugged his shirt up so I could feel his skin—which was warm, solid, and way too enticing.

Knowing I was only a few seconds from ripping his shirt all the way off, I groaned and pulled my mouth from his. Resting my cheek on his chest, I heard his heart beating as fast as my own. Our breaths came in ragged, uneven rasps, and his arms closed around me, locking me to him. Neither of us spoke for a while; we just stayed like that, pressed tightly together, waiting for the moment to calm.

And that was the second I knew something I'd been ignoring for weeks: I was more than attracted to Ethan Gallagher. Somewhere inside, on a gut level, I recognized him. And yeah, I was absolutely positive I was falling in love. Because this feeling? It beat the crap out of what I'd felt for Troy after a full year. Hell, it made all of my other relationships combined seem like a joke.

I was *this* close to tossing the warning aside, to letting myself fall in love, when my daughter kicked. And in that small, barely felt kick, all of my fears came rushing back. I was going to be a mother. I owed my daughter the best I could give her, and if for some reason Ethan wasn't that, what did that make me? Selfish. It made me selfish.

Separating myself from Ethan's embrace, I scooted to the side, my eyes not meeting his. Instead, they fell on his arm. At some point, in the midst of our kiss, his sleeve had gotten pulled up, and just below his elbow, on the inside of his arm, was a tiny white scar. "I thought you only had one scar," I blurted, my fingers touching the mark.

"Hmm? Oh, that? One of many accidents from my youth. I think that one was from tossing rocks with my friends."

"Tossing rocks?" I said lightly, barely daring to hope. "Grandma Verda said something about you only having one scar. On your leg? From glass or something."

"What? Oh, that's right. We had a rather strange discussion about scars and childhood injuries. I only told her the one story because I was on my way out to meet with a client." Then, as if he realized how odd our current conversation was, he paused. "Are you against scars?"

Relief flooded me. "Oh, not at all! I'm . . . curious. So, you have lots of scars?"

Humor edged his words. "I wouldn't say lots. Three or four, maybe. Why are you so curious?"

My mind flashed through all the answers I could give, but I came up blank. Remembering something my sister had said, I went with, "Scars turn me on. You know, they're hot . . . and dangerous . . . and sexy." I sounded like a loon, but so what? He had more scars. One could be on his shoulder!

"Every time we have a conversation, I learn a little more about how your mind works. And each and every time, it backs up my first conclusion of you."

"Oh yeah? What was that?"

"Funny, beautiful—and quite unique."

Leaning against him, I smiled. "Unique is good." There were more things about Ethan I wanted to know, but I let them slide away. Because sitting there felt so good, so right, that regardless of what happened in the future, it was a memory to cherish. No way, no how, was I going to screw it up.

Chapter Thirteen

"I wish to draw a picture of Kyle's wedding day," I murmured. Maybe, just maybe, it would happen and then I could cancel my lunch meeting with him; after yesterday's date with Ethan, the image of sitting across from Kyle Ackers for an entire hour didn't fill me with joy.

Nothing happened. Not even a zip of energy floated into me. But instead of becoming frustrated, I considered what I knew about the magic. Next, I pulled the limited knowledge I had about precognition together in my mind, which was basically nothing more than what Chloe had shared. That thread from earlier still existed, teasing me, skimming the edge of my awareness. I was absolutely missing something. But what?

Setting Kyle aside for now, I thought about Ethan. Drawing his future scared me, because if I weren't in it, I'd be crushed. I'd have no choice then but to seriously consider other alternatives. And while the intelligent way to proceed would be to gather that information as soon as possible, I couldn't do it. Not yet. Eventually I might not have any choice but to give that a shot, but for now I was skipping it.

Okay, so if I was too chicken to go down that road, what about Chloe's? There were similarities between her and Elizabeth. For one, I cared deeply about both of them. For two, both were going through emotional upheaval in their lives.

Excitement surged inside of me. I was close. So very close. The pieces suddenly seemed to click into place, and the end result was definitely something that made sense. So much so, I almost laughed. I'd been thinking too hard about things. The truth was so simple, I couldn't believe I hadn't realized it before: however my magic worked, it had something to do with my connection to the person, and to something they were experiencing at the time.

But was I right? No time like the present to find out.

Gripping my pencil, I thought of Chloe and how much she meant to me. I considered everything she was going through, and how much she needed answers. "I wish to draw a picture of Chloe and the man she marries," I whispered. The words had barely left my mouth before a swirl of electricity began at my toes. It curled through my body like wildfire, and in an instant, my pencil was moving across the page.

Oh my God. I'd hoped for this, but I hadn't actually thought it would happen. Lights and colors danced around me, around the pencil, just like with Elizabeth's drawing. The power whipped through the air, forceful and solid. And then, out of nowhere, a strong blast of wind hit my face. Okay, that was a new one. The magic undulated through my veins, and as it did, my pencil continued to draw, to shade, to put in detail where none had existed.

Chloe came into focus first. Her hair was longer, gently sweeping across her shoulders. Her eyes were large, luminous, and her happiness shone through. She wore an informal dress that stopped at the top of her knees. And even though it was just a picture, I could almost see how the dress moved around her like flowing silk. She held a large bouquet of flowers in her hands, and a small crown sat on top of her head as if she were a princess—and the pure beauty of the love I saw in her eyes stole my breath.

Then it was time to draw the man standing next to

her. Would it be Kyle? Scot? Someone else entirely? I didn't know what to hope for, because while seeing Kyle as her groom would give me a huge amount of peace, I didn't think he was the man for her any more than I thought he was the man for me. Still unable to breathe, I watched the pencil strokes become smaller, sketching in the fine details of the man's hair, eyes, nose, mouth, jaw . . .

In a giant rush, the energy burst through me one last time and evaporated. The colors disappeared, the wind stopped blowing, and my hand ceased to move. I stared at the picture, and a tremble not caused by magic crawled along my skin. This drawing was a close-up, featuring only the bride and groom. I couldn't see any of the room in which they stood, or any of the people around them. They took center stage. And the groom? He wasn't Kyle. He wasn't Scot, either. Rather, the handsome man smiling back at me from the page was a complete stranger. At least to me.

Wow. I didn't really feel disappointment it wasn't Kyle, because with Chloe beaming so brightly, how could I possibly be disappointed? Tears dotted my eyes. One blink and they cascaded down my cheeks in a hot rush. My friend was going to find her ever after, and I so couldn't wait for the day—the one right in front of me— to actually happen.

With a shaky hand, I reached for the phone. I needed to tell her, right now, so she could come over here and see for herself. She had to see the man, her husband, with her own eyes, so she knew not to focus on Kyle, or to worry about him any longer. But before I could dial the numbers, Miranda shimmered in front of me. No lights or colors, just her glimmering shape, not quite solid.

With a flick of her hand, my phone tumbled to the ground. "You can't show her this yet, Alice."

I frowned. "Why not? She needs to know, and it will make her so happy."

"Because she's not ready. If you show her this now, everything inside of her will be intent on finding him, but it's not the right time for them yet. And if she is able to find him now, this path will alter. It will change from the happy day you drew. You don't want to do that to your friend, do you?"

"You mean it won't happen? If she somehow tracks him down tomorrow, this day I just drew will never occur?" My chin dipped downward. I took in the drawing again, and my heart ached.

"That's exactly what I mean." Suddenly, Miranda was next to me. "Be very careful."

Anger and sadness collided. "Why do I even have this power? If I can't show it to those people I draw?" I so wanted to give Chloe this picture, but of course I wouldn't. Not if doing so would erase her glorious day.

"All power, all magic, has . . . hmm, what's the right word—Side effects? Repercussions?—if not used correctly. The magic is changing, and part of your magic is exactly what you've guessed. You have the power to see glimpses of the future, but you'll need to learn how to use those glimpses appropriately. I'll help you, and you will learn. I promise."

Understanding what she said didn't make it easier to take. "What about the wishes? Is that me or the baby?"

"A little of both. You have some power with wishes, more with the presence of your daughter. It will grow as she grows."

God. Chloe had basically been right about that too. Smart lady, my friend. "Okay then, what about *Elizabeth's* picture? Can I show her?"

A ghost of a smile touched Miranda's lips. "Yes. Because the steps to achieving that future have already begun. She might not want to know, though, so be careful before you show her."

Holding up the sketchpad, I stared at Chloe's beaming face again. It was there; I could see it—all of her dreams about love were going to come true. "When can I show her?"

Miranda sighed. "You'll know when. Trust me on this, Alice. When the moment arrives, you won't doubt it. If there is doubt, it's not the right time." And then, in her normal annoying way, she hazed out of my living room without another word.

"Come back! I want to talk to you about Ethan," I half shouted. Nothing. "Please?" Still nothing.

Honestly, if she weren't my great-great-great-grandmother, I'd have cursed the day she was born. Freaking ghost, blipping in and out with a mishmash of advice, warnings, and whatnot, but nothing real. Nothing tangible to give me what I needed to know.

Of course, that was probably because she couldn't tell me. Otherwise, just like Chloe, my happily ever after might never occur. And wow, I so wanted that future.

Very carefully, I ripped the Chloe picture out of my sketchbook and put it away, high up in my closet. For now, at least, I'd have to forget it existed, even if it went against every bone in my body. Me and Chloe? We'd never kept secrets. We'd never had anything we couldn't share. This was a first, in more ways than one. I hated it.

Deciding I needed some company, I figured a visit to my sister's would do the trick. Grabbing my sketchbook, I headed out the door without a backward glance. I hoped sharing her drawing with her would lift my spirits.

An hour later, I was at Elizabeth's place. We were seated on her couch in her tiny living room. And I do mean tiny. Elizabeth's apartment was about half the size of mine.

"I baked brownies yesterday. Do you want one?" She hadn't yet asked what I was doing there unannounced, but the question loomed between us.

"No, thanks. How are you? You didn't sound like yourself the other day." I eased in, trying to take the conversation slowly.

A wide smile broke. "Is that what this is about? I'm sorry I worried you. My past caught up with me, and I began to worry the same thing might happen again. But Nate's different, and what we have is special. I'm okay now."

"You're the happiest I've seen you in years. And I like Nate a lot." My eyes whisked over her apartment, which she'd completely redecorated not that long ago. It was stylish and chic, but homey too. Exactly right for my sister. "I still need to paint you a portrait. Maybe as a wedding gift . . ." I let the words trail off.

Her gaze narrowed. "Wedding gift? What are you talking about?"

"Um. Well, I have it on good authority—"

Before I could finish my sentence, she leaned over and lightly smacked her hand over my mouth. "No, Alice. If you know something like that—I don't want to hear. Let me be surprised if and when it happens."

Damn. There went that thought. I nodded, and she removed her hand. "I don't know anything for sure," I lied. "Mostly, I was prodding. You'll tell me right away if he proposes, right? Like, immediately? I've just been thinking about your situation and it seemed to make sense."

"Of course I'll tell you! Right now, I think we're good where we are. We might move in together soon, though. It seems wasteful for both of us to keep paying rent when we live right next door."

"Will you move to his apartment or will he move here?"

"No idea. I'd prefer here after all the work I've done on

the place, but what's important is being with the person you love. I'll go wherever." A light of knowledge danced into her brown eyes. "What's going on with you? Making any headway on the soul mate front?"

"Not really. Ethan and I had a date yesterday. It was really nice." Biting my lip, I asked a question I hadn't planned on: "How did you know you'd fallen in love with Nate?"

"That serious already? That must have been some date."

I gave my sister a glare. "Just answer. How'd you know?"

She shrugged, some of her chestnut hair falling into her eyes. Whisking it away, she said, "I can't answer that. I just . . . knew."

"That's no help! Can't you be more exact?"

I must have looked as miserable as I felt, because she squeezed my hand. "Aw, sweetie. Trust me. You'll know. When it comes right down to it, you won't have a question or a bit of doubt; your entire being will sing with the knowledge."

Weird, really, how her answer about love and Miranda's about magic were so very similar. Heck, it was even a little eerie. "Yeah. I've been hearing a lot of that lately."

"Come on. Let's get a brownie and a big glass of milk, and you can tell me all about your date. Sound good?"

"Yeah. I'd like that." And then, together, we talked it out over chocolate.

By the time I left, I was in a better frame of mind. If what Elizabeth said was true, then maybe I already had my soul mate question answered. Of course, a stupid little inner voice reminded me that, no matter how strong my feelings for Ethan were, it did not mean he was the man in my drawing. But that little voice? It pissed me off, so I tuned it out.

*   *   *

I waited for Kyle in a window booth at a local hamburger joint a few blocks away from Enchanted Expressions. I wasn't sure what I was going to glean from this meeting, but I hoped something would come out that would settle the Kyle-as-soul-mate subject once and for all.

When he loped into the restaurant, I saw him immediately. Today, he wore casual dress slacks, a tucked-in long-sleeved shirt, and a tie. A flutter of surprise had me taking a closer look. Dressed like this, he was actually fairly handsome, even with his apparently trademark sunglasses pushed up on his head. His gaze landed on me and he gave a small, tight smile.

Sliding into the seat across from me, he tipped his head in greeting. "Hey, Alice. Have you been waiting long?"

"No. Thanks for meeting me. I appreciate it."

The waitress stopped at our table, delivering two glasses of water and two menus. After she zipped away, Kyle opened his menu, his long fingers tilting it upright so I couldn't quite see his entire face. My stomach hurt, probably from the tension emanating off of Kyle. It appeared we were equally unhappy with this get-together. I knew what caused my stress, but I wondered what caused his.

As I watched him, I tried to imagine being with him the way I was with Ethan, but the image wouldn't take. It wasn't that I found him distasteful, because I didn't. Especially now that I knew more about him. There just weren't any sparks, any energy, any *anything* between us.

He set his menu down, and a hint of irritation existed in the way he sat, in his stiffly held shoulders. "What did you want to see me for?" he finally asked, his voice calm but abrupt.

"Um. Well, we're both friends with Shelby and Grant. And Chloe. I thought it might be nice to get to know each other a little better, that's all."

His eyes skittered to the window and then back to me.

Instead of the casual, even funny Kyle I'd seen at Shelby's, this Kyle was all about business. "This is probably a really rough time for you, isn't it? Being pregnant and the father skipping out and all. I'm sorry you're going through that."

"It hasn't been easy," I agreed, once again surprised.

"And you'd probably like to find someone else. Another man or . . . well . . . even a woman if you go that way, to help you out a little. I get that. I do." Fidgeting, he played with his napkin-wrapped silverware. "Do you go that way? Or are you set on finding a man? Maybe I can fix you up with some people, if you tell me what you're looking for. There're a couple of divorced guys at work who are seriously into the daddy scene."

Was he trying to match me up? Seriously? "Kyle? What are you talking about?"

"I'm just saying I understand." The words were said slowly, as if he were talking to a child.

"Understand what, exactly?"

"You've called almost every day for the past week. I thought by not returning your calls I'd have given you the message I wasn't interested. But you haven't gotten that." Slouching back, he watched me carefully. "You're not going to cry or something, are you?"

"No, I'm not going to cry." I took a slow breath to battle the annoyance rising up in me. Maybe he wasn't getting at what I thought he was getting at. "But you'll need to spell this out for me, because I'm a little confused."

"Look, Alice. There have been girls I've really liked in the past. I know how it feels to want to hook up with someone so much you can't get them out of your mind. If it weren't for Chloe, I might even think it was cool you'd chosen me." Now he fiddled with the saltshaker. "Not that I want to be a dad to your tyke-to-be, 'cause I don't. I'm not in that place right now, if you get my gist."

I stared at him, incredulous. He thought I wanted to hook up with him? Ew! Just . . . ew. The waitress appeared then, thank goodness. She took our orders and then rushed over to the table next to us. Unfortunately, the brief respite didn't give me one iota of clarity as to why he'd made this leap. "I've been calling because I wanted to *talk* to you. That's it."

"You're nearly stalking me! Chloe won't go out with me because of you. Shelby keeps asking if we've done anything together yet. And you drew a picture of me? It's crazy. The only reason I came today was to tell you in person I'm not interested." He shifted around in his seat, and a sideways grin popped out. "I know I'm nearly irresistible, so it's not even your fault. The ladies dig me, so you're in good company, but please chill out on the phone calls."

Okay, maybe it was rude, but I laughed. "You think I'm stalking you?" Another burst of laughter escaped. "Oh, Kyle, that is so far from the truth. I'm sorry if I . . . er . . . frightened you."

It was his turn to laugh, and he looked obviously relieved. "You didn't scare me. But between Chloe and Shelby, and you calling so much, it really felt weird. So . . . you're not on a daddy hunt?" He gave me another nervous look.

"No. I'm not on a daddy hunt. Chloe wanted us to get to know each other better, so that's what I'm doing." It was another lie by omission of some key facts, but somehow, I didn't think exposing the soul mate hunt to him would go over any better than a supposed daddy hunt.

"Uh . . . what's the deal with drawing me then? And why is Chloe so adamant about us talking?"

"I drew a picture that Shelby thought looked like you." At his doubtful glance, another laugh escaped. "Seriously, Kyle. I drew it before I even saw you at the cookout. As far as Chloe goes, we're close. Friends check out guys for their friends. She's a little nervous, that's all. With the past you two have, you can't really blame her."

Something—remorse?—trickled over his features. "I know I didn't treat her right. Shelby came along, and I was hooked. She was all I could think of. But that was high school. It's different now. I've grown up a little, believe it or not."

Both of us relaxed then, for real, and finally I was able to just talk to him. You know how they say first impressions can be deceiving? Well, in Kyle's case, that was definitely the truth. Sure, the guy had some *serious* hangups about commitment, but he was nice, smart, and really quite funny. By the time we finished lunch, I could honestly say that being Kyle's friend might be a cool thing.

But as far as the soul mate issue went, I thought I could safely cross him off my list, scar or no. Because that was the only fact lining up on his side. Attraction between us was nil, he was not seeing marriage in his near future, and, yeah—the daddy thing? Completely freaked him out. And the fact I hadn't been able to draw his wedding day made me think he wasn't going to have one. Ever.

Also, seeing as how the man in my drawing wore a wedding ring, well—that was something that made me feel oh-so-much better. We left the restaurant together, stopping outside to say our good-byes.

"It was nice hanging with you today." Bending down, he smooched me lightly on my cheek. "Now maybe Chloe and I can go out."

I almost told him that Chloe was on a different track, that she wanted to get married and have kids someday, but luckily common sense won out and I kept my thoughts to myself. If anything I said or did changed Chloe's future, I'd never forgive myself. "Good luck," was my only reply.

"Thanks! And hey, if it doesn't work out with her, maybe we can hang out some more." He winked. "You're pretty hot for a pregnant chick."

"Um. Thanks?"

Seeing as I already knew that things weren't going to pan out between Chloe and Kyle, his little statement gave me pause, even if it was only a joke. I strolled back to work slowly, thinking about Kyle and trying to be sure that I truly felt nothing for him. My emotions for Ethan were strong, intense, and had been almost from the beginning. Was that coloring my thoughts about Kyle? My attraction to him? No. I didn't think so. For now I was keeping Kyle crossed off the soul mate list. If following my heart didn't lead me to happiness, and I had to end my relationship with Ethan, well . . . maybe I'd give Kyle more consideration. But I didn't think that was going to happen, because everything about Ethan just felt right.

Returning to my office, I beelined for my desk, pushing all other thoughts straight out of my head. I needed to be able to concentrate. We had just gotten a new account that required my attention, and while the original meeting with Mr. Kendall had been delayed, the new date was fast approaching, so I had plenty to keep my afternoon occupied. When I pulled out my chair, a large manila envelope sitting on the seat grabbed my attention.

My heart stopped. Well, not literally, but for a second it felt like cardiac arrest. I opened the envelope and pulled out the sheaf of papers within. Yep, just what I'd figured. These were the papers from Troy requiring my signature to end his rights with our child. As if he'd never existed.

My fingers closed around the pages so tightly that my knuckles turned white and then pink. Even though this was what I wanted, pain still churned inside of me, because no matter how hard I tried, I couldn't understand how anyone—even someone as jerky as Troy—could ignore his child coming into the world.

Instinctively, I rubbed my belly with my other hand. "We'll be okay, kiddo. I promise."

She moved then, in a mixture of tiny kicks and butterfly wings, as if in agreement with my words. Silly to think that way, but it still put a smile on my face. "Yeah," I said with much more confidence, "One way or another, we'll be fine."

After I read the papers clear through, I made a copy of them and gave the originals already bearing Troy's signature to Ethan to pass to his attorney. Soon, at least one area of my life would be finalized. Not exactly something to celebrate, but hey, any progress was better than none.

And tonight, Ethan and I were meeting with Beatrice. Maybe, if I were really lucky, by the end of the evening I'd have a few more answers.

Chapter Fourteen

Beatrice Bellamy looked nothing like her son. Or, rather, he looked nothing like her.

Where Troy stood barely taller than I am, Beatrice towered over me. Compared to Troy's dark hair and eyes, Beatrice seemed faded. From her gray-dusted light brown hair, to her pale brown eyes, even to the lackluster tone of her skin, everything about her was just a tad washed out. And if she was a witch, I sure as hell couldn't tell. It wasn't like she wore a pointy black hat or had warts on her nose—which, by the way, hadn't twitched even once so far.

I'd partially expected her to be the woman from my rocking chair drawing, but she wasn't. Probably this should have relieved me, and I guess in a way it did. But I still didn't know who the mystery woman was, and I remained just as clueless as to what that specific drawing meant.

Beatrice ushered Ethan and me into her home. I scrunched up my nose at the odd mixture of lemon, coffee, and tuna scents that wafted in the air. Three meowing cats trailed along with us. Cats were said to be familiars for witches, so was their presence a sign of witchcraft or merely a lonely woman? Or just a cat lover?

Ethan's hand stayed firmly on my waist as we walked, his touch centering me. Even though I could have met Beatrice on my own, I appreciated that he'd wanted to come. And somehow, his being there with me seemed natural.

We stopped in a small room off the front hallway. The two back walls were lined with shelves, and books, stacked two deep, were crammed into them. She'd placed two small pink and beige chairs in the center of the room, with an octagon-shaped table between. Across from them rested a white and pink flowered love seat held up by wooden curlicue legs. A couple of embroidered throw pillows perched atop the cushions.

I chose the love seat. One cat immediately jumped into my lap, purring and rubbing its calico head against my hand. I scratched behind her ears, which brought forth even louder purring. Ethan sat on my left side, slinging his arm over my shoulders. A nervous tingle dotted my skin.

I reminded myself what my objectives were. Not only did I need to judge what sort of person Troy's mother was, but there was that whole magic thing to contend with. Was she or wasn't she?

Beatrice smiled, her round cheeks puffing out, the skin around her eyes crinkling into myriad little lines. "She must like you; she normally runs and hides when guests are here."

I didn't want to chitchat, so I forged ahead. "Missy said you want to be a part of the baby's life. I'm slightly uncomfortable with that idea. What with the way things are with Troy."

The woman seated herself, lacing her fingers together on her lap. "I understand that," she said, "but I'm not my son, and I haven't done anything wrong to you—or to the child, have I?"

"Well, no, but . . ." I glanced at Ethan, and then back to Beatrice. "Look, I'm just going to put this out there and get it over with." One deep breath, and then, "Troy said you're a witch, and that you used to put horrible spells on him when he was younger so that he'd behave."

Ethan flinched next to me but stayed quiet. I kept my attention firmly on Beatrice. Her left eyebrow arched in either humor or interest, but she didn't appear surprised or annoyed by my blunt question. Rather, she seemed to appreciate my forthrightness. "Oh, he told you that, did he?"

I lifted my chin. "Yes, he did. Is it true?"

Ethan sucked in a breath. His arm tensed.

Beatrice continued to stare at me, but she didn't speak. The silence grew uncomfortable, awkward, and I was about to suggest we leave when she slowly shook her head. "You're an interesting one, Miss Alice Raymond. I'll give you that. But to answer your question: No, I'm not a witch. I never bespelled my son, though I did tell him that on occasion—to keep him in line. He was a difficult boy to raise."

"So you don't have any magic? None at all?" The question flew from my mouth before I could edit it.

Tilting her head, her amber eyes deepened a shade. "I didn't say that. I'm not a witch. What I am is a woman with a minute amount of power. My mother had more, my grandmother even more, but it's become diluted over the years. It's nothing to be afraid of. I can't do anything to you, Alice . . . if that's what you're worried about."

"What kind of power?" I asked. She remained quiet, which frustrated me. "What can you do?"

Ethan shifted, leaning over slightly so I could see his face. "Alice, are you sure you want to have this particular discussion right now?" he asked softly. "Maybe it would be best to start off with normal . . . er, easier . . . topics, until you get to know each other a little. Like the weather, or your favorite television programs? Or even work?"

His strain came through loud and clear. Maybe bringing him with me had been a bad idea. My reasons had seemed sound at the time; I'd figured I could gauge what his reaction would be if I were to tell him about my family, about my own powers. But it was too late now to second-guess myself.

"I know this is awkward," I said to him. "I'm sorry, but Troy said things I need answers to. It's okay if you want to wait in the car, but I'd like to finish this conversation."

Doubt and something else—worry?—appeared in his eyes. He shook his head and said, "Why am I attracted to women like you? There are perfectly normal women all around, but I seem to be hooked on the unusual."

If he hadn't said the words lightly, and with a grin, I would have been concerned. Really, really concerned. But because he had, I smiled back. "I guess because you're smarter than the average bear," I teased.

Another flash of confusion. "What?"

I laughed. "It's a Yogi Bear thing. Never mind."

Beatrice cleared her throat. "Would you like my answer now, or should I wait for the young man to leave?"

Turning toward her, I gestured for her to continue. My skin itched with nerves. Whoever, whatever this woman was, her blood ran in my child's veins as surely as mine did. So hell yes, I wanted her to answer my question.

"It's not so much a 'power' as it is a very strong sense of intuition. Of knowing what a person is within seconds of meeting them. Of waking up in the morning and knowing I should stay home that day and receive an important phone call when I'd normally have been out of the house. Of driving to my weekly book club and knowing I should take a different route—and then finding out there was an accident along a road I would have been on." She shrugged, and a glint of humor skipped into her eyes. "It's come in handy over the years, but I can't control it. I can't force things to happen or not happen."

"So you make choices based on feelings? How often have you been wrong?" Ethan interjected.

"Oh, it's not foolproof, but I'm right far more often than I'm wrong."

"Sure, but how many of your choices are more than a

50 percent shot one way or the other? Maybe you're just a really good guesser." Ethan's arm left my shoulders. "Please don't take offense at my doubt. I've just found the simplest explanation is often the most accurate."

Beatrice's eyes flickered from me to Ethan. Her chin lowered in a nod. "Perhaps you're correct. It could very well be that I am nothing more than a really good guesser."

"I wouldn't call you a good guesser if most of your guesses were incorrect," Ethan prompted. His voice held humor, but also a great deal of skepticism.

Beatrice sighed. "They're not. And it's more than that. I know things about you and Alice already. Nobody has told me these things, but I know them as fact."

"Please, amaze us with your knowledge." I was more than a little surprised to hear censure in Ethan's voice. It wasn't strong, but it was there, threaded beneath the calm.

"Are you sure?"

"Absolutely. Hit me with your best shot."

"Remember that you asked. You're a good man with a good heart, but you've been hurt in the past by a woman you cared a great deal for. This woman hurt you so much that . . . elements you were raised to believe in, you've now set aside as rubbish."

A cynical laugh. "How many men have reached my age without being hurt by a woman at least once?"

"Again, you speak the truth. But in your case, it was more than a simple breakup or a romance gone bad." Beatrice's eyes narrowed. "I'm not a fortune-teller, but whatever happened with this woman altered your relationship with two other women tied closely to you. Your mother and grandmother, perhaps?"

A wave of silence crashed through the room, so fast, so heavy, my head pounded. I began to wonder what, exactly, had happened with the woman Ethan had proposed to. Was this the woman Beatrice spoke of? I wanted to ask. The words gathered in my mouth but I gulped them away.

"It seems you are, indeed, a very good guesser," Ethan acknowledged, his tone still calm, still doubtful, but without the censure.

"Thank you for playing," Beatrice said, a tad smugly. I didn't hold it against her, though, because let's face it, she hadn't initiated any portion of this conversation. I had, and then Ethan had pushed it along.

Ethan seemed to feel the same, because he chuckled.

I grabbed the reins of the conversation to bring everything back into focus. "So, that's it? Your power is completely passive?"

"Passive is a good word for it. I can't make anything happen; it just exists. Like any other sense we're born with. But you know as much about that as I do, don't you?"

I hurried the conversation on, giving a barely perceptible shake of my head. "How far will you take this visitation thing?"

"If you're asking if I'll go to court over it, the answer is no. A mother has the right to make her own choices about her child. I won't interfere with that, but I do hope you'll give it—*me*—a chance. I'd like to know your daughter in whatever way you're comfortable with." Emotion brightened her eyes, added color to her cheeks, and she no longer appeared faded.

Before talking with Beatrice, I'd been sure my answer would be a simple but unequivocal no. Now I didn't know what I thought. She seemed harmless, and my gut told me she wouldn't push, wouldn't try to force her way into my life or my daughter's. "I'll think about it," I admitted. "Maybe we can get together again, get to know each other better over the next few months. But I can't say yes or no right now."

"That's more than I'd hoped for," she replied. "I'm a good grandmother, Alice. Much better than I was a mother."

Suddenly, my mind flipped back and realized what she'd said. I hadn't told Beatrice I was having a girl. "Were you guessing just now? When you said 'daughter'?"

She winked at me. "What do you think?"

Clearing my throat, I said, "I think this has been a lot for a first meeting. We should get going."

Strangely, most of my worries surrounding Beatrice had evaporated. I still needed to know more, but that would come in time. And while she was a little odd, the same could be said for my own grandmother—heck, for most of my family—so that was something else I didn't hold against her. Really, the only black mark I saw was that she was Troy's mother. I shivered. It was a big black mark.

Baby steps, I reminded myself.

"That wasn't nearly as horrible as I thought it might be," I said to Ethan once we were back in his car.

He turned to me. "Are you thinking you're going to let her know the baby?"

"Maybe. I don't know yet. I'll spend more time with her before making a final decision, but she seemed sincere."

"She definitely seemed sincere."

"I hear a 'but' there."

"No 'but.' She was nice enough, up front about her wishes, wasn't wishy-washy about her beliefs. Even if I don't agree with some of what she said, those are good qualities." He put the car into gear and headed down the street.

"Um. About that. What she said to you? Was she right?"

Before he could answer, my cell phone buzzed. I tossed him an apologetic look and clicked the button. "Hello?"

"Alice? This is Grant. Grant Harris? Shelby's husband?"

"I know who you are, Grant. What's up?"

"We had the babies! Shelby's too out of it to talk right now, but she wanted me to call. Twin girls. They're early, but are doing well."

"Oh! Wow! That is amazing! Congratulations!"

Grant filled me in on their weights, names, and when I could visit. I asked him to pass my congrats on to Shelby, and then I clicked off, telling Ethan, "Grant and Shelby had their babies tonight. Twin girls. Isn't that cool?"

All of a sudden I thought of Miranda's twin daughters. I remembered what she'd said to me that night, something I hadn't focused on before. She hadn't said to *find* her other daughter's family; she'd used the word *recognize*. So . . . Wow. Did that mean I already knew them? Shelby and twin girls? Miranda and twin girls? Was it really that simple? Could Shelby be my family?

"You asked me a question," Ethan said, his voice pushing into my musings. "Yes, Beatrice was right about me being hurt, and about the fallout affecting my relationship with my mother and grandmother."

I switched gears, focusing on him. My eyes took in his tense jaw, the way he gripped the steering wheel. "Do you want to talk about it?"

"There's not much to say. I fell in love and proposed. She said yes; we began to plan our wedding. Two weeks before the event we went to a local fair, and one of the things we did that day was have our fortunes read. The fortune-teller said we were not meant for each other, and that if we married we would regret it."

I was pretty sure I knew what had happened, and it explained so much about Ethan. "Go on."

He slid the car to a stop at a red light. "Initially we both laughed over it. A week later, she ended our engagement and canceled the wedding. I actually thought she was joking at first." He choked out a laugh. "But she wasn't. She chose to trust in the mumblings of a so-called seer rather than the feelings we had for each other."

My heart climbed into my throat and I fought to swallow it back down. "That bites."

"There's more," he admitted. "I'm a logical guy. I like to see how someone gets from point A to point B, and so on. My ex felt that my logic was a fault. Even at the end, while she explained why she must leave me, I remained calm. Reasonable. She wanted me to show more emotion, to be passionate. She called me a cold fish." He cleared this throat. "I've wondered for years if she was right."

"No! She wasn't. I like that you're calm and logical. A lot; actually." Putting my hand on his knee, I squeezed. "Trust me, Ethan. I've never once thought of you as cold. But I'm so sorry you had to go through that."

"It's long in the past. But when Beatrice started talking about her power . . ." He shrugged. "I guess I still have an Achilles' heel about certain things."

"I get that." His revelation swirled inside me, mucking everything up. I almost confided in him then. I could taste the words on my tongue; they were that close to coming out. But I gulped them away, tried to even my breathing, the beat of my heart. How could I continue with Ethan, knowing that the fate of our relationship could very well end just like his previous one, because of a prophecy? "I'm sorry," I said again.

He brought his hand down to mine and clasped it. "You've done nothing wrong. You wouldn't leave a man you loved over something that flimsy. I'm sure of that."

I turned to stare out the window, saying the only thing that came to mind. "What happened with your mother and grandmother?"

"Nothing horrible. I was hurt when they thought my fiancée had made the correct decision. They . . . well, they've always had strong beliefs in almost all areas of the supernatural. From fairies to superstitions to magic." His hand tightened around mine. "I guess my experience has made me more cynical than ever, and I don't handle it all that well. To the chagrin of my female relatives. But we're still close. There's just this gray area between us now that wasn't there before."

"Oh . . . well, it's understandable that you'd feel that way." And it was. But as I thought about my family tree, my daughter and her legacy, and the power I held, it didn't exactly give me hope as far as Ethan went.

The knowledge that I should end this now came at me, but I couldn't. Not when everything inside of me, the very air around me, hummed in Ethan's presence. But yeah, I'd been stupid this whole time. Because I'd assumed that if Ethan were the right guy, my soul mate, that us getting together would be a fait accompli. But now? Not so much. Not by a long shot.

The same thoughts and worries plagued me as the week went on. By the time Friday rolled around, my emotions were one big jumbled mess. Okay, that wasn't completely true. My feelings for Ethan hadn't decreased. If anything, they continued to grow whenever we were around each other. But the rest of my emotions? They were flying out of control.

Tonight I'd decided to push myself to draw a picture of Ethan's future, and to hope it was *my* image that appeared next to his. If that fizzled, I'd have to come up with something else. Whether that meant dumping something over his head, ripping his freaking shirt off, or some other, as of yet undefined, plan of action, I hadn't decided.

Juggling my mail in one hand and my keys in the other, I heard my phone ringing as I unlocked my front door. I rushed in, dropping the mail on the table as I zipped by, and grabbed the phone the second it stopped ringing. Awesome. I clicked to check the caller ID, and was surprised to see the number of the art gallery where I used to work. Hmm. Maybe they'd sold one of the few paintings I'd left there.

I dialed the number, assuming that was the case. When my previous boss answered, I said, "Hey, Maura. It's Alice. You called?"

"Yes! I'm glad you called back so fast. I have a proposition for you." She went on to offer me a job at the gallery as its manager. Full-time, with benefits, at a decent wage.

"Are you serious? You've always managed everything; why the change?"

"I'll still be in and out, but with my husband retiring in a few months, I'd like to make some changes. What do you think? You don't have to decide today."

"I . . . Well, I don't know. When would you want me to start?"

"If you want the job, Alice, I'll keep it open until you're ready. So if you want to stay where you are until after the baby's born, that's fine. You can begin here after maternity leave." She paused for a second. "Oh! And a day care opened up a few doors down, so you'd be close to the baby. We might even be able to work it so you could have the baby here a few days a week."

Talk about a hard offer to turn down!

"Don't get me wrong," I said, "because it sounds perfect—but why me?"

"You already know how the place runs. You're dependable. And it saves me from looking for anyone else. I just wish I'd thought of it before you officially left. Are you interested enough to give it some thought and get back to me? Say, within a week or two?"

I hesitated. I'd be crazy not to consider it. "That sounds good. I'll talk to you soon." With hindsight, I added, "Thanks for thinking of me."

We hung up and I gave the offer more thought as I changed out of my work clothes. Even though I'd begun to find my groove at Enchanted Expressions, it still felt like just a job. Working at the gallery had always been fun, exciting, and had spurred my creativity. I hadn't painted anything—not even one measly stroke—in months. That, combined with the other, more practical reasons, should have made the decision easy. But it wasn't. Because by leaving Enchanted Expressions, I'd give up the ability to see Ethan every single day.

Pushing my thoughts in another direction, I meandered into my kitchen to start dinner. I'd left work early for my five-month doctor's appointment, and then had stopped to see Shelby and the babies at the hospital. Everyone was doing well, and even though the babies looked incredibly tiny, they'd be going home in the next day or two.

When I finished eating, the quiet started to get to me. I put on some music, and then took to the couch with my sketchpad. If I were really going to find some answers, like it or not, I needed to give this a go.

I opened the pad to a clean page and stared at it. And then I stared at it some more. Anxiety made my hand shake. I tried to steady it. I knew I needed to do this, but somehow I couldn't seem to make myself say or even think the Ethan wish. Which was stupid. I almost phoned Chloe to see if she'd come over for moral support, but just as quickly changed my mind. She had a date that night. With Kyle.

Again, my eyes found the page. "You can do this," I whispered. Reminding myself it was better to know, I forced my mouth to move. "I wish to draw a picture of Ethan and the woman he marries."

Nothing happened, so I said my wish again, putting more conviction into my voice. My baby kicked, but other than that, still nothing. Did my fears interfere with the magic? Or did this mean Ethan wasn't going to get married, like I'd thought about Kyle? Or was Chloe right and I couldn't directly draw my own future, which would then mean Ethan's future was with me? Ugh. The same could then be said for Kyle, couldn't it?

Sudden knocking at my door dragged my attention off the pad, off my worries. Stumbling a little, I opened the door to see Ethan standing on the other side, sexy grin and all. And in that second, everything in my world seemed right again.

"Hey! Come on in," I said.

He angled inside, one arm behind his back. "I hope you don't mind the unexpected visit. I was out, and you were on my mind, and then I saw these"—he brought his arm around to show me the bouquet of multicolored roses he held—"and I thought of you."

"Oh. Wow." Tears gathered in my eyes. I tipped my head so he wouldn't see. When was the last time a man had given me flowers? So long, I didn't even remember. "They're beautiful. I love them. I . . . um . . . should get them in some water."

He followed me to the kitchen. I found a vase, added water and then arranged the roses, all with my back to Ethan. Dipping my nose down, I breathed in the scent. Prickles whisked along my skin, because that scent? It reminded me of Miranda. And of course that brought everything to the surface.

"Thank you." I cringed when my voice cracked.

"Are you okay? Did I come at a bad time?" In a flash he stood behind me, his hands on my waist. His lips touched the top of my head. "Talk to me."

"There's nothing to say."

"Did something happen after you left work today?" His body tensed, tightened. "Honey? Did you get bad news at the doctor's?"

"No! Not that. Everything's fine there. I'll be having an ultrasound soon, even." He moved his arms so they encircled my waist, and pulled me against him.

"Then what? Do the roses upset you?" he asked

lightly. "Would another type of flower have been a better choice?"

"The roses are perfect." But then, because I didn't know how to tell him what was really bothering me, I told him about the job offer.

"Ah. And you're considering it?"

"It's a better fit for me, so yes. But . . . well . . . I hate the idea of not being around you."

A low chuckle tumbled out; the sound of it wrapped around me. "You can't get rid of me that easily. If this job is what you want, you should take it. But you'll still see me, Alice. At least, until you tell me to go away."

He loosened his grip so I could turn around. Lifting my chin, I looked into his eyes, and in a whoosh, the crazy stuff inside steadied. How could this man have such an effect on me if he *wasn't* my soul mate?

"I don't want to tell you to go away," I murmured.

"Then don't."

I reached my hands behind his head and tugged it down. Closing my eyes, I waited for our lips to touch. When they did, the kiss was hesitant, soft. I moaned and prodded his mouth open with my tongue. His hands slipped underneath my shirt, stroking my back, his touch searing into me, starting a heady stream of desire.

Our kiss deepened, and all I wanted was for it to continue, so I pushed myself closer to him, opened my mouth wider, and let myself just experience the moment. It was as if every sense came alive as we tasted, touched, consumed each other, and never before had I craved a man like I craved Ethan. I wanted more. So. Much. More.

He seemed to know my thoughts, my feelings, because he groaned. His lips left mine, trailing kisses from my mouth, to my cheek, and then to my ear, sending another wash of yearning cascading into me, through me. "You're entirely too enticing, Alice," he said. His voice was low, quiet, but with an edge of longing hanging on each word.

He wanted me as much as I wanted him: the realization nearly undid me. Separating myself from his embrace, I wiped my swollen lips and said, "What I feel for you . . . it goes beyond reason. I don't know how to quantify it."

Stroking the plane of my cheek with one finger, with eyes as dark as a stormy night, he looked at me, searching. "I believe I'm falling in love with you, and like you said not that long ago, it startles me. It *surprises* me. I never expected to feel this way again."

"Ethan . . . what we have is so strong, I'm still reeling from it. How can it be real? How can *this* be something I can believe in?" The question was unfair. What I really wanted to hear wasn't something he'd be able to say, because he didn't have all the facts. But my breath still caught as I waited.

"It's a little scary, isn't it? More so for you than for me, I imagine. All I know is I wake up each morning with you in my head, and you're still there when I go to sleep. I feel as if I already know you, that I have known you forever." He paused, as if struggling to find the correct words to say exactly what he wanted to say. "But even so, every facet of your personality intrigues me. You are a woman I can see spending my life with."

I nodded, unable to speak. The emotions in his eyes, in his voice, filled me with happiness . . . but also with confusion and worry. Because guess what? I felt the same way.

"Oh, Ethan," I murmured. I was this close to pulling him into the living room, to showing him the drawing, to explaining every last detail to him, when he dragged me into his arms again.

"I see your worry, Alice. Trust me when I say you can believe in me. I'll never lie to you, like Troy did. I'll wait for as long as you need to see that's the truth."

Oh, God. He thought my apprehension was over Troy. Well, duh, what else would he think? "I do believe in you."

"Good. That's all I want. Remember what I said: we don't have to hurry or rush into anything. But I will always be honest with you about how I feel." He kissed me again, and for a few minutes my fears abated. When we disengaged, he smiled and once again stroked my cheek. "As much as I don't want to, I should go. We have all day tomorrow, and it looks as if the weather is going to be perfect for my plans." I nodded again, and saw him to the door. One more kiss, and I was alone.

How could I be happy, hopeful, and filled with despair all at once? I shuddered. A weight sat there, on my shoulders, inside of me, as I brushed my teeth and washed my face. And when I crawled into bed, I curled one of my pillows up and held it close. Somehow I began drifting off. Right before I completely dropped into sleep, I murmured into my pillow, "I need to know what will happen if I ignore this warning, if I end up without my soul mate or choose a man that isn't. I wish . . . I wish I could see."

The tide of sleep swept me away to a place I didn't recognize. There were no walls, no air, no ground, no nothing, just a vast, empty space. I realized I was dreaming but couldn't shake myself out of it. Like before, yet different, I suddenly saw Miranda cradling her belly, thinking about her daughters—and then *their* daughters. The flash of faces began again, one after another, in lightning speed. Some of the people I recognized, some I didn't. They sped by so fast, I couldn't keep up.

When the final face staring at me was my daughter, the dream—vision—changed. Weirdly, what appeared before me, around me, was like a split screen, and I knew without understanding how one side of the screen was my daughter growing up in the best scenario: the one where I found my soul mate. The other side was the worst, where either he was never found or I ignored the warning. I didn't know which, but it didn't matter. What mattered was that

I was finally going to understand what Miranda's prophecy meant, and how it affected me and my child.

On the good side, my daughter grew up confident and sure about who she was, what her power was; and while I couldn't see actual details of her life, I felt her emotions, like I'd felt Miranda's. Oh, she was glorious, and the pride and love inside of me grew so large, so strong, that it almost made the other side of the screen disappear into nothingness.

But I had to know, so I forced myself to watch, to feel. And while the love for my daughter remained just as strong, fear for her sank in, drowning out the pride, because here her emotions were all about what she could do with her power, gaining more, going for whatever she wanted without thought or concern for those around her. Power-hungry. Addicted to magic. Seeking. This version of my daughter was always searching for something she couldn't find, believing she'd find it within her magic. Her desperation grew as she sought, suffocating those around her, creating chaos and havoc in her relentless search. I knew with every bone in my body that this outcome would ruin everyone with whom she came into contact: me, my family, my friends, and yes, even the Wrong Man. And eventually, my beloved daughter would self-destruct.

My heart breaking, agony tearing through me, eating at me, I focused on the other side again, where I could feel her happiness, her confidence, her belief in herself and in using her magic for good. I considered again the choices before me, and—

I woke with a start, sweat pouring down my face and back. Jumping from bed, I ran to the restroom and turned the cold water on full blast, splashing my cheeks with it. My life, my daughter's life, the lives of those I loved were in my hands. I splayed my fingers in the pouring water, watching the liquid run through.

Slowly, I lifted my chin and stared at my reflection in the mirror. Not only would my daughter destroy herself, she'd destroy Ethan if he wasn't my soul mate. I remembered Miranda's words, and her message about pure love and the guidance of the right man merged with what I'd just seen. Comprehension slid in, just like the water rippling over my hands. To my way of thinking, that meant my daughter needed something that only my soul mate and I *together* could give. Balance, maybe. Or it could be as simple as her being raised with that type of love around her from her very first breath.

I weighed this new knowledge, thought about it, and then considered my feelings for Ethan. As much as I believed he was, indeed, my soul mate, this changed everything. Drastically. If at any time it became obvious he wasn't the man in my drawing, I'd have to move on, I'd have to keep searching. Because not only would I do anything—everything—to protect my daughter from the destructive future I'd just seen . . . well, no way would I allow my family, my friends and even Ethan to be affected by the wrong choice.

I curled my hands around the still-pouring water, its coldness seeping into my skin, into my heart. For the very first time, I truly understood how high the stakes were.

"I'll protect you," I whispered, my wet hands going to my stomach. "I promise. I'll do what's right for you, no matter what."

Even if my own heart broke in the process.

Chapter Fifteen

The sun dappled the water, creating glistening sparkles of light almost as far as the eye could see. "This is amazing. I didn't know you sailed," I said to Ethan. He'd shown up that morning with a huge picnic basket in tow. I'd assumed we were heading out for a hike, but when he asked me if I had a problem with motion sickness, I knew I was wrong.

Luckily, I didn't. And with my morning sickness a thing of the past, so far everything had been . . . well, smooth sailing.

"It's a passion of mine. I've had this boat for about two years." We'd dropped anchor a few minutes earlier, and now we were both seated on deck. It wasn't a large space, but certainly big enough for the two of us. "I thought it would be nice to get away from everything and relax. So we could really talk."

"I love that." I took in the sights around me—the water, other boats dotting the horizon, even a few water-skiers—and sighed. "I love *this*. Thank you for bringing me here."

"You're very welcome." He dug out a bottle of sunscreen and offered it to me. "I don't want you to burn. The sun is stronger than it seems, and you're fairly pale."

Accepting it, I squeezed out a glob and began rubbing it into my legs, and then my arms, aware that his gaze stayed planted on me the entire time. We both wore khaki shorts and white T-shirts, a fact Ethan had found humorous, and I found . . . well, hopeful. Dumb, huh?

Like the accidental choice of similar clothes meant anything other than a weird coincidence.

When I finished, I tossed the bottle back to him. He caught it easily, and coated his own skin with a layer of the coconut-scented lotion. And then we just sat in silence for I don't know how long, and it was exactly what I needed after the previous night.

The quiet wasn't uncomfortable; it didn't make me feel like I needed to fill it with words or actions, so I didn't. I leaned back in my chair and stretched my legs as much as I could, the sun warm on my skin, the breeze light on my face, enjoying the gentle sway of the boat, and I did exactly what Ethan had suggested: relaxed. I didn't allow myself to dwell on my dream, because at that moment nothing had changed as far as Ethan went. And even though I knew what I had to do, and I planned on doing it, today was a gift.

After a while, I shielded my eyes with my hand and regarded the man sitting across from me. His eyes were closed, his legs stretched in front of him, his arms cradled behind his head. I sort of wanted to ease myself into his lap, caress his jawline, stroke his arms, and then drag him into the cabin and yank every bit of clothing off of him.

Okay, not sort of. That was exactly what I wanted to do.

I restrained myself, because while I'd have loved every freaking minute of it, I needed to gather some information. I'd thought long and hard about it all morning while getting ready. I'd continued to think about it on the car ride over, and even as I had watched him maneuver the sailboat to our present position. Obviously logic didn't have an iota to do with how I felt about him, because there was no logic; things were just what they were. And while I still wanted to see his shoulder, there were other avenues open to me until I did. For one, I could definitely learn more about the man, and maybe that would erase some of my questions.

Of course, it could open up other questions. But it was worth the chance. I couldn't wait forever.

The first thing was determining how closed off he was to the idea of magic. "Ethan?"

"Hmm?" His eyes remained shut.

"Why did you name your company Enchanted Expressions? What with your feelings about the supernatural and all?"

One eye opened and then the other. "That's an interesting question. Part of it was business-minded. People come to us and they want us to create magic for them, for their companies. I felt the name was appropriate, given that consideration."

"There's more, though?"

"As I said before, I grew up in my grandparents' house. My grandmother was a major influence on me, and she lives her life based much on old-world traditions, many of which are grounded in the supernatural." He blinked, and his smile broadened. "She's an incredible woman. I would have to say that part of the reason Enchanted Expressions has its name is because of her. In a way, it's meant to honor her and her beliefs."

"Even if you don't believe yourself?"

"I'm not a complete nonbeliever, Alice. It's a little hard to explain. Let's leave it that I'm open-minded, but prefer to make choices based on things I know and see rather than things that can't be proven. Does that make sense?"

"It does." It helped me feel somewhat better too. I mean, as long as he was open-minded, there was a chance he'd accept the power that existed in my family. "I think it's really great you love your grandmother so much."

"It's no more than the love I see between you and Verda. There's another woman who definitely has some out-there beliefs."

I laughed. "She's always been that way. I grew up hear-

ing about magic and wishes and now I understand why."
Oops. Big oops, because I hadn't meant to say that.

He'd caught on too. "What do you mean?"

I tried to make light of my words. "Just family stuff.
We have a long and varied history that I've only recently
learned about." Yay! Points to me for not lying.

"I think most families, if they search back far enough,
will find something." Curiosity gleamed for just a second
in his eyes, and I thought he was going to ask me more
about it, but he didn't. Instead, he said, "Anything else
you want to know? I feel further questions emanating
from you. I told you last night I'd always be honest, so
don't hesitate."

As much as I worried about the magic, my next question concerned me even more. I exhaled and sat up
straight. "Well. Just one more, actually, and it's probably
something I should have asked before now."

He must have noticed the seriousness in my voice, because he leaned toward me. "Okay. I'm listening."

"I'm having a baby," I blurted.

Humor darted over his features. "I know that, Alice."

"Yeah. Right. Of course you do. But if . . . well, if we
were to become even more serious, you'd have a certain
role in this child's life. I guess I need to know if you've
thought about that at all. Because that's important to me."

"Of course I have. I've given it considerable thought,
actually."

"And?" Everything inside of me tensed while I awaited
his response.

"I wouldn't be here with you now if I had any worries
on that front. I've felt this magnetic pull toward you since
the moment we met, and it hasn't eased." He paused,
watching me carefully, shoulders tensed.

"It's the same for me," I said, answering the question
in his eyes.

His body relaxed. "I already consider us serious, and I

have hopes for our future—and that future includes your child." He gave a slight grin. "And maybe others."

"Oh. Wow. Okay, then." A sense of surety floated in. I could see Ethan in my future, in my daughter's future, and not only did it feel right, I'd have bet money at that second that it *was* right. A little more of the fear from the previous evening slipped away.

"Feel better?"

"Yes. I mean, from a practical standpoint." Heat rushed through me. I didn't care. "Today makes me . . . happy."

"That makes two of us." His fingers brushed my knees and another blast of warmth saturated me. "Ready for lunch?"

At that point, talking was so not going to happen, so I nodded.

"Wait there. I'll call you when it's ready." He disappeared into the cabin.

"I can help," I called from behind him.

He popped his head back out and tossed me his sexy-as-sin grin. "Let me do this. I want to take care of you today."

Take care of me? Wow again. "Okay . . . I'll just sit here."

While I waited, I rehashed our entire conversation in my head, and the surety I'd felt earlier strengthened. Yes, I still needed to take the proper steps, to find the facts that would line up with my feelings, but really, I didn't think that was going to be a problem. At least, I hoped it wouldn't. Really, really hoped.

Less than twenty minutes later, Ethan returned and held out his hand. I gripped it and, with a gentle tug, he pulled me to my feet, his touch both electrifying and calming. We took the few steps down to the cabin in single file, with him leading the way. Curious, I stopped at the bottom and looked around.

The room was small but impeccably kept, which didn't surprise me. A little table sat on one side, surrounded by booth-type seats. The other wall held a sink, minimal counter space, and a tiny refrigerator. A narrow door led to the restroom, or as Ethan called it, the head. All in all, nice but nothing spectacular.

What staggered me was the attention he'd put into our lunch, into the scene he'd created. He'd found battery-operated candles somewhere, and two of them were on the table, softly glowing. Soft music from an MP3 player filled the air, and there were two champagne glasses with a bubbly, amber liquid in them. "Ginger ale?" I asked, nodding toward them.

"Yes. Someday, it will be champagne. After the baby."

One by one, he lifted the covers off of the food. There was a cold chicken pasta dish, fresh fruit, and some dinner rolls. There was also a container of chocolate chip cookies in a very recognizable box.

"You've met my sister?" I asked.

"I stopped by A Taste of Magic yesterday and quizzed her on your favorite foods. I wanted everything to be just right."

Another type of glow eased in. With a shot of surprise, I realized I hadn't been quite this content in a very long time. "It *is* right, Ethan. Exactly right."

"I'm glad." He picked up his ginger ale filled champagne glass. "To the most curious, intriguing, and breathtaking woman I've ever met. I hope we share many meals together."

Because I so seconded that, I lifted my glass and clinked his. "I couldn't have planned a better day. You . . . well, you continue to startle me."

I spoke too soon, because what he did next startled me even more. After we slid into our seats, he fed me my first bite of pasta, and then leaned over and kissed me. No man, ever, unless it was my father when I was a child, had ever fed me a bite of anything. And as weird as it might sound, not only did that one little action completely melt my heart, but it so turned me on. Who knew feeding someone could do that? Not me, that was for sure.

We ate our lunch and then returned to the deck. The rest of the day passed in a blur of laughter, more kissing, and by the time my head hit the pillow that night, I knew I was a goner.

I'd fallen in love with Ethan Gallagher.

Grandma Verda stared at me stubbornly, her frail shoulders set in a rigid line. "You *have* to do this. I hope you're right and Ethan's the one, but with what you experienced the other night, you can't chance it, Alice."

I'd planned on telling her and my sister about Miranda having twins, but it seemed that conversation wasn't going to happen today. I scrunched my hands into fists and returned her stare. "I'm not chancing anything, Grandma. But I'm not setting up any dates with these"—my gaze flipped over the files stacked on my dining room table—"models yet, either."

"What if you're wrong about Ethan? You're willing to risk everything on a hunch?" my grandmother demanded.

"The way I feel isn't a hunch." But still, her words twisted in my stomach, because no, I wouldn't risk *every*-thing.

Elizabeth cleared her throat. "There is a compromise." That is my sister, always the peacemaker. And yeah, I so appreciated that.

"Compromises are good," I said. "I can do a compromise."

"You don't have to actually set the dates up yet, but Grandma's right that you should be prepared . . . um . . . ready with a new plan in case everything with Ethan falls apart." She spoke tentatively, as if afraid of my reaction.

Sighing, I nodded. "I agree with that. I just don't think I'll need it."

Her eyes lit up. "Good! I like Ethan. I thought it was really sweet, his coming by the bakery, and I think the very fact that you're this confident is a terrific sign. But just in case, why don't we go through these"—she gestured to the files—"and look for scars that are similar to your drawing? That way, they're ready to go if you need them. You can set up the dates without any hassle then."

"That works. As long as you promise you won't hesitate if anything changes with Ethan," said Grandma Verda. "I want you and my great-granddaughter to be safe and happy."

"We're on the same side. I want the same things, and I already made that promise to myself." And I'd stick to it. But somehow, even considering an alternative plan felt wrong. Oh. So. Wrong. It was as if I were contemplating cheating—which was ridiculous, given how little Ethan and I had done together, but it still sat inside of me, churning away.

With a heavy swallow, I plopped down in one of my dining room chairs. "Separate them, but make four stacks because Chloe will be here soon."

Grandma nodded and gathered the files together in front of her. She'd just finished creating four even stacks when Chloe arrived. We filled her in, and she scooted into another seat at the end of the table. "So, I'm looking for photos that match the drawing, correct? Nothing else?"

"I think we each need to make three stacks," Elizabeth said. "One for those that are really close in all ways: medium to dark shade of hair, size, and the mark. One for those where the mark is close but maybe other things aren't, yet not enough to be completely ruled out. And then one for those that aren't similar in the slightest."

Before we started, I had scanned the beach drawing into my computer and then printed out four copies, so we'd each have one. After I passed them out, we got to it. I counted my stack, and came up with fifteen files. So that meant, altogether, we probably had around sixty possible soul mates sitting on my dining room table. That scared the hell out of me, because I couldn't see how that many men could be a close enough match to have warranted my grandmother putting them in a file.

But as I began going through them, my fears calmed. Grandma Verda had, indeed, created a large pool of men . . . and very few of them were even close. Thank God for that. Each file consisted of the paperwork the man had completed, along with several photos of his back and one of his face. By the time I finished sorting, I had two Really Close, three Not So Much But Maybe, and the rest were in the No Way in Hell category.

I shoved the piles away. "Okay, I'm done, but I only have two who are similar enough to even think about."

Chloe tipped her head up, smiled at me, and returned to the few files she had remaining. I watched her, thought about the picture I had of her in my bedroom, and so wanted to get it. Of course I didn't, because it wasn't the right time. I left it alone.

When all was said and done, there were only four men out of the sixty-plus I even had to be concerned with. One of them was Aaron, the auburn-haired man I'd met the day I'd walked in on Grandma. I didn't recognize the other three, and I didn't bother going through the Maybe stacks. If I had to later, they'd be there.

"Now, pass me all the Nos so I can deal with them." Grandma Verda winked. "Maybe there's a man for Chloe there."

A light pink blush tinged my friend's cheeks. "That's

not necessary, Verda. I'm sort of dating someone right now."

"That's okay, dear. You'll have these to look over later, if it doesn't work out."

"Um . . . Grandma? What are you talking about?" I glanced at Chloe again, and almost laughed at her expression. Hey, she wanted to be a part of a large family, and in *my* family Grandma Verda's manipulations were part of the package.

A twinkle sparkled in Grandma's blue eyes. "I went to a lot of trouble putting all of these together. It would be nice if someone could use them." She shrugged. "Besides, there's so much information about these men! You'll see their pictures, their medical histories, their résumés, and even how well they did on the IQ tests! What could be better?"

Good grief, the woman should open her own matchmaking service.

Surprisingly, Chloe didn't argue further. I didn't know if that was because she knew arguing with Grandma Verda was pointless, or if the idea intrigued her.

In minutes, Grandma was flipping through the files at breakneck pace, separating them into four distinct piles. Curiosity flared, and while I shouldn't have asked, I couldn't help myself. "Grandma? How are you separating those?"

She laid a hand on the pile farthest to her left. "This is the lemon stack. I wouldn't recommend dating these fellows based on what I see here."

Oh my God. It was her *fruit* thing.

She moved her hand to the next pile. "And these are the pears. Not horrible, but not all that good, either. Consider them just below average. But maybe with some work, they could move up the ranks a bit."

I bit my lip to keep from laughing.

On the third pile, she grinned. "These are the oranges.

They can go either way. They're usually above average to begin with, but you need to watch them carefully, because they can slip in the other direction. Elizabeth knows all about oranges. Marc was an orange when they married, but ended up being a lemon."

Elizabeth wrinkled her nose but stayed quiet.

Grandma Verda's smiled broadened, and the twinkle in her eyes brightened even more. "And these are the pomegranates. Well, I don't know for sure, so maybe it's better to say they have pomegranate possibilities. I'd have to spend more time with them to be absolutely sure."

"Pomegranate possibilities? I'm probably going to be really sorry for asking this, but how did this fruit thing get started? And how'd you decide that pomegranates were the top-shelf men? What about watermelons? Or Asian pears? Or even strawberries?" I pursed my lips, still fighting off laughter.

"Watermelons? Don't be ridiculous." She rubberbanded the Pomegranate pile and set it aside. "It's simple. Years ago, when I started dating again, after your grandfather died, I wanted a quick way to classify the men I met. Lemons were easy, if a tad cliché, so it started with that, and because lemons are fruit, I just took it one step further. Pomegranates are my favorite, so those are the best. The rest I just ranked accordingly."

My sister laughed. "That's it? That's all it is? So your pomegranate would be a pineapple for me, because those are my favorite fruit?"

"Well, no, dear. It's too late for that. The fruit ranking system is my idea and already in place, so you have to use the fruit I established. Otherwise it would just get too confusing." She snapped a rubber band around the orange pile. "Take these two stacks home with you, Chloe. Even if you don't need them, maybe a single girlfriend of yours will."

Chloe glanced at me but then shrugged. "Sure. Thanks for thinking of me."

Grandma Verda and Elizabeth departed shortly after, leaving Chloe and me alone. While we sat there and chatted, I went through the files Grandma had left for her. I wanted to see if the same man I'd drawn Chloe with was buried in there somewhere. Because with Grandma Verda? Well, I'd learned that sometimes there was much more she left unsaid than said.

But he wasn't. So in this case, it seemed what she'd said was actually what she meant. Refocusing on Chloe, I asked, "How are things going with Kyle?"

"Okay. We laugh a lot, and he's a great kisser, but it's not like I thought it would be. Not yet, anyway." Fleeting disappointment made her frown. "But I don't think he's changed all that much. Shelby says he's a commitment-phobe."

"What do you think?"

"Oh, he's not even close to being ready to settle down, but that doesn't mean he won't change for the right girl."

"Do you think he's the right guy for you? That's the more important question, because if he isn't, then it doesn't matter what he thinks."

"It's too soon to tell. I like him and we have fun together. That's enough for now, so don't worry. I'm not going to make the same mistakes I did last time, I promise." Her green eyes shone with interest. "Have you had a chance to do that drawing I asked you about? The one of me on my wedding day, or of the guy I'll end up with?"

My gaze darted downward. I hated lying to Chloe. "I did try. But it didn't work. I'm sorry. I'll try again soon, though."

Her unhappiness came through loud and clear. "I was so hoping you'd be able to do it. Nothing happened at all when you made the wish?"

"I'm sorry," I said again, not wanting to repeat my lie.

She sighed, and that made me feel worse. "Oh well, better luck next time, right? What about you and Ethan? Things are really going that great?"

A shiver of happiness slipped inside of me, briefly replacing my remorse. "Everything is amazing with him. I'm going to his place for dinner on Friday. I might even stay the night." Well, actually, I'd already decided, if the opportunity presented itself I was definitely staying.

"Ooh! That's wonderful. I have a good feeling about him."

"Me too."

We chatted for a while longer, and then I picked up the remaining files and dumped them into a brown grocery sack that I slid under my bed. You know, that whole *out of sight, out of mind* thing. Because what I couldn't see, maybe I wouldn't worry about.

After work the following Tuesday, I cruised over to Shelby and Grant's house. I had a present for the babies, and I also had something I wanted to show Shelby.

The night before, I'd drawn as many of the faces as I could remember from my visions, dreams or whatever, and I wanted to see if Shelby recognized any. I was surprised how easily they came back to me, and I hadn't even had to use magic to get it done. While Shelby identifying any of them might be a long shot, it was the only thing I could think of to see if she was the family *I* was supposed to recognize. It wasn't like I had a lot to go on, other than the twin daughters element, and I wasn't even sure if my thoughts about what Miranda said were right; but it was a start. Even better, it gave me something less heavy to focus on, at least for a little while.

When I got there, one of the girls was sound asleep in a bassinet in the living room. Shelby was tucked up on her couch, holding the other. "Who is who again? And how are you telling them apart?" I asked, taking a seat next to Shelby.

"This little peanut is Rebecca, and Jessica is snoozing away. And telling them apart is easy for me. I just know who is who." She grinned. "But Grant is worried we're going to mix them up, so we painted Rebecca's toenail with a little bit of pink polish, and Jessica's with red. And right now, Grant's ironing little patches with their names into their clothes."

"Good ideas! Gosh, she is so beautiful. How are you doing? Getting enough sleep?"

"Right now, but that's only because Grant is off for another week. When he goes back to work, it's going to be a little more difficult. We'll manage though."

I gazed at Rebecca, stroking the bottom of one bare foot with my finger. "She is just so . . . perfect. They're completely identical?"

"From what we can see right now, they are. Crazy, huh?"

"Yeah, but really cool."

"Do you want to hold her?"

"Oh. Um." Did I? "I'm a little nervous. What if I squeeze her too tight or something?"

Shelby laughed. "You'll be fine. Here." Gently, she passed the baby to me, and as soon as she was in my arms, everything inside of me turned into a big, mushy pile of goo.

"This is incredible! Everything is so tiny." I laid her down on my legs, so I could see her face. She scrunched her nose up and then turned her head to the side, moving her mouth. "She might be hungry."

"She's always hungry. But she just ate, so she's fine."

We talked a little about the benefits of nursing, and other things related to the care of newborn babies. I soaked it all in, knowing I'd be going through the same process myself not so far in the future. A moment of absolute calmness swept over me, and I smiled—both to myself and to the little one in my lap.

"You look natural holding her," said Shelby, as if reading my thoughts. "Less than four more months to go for you. It'll be awesome, seeing our kids grow up together."

"Yeah, it will." And that made me remember my drawing. "While I'm holding her, could you do me a favor? In my bag is a present for you, and I brought a picture I wanted your opinion on."

Shelby retrieved the wrapped gift and the drawing I'd folded into a square. She opened the present first, and exclaimed over the dresses I'd bought her girls. "I love these! Thank you for not buying two identical outfits too. I really don't want to do the matching clothes thing, but everyone seems to think I do."

Ha! I'd almost gone that route, but decided not to. Points for me. "You're welcome. You'll have to give me a picture of the girls when they're dressed in them."

"I will." Then Shelby carefully unfolded the drawing and looked at the dozen or so faces I'd sketched. "Wow, it's sort of like a collage. Are you going to paint this or something?"

"I might. Do . . . um . . . any of them look familiar to you?" All were females, but some were of women and some children. I'd just drawn what I remembered, and I didn't even know if the same person was depicted twice, once at a younger age.

She stared at the picture for a couple more minutes. I watched her intently, trying to read her reaction. "Hmm." She shook her head. "No. Should I?"

Like I said—a long shot. And it didn't mean Shelby wasn't the descendant of Miranda's other daughter. I'd mostly been operating on a hunch, even though it felt off to me. Besides, the pictures weren't exact, or even complete, because it wasn't like I had *that* great of a memory regardless, and definitely not when things flashed by at top speed in a dream state. "Probably not, but thought I'd ask."

Questions appeared in her eyes, and I was trying to figure out how I was going to answer them when Jessica squawked from the bassinet. "Now, *she* is probably hungry." Shelby stood and then scooped up the fussing baby into her arms. "I'm going to go upstairs to feed her. Are you okay with Rebecca?"

"Oh . . . if you want privacy, I can take off."

"Don't be silly. It won't take long, and then we can keep talking."

I nodded and watched her leave the room. I put my pinky finger in Rebecca's tiny hand, and she squeezed. "Maybe you and my daughter will be friends," I whispered.

She gurgled in a breathy, oh-how-sweet sort of way, and I smiled again. Because somehow, what had once terrified me now filled me with awe. And even with all the worries and fears I had, I couldn't wait to meet my daughter. I just had to ascertain that everything was how it should be when that day finally arrived.

Chapter Sixteen

It always seemed to take forever to get to five o'clock on Fridays, but this particular Friday was the slowest of my entire life. I swear. Because all I could think about was going to Ethan's place that evening. Thoughts, questions, and anticipation of the night ahead consumed me. So much so, concentrating on anything else proved to be difficult. Hell, it was nearly impossible.

When it was finally time to leave, I raced home as quickly as the speed limit allowed. Ethan had offered to pick me up, but I wanted to drive myself. That way, I could discreetly bring an overnight bag and leave it in my car, and run out and grab it if things went the way I thought they would. The way I wanted.

And yeah, I could have gone to Ethan's directly after work, but I wanted the chance to be a girl. So I soaked in a bubble bath, rubbed scented lotion into my skin, brushed my hair until it shone, and found the one and only dress I owned that was still somewhat sexy. Not only was my belly barely noticeable in it, but the black dress with its little spaghetti straps showed off my arms, my legs, and just the right amount of cleavage. A strappy pair of black heels completed the outfit. Pregnant or not, I looked pretty damn good.

Now I sat in my car outside of Ethan's apartment building. Getting there had been easy, as his directions had been perfect, but also because he didn't live that far from Enchanted Expressions. I drew in a breath and slowly released it. Getting out of the car? Not quite as easy. My hopes for tonight—for me and Ethan—were huge. Wonderful. Glorious. The potential I saw for us made my head swim.

On the other end of that was the very real possibility that it would all crash down around me. And that was the reason I found it so hard to unbuckle my seat belt and make my way to Ethan's door. But because going home was not an option I was willing to take, I gathered all of my fears and tucked them away.

Besides, if worse came to worst, I'd at least have tonight.

After climbing the steps to Ethan's building, I buzzed his apartment. In mere seconds, another buzz met my ears and the door unlocked. When I reached his actual apartment, he stood in his doorway, waiting. His eyes skimmed over me with an appreciative gleam. "Hey there, beautiful. No problems finding the place?"

"Nope, none at all." My voice quavered, just a little. Tonight he wore dressy black slacks and a dark purple—almost plum—button-down shirt. His cologne weaved around me, muddling my senses. "You are very handsome, Mr. Gallagher." And he was. Big time. Not that that was anything new, but somehow, every time I saw him, I realized it all over again.

His hand reached out. I grasped it, and he tugged me inside. Leaning down, he kissed me lightly. "I'm going to finish dinner. Make yourself at home," he said.

Putting my fingers to my lips, I nodded. He disappeared into the kitchen and I took stock of my surroundings. Ethan's apartment was a loft-style, with a black iron staircase leading to the bedroom upstairs, which overlooked the living room. I could just make out the edge of his bed from where I stood. An image of us making love made me shiver. Pushing it away, for now, I pivoted on my heel to take in the rest.

The dining room, with its dark hardwood floors, and

the living room, with its plush off-white carpeting, merged together, creating an open, inviting space. One wall was red brick, with the remaining walls painted a chocolate shade similar to his office. His sofa was large and comfortable looking, upholstered in a lush, suede-type brown fabric, and faced his wide-screen TV. Two chairs sat on either side, with gleaming end tables between. A ceiling lamp rested on top of one of these tables, with a toolbox sitting on the floor below. Grinning, I tipped my head up. Yep, a bunch of wires poked through the ceiling directly over the couch. Apparently, Ethan planned on playing Mr. Fix-it soon. My grin widened.

Other than that light, nothing was out of place. A desk rested against one wall, with his laptop and some papers sitting on top. Various pictures, a minimum of knick-knacks, and a few plants added color and rounded out his furnishings. I couldn't have imagined a better space for him, because everywhere I looked, I saw and felt Ethan. I sighed, and the last of my tension eased out of me.

At that moment, there was nowhere else I wanted to be, no one else I wanted to be with. That realization sifted in, relaxing me even more. Tonight was the night that everything I wanted and dreamed of would come true. I knew it, and that knowledge danced around inside of me, leaving me giddy—breathless, almost—with anticipation.

Not ready to sit down, needing to move, I walked across the room to a shelf where some photos were displayed. The first showed a man and woman standing arm in arm, with a little boy in front of them. My lips twitched. I recognized the boy immediately, as his dimples were a matching set to the adult Ethan's. And wow, was he adorable—and he appeared more than a little mischievous. I stared at the younger version of Ethan for a while, wondering about the day the photo had been taken. Was it a good day? Had he laughed that day? I hoped so.

My eyes moved on, finding a picture of Ethan as I knew him now, sitting on a porch swing with an elderly woman. Her face was lined, but it held a smile as bright as any I'd ever seen. Something about this woman tugged at my memory and made me take a second look. Ah. Her eyes . . . they reminded me of Ethan's, so she must be his grandmother. The love between them was evident in the photograph, and somehow, that too centered me.

I mean, come on: not only was Ethan sexy, funny, and oh-so-sweet, but he valued family in the same way I did. And that? Well, it solidified my feelings in a way that little else could.

I sensed him then, before I heard him. I turned just as he stopped beside me. His arm swung around my waist, and I shivered again. Funny, how the merest, gentlest touch from him could do that. "Ready for dinner?" he asked. "I can't promise it's the best food you'll ever eat, but I can promise it's edible."

"I'm not picky." Lifting my chin, I smiled. "Besides, I'm more interested in you than I am in food."

Humor mixed with desire, strong and fast. "Good, because I'm only proficient in making three meals. One is scrambled eggs, one is grilled cheese sandwiches, and the other is homemade pizza. Guess which we're having?"

Laughing, I let him lead me to the table. I don't know if it was the moment, the company, my emotions, or what, but Ethan's homemade pizza certainly was the best I'd ever had. Of course, he probably could have fed me dry bread and room-temperature water and I'd have said the same.

When we finished eating, we moved to the living room. He sat on the couch and opened his arms. I scooted into them, and we stayed that way for I don't know how long. He offered to put a movie on, but honestly? Paying attention to anything other than Ethan would have proved impossible. Because every part of my body was focused on *him*. From his scent, to the feel of his leg pressed against mine, to his hand touching my shoulder and every now and then playing with my hair—he was all I could see.

After a while he picked up a remote and in one click, soft music poured into the room. His gaze met mine, and anticipation once again quivered in my stomach. "Dance with me, Alice," he said.

I was surprised. "Really? I'm not the greatest dancer." I'd probably stomp on one of his feet hard enough that we'd end up in the emergency room. That was so not the way I wanted any evening, and this one in particular, to end.

Standing, he held his arms out. "Really. Just one dance."

"Okay. If you're sure."

I kicked my shoes off—for safety reasons—and then stepped into his embrace. My arms wrapped around his neck, his chin dipped down so it barely touched the top of my head, and my cheek pressed against the curve of his shoulder. Then we danced. Not just for one song, either, but for several. We fit together in a way I hadn't expected, and dancing with Ethan made me feel graceful, beautiful, and sexy as hell.

His fingers brushed the bare skin at my neck, and then my shoulders, moving down to stroke my back. The tiniest crawl of warmth grew in my stomach—each touch, each breath, each soft step made it branch out bit by bit until heat suffused my entire body. All I wanted was Ethan.

A tremble edged through me, and I pressed myself tightly against him, the firmness of his chest meeting the softness of mine. My nipples hardened beneath the thin fabric of my dress, and the heat inside of me floated out until every inch of my skin shivered. Without thinking, because any coherent thought process had long since left my brain, I gave voice to the feelings swirling inside of me. "I love you," I murmured.

I snapped my mouth shut immediately. Nervous ripples replaced the shivers of desire, of want, and a different type of warmth filled my face. When would I learn to think before I spoke? We stopped dancing, his arms locked around me, drawing me even closer. And in that one little movement, confidence soared. I knew what I felt, what I wanted, and really—why pretend I hadn't said what I'd just said?

Bringing my hands to his chest, palms flat, I pushed back just enough so I could tip my head up and look into his eyes. They were dark, almost black instead of their normal gray, emotions swirling there like heavy, brooding clouds just before a storm. "Ethan. I love you," I said again. My gaze didn't leave his, because I wanted him to see the truth of my words, what existed inside of me.

The intensity of his expression tore through me, but still he didn't speak. I tried to breathe, tried to calm the crazy beat of my heart, but I couldn't. Need, want, and something else flowed through his eyes, his features, like wildfire. His hand went to my cheek, stroking backward until it touched my hair. "Are you sure? You can take it back, right now, if you're not."

"I'm positive. And it's okay if you don't feel the same, but I had to say it, had to make sure you knew how I felt. Right now, right this instant."

His eyes darkened even more. He continued to stroke my hair, my face. "I fell for you before I even realized what was happening. I can't explain it, but for the first time in my life, I find I don't care much about logic. I don't need to understand this." He stopped speaking abruptly, but his gaze didn't leave mine.

My breath caught in my chest. I knew, for the rest of my life, that I would remember this moment in vivid detail.

And then he said words I so wanted to hear. "I love you too. The only reason I haven't said it before is because I didn't want to scare you off." His body quaked in a soft shudder. "I couldn't bear to scare you off. So I convinced myself we needed to move slowly, so you could handle the changes coming into your life without me confusing everything. But Alice, I can see us together—in every way."

"I can too. And right now, that's all that matters."

We didn't speak, just moved together, slowly taking the stairs to his bedroom. Not one movement was rushed or frantic. The space was dark, with the barest glow of light from downstairs melting the shadows. I turned, and he unzipped my dress. It fell to the floor in a pool of fabric. I stepped out of it and into Ethan. His head came down and his lips met mine, and the desire between us was bright, hot, and pure energy. But so much more existed in this kiss, in our need, in our touches.

I unbuttoned his shirt and dragged it off of him, wanting nothing more than to feel his skin against mine. With hurried yet steady hands, I undid his pants and tugged them down, until they too dropped to the floor. We tumbled backward, landing on the bed in a hot, melting rush.

We kissed again. Everything inside of me yearned for something I didn't understand, and while sex with Ethan was part of it, there was more, somehow, that I needed and craved. Trailing kisses from my mouth to my neck, and then down some more, his tongue found my breasts. I arched my back, a moan slipping out.

My hands roamed the length of his back, his muscles rippling at my touch, his skin growing hot beneath my fingers. He pulled at my panties, moving them down and off my legs. I moaned again, wanting more, wanting everything. He came back to me, wrapped his arms around me, and shifted my body against his pillows.

"I want you," I said. "I want to feel you inside of me." I didn't recognize the sound of my voice. It was thick, heavy with desire, with longing.

He growled and brought his lips to mine. I weaved my fingers into his hair and pulled him toward me, plunging my tongue into his mouth. We continued to touch, to kiss, to explore, and every second—every minute—strengthened my feelings. There was no way this man wasn't my soul mate. Every part of me recognized him.

He entered me in a soft, slow, sweet slide that took my breath away in a gasp. I wrapped my legs around his waist, tightened myself around him, and pulled him deeper with each thrust. He combed his fingers into my hair and groaned, thrusting again, sending trembles through both of our bodies. He took his time, didn't rush, bringing me to the peak of my desire and then slowing the pace again. One moment was soft and sweet, the next heady and hot, our bodies moving together in a synchronicity I'd never before experienced; and now that I had . . . well, I couldn't imagine anything else.

When I didn't think I could handle any more, when my body screamed for release, I tensed my legs again, pushing him in hard, tight. I moaned as everything inside of me, everything around me, my entire being exploded in a million little sensations that rocked everything I ever thought I knew about sex. "Oh!" I murmured, burying my head in Ethan's chest as he collapsed on top of me. Our bodies shivered, trembled, and we stayed that way for a long, blissful while.

And then he rolled to the side, his arms around me, his hands cradling my stomach, his breath warm on my neck. "Amazing," he whispered.

"What is?"

"That we found each other."

And because I agreed, I sighed in pure contentment.

Curling myself into him, I fell asleep to the sound, to the feel of Ethan. The man I loved.

Light streamed into the room, waking me with its brilliance. It took a second to realize where I was, but when it hit, when the memories flooded in, the room became even brighter. I turned in bed, looking for Ethan, missing his touch, only he wasn't there. Stretching luxuriously, I reveled in the way my body still hummed, the way my lips and neck still tingled from his kisses. My skin warmed as my mind played through the things we'd done to each other, the things we'd said. A mix of delight and satisfaction raised my temperature another notch.

Kicking the blankets off my legs, I stretched again, trying to work out the kinks that only a full night of sex, broken up with sporadic sleep, could give. Everything about last night had rocked. Would tonight be more of the same? My lips curved into a smile of anticipation.

Hell yes, tonight would be more of the same. Maybe we could even start early.

My stomach growled at the same time the scent of bacon and eggs drifted into the room. He was making me breakfast? Wow. Warmth spilled in, and I sat up in bed, yawning. I looked for my overnight bag, only to realize I'd never brought it in. But Ethan had thought of that too, because he'd left one of his T-shirts on the bed for me.

I slipped it on over my head and then stood, stifling another yawn. Taking the steps down slowly, quietly, I sneaked into the restroom. Using his brush, I smoothed my hair. I washed my face and hands, and gargled with a little mouthwash. I wanted to kiss him again the second I saw him, so no morning breath for me, thank you very much!

When I left the bathroom, it was to see Ethan emerging from the kitchen, dressed in nothing but a pair of boxers, a tray in hand. Many mornings yet to come flashed in front of me, as sure as the sun shining in the windows. Even better, the sight of his naked chest sent another tingling series of shivers across my skin. And his stomach? Tight. Taut. Beautiful.

His eyes found me, and he smiled. My stomach flip-flopped. "I was bringing you breakfast in bed," he said. "But since you're awake, why don't we stay down here?" He winked, and my shivers increased. "For now."

"That sounds perfect."

He walked forward a few steps, putting the tray on the table. When I got to him, I balanced on my tiptoes and kissed him. He tasted like sugared coffee, hot and sweet, and he pulled me close for a deeper kiss. I could have stayed that way forever, but at that instant, my stomach growled again. Loudly.

His eyes alight with humor, he laughed. "Sit down and eat. I left the orange juice in the kitchen; I'll be right back." Another quick kiss, and he turned around. My gaze fell on his back, and then moved up to his shoulder.

His completely bare, 100-percent mark-free, perfect-in-every-way, right shoulder.

The floor swayed. I gripped the chair next to me, holding on for dear life as everything I knew, everything I wanted, everything I'd believed in mere seconds earlier swirled down the drain as quickly as water streaming from a faucet. My chest tightened. My heart galloped. I tried to find distance, so I could think. So I could figure this out.

No scar. No birthmark. Not even a freaking freckle. How in the hell was that possible? I'd been so *sure*. So very sure. The air grew heavy; so heavy, it hurt to breathe. My chest tightened more, and I dragged a mouthful of air into my lungs and forced it back out. Queasiness spiked in my stomach, sharp and fast, crawling up my throat, almost making me gag. I swallowed hard, gripped the back of the chair harder.

The clinking of glasses in the next room floated into my haze. I needed to pull myself together. I needed to figure this out. But on the heels of that came the realization that there was nothing to figure out, nothing to do but leave. To walk away from the man I loved, who loved me, and go in search of someone else. Someone who was supposed to be the key to saving my daughter, my family, me . . . and yes, at this point, Ethan.

He reappeared then, a smile on his face, happiness in his eyes. At that moment, I hated myself, hated the fact I was going to hurt him.

"You didn't have to wait, sweetheart. Dig in. I know you're starving." He set the glasses filled with orange juice on the table, and then . . . well, then he looked at me. And he froze.

My mouth opened, but nothing came out. All I could do was stare at him.

"Are you in pain? You're completely white. Sit down, Alice." He pulled my hand free from the back of the chair and guided me into it. "Where does it hurt? Is it the baby?"

I shook my head. "The baby is fine," I mumbled.

He pulled another chair over, so we sat knee to knee. "What is it? What could possibly have occurred in the last three minutes to cause this?"

"Nothing. Everything." My chin trembled, my voice cracked.

"Are you sorry about last night?" He paused, inhaled deeply, and then asked, "Did I disappoint you?"

"No!" I couldn't let him think that. Not only because it wasn't true, but because I wouldn't leave that legacy behind. "Making love with you was incredible. I'm not sorry about that in any way."

"Then what is it? Are we moving too fast?" Confusion merged with concern. "We can go back to taking it slow. No pressures. No worries."

"That's"—I gulped air—"not it."

"Then what? Talk to me."

I said the only thing I thought, the only thing I could. "You don't have a scar." A big, fat tear dripped down my cheek. And then another, and another. The tightening in my chest let loose, and the tears turned to sobs. Gasping, I tried to form words, tried to talk, but I couldn't. How could I have done this? How could I have made such a massive mistake?

"Are scars that important to you? Because I do have plenty, you know." His voice was light, but his eyes were filled with worry. Standing, he put one foot on the chair. "Look, there's one here on my thigh. See?" He held his arm out. "And here. There's the one you saw the other night." Swiveling at the waist, he pulled the band of his boxers down, just a little. "And look here, sweetheart, that's a nice one. Plenty of scars, so nothing to cry over."

I heard the humor in his tone, his way of trying to make me laugh, and wow—I loved him even more, if that was possible. But of course, that didn't help. It didn't stop the sobs from tearing out. It didn't change the fact that he didn't have the one scar I so needed him to have. The one scar I'd somehow talked myself into believing he *would* have.

Stupid. So stupid of me.

He sat down in his chair again, lightly grasping my arms, his gaze seeking, searching. "Since it's not our compatibility in bed, I can fix anything. I hate to see you this upset. What is it? Tell me and I'll fix it. Give me the chance to try."

I angled away, not able to look into his eyes. "It's not fixable. I've made a terrible mistake, Ethan. I am so sorry."

His breath caught. "Do you love me?"

"I do."

"Well, then, it can't be too horrible. Because I love you back!" He tipped my chin, so we were eye to eye. "You can trust me. What is this about?" Cupping my face in his hands, he leaned over and kissed me.

I pulled back, wiped my hand over my lips, and then my cheeks, trying to dry the tears that refused to stop. "You're not going to want to hear this. I don't want to say it. I don't want to believe it."

For the first time, his eyes hardened. "Maybe not, but if this is going where I fear it is, then I need to."

He was right, so I nodded. I reined in my emotions, calmed my breathing, and steadied my voice. None of this was easy, because all I wanted to do was tell him everything was okay, that I loved him and that was that. For a second, I actually considered it, but then . . . the dream came back in all its vivid heartbreak. So I told him everything, beginning with Miranda's warning and ending with my dream about my daughter. It was hard. Harder than anything else I'd ever done, getting it all out, saying everything I knew, thought, and believed. Telling the amazing man I'd fallen in love with that I couldn't be with him.

Through it all, he listened and didn't ask any questions. At the end, when there was no more to say, his face was impassive. A shield had dropped into place. "You're leaving me because I don't have a scar on my shoulder; is this correct?"

"I don't want to. But this is bigger than me. More important than me." My throat closed, and the pain grew and grew inside until I could hardly stand it. "This is about my daughter."

He cleared his throat, his eyes moving past me. "I understand that, Alice. I'm even willing to set my skepticism aside and believe in . . . magic. What I can't comprehend is how you can't believe in what you feel for me. What I feel for you. And that *on the basis of a drawing,* you're willing to walk away."

"I have no choice. I promised myself—" It didn't matter what I said, because there was no way I could make him understand what I barely could.

"The other night, I told you I wouldn't go away unless you told me to. And now, that's what you're doing," he clarified.

"I don't want to," I said again.

"Then don't." When I didn't respond, he grabbed my hand. His mask slipped a little. "There is nothing I can do or say to convince you to give us more time, to see where this leads? To trust in how we feel?"

His willingness to try, despite what I'd said, made it worse. Why couldn't he hate me for being like his fiancée? Push me away for being insane? No, he had to be understanding and loving and I so wanted to say yes. More than I'd ever wanted anything else. But I thought again of that dream, and the horror that awaited my daughter, awaited Ethan and me, if I followed my heart. The tears came again, and I tried so hard to hold them back. "I can't."

He released my hand. In a flat, emotionless voice I'd never before heard from him, he said, "That's that, then."

Everything inside of me bottomed out. "I'm sorry."

A light of anger flashed in his eyes so fast it surprised me. "It's your choice, Alice. I love you, but I can't—won't—force you to stay with me. To give us a chance." Just as quickly, the anger subsided. "I hope you find what—who—you're looking for."

There wasn't anything more to say. I grabbed my purse, ran out of his apartment, and drove home. My body shook the entire time, and I could hardly see through the fog of tears that continued to flow. It didn't matter that I'd made the only decision I could, because now all I felt was an empty, gnawing pain deep inside.

It wasn't until I got home and collapsed on my bed that I realized I still wore Ethan's shirt. Lovely. I'd run from his place like a maniac in nothing but a T-shirt.

But then I pulled it up over my face so it covered my nose and mouth and breathed in. In barely the beat of my heart, he was there with me, just by the scent of his shirt. I curled up, held myself as tightly as I could, and tried to imagine my life without him. The pain grew even stronger, so instead I pretended he was holding me, and that when I woke up he'd still be there lying next to me.

It was still just pretend.

Chapter Seventeen

Grandma Verda waved her files in the air. "I know this hurts, but it's been a week. You need to set up some of these dates."

I blinked but didn't respond. The past seven days had been hell. I'd almost called in sick the Monday after ripping my heart and Ethan's to shreds, but I'd missed him so much, even with the pain, I had to see him; so I'd forced myself to go. Only to find *he* was the one who'd called off—for an entire week. The rumor was he'd gone to Ireland to see his family, but I had no clue as to whether that was the truth. He'd missed several important client meetings, though, the Kendall account for one, so likely the rumor held weight. But that didn't make me miss him any less.

Elizabeth put her arm around my shoulders. "Sweetie, you don't have to do this yet. Take the time you need."

"She can't. It might not be any of these men, either," Grandma interjected, as stubborn as ever. "This isn't a game."

Chloe laced her fingers together, watching me. She'd stayed with me the entire week, only leaving my side for work, returning the favor I'd done for her so long ago when Kyle had broken her heart. I focused on her. "What do you think?"

She stared at me, sadness lurking in her eyes. "I don't know. In any other circumstance, I'd say it was too soon."

I blinked again, still surprised the crying had stopped.

Oh, the pain hadn't lessened; if anything, it had gotten worse. But somehow, I'd drained myself of tears.

"There're only four men to begin with." Grandma Verda yanked off the rubber band holding a particular stack of files together. "One afternoon is all it will take. We can set up . . . what's it called? Where you meet one right after another for an hour or so each?"

"Usually it's only like fifteen minutes, but you're talking about speed dating," said Chloe. "But you can't push her, Verda. That isn't fair."

"None of this is fair. But she left Ethan for a reason, didn't she?" Grandma turned to me. "Didn't you? If you're unwilling to move forward, then you might as well have stayed with him and been happy until the doo-doo hit the fan."

Her words hit hard, like being slammed by a Mack truck. Because she was completely correct. And no way was all this pain going to be for nothing. "Fine. But I can't set it up. Someone else do it and just tell me where to go and when to be there." I paused, realizing I was really going to do this. "And if any of you has a clue as to how I'm supposed to recognize the right man when I'm in love with another, please let me in on it."

Chloe reached her hand out toward Grandma, accepting the files. "I'll do it. I can talk to them on the phone and feel them out a little, maybe."

I almost asked how that would help, but then the doorbell rang. I didn't think, I didn't take a minute to consider why a blast of hope rushed through me; I just ran to the door and swung it open. Disappointment settled in, but I slapped on a smile. It was my brother Scot. With his slightly damp-at-the-edges hair, flushed cheeks, and overly bright eyes, he could have just run a marathon. Even with my misery, that should have been my first clue. "What's wrong? You don't look so good."

"Nothing's wrong. Why would you assume something

is wrong just because I'm visiting you on a Saturday?" He strode into the dining room. "I tried calling you. Twice. Don't you ever answer your phone?"

Before I could respond, let alone close my door, I saw our mother approaching at top speed from down the street, our father following at a slightly slower pace. I squinted, in case I'd imagined it. I hadn't. "Um, Scot? Why are Mom and Dad here?"

"Shit. How'd they get here so fast?" He came up behind me and shut the door—not quite in my mother's face, as she hadn't actually gotten there yet, but pretty dang close. He leaned back, as if barricading it. "Listen to me."

Crossing my arms, I tried very hard to disregard the dread I felt. "Talk fast. You have, like, ten seconds."

"Um. Okay. She called me this afternoon and I accidentally let it slip that you're pregnant." Sweat beaded on his forehead. "I didn't mean to. It just came out."

"Seriously?" Like I needed this in the middle of everything else! "Awesome. Thanks for the notice."

"Hey. I tried calling you. It's not my fault you didn't answer." He tossed me a sheepish grin. "Want to escape out the back? We can probably make it if we go now."

"She'd just chase us down." I sighed. This wasn't his fault; it was mine. I'd turned my ringer off, and I'd continued to ignore something I shouldn't have. But still, why today? Why now? "It's probably better to have it out in the open. But geez, Scot, learn to keep your mouth shut."

The doorbell rang. We both ignored it.

"I'm glad you're not mad at me." He bent over to give me a quick hug. "Okay. I'm gonna take off. Good luck with Mom and Dad."

Grabbing his arm, I pulled him toward me. "What? You really think I'm going to let you leave? Not hardly."

"I . . . uh . . . thought you'd want to handle the rest yourself."

"Um. No." I didn't let him argue, just opened the door.

My mother's gaze went directly to my stomach. "How could you not tell us?"

"Isobel, calm down. She's a grown woman. We should have waited and let her come to us when she was ready." My father smiled at me, but concern gleamed in his eyes. "I'm sorry. I tried to stop her from coming over, but she wouldn't hear of it."

"It's okay, Dad. She's right. I should have said something a long time ago. Let's go into the living room. Grandma, Elizabeth, and Chloe are here."

"Do they know?" my mother asked.

"Yes. They've known for a while," I admitted, leading the way.

Elizabeth was in the papasan chair. My parents took the couch, next to my grandmother. Scot sort of eased himself against the wall, next to Chloe, and I sat in the chair across from everyone. "Okay, should I talk or do you want to?" I asked my mother.

Her gaze softened, and the tight way she held her shoulders relaxed. "I just want to know if you're okay. And when you're due. Oh, and who the father is."

The calmness in her tone surprised me. Kudos to her for keeping it together. And somehow, it helped me too. "I'm okay. The father is Troy. Remember him? And I'm due in September."

She pushed a strand of hair behind her ear in a nervous gesture. "You never introduced us, so no, I don't remember Troy. And if he's the father, why isn't he here?"

"He's the guy whose wife totaled your apartment?" Scot asked.

"Yes, and he's not here because he's not going to be involved. And it's better that way."

My mother asked more questions; so did my dad, and I answered them all. Honestly, it wasn't nearly as difficult as I'd thought. Really, it was the only thing that had gone right lately, because as soon as our conversation ended, a huge amount of relief slid in.

That is, until my mother said something that pushed me back over the edge. "I'm glad to know now, but I wish you'd told us earlier. You've always been so secretive. I don't understand where you get that from."

I sighed, exasperated. "It seems that keeping secrets is something this family is good at. Including you."

Her eyes narrowed. "What are you talking about?"

I narrowed mine right back. "Miranda. And the little family gift that I should have known about forever ago. Why'd you keep that a secret, Mom?" I bit my lip. I hadn't meant to sound so harsh. But dang it, the *secret* comment really got to me.

"Alice! Mom isn't a part of that," Elizabeth said.

"That's her own fault," said Grandma Verda. "I certainly gave her the gift. It's about time all of this came out. I'm so proud of you, Alice!"

"I have no idea what you're going on about." My mother looked at my father. "Marty? Do you know what's going on?"

"This has nothing to do with me. But maybe you should listen to them." He leaned over and picked up my newspaper. *Great.* This was my father's number-one technique for tuning everyone out. Well, that or the TV, but he wouldn't turn that on now. Not without serious repercussions from my mother.

Refocusing on her, I asked, "You don't know? Seriously?"

"She knows; she just doesn't believe. It didn't work for her and it came back to me." Grandma Verda shrugged. "You have to be willing to accept it, and she never was. Even worse, she thinks I'm a batty old woman who just made everything up."

"Mom! That's not true. I've never called you batty. A

little eccentric, maybe." My mother curled her arms around herself, as if warding off a chill. "It's nonsense."

"It's not nonsense. Every woman in this family has had the magic. Except for you, which is just fine, Isobel. It's not right for everyone." Grandma Verda squared her narrow shoulders. "But don't you go mocking it, or Miranda, just because you don't understand."

Confusion zipped over Scot. "Magic? Miranda? What's going on here? Have you all lost your minds?"

"It's real, Scot," Chloe said. "I've seen things myself."

My dad stood, still holding the newspaper, and beckoned to my brother. "This is something that doesn't concern us. Let's go to the kitchen and let them talk." When Scot hesitated, my father said, "Now, son."

After my dad and Scot had escaped the madness, I collapsed on the couch next to my mother. "Why don't you believe?"

"Because it's ludicrous. That's why."

"And why did Dad leave? It sort of seems like he knows."

"I told him about it a long time ago, when I tried to give it to Isobel. Joe knows too, but that was an accident." Grandma Verda frowned at my mother. "They both believe, and Marty has asked me to help him out with a spell here and there over the years."

My mother gasped. Elizabeth's jaw dropped. Shivers sheathed my skin. "This is getting weirder by the second," I mumbled. I'd never have guessed, in a million years, that my brother and father already knew about the magic. About Miranda.

Covering her face with her hands, my mother sighed.

Ack. She wasn't handling it well. I even felt bad about bringing it up. I glanced at Elizabeth, Grandma, Chloe, and then back to Mom. "We don't have to talk about this around you. I should never have said anything."

A hard shiver rippled through Mom. Slowly, she re-moved her hands. "Thank you."

That should have been the end of it, at least for now, but of course it wasn't. Because at that instant, the scent of roses filled the air. I glanced at Elizabeth, and she noticed too. Strangely, so did Chloe, if her expression was anything to go by. I didn't have a chance to wonder why, because almost immediately, a kaleidoscope of colors swirled into the room, tiny glimmers of light darting every which way.

Of course. I'd been trying to get Miranda's attention for a week, and *now* she decided to show up. My ghost grand-mother had the most interesting, and frustrating, sense of timing.

My mother's cheeks whitened. "What is that? What's going on here?"

Grandma Verda clapped her hands. "Oh! It's her. She's coming!"

"Who's coming?" asked Chloe.

"Miranda." And wow, was she putting on a show. She certainly had a . . . gift in the special-effects department. The colors zipped around the room, the lights danced, and then there she was, in the center of all of it. I sort of wanted to strangle her; not that ghosts could be stran-gled, but . . . well, I wasn't very happy with her.

Grandma Verda stood, her body trembling with ex-citement. "I wondered if I'd ever see you again. I've wanted to see you again."

The light around Miranda pulsated. "I told you that you would, Verda. I don't break my word."

Chloe shrank against the wall. Not in fear, or even shock, but by the look in her eyes, pure amazement. "Wow. Just wow."

My ghostly grandmother laughed in her tinkling way. "Hello, Chloe. Thank you for taking such good care of

Alice. She needs you, and you need her. I'm so glad you have each other."

Chloe nodded, but continued to stare, wide-eyed, at her.

Miranda smiled in my sister's direction. "Elizabeth . . . I'm pleased to see how happy you are. Things are going well for you, yes?"

"For me, but not for Alice. She could use some help." Elizabeth's eyes beseeched our ancestress. "Can you please help her?"

She shook her head, a glimmer of sadness in her eyes. "I've done all I can do. The rest is in her hands."

"I'm right here. Talk to me! I've been trying to get you to all week. Why haven't you come?" The shaking in my voice pissed me off. "Do you know what's happened? Do you know how I feel?"

"I'm so very sorry you're in such pain, Alice. But I can't interfere. You need to find the solution for yourself. Nothing has changed there."

I wanted to argue with her. Hell, I wanted to—somehow—force her to answer my questions, to make everything better, to tell me that my feelings were right, even without a scar. But how do you make a ghost do anything she doesn't want to do?

Gliding to my mother, Miranda's form shimmered, and she smiled again. More pulsating lights and colors surrounded her, like a rainbow on speed. "Isobel, I've watched you for your entire life. Everything Verda has told you is the truth, but listen carefully: My love for you has nothing to do with the magic or the gift. It's within your rights to turn it away."

My mother nodded, and she seemed calm enough, but her complexion scared the hell out of me. This was probably way too much for her. What amused me, though, was how her good manners overrode her fear, her skepticism. "It's nice to meet you, Miranda. Uh . . . you look very nice today."

Elizabeth chuckled. Grandma Verda shushed her. Me? I just stayed quiet. I couldn't speak, but I couldn't turn away, either.

"If you ever change your mind about the gift, it's there for you . . . whenever you want it," said Miranda. "You don't need to be afraid."

My mother stared at Miranda, and questions dotted her eyes but she kept them to herself. "Okay, then. Well. It was nice meeting you," she repeated. "I'm going to go to the kitchen now and talk to Marty and Scot." Standing, she took one more long look at Miranda and then quietly, and quickly, left the room.

Once she'd disappeared, Miranda turned back to us. "She'll have questions eventually, but not yet. Be ready for them when they do come, answer them honestly, and she might surprise you."

Chloe stepped forward. "Isn't there anything else you can tell Alice? She's in love with Ethan and he doesn't seem to be the man in her drawing. How can that be?"

Miranda's form hazed out, the lights and colors dimmed, but her voice remained. "Alice has her answers . . . if she knows where to look, if she lets herself believe."

As quickly as she'd arrived, she left. The scent of roses disappeared, and the chaotic energy in the room ebbed. Annoyed I'd gotten nothing new from her, I slumped forward.

"That was so cool!" Chloe rubbed her arms. "I can't believe I met a ghost. How do you think your mom's handling it?"

Good question. "I don't know. She'll either pretend it never happened or wait to bring it up." I hoped she'd wait. I mean, eventually I'd be excited to talk to her about

Miranda, about everything that existed in our family, but not now. Not when I could barely breathe.

Elizabeth aimed her gaze my way. "Did anything Miranda said make any sort of difference for you?"

"It's the same stuff she always says. So, no."

This wasn't quite the truth, though, because all at once, something hung there right on the edge of my comprehension. I didn't give it too much thought, because unless I could find a way to make Ethan my soul mate, or turn back the clock to stop myself from falling head over heels . . . well, I just flat-out didn't care.

The staff meeting came to an abrupt end the following Tuesday afternoon. I was grateful for it, because listening to Ethan talk for a full hour had been agony through and through. Even worse, he'd barely glanced my way the entire time. In fact, he'd only spoken directly to me once, and that was to state that while Mr. Kendall had been impressed with both campaigns, he'd decided to go with Missy's ideas for the Frosty's Ice Cream Shoppe account. Most of his customers were families with kids, so he thought Missy's kid-focused campaign was a better fit.

Maybe this should have disappointed me, but it didn't. Seeing as I'd decided to accept the job at the gallery, it was better for Missy to get the accolades, anyway. That decision had become an easy one, at least. Not so much because of Ethan, but because I could now admit the gallery just fit me and my life better than Enchanted Expressions.

But I'd be lying if I said Ethan had *nothing* to do with it. How could he not? After all, he was all I could think of.

I shuffled out of the conference room, intent on making it to my desk. I hadn't put my notice in yet, because after talking to Maura, it definitely seemed better to wait until after the baby was born to make a change. I'd make it official soon, though, so Ethan would have plenty of time to find a replacement.

"Alice? Could I see you in my office, please?" Ethan's voice hit me from behind and a tight knot of anxiety curled in the middle of my back.

"Of course. Let me drop this stuff off at my desk and I'll be right there." I didn't turn around, just kept walking. What did he want? Was it personal or business?

Dumb question, because anything to do with Ethan was acutely personal.

I took my time, but even so, less than fifteen minutes later I approached Grandma Verda's desk. It was her last week helping out, as Ethan's new assistant was set to begin the following Monday. Rather than being relieved, it made me a little sad. I'd enjoyed having her in the office. She did little things that I appreciated, like ordering my favorite brand of herbal tea for the break room, stopping by my desk in the mornings with a treat of some sort, and sending me funny e-mails just to make me laugh.

Beyond that, she'd systematically impressed one person after another at Enchanted Expressions. Accounting loved her because she'd gotten several delinquent accounts to pay up. The administrative staff thought she walked on water because she'd fixed their temperamental copy machine. And she'd mediated several crises between creative and whoever they were arguing with at any particular moment, making her the most wanted person in the office.

All in all, Grandma Verda rocked. Plain and simple.

I stopped in front in of her. "Is he in there?" I nodded toward his closed door.

"He is. Waiting for you." Her blue eyes shifted away for a second. "If you don't want to talk to him, I can make up an excuse."

"No, Grandma. I'm still an employee here. So that means if the boss wants to talk to me, the boss gets to talk to me. I'll be fine." Or, at least, I'd pretend to be fine. Somehow.

Worry clouded her gaze. "Okay, then. Good luck, sweetie."

I rapped on the door once and then pushed it open. Ethan sat behind his desk, ramrod straight. I hovered at the threshold, ignoring the urge to run to him, to kiss him, to tell him I'd made a horrible mistake and I was sorry. Oh-so-sorry.

Jaw tense, eyes shielded, he nodded toward a chair. "Take a seat, Alice."

He spoke in his take-charge, all-about-business voice. My palms were moist, so I slid them down my skirt. Attempting to look poised, in control of my feelings, I crossed the room. In all likelihood I failed, but points to me for trying.

"If this is about the Frosty's account, it's cool," I said. "I'm not upset he chose Missy's campaign ideas."

"That's not it." Ethan's gaze drifted down to the open file on his desk and then back to me. "I have Troy's papers back from my attorney. There's a problem with them. I can tell you, or if you prefer I can set up an appointment with the lawyer."

Okay, this was not what I'd expected. The urge to kiss Ethan fled, because now, worry about my daughter crept in. "Go on. It'll drive me nuts if I have to wait. What's the issue?"

"It appears that, until the baby is born, Troy has no rights to give up." He tapped his fingers on the file as he spoke, his voice flat. "My attorney assures me that these papers are worthless until you, or a court, designate Troy as the father. Even then, they might not do you much good."

His words bounced around in my head. Worthless? How could they be worthless? "I don't understand. He *is* the father. This is what *he* wants."

"Correct, but paternity hasn't been legally established, and what he wants might not matter to the court," he said, an edge of anger evident.

"Oh." I focused on the first part, trying to think logically. "So basically, once she's born and I put his name on her birth certificate, then the papers can be submitted?"

"Correct," he repeated. "The possibility then exists, however, for a judge to rule against these documents. It's actually very unlikely a court will remove his parental rights, even with his wishes, unless he is deemed an unfit parent."

"But he doesn't want anything to do with her! Why go through all of this if that's the case? I don't want to force him to do anything."

Compassion flickered. "The attorney had a suggestion, but it's chancy."

"What is it?" Not only didn't I want to force Troy into anything, I really didn't want to have anything to do with him.

"If you're absolutely sure that Troy doesn't want to be a father, then don't put his name on the birth certificate. He can come back at a later date if he changes his mind, and ask for DNA testing, but it gets both of you off the hook to begin with."

Ew. The idea came off as shady to me, but maybe if I talked to Troy and he agreed, I'd feel better about it. And let's face it: there was no way Troy wouldn't agree.

"Maybe," I said, releasing a breath.

"I also have a suggestion." The timbre of Ethan's voice deepened, and something in his eyes made my heart flutter. Every part of me focused on him.

"What?" I reminded myself to breathe.

He stared at me, as if weighing his words, and my belly quivered. "We've both talked about how strong our connection is and how quickly it emerged. I've told you before that you're a woman I can see spending my life with.

Nothing has changed for me, so I'd like you to reconsider your decision. I'd like you to trust in our feelings." He inhaled deeply and then exhaled. "Marry me, Alice. Let me adopt your baby."

He was proposing? After everything I'd told him, after walking away from him, hurting him, he wanted to marry me? A rush of dizziness had me clenching my fists, my nails digging into my palms. My eyes welled and I held them open as wide as possible, knowing if I blinked, I'd cry.

"I didn't fight before. I'm fighting now. For us." He wiped his hands over his face. When he dropped them, the hope that existed there tore into me, ignited my own hope . . . and then slowly fizzled out. Because he was right: nothing had changed.

Why oh why couldn't I say yes? Everything I wanted was right here, right in front of me, just waiting for me to grab it. But I couldn't. No matter how much I wanted to, I just couldn't. "Ethan . . . I—"

"Right." The word erupted like a clap of thunder. "Still no scar. And that's the only thing that will change your mind, isn't it?" He slid the file with Troy's papers across the desk. "Save these, so if you ever need to prove Troy's intentions, you can."

And so it seemed, just like he'd said the other day: that was that.

Chapter Eighteen

Aaron wiped at the coffee he'd spilled on his shirt, little bits of paper napkin sticking to the wet fabric. "So... uh... when do you think you'll make a decision on the model thing?"

The last of my oh-so-not-fun speed dating sessions appeared to be ending pretty much like the first three had. Zilch for sparks, zip for interest, and nada for getting over Ethan. Basically, I was still screwed and in love with the wrong guy.

I sighed and handed him another napkin, just wanting this over with. So I could go back home and try to think of new ways to prove I was supposed to be with Ethan. "Well. The thing is... there isn't really a job." While I hadn't told any of my other "dates" the truth, Aaron was just so adorably cute—like a puppy dog—that keeping up the pretense somehow rubbed me the wrong way.

Giving up on his latest wet splotch, he frowned. "What is this about then?"

I wiggled in my seat. "Well," I said. "It's more like a date thing."

Green eyes bugged out behind his glasses. "You've gone through all of this to meet men? Why would you do that?"

"I didn't place the ad; my grandmother did. It's lame, and I'm sorry, but there you have it." Probably, he'd threaten to sue—or dump his coffee on my head. Neither of which would surprise me. Well, not that I actually thought he *could* sue. Could he?

He blinked. "This is odd. I can't completely decide if I'm flattered or creeped out."

"Be creeped out. I would be," I confided. "And I'm sorry. It was a bad idea and I should have stopped it immediately." Because come on, I'd known nothing would come from it.

"Why did you come then? Why not stand me up? Or call to cancel and tell your grandmother it didn't work out?"

"All very good points." I hesitated. Sure, the practical reasons for keeping the dates were sound, but he didn't need the *whole* truth. Finally, I shrugged. "Sometimes my grandmother knows what she's talking about, so I figured I'd give it a shot."

"Alrighty then. I'm sorry too. The job would have been cool, but I'm not in the market for a girlfriend." He cleared his throat. "My current girlfriend will think this is hilarious." Standing, he smiled, though it was a bit tentative. "I'm going to take off, since there isn't a job and all. But . . . uh . . . thanks for the coffee."

"No problem on the coffee, and thank you for being decent about this."

He nodded and left. Leaning back, I put my feet up on the chair he'd vacated and sipped my chai tea, trying to ignore the ache that refused to leave. Beyond that? Well, going home and informing Grandma Verda the dates had been a bust didn't thrill me. She'd come up with something new. Likely something else I'd hate.

Wow, the dates had definitely been a bust. Not just in the lack-of-feeling department, but also in the what-else-can-possibly-go-wrong department. The first guy's chair had broken for no apparent reason. Number two had suffered some sort of allergic reaction halfway through and spent the remaining time scratching his arm like crazy. Three couldn't stop sneezing—maybe another allergy? And poor Aaron had spilled coffee on himself repeatedly.

Yeah, all in all they'd been more than weird. More than a little humorous too. Part of me thought my daughter was exerting her magic to point out these men were wrong for me, but that was silly. Wasn't it? Or maybe it was just overly hopeful, because other than the sprinkler thing in the beginning, all of my dates with Ethan had been accident-free. And yeah, Chloe would definitely say the mishaps were a sign of some sort. And hey, maybe they were. Who was I to argue with fate?

My thoughts, as usual, reverted to Ethan, his proposal, and the look in his eyes when I'd walked out his door. Pain curled inside of me again, just as fresh as it had at that moment. In my heart, I still couldn't believe he wasn't my soul mate. Did that mean I was missing something, or wanted it to be true so badly I only hoped that was the case? Miranda had told me to believe, but that could mean anything. She'd also said the answers were there, if I'd only look for them.

But I *had* looked. Repeatedly. And kept coming up blank. Even my new understanding of my magic hadn't made a difference. Honestly? I was kind of sick of the whole magic thing, because if it couldn't help me, if it couldn't point me to Ethan, what good was it?

Ugh. I hated this. I hated how much I missed him, how drained and empty each and every day felt. Not to mention how much it freaking hurt.

Weird, how not that long ago, all I'd wanted was to find some measure of control in my life, and now . . . well, I'd give up any and all control if doing so would give me Ethan back. The barest image flickered into my mind, but before I could really grasp it and bring it into focus, I saw someone—a man—out of the corner of my eye. And it was *him*. The man I'd drawn with Chloe. Her ever after!

He strolled toward me, toward the exit, holding a take-out cup. My pulse sped up as I stared at him, trying to be sure. Was it really him? Light hair, chiseled cheekbones, strong jaw—oh yeah, definitely and without a doubt it was the same guy.

Should I say something? Try to get his phone number? His name? I didn't know what to do. He was almost to me, and because there was no way in hell this opportunity was going to slip through my fingers, I jerked my legs off the chair, thinking I'd wave him over and maybe, just maybe, he'd sit down. The chair fell to the ground with a crash.

Chloe's guy stopped in front of me, knelt down, and grabbed the chair. Setting it upright, he smiled—"There you go!"—and kept walking.

No. I couldn't let him just walk away! Shoving my phone into my purse, I jumped up and followed him out the door. I was about to yell at him to stop, when I had second thoughts. Miranda had said he wasn't ready. That if I told Chloe about him now, I could change their future. What if, simply by talking to him, I'd still screw it up?

That thought gave me pause. Enough pause that, while I continued to follow, I did so at a distance. I mean, I had to think about this. Luckily, a good number of pedestrians roamed the street, so keeping him in sight without showing myself proved fairly easy. And he didn't go far. At the end of the block, he stopped in front of a black-windowed office building and swiped a card into the locking mechanism at the door, letting himself in.

After he disappeared, I waited a few minutes and then rushed to the building. My gaze swept over the lettering on the door and excitement eased in. I smiled the first real smile I'd had in what felt like forever. Okay, then. I might not know his name, but I knew where the guy was employed. It looked like Chloe's ever after was an architect, and seeing as how he had access to the building on a Saturday, probably a highly ranked architect, at that.

For the first time in two weeks, a hint of positive anticipation whisked over me. When the day came that I could finally share the drawing with Chloe, I'd at least be able to send her in the right direction. So she, unlike me, would know who her soul mate was right from the get-go.

Maybe my magic didn't completely bite, after all.

Every part of me refused to relax. I'd taken a bubble bath, only to be reminded of Ethan and the night we had made love. Then I'd done a load of laundry, only to find his T-shirt, which I'd yet to wash, and that also reminded me of Ethan. Next, I'd flipped on the television, only to see a commercial for a local boating club's upcoming regatta. Yep, you got it—memories of being with Ethan on his sailboat flew back at me.

Everywhere I looked, I saw him. And because of that, relaxing wasn't going to happen.

Maybe when Chloe returned from her date with Kyle, she'd play a game with me. Or watch a DVD. Anything to pull my thoughts away from him, from what I'd lost, from what I still craved. Thank God she was still staying with me.

"Screw this," I muttered. There had to be *something* I could do. Something to prove everything I felt. Because my love for Ethan? It was alive, bright, and so very real.

Grabbing my sketchbook, I reclined on my bed and flipped through all of the drawings again. There had to be a clue in there somewhere, if I just looked hard enough. Thirty minutes passed during which I mentally dissected each and every picture, pulling them apart in my mind and then putting them back together. My answer was here. I knew it. I just couldn't find it.

Exasperation floated in. I dropped the sketchpad with a sigh. I wouldn't figure anything out if I remained an emotional basket case. Maybe if I focused on something else, and put the whole soul mate thing on the back burner, my subconscious would work it out? It was worth a chance—hell, anything was worth the chance I was after—so I laid back against my pillows, closed my eyes, breathed evenly and emptied my brain of all thoughts, all worries.

The first face that popped up was Kyle's. That ticked me off and nearly undid the whole calm thing I was going for. Not only because I'd already crossed him off the list, but because noway, nohow was it him. I knew that to the core of my being. I didn't need to know *why*; I just knew. And I didn't want him in my head, so I shoved him away.

Some more deep, even breaths: in, out, in, out. Chloe's image came drifting in, and my love for her. And then Miranda. The thing that had bothered me the other day but I hadn't paid attention to rolled in next. This time, I paid attention. You know, the weird fact that Chloe had been able to smell the roses, followed by what Miranda had said to her.

She needs you, and you need her.

Maybe? I mean, we did need each other . . . but coming from Miranda, well, it likely wasn't that simple. And then, suddenly, I realized what it was. The rush of clarity propelled me forward and I jumped from the bed like a crazy person. Retrieving the drawing I'd shown Shelby from my purse, I unfolded and stared at it. Every single person on the page in front of me was a female somehow connected to me by blood. Family.

My family.

Chloe had certainly seemed like family from almost the moment we'd met. But was I right? Adrenaline pumped through me. I searched each and every face, recognizing some but not all. *Damn it*. For a minute, I'd actually believed Chloe's face would be there . . . hiding in the masses, somehow. And that would prove she *was* my family. For real.

She wasn't.

I bit my lip, trying to bring back the rush of faces from the vision. Ha. That was so not going to happen. There were too many for me to remember clearly, and the real problem was I didn't recall seeing Chloe in *that* jumble, either. No way had I gotten every face from that vision in the drawing, though I'd managed to get quite a few. I scanned the page again, taking it all in. Some were of babies, some of little girls, some as young women, and others as old. Making sense of it was nearly impossible.

The paper crinkled in my hand, I was squeezing it so tight. I almost let go, let it flutter to the ground, but I was so close, I could feel the truth of that spinning around inside of me. So instead I relaxed my grip and thought about my magic, about what I'd been able to do and what I hadn't. What was it Miranda said? "The magic is changing," I whispered. And while I had some ability with wishes, it was . . .

Wait. *Part* of it was seeing glimpses of the future. A little more of the puzzle clicked into place; my daughter kicked and shivers poured down my spine. Part was seeing the future. So, what was the other part? And then, as if I'd reached out and plucked an apple off of a tree, I had my answer. Or I thought I did.

The past. Could I use my magic to draw scenes and images from the past? Might as well try.

I turned to a clean page in the sketchbook, picked up my pencil, and said, "I wish to draw a picture of Chloe's mother when she was a baby, and then as a little girl, and then as an adult."

Bam. The magic flew into me, though without the sparkles of light or color; sheer energy whipped in, through my hands and into the pencil. I began to draw. These pictures came forth rapidly, even quicker than either of the wedding drawings had. Maybe because the past was done and over and therefore a definite fact?

I didn't know. It made sense, but it didn't matter.

My hand continued to draw, to shade, adding some detail here and a little there. Tingles of electricity sped through me as I worked, as I drew. I so wanted to compare what I was now drawing with what I'd already drawn, but didn't want to turn my eyes away for fear I'd screw something up. So I stayed focused, kept drawing, and let the tide of magic do its thing.

When the pictures were finally complete, the trembles washed away, and there in front of me were three very clear images. Supposedly, each of them was Chloe's mother at a different stage in her life. Of course I had no way of knowing this for sure, at least not until Chloe returned, because I'd never met Chloe's mother. Heck, I'd never even seen a photograph of her.

With the original drawing in one hand and the sketchpad in the other, I compared each and every face with the three I'd just drawn. About halfway through the page, the wide-eyed grin of a little girl stared at me; and while she wasn't an identical match to the little-girl version of Chloe's mother, she certainly appeared to be the same child.

Oh. My. God. If I was right, then Chloe really was my family. Not Shelby.

A whoosh of air hit me, and Miranda appeared. No colors. No weird, chaotic energy, either. Apparently, my ghostly grandmother didn't feel the need to impress me with her optical or sensory illusions this time. That was fine by me.

"I knew you were strong enough to find the answer on your own. It was necessary for you to do so, because in this case I'd already stepped out of bounds once. My hands were tied, so to speak." Happiness edged her every word, and if ghosts could bounce, well . . . she bounced.

"So, this is all real? Chloe has been in my life for what

feels like forever. How . . . how did that happen? And don't tell me it was a coincidence!"

"No, Alice. It was fate." She winked at me and I almost laughed. Since when did ghosts wink? "Well, let's just say it was fate with a little nudge on my part."

"How? What did you do?"

Miranda laughed. "Why does it matter how it happened? I wanted you two girls to grow up together, to know each other, to be the family you were meant to be. And you did—you are. Even so, it took you forever to meet up. It was rather upsetting for me."

"So sorry." I narrowed my eyes and frowned. "Am I allowed to tell her about *this?*"

"Of course you are! And eventually I'll visit her and help with what she has coming toward her."

Okay, that phrasing worried me. In a huge freaking way. "Is it bad? What's 'coming toward her'?"

"She should be fine. Especially now! You've done so well." Miranda shimmered, as if she were about to haze out. But, no way in hell.

"Don't leave! I can tell you're about to, so just don't. We are going to talk."

"But you don't need me now . . . not for the question you're going to ask. Alice, listen to me carefully: Just as I was right about this, I'm right about your soul mate. You have the answer already. Look harder for it. It's all connected."

Standing, I put my hands on my hips, furious. "I get that you can't tell me everything, but I'm sure there is *some*thing you can say. Something to lead me in the right direction. So, think of it. Now. Because otherwise I'm tossing this whole soul mate crap out the window and doing what I want." Wow. That was way, way more than I'd meant to say.

A smile of satisfaction curled Miranda's lips. "Let

me see. I've already told you the magic is changing . . . and this will continue to happen each time the gift is passed on."

"Miranda!" I snapped.

"Ohhh." She played coy. "You want me to tell you about your soul mate. About why you feel what you do for Ethan when he doesn't match your drawing—is that it?"

"You *know* that's it." I ground the words out. Heavens, she was pushing my buttons, and apparently enjoying it.

"I suppose there is one thing I can tell you." She shimmered again, and I was afraid she was going to disappear, but thankfully, her image resolidified. "Though it's something you already know."

"Go on. I can tell you're losing power, or whatever."

Another shimmer. "The beach drawing, Alice. Was that your magic or Elizabeth's?" Before I could answer, she nodded. "That's right. So if it isn't your magic, then why are you using that as your guide? Look to *your* magic."

"My magic? But all my magic has done is wedding pictures that aren't of me."

"Really? Look again. Try again. Now I have to leave. I'll see you soon, dear granddaughter, but not until after your daughter is born. Be safe and do what's right."

And then she vanished.

I wasn't upset this time, because it was fairly obvious she'd hung around as long as she could. Strangely, though, the thought of not seeing her for months saddened me a little. Somehow, I'd gotten used to her. Oh well, when she did show up again, she'd probably drop another bomb on my head, so maybe I should be grateful.

Once again, I grabbed my sketchbook, intent on flipping through it, on trying to figure out what Miranda had alluded to, when Chloe barged in. "There you are!" Her face split in two, she was smiling so hard. "I need to tell you something."

"Oh yeah? I need to tell you something too." And what a something! "You go first, though."

"Kyle got a tattoo of an eagle," she blurted. "It's his spirit animal, but that's not what's important."

"Then what is?" I asked, wanting her to hurry so I could give her my news.

"The tattoo is in the middle of his back! You know what that means . . ." She looked at me expectantly.

"Yay for Kyle?"

She laughed. "Don't be so sarcastic. Don't you see? There's no way Kyle can be your soul mate, because the guy in the drawing doesn't have a tattoo."

"I already knew he wasn't my soul mate, Chloe. I told you that . . . which is why you're dating him, remember?"

"Yeah, but now I know 100 percent for sure. It's made me feel loads better. Because things are . . . well, they're kind of nice right now with him."

"Then I'm glad." And yeah, even though I'd settled the Kyle issue, it relieved me too. Though her other comment jarred me, knowing what I did about her future. Not that I could do a thing about it. Well, not now anyway. "So, come here and sit down. I want to show you something."

Curious glints sparkled in her green eyes. She plopped down next to me. "What's up?"

I picked up the drawing I'd just completed and put it in her hands.

Her chin dipped down as she took it in. "Um . . . Alice? This is my mother. Why did you draw her?" Confusion squinted her eyes. "Is it a gift?"

"It wasn't meant to be, but you can certainly have it." I picked up the other drawing, the one with all the faces, and passed it to her. "Look at this one."

Her mouth scrunched as she appraised the picture. Her eyes darted from one face to another, and the minute she saw what I wanted her to see, another bolt of confusion swept over her. "What is this? I see Elizabeth here. And your grandmother. Why is my mother here too?"

I tried to keep my voice light. "You're my family."

"Well, duh. Haven't we gone over this?"

My lips quirked. "No. I mean you're *really* my family." And then I told her the truth about her connection to me, and mine to her. I shared with her everything Miranda had said, word for word. "So, I don't know how she got us together. But it seems our hearts knew all along what our brains didn't. We're family," I said in a rush.

"Family? Not just me, my aunt, and my sister . . . but you. Elizabeth. Verda. Oh my God, this is . . . unexpected. And terrific! And wow. Just wow." She blinked, and while she didn't actually cry, her green eyes were way shinier than normal. Something else occurred to her, because her jaw dropped. "Do you realize what this means? Oh my God, Alice! I can have the magic. I can be like you and Elizabeth."

I barely heard her, because instead what I heard was my own voice coming back at me: *It seems our hearts knew all along what our brains didn't.* Was what I thought I knew about Ethan all along the actual truth, just like with Chloe, but I'd been too blind to see? To believe?

Maybe.

I wanted to grasp on to that and run with it, but it wasn't enough. I needed more. But then, I thought of Kyle's back and the tattoo he'd decided to get. The beach picture was in the future, which I'd always known, but it had never occurred to me that maybe, just maybe, the scar on my soul mate's back wouldn't exist in the present. And honestly? The only real reason it occurred to me now was because of Miranda questioning why I'd used it as my guide.

A long, hard tremble took me. "Maybe the scar happens a year from now. Or two years. Hell, who knows?" I mumbled.

"You're on to something, aren't you?" said Chloe.

"I think so, but . . ." I was about to say I didn't have all of it yet, that it was still coming, when it slid into my comprehension. "Oh! I know! I know how to prove it is or isn't Ethan once and for all . . . and it has nothing to do with that damn scar."

See, the pieces of what Miranda had said came together, and suddenly I just got it. It was about the *other* part of my magic, the past part. All I had to do was draw a picture of my soul mate's past. Like I'd done with Chloe's mom. And if it were Ethan—well, I'd recognize him as surely as I had the photograph at his place.

"I need to go see Ethan. Right now." I grabbed my sketchbook and my purse and headed for the door, because while I could use my magic to create the picture here, I wanted to do it with him.

Remembering Chloe, I stopped in my tracks and turned around. "I'll be back to explain everything. I promise!"

"Just go!" She shooed me on my way.

I couldn't wait to see Ethan. To tell him I loved him and that he was my soul mate—and that we were one little drawing away from our happily ever after.

I only hoped it wasn't too late.

Chapter Nineteen

My hand shook as I knocked on the door to Ethan's apartment. I'd half expected him to refuse me when I'd buzzed him from the outside, but he hadn't. Thank goodness. The door opened, and there he stood—all tall, strong, sexy, and delicious—and my first instinct was to wrap my arms around him and lay a huge, fat, wet kiss on his lips.

Luckily, common sense won out, because he didn't look happy to see me. He didn't appear unhappy, either. More like a statue, stiff and unyielding. That mask was in place, shielding his eyes. And instead of the smile I'd hoped to see, his mouth was spread into a taut, straight line. Well, who could blame him? I'd turned him away. Not once, but twice.

We stayed there for a second, the air between us heavy with unsaid words, emotions. Finally, because I couldn't stand the quiet any longer, and because the ball was oh-so-firmly in my court, I forced a smile. "Can I come in? I'd really like to talk."

Nodding, he stepped aside. "Do you want to sit down?" he asked.

"Yes . . . no . . ." I pulled in a breath. "Yes. That would be nice. Thanks."

I followed him on shaky legs. A stepladder stood in the living room, in front of the couch. Looking up, I saw the light fixture from the other night hanging in place. Scooting around the ladder, I balanced myself on the edge of the sofa. Ethan took one of the chairs. My gaze fell to my hands, to the sketchpad I clutched. The words I needed to say were there, inside of me, but they were all jumbled up, and I didn't know what order they should go in, where to start, how to say what needed to be said to make everything right. And that scared me, because for something this important, I should know.

"You obviously came here for a reason, Alice. What is it?"

I scraped my bottom lip with my teeth, and then just pushed the words out as they came. "I made a mistake. But I know how to fix it, if you'll let me. If you still want me."

He drew in a breath. "Please be more precise. What mistake have you made?"

Rallying every bit of courage I had, I lifted my gaze to his. "I love you. My mistake was in walking away from you on the basis of that drawing. You were right about that."

A glimmer of something—hope?—teased at his expression. "I love you as well. However, my shoulder remains scarless. Is that still a deal breaker?"

"No! Not anymore. Because, Ethan? You *will* have a scar there someday. I don't know when exactly, but I know you will."

A light of interest gleamed and his voice softened a tad. "You sound quite sure of yourself. How do you know?"

"When I drew the beach drawing"—I flipped to the appropriate page in my sketchpad—"it wasn't with my magic. It was with Elizabeth's, and I was supposed to use *my* magic to find my soul mate. Not hers." I handed him the pad. "But I didn't know that and I focused too hard on that one little thing, when I shouldn't have."

He barely glanced at it. "Please understand my confusion here. You've been very clear about the ramifications of being with me if I'm not the man in this drawing. What has changed?"

"This isn't coming out right. Let me start from the beginning." My heart raced, and probably I spoke too fast, but I managed to get all of it out. Unlike before, this time he stopped me often to ask a question or for clarification. Weirdly, the idea of the magic didn't seem to bring forth censure. Oh, there was still a bit of skepticism there, but for the most part, he—outwardly, at least—accepted what I told him.

When I finished, I waited for him to smile. To be happy. To pull me into his arms and tell me he loved me, that he wanted to be with me. My entire body zinged with excitement. Everything I wanted was just around the corner. So close, I could see it.

But when several minutes elapsed, and he didn't do any of those things, the first flicker of real fear trickled in. "What's wrong? All I have to do is use my magic to draw a picture of my soul mate's past. I know it will be you! And then we'll know for sure, and we can be together. Isn't that what you want?"

Slowly, he shook his head. "No, Alice. Not like this. I'm sorry, sweetheart, but I won't go down that road again."

"But it's so simple." Oh my God. I was losing him, but I didn't understand why. "I thought . . . well, I thought you wanted to be with me. I mean, I get it if you don't. I really screwed up. I turned down your proposal and I'm so sorry I did that. But I'm here now."

In barely a breath, he was next to me. Cradling my hands in his, his gaze soaked into me. "Of course I want to be with you. But not because of a drawing—*any* drawing. I need you to make this decision based on our feelings. I need you to trust in me. To trust in us."

"But it's just that one drawing to set all my fears to rest. So there are no doubts, no worries." I wanted to draw that picture so badly, my fingers twitched.

"Ah, sweetheart. If only it were that simple. Maybe

I'm selfish, because I want you to love me enough, to be so sure of us, that *you'll* decide our fate is to be together. Not some drawing. Not magic. Just me and you and how we feel."

"But it's just one little drawing," I repeated, my mind stuck on the ease of getting the proof I needed. "I love you, Ethan. I *am* sure about that. But don't you see? If you're not the right man, then being with me will hurt you too."

Steady gray eyes centered on me. "Take a breath. Calm down. Have faith in us."

I focused on him, on his voice, and slowly the worst of my nerves eased. As I sat there with my hands in his, a realization slid into place. He wasn't going to change his mind. It wouldn't matter what I said, how I pleaded. He'd made his decision and that was that. And if I wanted us to be together—and oh, I did—then I'd have to do it his way.

But could I? Could I give up that one measure of control, of absolute surety, that he was my soul mate? Was I willing to gamble *everything* on the love I felt for Ethan? On the love he felt for me? The fear came back, crawling through me with a vengeance.

"Let me think," I whispered. "I need to think."

"Take all the time you need. I'm right here."

Closing my eyes, I willed myself to relax. I fought to find the clarity that had come so easily earlier. I almost turned away again, and walked out that door, because as much as Ethan didn't want or need any more proof than how he felt, I couldn't let go of the desire for absolute certainty. I knew it was asking a lot. Normal people never have absolute certainty. But I *could*, and not reaching for it was terrifying. Almost too terrifying.

But because it—because *he*—was so important, I forced myself to stay, forced myself to breathe, and let the tide of emotions rip through me.

I could see my future with him clear as day. It was

there, all around us, inside of me, just waiting for me to say the words to make it so. I thought them in my head, tried them on for size, let myself feel the way I would feel if I spoke them out loud. That feeling? Glorious, perfect, and oh-so-wonderful.

So then I imagined saying no, leaving and going back home. Without Ethan. The pain came so swiftly, so unrelenting, I gasped from the strength of it. I didn't want that. I couldn't choose that. Not just because it hurt. Not only because the thought of days, months, years without Ethan seemed incomprehensible. But because it just felt *wrong*. More than that, it felt stupid. How incredibly idiotic to run away from him—over what? A drawing?

But it all came back to that dream . . . to the prophecy. And how could I make a choice that could hurt my daughter? I wanted a sign that I was supposed to stay with Ethan, something to push me over the edge I stood on. Something to allow me to believe in my feelings, in everything I thought I saw with Ethan.

My daughter kicked then, and just like in that first vision, this kick had far more strength than it should have had. It startled me. It rocked me. And weirdly, just like it had with Miranda so long ago, it brought every last thing into focus. The tears started then, dripping down my cheeks, one after another. And I knew, in every breath I took, in the beat of my own heart, that yes, Ethan was that man. Nothing . . . no magic, no warnings, nothing would ever change that.

I opened my eyes, wiped at my tears. "Yes. I say yes. I won't do the drawing. I won't doubt what we feel. I trust you. I trust us."

All impassivity dropped away, and the tension emanating from Ethan evaporated. "Thank God. You nearly scared the life out of me there, sweetheart." His hands touched my cheek, my lips, my hair. "You're quite sure this time, correct?"

"Oh, yes. Quite sure." I leaned toward him. "Kiss me. Love me. I'm yours for as long as you want me."

And he did. Kiss me, that is. Sparks of desire, longing, whipped through me, just like always. His arms tightened around me, pulling me closer, locking me to him. His scent punched into me, and every bone in my body went weak, every muscle melted. Because kissing Ethan? Well, it was the stuff dreams were made of.

He pulled back and stood up, and immediately his absence chilled me.

"What's wrong?" I gasped. "You haven't changed your mind, have you? I mean it: I'm in this for good. I promise."

Deep laughter tumbled out. "Not at all. You're stuck with me. But I do have a present for you. I'll be right back."

Confusion clouded my brain, but he was back so fast, I didn't have to wonder for long. A wrapped, flat box in his grasp, he sat down next to me. "When you left here that day, I couldn't breathe. I couldn't believe that I'd fallen, yet again, for a woman who would leave me over . . ." His voice caught. "Never mind that. I went home to see my mother and my grandmother. I hadn't planned on telling them anything about you, but my grandmother sensed something. And one day over tea, I told her everything."

"Okay . . ."

"She gave me this present for you. She said it would give you what you needed to know to move forward with me." The darkness from earlier crept into his gaze, and he blushed. "I even visited Beatrice to see what her intuition said." He shook his head and chuckled. "She knew I was coming, and backed up what my grandmother told me—that I should give you this to fix everything. But I couldn't do it . . . because I needed you to believe in your feelings, to believe in me. So I've held on to this, hoping you'd come to me on your own. And you have. So here. Please accept this gift from my grandmother."

My hand trembled. I ripped the paper off carefully, for some reason apprehensive about what I would find. Silly, but there you have it. Beneath the paper was a plain brown box. I picked off the tape that held the lid shut and slowly opened it. Gasped. Stared. "Oh my God. Do you know what this is?"

He angled himself so he could see the framed photograph. "That photograph has sat on my grandmother's mantel for most of my life. Why, Alice? What does it mean to you?"

I shook my head, not able to talk, barely daring to breathe. Because somehow, his grandmother had known the exact right gift to give me. And even though I didn't need it now, even though the proof wasn't necessary for me to move forward, I was still oh-so-grateful to have it.

The picture? It was a photograph of a woman rocking a baby to sleep. And it was the same picture I myself had drawn. "This baby is you. Not my daughter. And the woman is your grandmother. Oh, my."

Confusion crinkled his eyes. "You'll have to fill me in—" He looked up toward his ceiling, and the timbre of his voice changed. "Move, Alice! Now."

"What?"

Everything happened at warp speed. He pushed me down, flat on the couch, his body covering me. A loud crack reverberated, and then another. I tried to squirm out from under him, but he held me tight, secure. Then came a crash, and Ethan's body tensed and then jerked, and the weight of something slammed onto him. A curse ripped out of his mouth.

Slowly, too slowly, he moved. Chunks of glass fell to the ground as he righted himself. That was when I finally saw what had happened. The ceiling light had come loose and crashed down upon us. Well, it would have landed on me if Ethan hadn't moved so fast.

"Are you okay?" I asked.

Pain lit his eyes. "I think so. Can you take a look?" He turned his back to me, and carefully slipped his shirt up. "How bad is it?"

Blood dripped from his shoulder, but it was a fairly clean cut. "Not too bad, but you're going to need stitches. We should go to the ER."

"So I'll live?"

I took another look and had to suppress a laugh at the absurdity of my life. "Oh yeah, you'll live. But that cut? It's so going to leave a scar."

Chapter Twenty

The music drifted around me as I made my way across the room, looking for Ethan. I had something to tell him, something incredibly important. Vital, even. But as luck would have it, he seemed to have disappeared. My gaze swept the dance floor, wondering if perhaps Grandma Verda had shanghaied him again. Nope, not there either.

Elizabeth and Nate still danced, though. They'd been out there most of the evening, as well they should be. It *was* their engagement party, after all. My sister had never been so happy. I'd begun painting a portrait of their wedding day, based on the picture I'd drawn so many months ago, and I couldn't wait to give it to them. Delightfully, she still didn't know about it.

Moving on, I turned the corner, searching the many faces, wanting to find just one. Chloe and Kyle sat at a table, laughing and talking with Shelby and Grant. I no longer worried about Chloe—as far as Kyle went, anyway. I had to believe her future was as secure as mine, and that, when the time was right, she'd find *her* ever after. My lips twitched. Besides, I knew where Mr. Architect worked, and when the day came, she'd know it too.

Regardless, she was happy right now. My family had welcomed Chloe with open arms. And Scot? Well, he'd actually begun dating again, to my and Elizabeth's utter delight. In fact, the only blight, in Chloe's opinion, was that our magic, our gift, hadn't seemed to take hold for her. Both Elizabeth and I had tried to pass it on, but so far, nothing. Grandma Verda said not to stress, that when Chloe needed it, it would be there.

Yep, I pretty much agreed with that.

Besides, I kind of thought I'd already given it to her. Back before I'd known she was family, related by blood, on that day we had argued about Kyle, my promise, and the words I'd said to her in frustration: *I wish you had the magic, Chloe.* I was sure she'd gotten some.

I stopped and took a deep breath, centering myself. When it was easier to walk again, I moved forward, still seeking Ethan. Thoughts of that day at his place when I had almost made the biggest mistake of my life returned. I shivered from the memory. Thank God I'd made the decision I had. And thank God he hadn't been seriously injured. Though the scar that had developed? Yep, an exact match.

Ugh. The pain was coming quicker. Where the heck was he? My hand went to my stomach, and there, glistening in the lights, was the shine of my engagement ring. You see, we were planning a wedding too, but not until later, not until after the baby was born. In Ireland, when I could travel again. When we were a complete family.

And even though Troy had maintained his decision to not be a part of his daughter's life, Ethan and I weren't taking any chances. After a lot of talking and soul-searching, we'd decided to follow the law to the letter. While Ethan wouldn't officially be my daughter's father until he could adopt her, he'd be her daddy in every way that mattered—from her very first breath.

Finally, my eyes found him: the man I loved. He was leaning against a wall, talking to my father, possibly about Miranda and the magic, as he'd quizzed everyone except for my mother about their experiences with it. My mother still hadn't said a word about that day, which was fine. She would at some point.

A smile touched my lips as I thought again about

Ethan and his growing acceptance of my wacky family. Well, except for one thing. My big, handsome, sexy guy was all nervous over meeting Miranda. Which I thought was sweet.

When I reached him, I grasped his hand. "I love you."

"I love you too, sweetheart." His arm came around my waist, and he pulled me to him. "Your father and I were just discussing a house that's come up for sale near theirs. We should go take a look tomorrow. What do you think?"

I leaned in very close and whispered, "We'll be busy, as it appears Beatrice was right. I'm not going to make it through the weekend."

We'd spent quite a bit of time with my daughter's other grandmother lately, and slowly she was becoming an integral part of our family. Odd, maybe, but also very cool.

And yes, she truly was "a very good guesser."

Confusion zapped into his gaze, and then comprehension dawned. "Now? Right this second?"

I laughed. "Well, I think we have time to get to the hospital." My stomach tightened again. "But we should probably go." Another spasm rolled through me. So strong, so fast, I bit my lip, hard. "Um. Soon, actually."

The love in his eyes took my breath away. "Well, then. Let's go meet our daughter. We should probably finalize her name tonight, don't you think?"

Another laugh slipped out as he guided me away from the party. "We'll know, when we see her, what name suits her best. And I think, sometime tonight, we'll have another visit—this one from Miranda."

He kissed me, first on the forehead and then on the lips. A tingle swept over my skin, just like always. And then, hand in hand, we began walking toward our future. Gypsy magic might have gotten us started, but the magic we created together would see us through. One day at a time, for the rest of our lives.

What could be better than that?

☐ **YES!**

Sign me up for the Love Spell Book Club and send my
FREE BOOKS! If I choose to stay in the club, I will pay
only $8.50* each month, a savings of $6.48!

NAME: _____

ADDRESS: _____

TELEPHONE: _____

EMAIL: _____

☐ I want to pay by credit card.

☐ **VISA**　　☐ **MasterCard.**　　☐ **DISCOVER**

ACCOUNT #: _____

EXPIRATION DATE: _____

SIGNATURE: _____

Mail this page along with $2.00 shipping and handling to:
Love Spell Book Club
PO Box 6640
Wayne, PA 19087
Or fax (must include credit card information) to:
610-995-9274
You can also sign up online at **www.dorchesterpub.com**.
*Plus $2.00 for shipping. Offer open to residents of the U.S. and Canada only.
Canadian residents please call 1-800-481-9191 for pricing information.
If under 18, a parent or guardian must sign. Terms, prices and conditions subject to
change. Subscription subject to acceptance. Dorchester Publishing reserves the right
to reject any order or cancel any subscription.